†HE
SACRED
B⊕NES

Michael Byrnes is the founder and CEO of a highly successful multi-million dollar insurance brokerage firm. He lives in Florida with his wife and two daughters. *The Sacred Bones* is his first novel.

✝THE
SACRED
B⊕NES

A NOVEL
MICHAEL BYRNES

POCKET
BOOKS

LONDON · SYDNEY · NEW YORK · TORONTO

First published in the United States of America by
HarperCollins Publishers Inc., 2007
First published in Great Britain by Simon & Schuster UK Ltd, 2007
This edition published by Pocket Books UK, 2008
An imprint of Simon & Schuster UK Ltd
A CBS COMPANY

1 3 5 7 9 10 8 6 4 2

Simon & Schuster UK Ltd
Africa House
64-78 Kingsway
London WC2B 6AH

www.simonsays.co.uk

Simon & Schuster Australia
Sydney

A CIP catalogue record for this book is available
from the British Library

ISBN: 978-1-84739-012-7

Typeset in Janson by M Rules
Printed and bound in Great Britain by
Cox & Wyman Ltd, Reading, Berkshire

For Caroline, Vivian, and Camille

†HE
SACRED
B⊕NES

PROLOGUE
LIMASSOL, CYPRUS
APRIL 1292

Looking out from the eastern parapet of Kolossi Citadel's square tower, Jacques DeMolay gazed across the open expanse of the Mediterranean, his white mantle and thick auburn beard fluttering against a warm breeze. For a knight nearing fifty, his regal features – long nose, penetrating grey eyes, firm brow, and sculpted cheekbones – were surprisingly youthful. His cropped hair was thick and peppered with grey.

Though he couldn't actually see the shores of the Holy Land, he swore he could smell the perfume of its sweet eucalyptus trees.

It had been almost a year since Acre, the last major Crusader stronghold in the eastern Kingdom of Jerusalem, had fallen to the Egyptian Mamluk's. The siege lasted six bloody weeks, until the then Grand Master, Guillaume DeBeaujeu, had thrown down his sword and retreated from the citadel wall to the rebukes of his men. DeBeaujeu had responded: *'Je ne m'enfuit pas . . . Je suis mort.'* – 'I'm not running away. I am dead.' Raising up his bloody arm, he had shown them the arrow plunged deep into his side. Then he had fallen, never to rise again.

Now, DeMolay wondered if DeBeaujeu's death had foretold the fate of the very Order itself.

'*Monsieur*,' a French voice called over to him.

He turned toward the young scribe standing by the steps. '*Oui?*'

'He is ready to speak with you,' he announced.

DeMolay nodded and followed the boy down into the belly of the castle, the chainmail body armour worn beneath his mantle jingling as he descended the stone steps. He was led into a vaulted stone chamber where the new Grand Master, a haggard Tibald DeGaudin, lay in a bed positioned at its centre. The fetid air reeked of physical neglect.

DeMolay tried to not focus on DeGaudin's bony hands, covered with open sores. His face was equally appalling – ghastly white with yellow eyes bulging from sunken sockets. 'How are you feeling?' The attempt at being cordial sounded forced.

'As well as I look.' He contemplated the blood-red pattée cross that decorated DeMolay's mantle, just above his heart.

'Why am I here?' Regardless of the Grand Master's unfortunate condition, he was first and foremost DeMolay's rival.

'To discuss what will happen when I am gone.' DeGaudin's voice was scratchy. 'There are things you need to know.'

'I know only that you refuse to gather a new army to take back what we have lost,' replied DeMolay defiantly.

'Come now, Jacques. This again? The pope is dead and with him, any hope of another crusade. Even you can admit that without the support of Rome, we have no chance of survival.'

'I will not accept that.'

Pope Nicholas IV, Catholicism's first Franciscan pope and an advocate of the Knights Templar, had tried in vain to garner support for another crusade. He had held synods attempting to unite the Templars with the Knights of St John. He had raised funding to equip twenty ships, even sending emissaries as far as China to foster military alliances. Only days earlier, the sixty-four-year-old pope had died abruptly from natural causes in Rome.

'Many in Rome claim that Nicholas's death was no accident.' DeGaudin's tone was conspiratorial.

DeMolay's face tightened. 'What?'

'The pope's devotion to the Church was undeniable,' he continued. 'But he made many enemies, particularly in France.' The Grand Master raised a faltering hand. 'As you know, King Philip has been taking drastic measures to fund his military campaigns. Arresting Jews in order to seize their assets. He's levied a tax of fifty per cent on French clergy. Pope Nicholas protested these things.'

'Surely you are not saying that Philip had him killed?'

The Grand Master shielded a cough with his sleeve. When he pulled it away, spots of blood dotted the fabric. 'Just know that Philip's ambition is to control Rome. The Church has a much bigger problem to contend with. Jerusalem will have to wait.'

For a long moment, DeMolay was silent. His gaze shifted back to DeGaudin. 'You know what lies beneath Solomon's Temple. How can you ignore such things?'

'We are only men, Jacques. What lies there, only God himself protects. You would be a fool to think that we have done anything to change that.'

'What makes you so certain?'

DeGaudin managed a thin smile. 'Need I remind you that for centuries before we arrived in Jerusalem, many others had also fought to protect those secrets? We have only played a small role in this legacy, but I am certain that we are not to be the last.' He paused. 'I know your intentions. Your will is strong. The men listen to you. And when I am gone, you will no doubt try to have your way.'

'Is that not our duty? Is that not why we swore an oath to God?'

'Perhaps. But maybe what we have hidden all these years needs to be revealed.'

DeMolay drew close to the Grand Master's haggard face. 'Such revelations would destroy everything we know!'

'And in its place, something better may emerge.' DeGaudin's voice dropped to a whisper. 'Have faith, my friend. Put down your sword.'

'Never.'

1.

Salvatore Conte never questioned his clients' motives. His many missions had taught him how to remain calm and keep focused. But tonight was different. Tonight he felt uneasy.

The eight men moved through the ancient streets. Entirely clothed in black, each was armed with lightweight Heckler & Koch XM8 carbines equipped with 100-round magazines and grenade launchers. Padding along the cobblestone in soft boots, every man scanned his surroundings with infrared night-vision goggles. History loomed all around them.

With an abrupt hand signal to hold position, Conte paced ahead.

He knew that his team was just as apprehensive. Though Jerusalem's name meant 'City of Peace', this place defined turmoil. Each silent road was bringing them closer to its divided heart.

The men had travelled separately from a handful of European countries, convening two days earlier at an apartment leased in a quiet part of the Jewish Quarter overlooking Battei Makhase

Square, their accommodation booked under one of Conte's numerous aliases, 'Daniel Marrone'.

On arrival Conte had played tourist to familiarize himself with the web of alleyways and winding streets surrounding the thirty-five-acre rectangular monument in the centre of the fortified Old City – a massive complex of bulwarks and retaining walls standing thirty-two metres high that resembled a colossal monolith laid flat upon Mount Moriah's steep ridge. Easily the world's most contested parcel of real estate, the Islamic *Haram esh-Sharif*, or 'Noble Sanctuary', was more familiar by another name – Temple Mount.

As the cover of buildings gave way to the towering western wall, he motioned two men forward. The wall-mounted floodlights cast long shadows. Conte's men would blend easily into the dark pockets, but then so could the Israeli Defense Force soldiers.

The endless dispute between Jews and Palestinians had made this the most heavily guarded city in the world. However, Conte knew that the IDF was rife with conscripts – teenage boys whose sole purpose was to fulfil three-year service requirements and no match for his hardened team.

He peered ahead, his night-vision goggles transforming the shadows to eerie green. The area was clear except for two soldiers loitering fifty metres away. They were armed with M-16s, donning standard-issue olive green fatigues, bulletproof vests, and black berets. Both men were smoking Time Lite cigarettes, Israel's most popular – and, to Conte, most offensive – brand.

Glancing over to their intended entry point at Moors' Gate, an elevated gateway on the platform's western wall, Conte quickly surmised there was no way to gain access to the Temple Mount without being detected.

Shifting his fingers along the barrel, he flicked the XM8 to single-shot mode and mounted the rifle on his left shoulder. He targeted the first green ghost with the red laser, aiming for the head, using the glowing butt of the dangling cigarette as a guide. Though the XM8's titanium rounds were capable of piercing the soldier's Kevlar vest, Conte found no sport – let alone certainty – in body shots.

One shot. One kill.

His index finger gently squeezed.

There was a muffled retort, slight recoil, and he saw the target buckle at the knees.

The scope shifted to the remaining man.

Before the second IDF soldier had begun to comprehend what was happening, Conte had fired again, the round penetrating the man's face and cartwheeling through the brain.

He watched him collapse and paused. Silence.

It never ceased to amaze him just how token the expression 'defence' really was – offering little more than a word to make people feel secure. And though his native country had a laughable military competence, in his own way, he felt he had become its equalizer.

Another abrupt hand signal ushered his men onto the sloping walkway approaching Moors' Gate. To his left, he glimpsed the Western Wall Plaza nestled along the embankment's base. Yesterday he had marvelled at the Orthodox Jews – men separated from women by a curtained partition – who gathered here to mourn the ancient temple they believed had once graced this holy place. On his right lay a small valley littered with excavated foundations – Jerusalem's oldest ruins.

A substantial iron gate sealed with a deadbolt denied access to the platform. In less than fifteen seconds the lock had been picked and his team funnelled through the tunnelled entrance, fanning out across the broad esplanade beyond.

Slipping past the stout El-Aqsa Mosque abutting Temple Mount's southern wall, Conte turned his gaze to the esplanade's centre where just over tall cypress trees, a second and much grander mosque stood on an elevated platform, its gilded cupola illuminated like a halo against the night sky. The Dome of the Rock – embodiment of Islam's claim over the Holy Land.

Conte led the team to the esplanade's south-east corner where a wide opening accommodated a modern staircase, cascading downward. He splayed the fingers of his gloved right hand and four men disappeared below the surface. Then he signalled the remaining two men to hunker down in the nearby tree shadows to secure a perimeter.

The air in the passage became moist the further the men descended, then abruptly cold, giving off a mossy aroma. Once they had assembled at the base of the steps, rifle-mounted halogen lights were switched on. Crisp, luminous beams bisected the darkness to reveal a cavernous, vaulted space with arched stanchions laid out on neat avenues.

Conte remembered reading that twelfth-century Crusaders had used this subterranean room as a horse stable. The Muslims, its latest occupants, had recently converted it into a mosque, but the Islamic décor did little to mask its uncanny resemblance to a subway station.

Running his light along the room's eastern wall, he was pleased to spot the two brown canvas bags his local contact had promised. 'Gretner,' he addressed the thirty-five-year-old explosives expert from Vienna. 'Those are for you.'

The Austrian retrieved them.

Slinging his carbine over his shoulder, Conte took a folded paper from his pocket and switched on a penlight. The map showed the exact location of what they'd been charged to procure – he didn't favour references to 'stealing' – the term demeaned his professionalism. He aimed the penlight along the wall.

'Should be just ahead.' Conte's English was surprisingly good. To keep communications consistent and less suspicious to local Israelis, he had insisted that the team converse only in English.

Securing the penlight between his teeth, he used a free hand to unclip the Stanley Tru-Laser electronic measuring device from his belt and punched a button on its keypad. A small LCD came to life, activating a thin red laser that cut deep into the darkness. Conte began to move forward, his team trailing closely behind.

He continued diagonally through the chamber, weaving between the thick columns. Deep into the space Conte abruptly stopped, verified the measurements on the LCD and swung the laser till it found the mosque's southern wall. Then he turned to face the northern wall, the gut of the Temple Mount.

'What we're looking for should be just behind there.'

2.

Salvatore Conte rapped a gloved hand on the wall's limestone brickwork. 'What do you think?'

Setting down the canvas bags, Klaus Gretner unclipped a portable ultrasound device from his belt and held it over the wall to gauge density. Seconds later the result appeared on the unit's display. 'About half a metre.'

From the first bag, Conte pulled a sizeable handheld coring drill – the Flex BHI 822 VR model he'd specified – the chuck already fitted with an eighty-two millimetre diamond drumbit. Glinting beneath his penlight, it looked like it had just come out of its box. He passed it to Gretner. 'You should have no problem dry-cutting it with that. Plenty of outlets along the wall there,' he said, pointing. 'The extension cord and adaptor are in the bag. How many cores you going with?'

'The stone's soft. Six should do it.'

From the second bag, Conte took out the first brick of C-4 and began moulding the grey putty-like explosive into cylinders while the Austrian drilled into the wall's mortar seams.

Ten minutes later, six neat cores were packed and plugged with remote detonating caps.

Wiping down the drill, Gretner discarded the Flex by the wall. Then he and Conte took cover with the others behind the columns, covering their faces with respirators. Using a handheld transmitter, Gretner triggered a coordinated detonation.

The ear-numbing blast was immediately followed by a rush of debris and billowing dust.

After pulling away some more loose bricks to widen the blast hole, Conte climbed through the gaping opening, followed by the others.

They found themselves inside another chamber, its details obscured by the clouds of dust. Stout stone pillars could be made out supporting the low ceiling. Even with respirators, the air was thin and difficult to inhale, tinged with the lingering fumes of cyclotrimethylene, which smelled like motor oil.

This place had obviously been sealed for a long, long time, Conte thought and for a brief moment he wondered how his client could have possibly known it even existed. He turned sharply to the man next to him. 'Give me some light.'

Moving forward into the gloom, the lights played across a row of ten rectangular forms resting on the floor against the chamber's side wall. Each was about two-thirds of a metre in length, cream-coloured, and slightly tapered from top to bottom.

Perusing the inventory Conte paused over one at the end of the row, kneeling down to get a better look. Choosing the correct one was much easier than he'd have thought. Unlike all the others, this was covered in ornate, etched designs. Tipping his head to view the left side of the box, he compared the distinctive carved symbol to the image on a photocopy he pulled from his pocket. A perfect match.

'This is it,' he announced to the others, pocketing the papers. 'Let's keep moving.' Though they were deep beneath the Temple Mount, Conte knew that the sound of the explosions would have been heard beyond the outer walls.

Gretner stepped forward. 'Looks heavy.'

'Should be about thirty-three kilos.' Somehow, his client knew that as well. Rising up, he stepped aside.

Slinging his XM8, Gretner laid a web of nylon strapping on the floor. He and another man lifted the box onto the webbing, hoisting it off the floor.

'Let's get out of here.' Conte waved the team forward.

They worked their way through the blast hole and back into the mosque. Before ascending the staircase Conte collected their respirators, stuffing them into his bag.

Emerging onto the esplanade, Conte scanned the area intently and verified that his two sentries remained posted securely in the shadows. He signalled to them and both men sprinted ahead.

The rest of the team assembled on the esplanade.

Moments later, when the sentries' silhouettes swept across the opening of Moors' Gate, they were instantly forced back by automatic gunfire emanating from the plaza below.

A pocket of quiet.

Distant screams, then more shots.

Motioning for the others to remain, Conte ran over to the gate, dropping onto his elbows as he neared the opening. Peering out he saw Israeli soldiers and police swarming into the vicinity, blocking the walkways down by the Western Wall Plaza. Someone must have either found the two dead IDF soldiers or heard the detonation.

The Israelis were hunkered down, waiting for them to make a move. Other entrances provided access to Temple Mount and

Conte rapidly considered a revised exit strategy, but he was certain the IDF would be sending reinforcements to those gates as well. It wouldn't be long before they scaled the platform.

He knew that using the rented van parked in the Kidron Valley was no longer an option. Turning back from the gateway, he signalled for the sentries to follow him back to the group.

As he ran by the El-Aqsa Mosque, Conte grabbed the encrypted radio transmitter from his belt. 'Come in Alpha One. Over.'

Nothing but static.

He moved away from the interfering mosque wall.

'Alpha One?'

Through the haze a choppy voice was just audible.

Conte cut in with the transmitter button. 'If you can hear me, we've got a change of plan. We're under fire.' Raising his voice, he carefully articulated his next command. 'Pick us up on the south-east corner of the Temple Mount esplanade, beside the El-Aqsa Mosque. Over.'

A pause.

More static.

'Roger. On my way,' a faint voice crackled back. 'Over.'

Conte concealed his relief. Just over the jagged mountain range to the south he detected a dark shadow against the night sky.

The chopper was approaching rapidly.

He clicked his XM8 to fully automatic, activating the grenade launcher and the others did the same. Fearing they might inflict damage on this sacred place, he knew that the Israelis would be reluctant to fire heavily on them. But his team wouldn't be nearly as accommodating.

'We'll need to take those guys down to clear the area,' Conte commanded. On his signal, the mercenaries rushed toward the gate in neat formation, carbines drawn.

The chopping sound of rotor blades now had the Israeli's attention, many gazing skywards at the black shadow gliding low and fast toward Temple Mount.

From their shadowed position high up on the retaining wall, Conte and his men sprayed the soldiers with a curtain of fire-power. Within seconds, eight had fallen. Others were scurrying for cover in the open plaza below, while reinforcements spilled into the area from the network of narrow streets feeding in from the Jewish and Muslim Quarters.

The Israeli air force Black Hawk suddenly rose over the embankment's south-east corner, its profile decked out in desert camouflage temporarily confusing the IDF soldiers with its familiar markings. But Conte could also see a group of men manoeuvring to better positions along the embankment's south-west corner. Immediately to his right, Doug Wilkinson, the assassin from Manchester, England, suddenly recoiled, clutching his upper arm, dropping his XM8.

Sliding his finger to the carbine's second trigger, Conte centred his sights on the cluster of soldiers below and fired. The grenade rocketed off its rifle mount streaming an arc of smoke and orange sparks until it exploded, hurling fragments of stone into the air. Other grenades followed with a fiery barrage of exploding stone and shrapnel that forced the Israelis back in chaos.

The rotor blades were close behind the team now, throwing up a dust storm. The Black Hawk bounced down on the plat-form, coming to rest beside the El-Aqsa Mosque.

'Go now!' he yelled, waving the team toward the chopper. 'Get the cargo on board!'

Retreating from the gate, Conte spotted yet more IDF soldiers between the cypress trees on the opposite side of the Temple Mount, quickly closing in on the vicinity surrounding the Dome of the Rock platform.

It was going to be close, he thought.

The box was rapidly stowed in the chopper and then his men clambered aboard. He ducked under the rotor blades, jumping inside.

Under heavy gunfire, the Black Hawk lifted off the platform and tore away from Temple Mount. Hugging the Ha-Ela Valley floor, it swept across the barren expanse of the Negev Desert, heading south-west. The chopper's low flight path was well beneath radar range, but even at higher altitudes its state-of-the-art cloaking technology would render it virtually untraceable.

Within minutes the lights of the Palestinian settlements along the Gaza Strip came into view. Then Gaza's beaches rapidly gave way to the dark expanse of the Mediterranean.

Eighty kilometres off Israel's coast, a custom-built twenty-metre Hinckley motor yacht had been anchored at precise coordinates programmed into the flight console. The pilot manoeuvred the Black Hawk over the yacht's aft deck, easing down to hover in the hold position.

The box was carefully lowered to the Hinckley's crew, then one by one the team rappelled down the line. Wilkinson tucked his wounded arm tightly to his side as Conte clipped him to the line. All things considered, the wound was relatively minor. When Wilkinson had made it on deck, Conte went next.

Setting the autopilot controls to hover, Conte's pilot evacuated the cockpit, stepping over the two dead Israeli pilots who earlier that evening had set out from Sde Dov airbase on a routine surveillance mission along the Egyptian border, blissfully unaware of their heavily armed replacement hidden in the rear.

With cargo and passengers secured, the Hinckley's engines fired up and the craft moved off, slowly gathering speed. Conte loaded another grenade and found the chopper fifty metres away. A split second later the latest state-of-the-art in American military technology ripped apart, lighting up the night sky in a flaming ball.

The yacht accelerated to its cruising speed of twenty-two knots and headed north-west across the Mediterranean's choppy waters.

There would be no more fighting that night. As Conte had anticipated, the Israelis had been totally unprepared for an orchestrated stealth attack. But the messy confrontation and high death toll meant his fee just went up.

MONDAY
THREE DAYS LATER

3.

TEL AVIV

As the El Al captain announced the flight's final descent into Ben Gurion International, Razak bin Ahmed bin al-Tahini gazed out of his window to watch the Mediterranean yielding to a desert landscape set against an azure sky.

Yesterday, he had received a disturbing phone call. No details had been provided, merely an urgent request from the Waqf – the Muslim council that acted as the Temple Mount overseers – summoning him to Jerusalem for assistance in a sensitive matter.

'Sir,' a soft voice called to him.

He turned from the window to find a young flight attendant dressed in a navy suit and white blouse. Razak's eyes were drawn to the El Al insignia pin on her lapel – a winged Star of David. 'El Al' was Hebrew for 'skyward'. Yet another reminder that here, Israel controlled more than just the land.

'Please bring your seat to the upright position,' she politely requested. 'We'll be landing in a few minutes.'

Raised in the Syrian capital of Damascus, Razak was the oldest of eight siblings. Growing up in a close-knit family, he frequently helped his mother shoulder household responsibilities since his father was an ambassador for the Syrian embassy and travelled endlessly. With his father's help, he had begun his political career as a liaison between rival Sunni and Shiite factions in Syria, then throughout the Arab region. After studying politics in London, he'd returned to the Middle East, where the scope of his duties had broadened to include diplomatic missions to the UN, and liaising between Arab and European business partners.

For almost a decade now, Razak had been intimately involved in Islam's most problematic issues, becoming a reluctant – yet increasingly influential – political figure. Faced with its maligned association to radical fanaticism and terrorist acts, and the neck-breaking onslaught of globalization, the sanctity of Islam in the modern world was increasingly difficult to preserve. And though Razak's aspiration in accepting his role was to focus on the religious aspects of Islam, he had quickly learned that its political components were inseparable.

And at forty-five, his responsibilities were showing. Premature grey streaks had sprouted from his temples, spreading through thick black hair, and a permanent heaviness showed under his dark, solemn eyes. Of medium height and build, Razak wasn't one to turn heads, though in many circles, his knack for diplomacy was sure to leave a lasting impression.

Substantial personal sacrifice had quickly transformed his youthful idealism into tempered cynicism. He constantly reminded himself of the wise words his father once told him when he was just a young boy: *'The world is a very complicated thing, Razak, something which is not easily understood. But surviving out there'* – he had pointed somewhere far out into the distance – *'means never compromising your spirit, because no man or place can take that from you. It is Allah's most precious gift to you . . . and what you do with it is your gift to Him.'*

As the Boeing 767 touched down, Razak's thoughts shifted to the mysterious altercation in Jerusalem's Old City three days earlier. The worldwide media was circulating reports about a violent exchange that had taken place at Temple Mount on Friday. Though the nature of the altercation was still highly speculative, all accounts confirmed that thirteen Israeli Defense Force soldiers had been killed by an as-yet unknown enemy.

Razak knew it was no coincidence that his services were now required here.

As he retrieved his suitcase from the baggage claim carousel inside the terminal, his watch alarm beeped. He had programmed it to ring five times a day, and in five differing tones.

Two thirty.

After stopping in the men's room to ritually wash his face, hands, and neck, he found a clean spot along the concourse and set his bag down. Re-examining his watch, he referenced a miniature digital readout data-fed by a global positioning microchip. A small arrow shifted on the face pointing him in the direction of Mecca.

Raising his hands up, he declared '*Allah Akbar*' twice, then crossed his hands over his chest and began one of the quintet of daily prayers compulsory in Islamic faith.

'I bear witness that there is no God but Allah,' he softly muttered, easing down on his knees then bowing in submission. In prayer he found a solitude that silenced the noise around him, reconciling the compromises he was asked to make in the name of Islam.

Deep in meditation, he blocked out the group of Western tourists scrutinizing him. To many in the modern world, devout adherence to prayer was a foreign concept. It didn't surprise him that the sight of an Arab man in a business suit kneeling in submission to an invisible presence so easily captured the curiosity of most non-Muslims. But Razak had long ago accepted the fact that piety was not always convenient or comfortable.

When he had finished, he stood and buttoned the top button of his brown suit jacket.

Two Israeli soldiers watched scornfully as he made his way through the exit, staring at his rolling suitcase as if it contained plutonium. To Razak, it was indicative of a much broader tension that defined this place and he ignored them.

Outside the international terminal he was greeted by a Waqf representative – a tall young man with dark features who led him to a white Mercedes 500.

'*Assalaamu 'alaykum.*'

'*Wa 'alaykum assalaam,*' Razak replied. 'Is your family well, Akil?'

'Thank you, yes. An honour to have you back, sir.'

Akil took his bag and opened the rear door. Razak dipped into the air-conditioned interior, and the young Arab took his place behind the wheel.

'We should be in Jerusalem in under an hour.'

Approaching the towering ancient limestone block wall that wrapped around Old Jerusalem, the driver turned into a parking lot and reclaimed his reserved spot. They would have to make it the rest of the way on foot since the Old City, with its prohibitively narrow streets, was off-limits to most vehicular traffic.

Outside the Jaffa Gate, Razak and the driver were queued into a long line by heavily armed IDF guards. Nearer the opening, they were subjected to a thorough body pat down while Razak's bag was inspected and passed through a portable scanner.

Then came an exhaustive verification of their credentials. Finally, they took turns being funnelled through a metal detector, all the while being monitored by a set of surveillance cameras mounted high up on a nearby pole.

'Worse than ever,' Akil remarked to Razak, relieving him of his luggage. 'Pretty soon we'll be locked out all together.'

They went through a narrow, L-shaped tunnel – a design from centuries earlier meant to slow marauding attackers – and emerged into the busy Christian Quarter. Climbing the sloped cobblestone walkways into the Muslim Quarter, Razak breathed in the complex aromas of the nearby *Souk* – fresh bread, spicy meat, tamarind, charcoal, and mint. It took them fifteen minutes to reach the high staircase on Via Dolorosa that climbed up to the Temple Mount's elevated northern gate. There, a second security check was required by the IDF, though not nearly as intrusive as the first.

As Akil led him across Temple Mount's expansive esplanade, Razak could hear the raucous cries of protestors down near the Western Wall Plaza. He didn't need to see them to know that Jerusalem's district police and reinforcements from the IDF would be there in large numbers, holding the crowds at bay. Focusing on the spectacular mountainous panorama afforded by the Temple Mount's high vantage point, he tried to block out the distressing sounds.

'Where will we be meeting?' Razak asked.

'Second floor of the Dome of Learning building.'

Taking his bag, Razak thanked Akil, leaving him at a free-standing archway and headed toward a squat, two-storey building situated between the sacred Dome of the Rock and El-Aqsa Mosques.

Entering the northern door, he climbed a flight of stairs and strode down a narrow corridor to a private room where he could already hear the voices of the Waqf officials awaiting him.

Inside, nine Arab men – middle-aged and older – were convened around a heavy teak table. Some wore traditional *kaffiyeh* head wraps and business suits; others had opted for turbans and colourful tunics. When Razak entered, the room fell into a hush.

At the head of the table, a tall bearded Arab wearing a white headdress stood and raised a hand in greeting.

Making his way over to him, Razak raised his own. *'Assalaamu 'alaykum.'*

'Wa 'alaykum assalaam,' the man responded with a smile. Farouq bin Alim Abd al-Rahmaan al-Jamir had presence. Though his real age was unknown, most would correctly place him in his mid-sixties. Lucid grey eyes revealed the burden of many secrets, but showed little of the man within. A thick scar ran across his left cheek and he wore it proudly as a reminder of his days on the battlefield. His teeth were unnaturally symmetrical and white, obviously replacements.

Ever since Muslims regained control of the Temple Mount in the thirteenth century, the Waqf had managed this sacred shrine and a 'Keeper' had been appointed as its supreme overseer. That responsibility, entrusting all matters concerning the sanctity of the site, now lay with Farouq.

As they took their seats Farouq reacquainted Razak with the men around the table then quickly got to the matter at hand.

'I make no apology for summoning you here on such short notice.' Farouq stared round the table, while tapping a ballpoint pen against the polished teak surface. 'You all know about the incident last Friday.'

A male servant bent to pour Razak a cup of spicy Arabian coffee – *qahwa*.

'Enormously troubling.' Farouq continued. 'Sometime in the late evening, a group of men broke into the Marwani Mosque. They used explosives to access a hidden room behind the rear wall.'

The fact that the crime had occurred on a Friday, when Muslims from all over Jerusalem would gather on Temple Mount for prayer, was particularly troublesome to Razak. Perhaps the perpetrators meant to strike fear into the Muslim community. He settled into his chair, trying to compute the audacity it would take to desecrate such a sacred site. 'For what purpose?' He sipped his coffee slowly, letting the smell of cardamom fill his nostrils.

'It seems they have stolen an artefact.'

'What kind of artefact?' Razak preferred forthright answers.

'We'll get to that later,' Farouq said dismissively.

Not for the first time Razak wished the Keeper didn't play his cards so close to his chest. 'Professional job then?'

'It appears so.'

'Did the explosions damage the mosque?'

'Luckily, no. We immediately contacted a structural engineer. So far it seems the damage is contained to the wall.'

Razak frowned. 'Any idea who could have done this?'

Farouq shook his head.

'It was the Israelis I tell you!' one of the elders burst out, quivering with rage, his lower lip dramatically curled.

All heads turned to the old man. His eyes shifted away and he eased himself back into his seat.

'That is not certain,' Farouq firmly cut in. 'Though it's true that eyewitnesses reported an Israeli Black Hawk was used to transport the thieves.'

'What?' Razak was stupefied.

Farouq nodded. 'It landed in the esplanade outside the El-Aqsa Mosque and took them away.'

'But isn't that restricted airspace?'

'Absolutely.'

Though he wouldn't admit it, Razak was impressed that anyone could pull off such an operation, especially in Jerusalem. 'How?'

'We don't have details.' Farouq's pen resumed its tapping. 'All we know is that the helicopter was spotted over Gaza minutes after the theft. We're awaiting a full report from the IDF. But let's not forget that thirteen Israelis were killed during the attack and many more injured,' Farouq reminded the assemblage. 'Policemen and IDF soldiers. To assume Israelis were responsible . . . For now that wouldn't seem to make sense.'

Another elder spoke up. 'This situation's very complicated. Clearly this theft has occurred within our jurisdiction. However, that so many IDF soldiers were killed does matter greatly.' He spread his hands and paused. 'The Israelis have agreed to keep this quiet, but ask that we cooperate in sharing all information uncovered through our internal investigations.'

Razak fingered his cup and looked up. 'I'm assuming the police have already begun preliminary investigations?'

'Of course,' Farouq interjected. 'They arrived minutes after the episode occurred. Problem is they've yet to present any definitive evidence. We suspect important facts are being withheld. That's why we've summoned you. Confrontation seems inevitable.'

'If only – ' Razak began.

'Time's limited,' another Waqf member with a thick head of silver hair overrode him. 'Both sides are concerned it won't be long before the media starts drawing its own conclusions. And we all know what that will lead to.' His grave eyes circled the table to draw support. 'Razak, you know how fragile our role is here in Jerusalem. You see what's happening outside on the streets. Our people rely on us to protect this place.' He stuck out an index finger and tapped it on the table twice. 'There's no knowing how they'll react. Unlike *most* of us,' he eyed the first outspoken elder, still purple from rage, 'they will assume the Israelis are responsible.'

Farouq came in again. 'You can well imagine that Hamas and Hezbollah are both anxious to lambaste the Jews for this.' His face darkened. 'They're asking for our support implicating the Israelis to further Palestinian liberation.'

The situation was far worse than Razak had imagined. Tensions were already running high between the Israelis and Palestinians. Both Hamas and Hezbollah had garnered much support over the past few years in their efforts to outwardly oppose Israeli occupation and this incident would surely bolster their political agenda. Razak tried to not think about even more drastic consequences that were likely to occur. The Waqf was now stuck in the middle of a very precarious political situation – one that felt impossibly fragile to Razak. 'So what do you wish of me?' he asked, looking round the table.

'Determine who stole the relic,' replied the soft-toned elder. 'We need to know who committed this act so justice can be served. Our people deserve an explanation as to why such a sacred place has been so maliciously violated.'

In the ensuing silence Razak could hear the taunting, muffled sounds of protestors through the window, like voices from the grave. 'I'll do whatever's necessary,' he assured them. 'First I'll need to see where this happened.'

Farouq rose to his feet. 'I'll take you there now.'

4.

VATICAN CITY

Charlotte Hennesey was battling the unforgiving eight-hour time difference, and three espressos earlier that morning hadn't helped to settle her.

As instructed, she was waiting in her guest suite until summoned. Unlike the limousine and first-class service that had whisked her from Phoenix to Rome, her accommodation at the Vatican City's Domus Sanctae Marthae residence hall was austere. White walls, simple oak furniture, twin bed and nightstand, though she did have her own bathroom and a small refrigerator.

Seated at the sun-filled window, she gazed out over the tiled roofs of Rome's western sprawl. Having finished her novel on the plane—Anne Tyler's *Saint Maybe* – she'd now had to settle for the English edition of *L'Osservatore Romano*, reading it from cover to cover. Sighing, she set the paper down and looked over at the nightstand's digital alarm clock – 3:18.

She was anxious to get to work, but wondered what purpose an American geneticist could possibly serve here. As the head of research and development at BioMapping Solutions, Charlotte typically made off-site visits to pharmaceutical and biotech companies looking to apply the latest discoveries in the human genome to their research.

It was her boss, BMS founder Evan Aldrich, who had taken the call almost two weeks ago from a Vatican cleric named Father Patrick Donovan. Having heard the priest's compelling proposal, Aldrich had volunteered her services for a highly secretive project. Few things could divert Evan Aldrich from his work, especially when the request required him to hand over his best researcher.

Clearly this was one of them.

At thirty-two, Charlotte was a lithe five-nine with striking emerald green eyes and a smooth, healthily tanned face framed by shoulder length curls of chestnut hair. With a rare balance of intellect and charm, she'd become her company's chosen spokesperson for an industry typified by grey scientists. Human genetics was often misunderstood and always controversial. With BMS aggressively promoting its latest gene-mapping technology, the right public image was important.

Recently she had added media appearances to her arsenal of talents – talk shows and news programmes. Aldrich had told her that the Vatican priest mentioned seeing one of her most recent interviews concerning the reconstruction of maternal lineage through mapping mitochondrial DNA, prompting his request for her services.

Now that her time was split between research and public relations, she wondered exactly what role she'd be asked to play here. After all, the conservative papacy was surely not one of her biggest supporters.

Her thoughts drifted back to Evan Aldrich.

Aldrich had abruptly shifted career ten years ago, abandoning his secure tenure as a Harvard professor of genetic science to enter the uncertain world of business. And he had handled the switch brilliantly. Not for the first time, Charlotte mused about what made Evan tick. Not money, though when BMS eventually went public he would make a great deal of it. What really drove the man was his sense of purpose, his belief that the work they did and the choices they made really mattered. It was his passion and genuine charisma that first attracted her to him. The fact that she thought he looked like a movie star didn't hurt either.

Almost a year ago, she and Evan had begun dating, both very cautious about the potential work-related conflicts such a relationship might bring about. But if there could exist a natural fit between two people, Charlotte had certainly found it – like the inevitable laws of physics she found herself hopelessly drawn to him. Only four months ago, things between them seemed perfect.

Then fate decided to intervene.

A routine blood test taken during her annual physical detected abnormally high protein levels in her blood. Further testing followed that included a painful bone biopsy. Finally came the devastating diagnosis: *multiple myeloma*.

Bone cancer.

At first, she was angry. After all, she was practically a vegetarian, rarely drank, and exercised like a fiend. It just didn't make sense, especially because at the time, she felt perfectly fine.

That wasn't the case now. Just a week earlier, she began taking Melphalan – her first round of low-dose chemotherapy. Now she felt like she was battling a permanent hangover, complete with intermittent waves of nausea.

She didn't have the heart to tell Evan. Not yet, at least. He had already been talking about a more permanent future, even kids.

None of that seemed possible now and it crushed her. Over the past few weeks, she had grown more despondent. In all fairness to him, she needed to be absolutely certain that she would be among the ten per cent who actually beat this disease before she could commit to anything more serious.

A discreet knock pulled Charlotte from her thoughts.

Reaching the door in four strides, she opened it to see a bespectacled bald man barely her height, dressed in a black suit and shirt. His complexion was smooth and pale. Maybe in his late forties or early fifties, she guessed. Her eyes were immediately drawn to the white priest collar.

'Good afternoon, Dr Hennesey. I'm Father Patrick Donovan.' His English was flavoured with an Irish brogue. Smiling pleasantly, he extended a thin hand.

My Vatican admirer, she thought. 'A pleasure to meet you, Father.'

'I so much appreciate your patience. I apologize for the delay. Shall we go?'

'Yes, of course.'

5.

TEMPLE MOUNT

Deep beneath Temple Mount, Razak and Farouq stood amidst the rubble-strewn floor of the Marwani Mosque. As the Keeper had indicated, the damage to the site had been considerable, yet contained. Pole-mounted spotlights had been erected to illuminate a gaping hole in the rear wall about a metre-and-a-half in diameter. On seeing it, Razak felt his stomach twist into a knot.

The first time he had seen this place was in the late 1990s. Back then, rubble and debris had completely filled the space, floor to ceiling. But that was before the Israeli government had allowed the Waqf to initiate excavation and restoration. In exchange, Jewish archaeologists had been permitted to excavate the Western Wall tunnel – an underground passage far beneath the buildings of the Muslim Quarter, connecting the southern Western Wall Plaza to the Via Dolorosa on the embankment's north-west corner. As usual it was a compromise that wasn't without bloodshed. Riots had broken out between Palestinians and Israelis opposing the excavations, resulting in the deaths of over seventy soldiers and civilians, including Razak's closest friend, Ghalib, who vehemently opposed Israeli digging beneath his home that abutted the Temple Mount's western retaining wall.

Some Muslims had clung to the belief that a demon called the *Jin* had deliberately filled this underground room with rubble to deter entrance. And now that its restoration was nearing completion, Razak couldn't help but feel a malevolent presence still lurked here in the shadows.

Approaching the aperture, he ran his fingers along its jagged edge, feeling a gummy residue. He peered into the secret chamber beyond where the rubble was minimal.

Farouq appeared beside him holding a piece of masonry and handed it to Razak. 'See this?' He indicated a smooth arc that ran along one edge of the brick. 'The Israelis found a drill the thieves left behind, used to make cores that were then packed with explosive.'

Razak examined the brick. 'How could explosives be smuggled into the heart of Jerusalem, past all the checkpoints?'

'Explosives *and* guns. These people were smart.' Farouq leaned through the hole and peered into the chamber. 'I didn't want to mention it in front of the others, but this seems to suggest that someone on the inside helped them. Perhaps the Jews did have something to do with this.'

Razak wasn't so sure. 'You said the police have already seen this?'

'The police and the IDF's intelligence people studied it for two solid days following the theft.'

Their thoroughness didn't surprise Razak.

'We've been awaiting a full report,' Farouq added. 'It has yet to come.'

Both men climbed through the hole into the space beyond. Additional pole lights illuminated the inner chamber clearly carved from Mount Moriah's soft limestone bedrock with thick stone pillars supporting its rocky ceiling. The walls were bare of any ornamentation. Here the stagnant air still smelled of explosives.

Razak turned to face the Keeper. 'Did you know about this chamber before?'

'Absolutely not. Our excavations were contained within the mosque itself. Any unauthorized digging would have been strictly forbidden.'

Farouq's gaze was steady, but Razak was well aware that, when it came to excavations, the Waqf had taken some liberties in the past.

Against the east wall, Razak detected a line of nine compact stone boxes, each etched in a language that looked like Hebrew. He moved closer. At one end, a rectangular depression in the earth suggested a tenth box had been removed and he moved closer.

Unexpectedly, a voice broke in from the other side of the blast hole. 'Gentlemen. Can I have a moment?'

Razak and Farouq whirled round to find a plain-looking middle-aged man peering through the aperture. His face was pale and streaked by sunburn, topped off by a nest of unruly brown hair.

'Sorry, do you speak English?' The stranger had a refined English accent.

'We do.' Razak rapidly approached the hole.

'Marvellous.' The stranger smiled. 'That'll make things easier. My Arabic's a little ropey.'

Farouq elbowed Razak aside. 'Who are you?'

'My name is Barton.' He moved forward through the opening. 'Graham Barton, I—'

Farouq threw oversized hands in the air. 'You dare come in here? This is a sacred place!'

Barton stopped in his tracks, looking like he had just stepped on a landmine. 'I'm sorry. But if you'll just let me—'

'Who let you in?' Razak moved past Farouq to shield the chamber.

'I was sent by the Israeli Police Commissioner, to assist you.' He pulled out a letter on police department stationery.

'An Englishman!' Farouq was gesticulating wildly. 'They send an *Englishman* to assist us. You see where that got us in the past!'

From the extensive time Barton had spent on projects in Israel, he was painfully aware that here the English were still best known for their botched colonization efforts in the early 1900s – a debacle that only served to deepen Palestinian resentment toward the West. He grinned tightly.

'Need I remind you,' Farouq warned, 'that non-Muslims are banned here?'

'My religious affinities aren't so easily defined,' Barton scowled. There was a time when he regularly attended Anglican services at Holy Trinity Church near his Kensington home in London. But that was a long time ago. Now he considered himself a more secular believer who shunned the establishment, but still sought a better understanding of his belief that there was indeed something bigger than himself in this miraculous universe. That search had yet to exclude elements of most faiths, including Islam, which he regarded highly.

'So what is your purpose here?' Razak demanded.

'I work with the Israeli Antiquities Authority,' Barton persisted. He was already feeling that accepting this job had been a very bad idea. The guppy was now in the piranha tank. 'Ancient Holy Land antiquities are my speciality.' *Biblical* antiquities was more like it, he thought. But mentioning that to this pair didn't seem smart. 'I'm well regarded in my field.' Renowned, in fact, he thought. Trained at Oxford University, head curator of antiquities for the Museum of London, and a résumé that read like a novella – not to mention the countless archaeological digs he'd managed in and around Jerusalem and his regular pieces in *Biblical Archaeology Review*. And just prior to the theft, the IAA had commissioned Graham Barton with a generous stipend to oversee a massive digitizing campaign that would catalogue the entirety of its priceless collections throughout Israel's museums. Wisely, he chose not to elaborate on those details.

Farouq was dismissive. 'Credentials do not impress me.'

'Right. But I can save you a lot of time,' Barton added, dodging the Keeper's outright hostility. 'Besides, the IDF and Israeli police have retained my services. I've been told you're committed to full cooperation in order to determine what happened here. I have a letter of introduction.' His tone was more assertive now.

Farouq's eyes met Razak's, registering displeasure for the Israelis' sneaky tactics.

'I was informed that the incident here possibly involved an ancient relic.' Barton was trying to peer over Razak's shoulder.

The two Muslims were still grappling with what was happening.

'The thieves must have had very precise information,' Barton forged on, 'to know the exact whereabouts of a room so well hidden beneath Temple Mount. Wouldn't you agree?'

'A moment, please.' Farouq raised a finger and motioned to the archaeologist to move back through the blast hole.

Sighing, Barton retreated into the mosque. The tricky politics of this place exasperated him.

Razak watched him go. 'Strange. I wonder if they—'

'An outrage!' Farouq's face was close.

Razak's voice sunk to a whisper. 'Did the Israelis mention this to you?'

'Not at all. And I will not permit this.'

Razak drew a deep breath. He didn't like the idea of allowing this Barton – apparently a delegate from the Jewish authorities – to intervene in such a sensitive investigation. After all, the Israeli police and the IDF had already spent two days inspecting the crime scene without apparent results. Now they were sending in an outsider? Perhaps Barton would not simply replicate the investigation. There was no telling what their motives could be. However, time wasn't on Razak's side and his knowledge of archaeology and antiquities was limited at best.

Farouq drew even closer. 'What are you thinking?'

'We don't have much time. Since Barton claims to be an expert . . .'

'Yes . . .'

'Well, it's obvious the Israelis already know what happened here. Perhaps he can give us information. Something to start with. It's in everyone's interests to resolve this quickly.'

Farouq stared at the floor. 'Razak. Trust requires merit. Every man needs to prove his character. You are a virtuous man. But not everyone's like you. You and I – we trust each other. But with this Barton we have to be very careful.' He marked the point with a raised finger.

Razak raised an eyebrow. 'Of course, but do we really have a choice?'

Farouq returned Razak's gaze. Finally, the creases in his brow softened. 'You could be right,' he relented, sighing dramatically. 'I just wish he wasn't an Englishman.' The Keeper forced a smile. 'Take his letter and check his credentials with the police. Proceed how you see fit. I'm leaving.'

Back out in the mosque, Razak took the letter and instructed the Englishman to wait for him to return, then walked Farouq to the stairs.

'Keep a close eye on him,' Farouq reminded Razak, leering back at Barton.

Taking off his suit jacket, Razak asked Farouq if he wouldn't mind taking it back to his office. He watched as the Keeper disappeared into the sunlight above.

After rolling up his sleeves, Razak pulled out his cell phone and punched in the number for the Israeli police commissioner who had signed the letter. Two transfers later he was put on hold and subjected to a banal Israeli pop song. Watching Barton pace in small circles in the Marwani Mosque, he shifted back and forth on his feet, holding the phone at arm's length, trying his best to tune out the song's headache-inducing techno beat. A minute later, there were two distinct clicks followed by a ring.

A strong, nasal voice came on. 'Major Topol speaking.'

Razak did his best to filter out the Arabic undertones from his near-perfect English. 'My name is Razak bin Ahmed bin al-Tahini. I've been commissioned by the Waqf to oversee the investigation at the Temple Mount.'

'Been expecting your call,' Topol said between sips of burned coffee from a paper cup, clearly unimpressed. 'I take it you've met Mr Barton?'

Razak was thrown by the man's directness. 'Yes, I have.'

'He's good . . . used him before. Very objective.'

Razak refrained from comment. 'I must inform you that his presence wasn't well received. We understand the need for your

40

department's intervention, but Mr Barton entered the mosque without authorization.'

'Apologies for not notifying you sooner,' Topol replied, stifling a yawn. 'But Graham Barton has been authorized to act on our behalf. It's all in the letter he's carrying. I'm sure you'll understand that the nature of this crime requires us to play an equal role in the investigation.'

'But he's an archaeologist, not an investigator,' Razak challenged. 'Israeli police have already analysed the crime scene.'

'Sure, our people have been there,' Topol admitted, 'but this crime seems to centre on a missing artefact. We're the police. Stolen cars, burglaries, murders, we understand. We don't know about artefacts. So we felt the investigation could benefit from Barton's knowledge of archaeology.'

Razak said nothing. It was routine for him to choose silence over confrontation. When negotiating, the opposition often blurted out significant information just to fill the silence. The pause allowed him to consider Topol's argument. For the most part it seemed sensible.

The policeman lowered his voice and spoke conspiratorially. 'I think we'll both need to put aside our differences, so that justice can be served.'

'My colleagues and I share your concern. Can we trust all information will remain confidential until our investigation is complete?'

'You have my word on that. We're looking for a quick, peaceful resolution here. Rumours are spreading like wildfire. We could soon have a much bigger problem on our hands.'

'I understand.'

'Good luck to you.'

The line went dead.

Razak returned to where the Englishman stood near the blast hole, hands folded behind his back, whistling and admiring the Marwani Mosque's impressive interior. Barton turned to him. 'Everything okay?'

He nodded and offered his hand. 'Welcome, Mr Barton. My name is Razak.'

6.

VATICAN CITY

At the end of the dimly lit corridor Charlotte Hennesey and Father Donovan descended two flights of switchback steps and emerged into the Domus's modern lobby. They strode across the expanse of white marble tile, passed a bronze bust of Pope John Paul II, and exited the building into bright afternoon sunshine.

Charlotte was accustomed to the dry desert heat of Phoenix. Rome's heat came with oppressive humidity. And then there was the Vatican's strict dress code – arms, legs, and shoulders had to be covered at all times. No shorts or sleeveless tops. It was like high school – no tube tops or halters. For the next few days it would be khaki pants and long-sleeved blouses with uncomfortably high thread counts. Back home, she typically ended her day lying poolside in the backyard of her Spanish-style ranch, sporting a bikini. At least, when she was feeling up to it. It was quite evident that wouldn't be happening here.

'I'm sure you're curious as to why you've been asked to come here,' Father Donovan said.

'The thought had crossed my mind,' she politely replied.

'The Vatican is proficient in theology and faith,' he explained.

'However, you won't be shocked to hear that in the field of natural sciences, there are some obvious deficiencies in our capabilities.' He offered a self-deprecating smile.

'That's perfectly understandable.' The priest had a gentle spirit, she thought. His Irish accent was calming and she noticed that he gesticulated often, the by-product of years behind a pulpit.

They strolled past Piazza Santa Marta, circling the rear walkways along the apse of the basilica. Charlotte marvelled at its marble and stained-glass exterior.

'Take me for instance,' he offered. '*Prefetto di Bibloteca Apostolica Vaticana* . . . a fancy way of saying head curator of the Vatican Library. My expertise is books and Church history. I must confess that I know little about your field. But when I saw you on television, I was convinced that you could really help me with a project I've been asked to undertake.'

'If you don't mind me saying so, I'm surprised my field intrigues anyone in Vatican City.'

'Indeed, many within these walls would have reservations about the intentions of genetic research. I, however, like to keep a more open mind.'

'That's good to know,' she said, smiling. 'So what exactly is it that I'll be studying?'

The priest didn't respond right away, allowing a pair of strolling clerics to pass a comfortable distance before quietly saying, 'A relic.' He considered enlarging on the idea, but decided against it. 'It's best to see it with your own eyes.'

Heading north on Viale del Giardino Quadrato, they crossed through the lush greenery of the Vatican Gardens, passing the Casina of Pius IV, the lavish sixteenth-century neoclassical papal summerhouse.

The straight pathway ran behind the massive Vatican Museum. Charlotte remembered reading that the Vatican's extensive art collection was housed there, within the former palace of Renaissance-era popes. It was also the place where countless visitors from around the world came to marvel at the city's most famous exhibit – the Sistine Chapel – its walls covered in narrative frescoes; its ceiling painted by Michelangelo.

She could tell Father Donovan wasn't yet ready to divulge any more. Though she wanted to enquire why the librarian was handling the study of relics, she decided to change the subject. 'This place is enchanting,' she said, gazing at the flowers, ornate fountains, and fantastic Renaissance architecture. 'It's like a fairytale. Do you actually live here?'

'Oh yes,' he said.

'What's it like?'

The priest looked up at her, grinning. 'The Vatican is its own world. Everything I need is right within these walls. It's kind of like a college campus, I guess.'

'Really?'

He held up both hands. 'Without the night life, of course,' he said with a laugh. 'Though I must admit, we do have our own equivalents to fraternities.'

They were just approaching the museum's service entrance. Even at a leisurely pace, in less than ten minutes they had walked about six hundred metres – almost the entire width of the country.

7.

TEMPLE MOUNT

Razak led the Englishman over to the blast hole, motioning him through the aperture.

Stepping inside, Barton's analytical gaze immediately swept the chamber.

Coming in behind him, Razak remained standing near the opening, uneasy with the gloomy, subterranean atmosphere.

Energized, Barton didn't hesitate to start airing his thoughts. 'In the late first century BCE, King Herod the Great employed master architects from Rome and Egypt to design the Temple Mount. It was a huge undertaking that required the construction of an enormous platform that incorporated solid bedrock at the northern end' – he gestured behind him – 'and expanded south, using vast retaining walls where Mount Moriah's bedrock slopes down.' He swivelled round, pointing in the opposite direction. 'That's why the southern end of the platform can easily accommodate vaulted rooms, like the space that is now the Marwani Mosque. And archaeologists have long theorized that other similar spaces existed beneath the Mount.'

'Are you telling me the Israelis were aware of this room's existence?'

Barton knew Razak was looking for suspects so he knew he had to tread lightly. Though he was aware that Jewish archaeologists had performed thermal scans on the Mount that had shown questionable subsurface anomalies, he was fairly certain that this particular chamber had remained completely undetected. 'Absolutely not. I'm sure that if they had, the Waqf would have been informed.' He could tell that Razak didn't believe a word of it.

Barton focused his attention on the stone boxes, crouching down to get a better look, moving from one to the next, his excitement building with each new discovery.

Meanwhile, Razak's haunted gaze wandered over the stone walls. 'So what is this place?'

Barton stood and let out a prolonged breath. 'You're standing in what appears to be an ancient Jewish crypt.'

Razak crossed his arms tightly across his chest. The idea of being amidst death and unreconciled souls was unnerving, only underlining his sense of foreboding. And Jewish, to boot! The place felt instantly smaller. Suffocating.

'And it looks like your thieves removed one of the permanent occupants.' Barton was shifting from foot to foot, pointing to the rectangular depression in the dirt at the end of the row.

'But aren't those boxes far too small to be coffins?'

'Let me explain.' The archaeologist paused to gather his thoughts. 'During the ancient Jewish burial ritual – the *tahara* – bodies of the deceased were cleaned, then covered with flowers, herbs, spices and oils. Next, the ankles, wrists, and jaw were bound and two coins placed over the eyes.' He cupped his hands over his eyes. 'Finally the entire body would be wrapped in linens and covered with a shroud.' At this stage Barton knew that the prepared body would be placed inside a long niche, or *loculus*. There were none here, but variations in tomb design weren't uncommon and he didn't want to complicate matters.

Trying to visualize the inner dimensions of the box, Razak couldn't compute how a body could fit in such a cramped vessel. 'But I still don't see—'

Barton held up a hand. 'Please,' he gently cut in. 'They believed that the body needed to expiate sin, shed it through the process of decaying flesh. So the family would allow the corpse to putrefy for a year, after which, they would come back to place the bones in a sacred stone box – a miniature coffin called an ossuary.'

Razak stared at him. Islamic burial practice – interment within twenty-four hours in a modest tomb facing Mecca, preferably without a casket – was in stark contrast to elaborate ancient Jewish rituals. 'I see.' Razak fingered his chin.

'This type of burial was common in this region,' Barton continued, 'but only practised during a very brief period – roughly 200 BCE to 70 CE. That helps us to date ossuaries pretty accurately, even without fancy tests. As you can see,' Barton pointed to the row, 'the boxes are just large enough to accommodate a dismembered skeleton.'

'Why did they save the bones?' Razak thought he knew the answer, but wanted to be sure.

'The ancient Jews believed strongly in their eventual resurrection, ushered in by the coming of the true Messiah.'

Razak nodded. The bodies of Muslims also waited in the grave for a Day of Judgement, reminding him how Judaism and Islam shared many common roots.

'The same Messiah,' Barton added, 'whom the Jews believe

will rebuild the third and final temple up there,' he pointed above his head toward the Temple Mount esplanade.

'That will never happen,' Razak defiantly stated.

That's precisely what Barton would have expected the Muslim to say. 'Yes, well, anyway, this was considered preparation for that day. Without the bones, there would have been no chance for resurrection.'

'Are ossuaries valuable?'

'Depends. The stone would need to be in pristine condition.' Barton surveyed the nine remaining relics. 'And these look to be in excellent shape – no obvious fractures, plus they all have their lids. Etchings can be important too. Often an engraver would mark the surface with the corpse's identity. Sometimes they'd have decorative patterns and scenes. If the engravings are impeccable, it pushes the price up.' Barton had seen hundreds of similar boxes that had been recovered throughout the region, many more impressive than these. 'These ossuaries look fairly standard.'

'Then what would one of them be worth?'

Barton pursed his lips. 'Depends. Maybe six thousand pounds, or perhaps ten thousand dollars, assuming it could be sold in the antiquities market. Big problem is that the relic probably wouldn't be particularly unusual. To fetch a high price, it would need to be in perfect condition and purchased by an avid collector or museum. But these days museums tend not to like pieces obtained through the antiquities markets.'

Razak was starting to get used to the archaeologist's English accent. 'Why not?'

'Well, desirable artefacts would be those with a high degree of provenance. A serious buyer needs adequate proof that a relic had been excavated from a specific site, validating its authenticity.

The earth and commingled artefacts around an archaeological dig provide lots of clues to an artefact's age. Remove the relic from the earth, and . . .' He shrugged his shoulders.

Razak squatted down. This was a lot to absorb. 'So what you're really saying is . . . since its value can depend on substantiating its origin, this stolen ossuary might not be worth much at all on the open market?'

Barton nodded. 'Absolutely. Value also relies heavily on the credibility of the seller. If its provenance is suspect, the ossuary's value would be severely reduced, which means we can rule out the possibility of a museum or well-known collector as the thief.' Barton eyed the squatting Muslim, considering whether or not he should reciprocate by sitting. Would he expect that? Unsure, he decided to remain standing. 'The potential consequences are too severe. I might also point out that many relics that have come out of Israel in the past two decades have been proven fakes, only after European museums paid exorbitantly for them.'

Razak looked up at him. 'So putting the ossuary on display in a gallery would be a waste of time for them?'

Barton nodded.

The Israeli death toll just didn't tally with the relic's questionable market value. 'Why would someone go to so much trouble – with such violence – to steal just one?' he countered. 'Why not steal them all?'

'Good point,' Barton concurred. 'That's what you and I will need to determine. I'll need to analyse the etchings on these. I will also need to study this crypt for clues as to whose family was buried here. My guess is the thieves knew precisely which ossuary they wanted and were unconcerned about establishing provenance. That rules out serious archaeologists, who are not known to blast holes through walls.'

Razak allowed himself a smile. 'What does one of those things weigh?'

'Probably about twenty-two kilos, plus the bones . . . around thirty-five in total.'

'And how would one go about shipping it?'

'A standard crate, I'd guess. You'd need to wrap it in a fair amount of packing material. If it left one of Israel's ports, the contents would have to clear Customs. And I've been told that since Friday, all cargo awaiting shipment is being inspected piece by piece. It would never get through.'

'Most likely the IDF secured all roads immediately following the crime,' Razak added. 'That would rule out the ossuary being driven from Israel.'

Quizzically, Barton eyed the Muslim. 'Yes, but aren't the police saying a helicopter was used during the theft?'

Razak nodded. 'That's what eyewitnesses have been saying.'

'I don't mean to state the obvious, but don't you think they probably flew it directly over the border somewhere?'

Razak's expression was squeamish. He had thought the very same thing, but didn't even want to consider that prospect. 'Anything's possible.' The idea that the relic might already be far from reach was daunting. This was way beyond his usual role and he silently cursed the Waqf for involving him in all this. 'And apparently eyewitnesses reported a helicopter over Gaza shortly following the theft.'

'Oh dear, that's not good,' Barton said.

'No it's not,' Razak sombrely replied. 'Not when the helicopter is yet to turn up.'

'There's always a remote possibility that the ossuary is still in Israel,' Barton offered.

Standing, Razak brushed away dust from his pants. 'I think that's unlikely.'

Sensing that the Muslim delegate seemed overwhelmed, Barton thought it wise to shift gears. 'I'm no expert on crime scenes,' Barton continued, 'but I believe the ossuary contained more than bones. I would wager those thieves knew exactly what was in it.' He placed a hand nonthreateningly on Razak's shoulder. 'We'll get to the bottom of this. I'll do my best to see what these inscriptions say.' Seeing the Muslim's discomfort with the gesture, he pulled his hand away.

'How much time will you need, Mr Barton?'

'About an hour should do it.'

'Let's reconvene in the morning,' Razak suggested. 'I'll have one of our men from the Waqf, Akbar, meet you at the top of the steps. He'll escort you down so you can get started.'

'You mean watch me.'

Razak ignored him.

'Look, I don't blame you.' Barton held out his hands, palms up. 'I know this place is sacred. And I'm not a Muslim.'

Silence, not confrontation, Razak reminded himself. 'Shall we say around nine o'clock?'

'Right.'

Razak passed him a business card. 'In case you need to contact me.'

Barton glanced at it. Just the name and mobile phone number. 'Thanks. And just for the record, Razak . . . I'm not interested in politics. I'm an archaeologist. Please remember I'm here to help you. Thirteen men died on Friday and I'm confident that the clues here will help to determine why.'

Razak nodded affably and the two men made their way out of the crypt.

8.

VATICAN CITY

Father Donovan and Charlotte rode a noisy freight elevator down one level beneath the Vatican Museum.

When the doors opened, the cleric led her out into a wide, fluorescent-lit corridor that she would have expected to see in a hospital. Their feet echoed off the vinyl tiles and blank white walls. The place was a gallery of doors. Most likely storage, she guessed.

'We're just up ahead,' Father Donovan said, pointing to a wide metal door situated at the end of the hall.

The priest slid a key card through a reader mounted on the doorframe and a heavy lock disengaged. He opened the door and motioned her inside.

'You can keep this key.' The priest handed it to Charlotte. 'It also opens the rear service door after hours. Please don't lose it.'

She nodded, pocketing it.

Beyond the threshold was a spacious laboratory. The walls were lined with sleek, glass-panelled cabinetry that housed a broad range of chemical containers, bottles, and small boxes. The cupboards beneath boasted an armada of state-of-the-art scientific gadgetry. Crisp halogen lighting illuminated every surface and hulking stainless-steel workstations dotted the main floor like islands. An air-conditioning and purification system hummed quietly in the background, removing dust and microscopic contaminants, while regulating the laboratory's humidity and temperature.

If the Vatican wasn't interested in science, it sure didn't show down here. This was one of the most impressive workspaces she had ever seen.

'It's our newest addition to the museum,' Donovan explained. 'Hasn't even been opened to our residents yet.'

'Impressive.'

'Our art collection requires constant maintenance,' he went on, as if in justification. 'Lots of marble sculptures, paintings, tapestries.' His hands were moving again as if delivering a sermon. 'This is where our most precious treasures will be maintained so that the coming generations can enjoy them.'

A man emerged from a doorway to an adjacent room in the rear of the lab. Seeing him, the priest smiled.

'*Ah, Giovanni, come sta?*'

'*Fantastico, padre. E lei?*'

'*Bene, gratzie.*'

Hearing the Irish priest effortlessly switching languages impressed Charlotte. She watched the middle-aged man, dressed in a crisp white lab coat, as he approached to shake the priest's hand. With hazel eyes and thick whisps of black and grey hair, he had a pleasant face that was wrinkled only in the areas where his continuous wide smile had left its marks.

'Dr Giovanni Bersei, I'd like you to meet Dr Charlotte Hennesey, a renowned geneticist from Phoenix, Arizona.' Donovan placed a hand on Charlotte's shoulder.

'A pleasure to meet you, Dr Hennesey,' Bersei kindly replied, in accented English. He offered a handshake. Like many others who had met Charlotte Hennesey for the first time, he too was captivated by her striking green eyes.

'Likewise.' She shook his smooth hand and offered a warm smile. Wishing she could say something nice in Italian, she realized how she, like most Americans she knew, was deficient when it came to linguistic skills, although in Phoenix, she had learned some basic-survival Spanish.

'Dr Bersei has helped us many times in the past,' Father Donovan informed her. 'He is an anthropologist whose speciality is ancient Roman culture.'

'Fascinating.' Immediately she wondered how their diverse disciplines could possibly complement one another. Now she was even more anxious to see this mysterious relic Donovan had alluded to earlier.

Donovan held out his hands, as if an invisible communion chalice had been set before him. 'I actually have to leave for about an hour to go and pick up our delivery from Termini. I thought the two of you might get acquainted while I'm gone.'

'Great,' Charlotte said, eyeing Bersei who also seemed pleased with the recommendation.

Before making his way out the door, Father Donovan added, 'I'll see you both shortly.'

The priest left.

Charlotte turned to Bersei wearing a puzzled look. 'Any idea what this is all about?'

'No idea,' the anthropologist shrugged. 'I have to admit, I'm a bit curious. I've done plenty of work for the Vatican in the past, but never had to sign confidentiality agreements. You too, I suppose?'

'Yes. I thought that seemed odd.' Three pages of legal disclaimer stamped with a raised papal seal and witnessed by a Vatican notary. Obviously, the project's secrecy was more than just a tacit request. She was tempted to ask about the financial retainer, but felt it might be inappropriate. Aldrich didn't say exactly how much money had been wired to BMS's corporate account, but she guessed it was plenty.

'And I've certainly never been paired up with a geneticist,' he said, puzzled. 'Not that I'm complaining, of course,' he quickly added.

'Do you live in Rome?'

'Two kilometres away. I ride my Vespa when I do work here.' He flitted his eyebrows.

Charlotte laughed. 'I hope you're careful. Everyone seems to drive pretty fast around here.'

'Craziest drivers in all Europe.'

'So tell me, what type of work have you done here in the past?'

'Oh, a few different projects,' he said. 'I suppose my claim to fame is my papers on the ancient catacombs throughout Rome. A Vatican commission oversees the sites, so I interact with them quite often. But I'm rarely called inside the Vatican itself. It's a bit intimidating, no?'

'Certainly is,' she agreed. 'Lots of guards.'

'So you're a geneticist? Sounds exciting. Very modern.'

'I mainly do human genome research, analysing cell structure and DNA to spot genetic flaws that cause disease.'

Bersei stroked his chin. 'Amazing. So remarkable, the human organism.'

'It's always fascinated me, ever since I was a girl.'

'Well Dr Hennesey, I'm not sure why fate has brought us together, but I certainly look forward to working with you.'

'Thanks. And please, call me Charlotte.'

'Come,' he turned and motioned for her to follow him to the rear room. 'Let's get you a lab coat. I'm sure Father Donovan will be anxious to start as soon as he returns.'

9.

JERUSALEM

Returning from his meeting with the archaeologist, Razak found Farouq in the same room the Waqf council had convened earlier that afternoon. The Keeper wound up his phone call and placed the receiver back in its cradle.

'So what did you think of Barton?' Farouq eased into his chair.

'Seems to know what he's talking about,' replied Razak.

'That was Topol.' Farouq nodded toward the phone. 'Apologizing he hadn't contacted us earlier. Offered to pull Barton if we weren't comfortable. I told him I'd speak to you.'

Razak knew Farouq was indirectly asking if he was willing to take responsibility for Barton's actions. 'I think we can trust him. He's already given me valuable information.'

'Should I tell Topol we'll cooperate?'

'It would show good faith,' Razak urged. 'After all, this affects both sides. If we keep the Israelis involved, it will alleviate suspicion – delay any violent protest.' Sometimes politics, like inner peace, was largely about damage control.

'Just be sure to keep a close eye on him,' Farouq reiterated. 'Does he know what was stolen?'

'Yes. An ossuary.'

'A burial box? Why so much trouble for such a thing?'

'Still unclear.' Razak shook his head. 'Barton needs time to determine exactly what was in the ossuary. He'll be conducting a study of the crypt tomorrow morning to understand more.'

'I see.'

'Heard anything else about the helicopter?'

Farouq shook his head.

'Until it's determined what happened,' Razak said, 'we should request copies of all outgoing shipping manifests at the ports for the past three days, starting with Tel Aviv. Also check the airports. According to Barton the consignment would weigh about thirty-five kilos. Most likely the crate would be about a metre in length, about two-thirds of a metre in height and width. That should narrow things down.'

'I'll request copies of shipping records for air, rail, and water transport,' he said unenthusiastically. Putting on a pair of glasses, Farouq jotted some notes on a pad.

'Is it safe to assume all the roadway checkpoints have been secured?'

Farouq grimaced. 'Come now, Razak. When has that ever been a safe assumption? Nonetheless, all vehicles are being thoroughly inspected. But I highly doubt they'd risk driving this thing out of Israel.'

'Do you think the helicopter may have flown it out of the country?' The fact that Barton had himself mentioned the idea really had Razak thinking it through more seriously now.

'It hasn't turned up in Israel yet, so the odds are it's already gone. By the way,' Farouq continued without pause, 'the police are looking into a call from a landlady in the Jewish Quarter. Told them a stranger had rented a room from her. He shared it with several men she thought were part of a tour group. They all disappeared late on Friday evening some time before dawn. The chambermaid's agreed to meet with a police photofit expert first thing tomorrow.'

'Think it's anything?'

'Perhaps. But it's taken this woman three days to come forward. Seems odd.' Farouq eyed his notepad. 'The name on the room was Daniel Marrone – the same one used to lease a rental van found abandoned on Haofel Road. No surprise that it appears to be an alias. The Israelis also ran ballistics tests on the munitions,' he continued. 'The thieves were armed with XM8 assault rifles, apparently very sophisticated weapons, manufactured by Heckler & Koch for the United States military.'

'Interesting.' The Israeli forensic crime labs never ceased to impress Razak. As a matter of ongoing national security, they'd invested heavily in counter-terrorism technology that included a highly sophisticated database with profiles of every known manufactured weapon. 'But that doesn't seem to make sense.' Razak was frowning.

'What do you mean?'

'Barton says the ossuary is probably only worth a few thousand dollars.'

'Hmm.' Farouq considered it. 'Let's wait and see what the archaeologist comes up with.' Farouq looked at his watch. 'Before this relic is completely out of reach.'

10.

ROME

On the wide cement walkway along Stazione Termini's loading zone, a young baggage clerk was working a bulky wooden crate onto a hand truck.

'*Tananài*,' a sharp Italian voice cut the air, 'make sure you handle that with care.'

Squinting into the bright summer sunlight, the clerk looked up to see who had just called him a dickhead. Standing stiffly against the backdrop of the terminal's modern glass and steel structure was a tall, thickset man dressed in chinos and a white shirt. The brawny stranger didn't look like the type who would respond well to a smart reply. '*Si, signore.*'

Turning slightly off Via Giovanni Giolitti's busy thoroughfare, a white Fiat van pulled up and parked along the kerb. Father Patrick Donovan jumped out and excitedly went over to meet Conte. 'Everything all right?'

'Would be if baggage handlers gave a damn about doing their job right.'

The young clerk rolled his eyes, careful to not let the impatient Italian see him.

Conte eyed the priest disapprovingly. 'Did you have to wear that get-up? Do you really need to be so damn obvious?' He eyed the van's tags. They weren't Vatican City plates. At least Donovan had got that part right.

Father Donovan shrugged and let out a long breath.

Conte stared for a moment at the priest's bald scalp, glistening in the sun. 'You should put some lotion on that thing before you burn my eyes out.'

The clerk laughed.

The priest was not amused.

'Make yourself useful and open the doors,' Conte instructed Donovan.

Silent, Donovan made his way to the van's rear. Such a brash man, he thought. Though he wouldn't expect anything less from the Vatican's notorious hired gun. He hated the idea of working with Conte – a thief, a killer. It all made him feel unclean. But he reminded himself how critical it was to make this work. So much was at stake. And if having to contend with the Contes of the world was part of it, then so be it.

'I'll take it from here,' Conte huffed, urging the handler to the side with the wave of a hand. The mercenary stepped behind the hand truck and raised the load, his thick, corded arm muscles flexing.

Conte was still irritable from the return trip. If getting the secret cargo out of Jerusalem had been a harrowing experience, the two-day crossing of the Mediterranean in rough seas hadn't been much better. Seasickness and a confrontation with team member Doug Wilkinson – those were the *high* points. After some heavy drinking, the young twat had dragged Conte out to the aft deck for a 'friendly' discussion regarding the bullet he took to his right arm. *'It's my good arm for Christ's sake,'*

Wilkinson protested. '*Now I'm going to have a fucking infection. You should be paying me triple for this. It's only right,*' he'd insisted in a slurred growl. That was right before Conte coldcocked him and pushed him over the deck rail into the Adriatic. Shark bait.

Yes, after all that nonsense, Conte wasn't about to risk having some pimply faced station porter dropping the damn cargo now.

Wheeling the crate off the kerb and to the rear of the Fiat, Conte motioned for Donovan to help him lift it into the van. Stowed securely inside, Conte slammed the doors and returned the hand truck to the porter. No tip.

In the meantime, Donovan had made his way into the driver's seat and started the engine, but Conte was having none of it. Sighing, he paced over to the driver's side window and motioned Donovan out of the van.

Confused, the cleric hopped out onto the roadway.

'When I'm here, you're over there,' the Italian said gruffly, pointing to the passenger seat. 'Get moving.'

Weaving through Rome and heading south on Lungot Marzio, the van hugged along the riverbank of the sparkling Tiber. Donovan gazed out the window trying to calm himself, his thoughts tortured by the box in the rear compartment, hoping, praying that its contents were indeed genuine. Only the scientists whose services he had convinced the Holy See to commission could inevitably make that determination.

For the past three days, the priest had been closely monitoring news reports flooding out from Jerusalem. Every time he heard the death toll, a wave of nausea swept over him and he prayed to God for forgiveness in allowing such a thing to happen. But having lobbied for a more diplomatic way to extract the relic, he was once again swept aside. The political manoeuvring he had witnessed in his twelve-year tenure at Vatican City would have made even Machiavelli gasp.

Fifteen minutes from Termini and Conte had yet to make small talk. Certainly not a man concerned about first impressions, Donovan thought, glancing over at the brooding mercenary. He directed his attention back outside.

Rising like a mountain on the Tiber's western bank, Donovan's eyes reached out to the brilliant white cupola of St Peter's Basilica – the heart of Vatican City – a beacon that could be seen from all over Rome. In 1929, the Vatican's governing body, The Holy See, had been granted full property rights and exclusive sovereignty by Italy's fascist dictator Benito Mussolini, thus making this place the world's smallest independent nation – a country within a country. Amazing, Donovan thought. Here the supreme Catholic monarch, the Pope, and his trusted advisors, the College of Cardinals, managed worldwide operations for over one billion Catholics and diplomatic relations with almost two hundred countries around the globe.

Crossing Ponte Umberto I, Conte angled his way around the massive ramparts of the Castel Sant' Angelo riverfront citadel.

Heading down Borgo Pio, the Fiat approached the Sant' Anna Gate – one of only two secure vehicle entrances through the continuous fifteen-metre high wall that formed a tight three-kilometre perimeter around the Vatican City's 109-acre complex. The van stopped behind a short queue of cars awaiting clearance from the Swiss Guards.

'Look at those guys,' Conte scoffed. 'They're dressed like clowns for fuck's sake.'

Though the routine garb of the Vatican City's 100-man Swiss

Guard battalion was blue coveralls and black berets, it was their official uniform that had earned them the status of 'the world's most colourful army' – a sixteenth-century purple-and-yellow-striped tunic and matching pantaloons with red arm cuffs and white gloves, all topped off with a red felt beret.

Explaining to Conte that the tradition meant something would be fruitless so Donovan remained silent. Up ahead, he watched the guards shuffle in and out of their barracks just inside the gate. There was nothing to fear, but as the van was waved to the gate his heartbeat quickened irrationally.

Conte gently accelerated to cross the threshold into Vatican City. A guard motioned for him to stop, checked the licence plates, then paced around to Conte's open window. 'Your business here?' he rigidly enquired in Italian.

Conte smirked. 'You don't really want to know that,' he answered coyly. 'Why don't you ask him?' He leaned back and pointed over at the priest.

The guard immediately noticed Father Donovan.

'It's okay, he's with me.' Donovan nodded.

'Of course, Father,' the young guard replied, suspiciously eyeing Conte again. 'Have a good day.' Stepping back from the van, he waved them along.

Conte sighed. 'What a bunch of buffoons. That kid's not even shaving yet. Even more pathetic than the Israelis.'

Donovan cringed at the man's callousness, deeply regretting that Cardinal Antonio Carlo Santelli – the *Segretaria di Stato*, or Vatican secretary of state – had commissioned the ruthless mercenary for such a momentous task. It was whispered that Cardinal Santelli was the reckoning force behind numerous Vatican scandals. But no one in the Curia, including Santelli, seemed to know much about Salvatore Conte, even if that was his real name. Some speculated that he was a retired Italian Secret Service operative.

According to Santelli, the only sure things about Salvatore Conte were his reliability and his mission-specific twenty-four-digit Cayman Islands bank account number. Lord only knew how many of those accounts a man like Conte had, Donovan wondered. Having seen the generous financial enticements that secured the scientist's services, it was obvious that Santelli had spared no expense – in money or lives – to ensure this project's success.

The Fiat lurched forward down the paved roadway that ran behind the Apostolic Palace and through a village of low buildings that included a post office, emissary, and television broadcast studio. Following Donovan's directions, Conte continued through a short tunnel that led out onto a narrow driveway that snaked around the towering edifice of the Vatican Museum complex.

Near the service entrance, Conte parked the van, then unloaded the secret cargo onto a compact dolly. The priest escorted him inside to the elevator and down one flight.

Entering the lab, Conte parked the dolly to one side. Father Donovan trailed in as the two scientists made their way over.

'Thanks so much for waiting,' Father Donovan said in English. 'Dr Giovanni Bersei, Dr Charlotte Hennesey' – he motioned to them, then over to the mercenary – 'this is Salvatore Conte.' Anything beyond a name for this killer would be too much, so the priest chose not to elaborate.

Keeping his distance, Conte straightened, hands on hips. His eyes immediately glued to Charlotte, roving up and down her body, trying to assess what lay beneath her draping lab coat. He grinned. 'If my doctor looked like you, I'd be sick every week.'

Charlotte smiled tightly and diverted her attention to the bulky wooden crate. 'So this is it?' she asked Donovan.

Clearly embarrassed by Conte's crassness, the priest said, 'Yes. I think it would be best to open the crate now.' He turned to Conte expectantly.

'You're a man of God, not a cripple,' Conte grumbled. 'So give me a hand.' He leaned over and grabbed a crowbar off the dolly.

11.

The wooden shipping crate was a sturdy, four-foot cube with a *Eurostar Italia* logo plastered on its lid. Conte worked one side of the lid, jerking the crow bar up and down, while Donovan steadied it to prevent it from flying off and damaging the new lab equipment.

Charlotte noticed that Father Donovan's hands were shaking. If she hadn't known any better, she'd have sworn that he suspected the container might be empty. Then again, maybe this character, Conte, had unnerved him.

Less than thirty seconds later Conte stripped the lid away. Father Donovan gently placed it on the floor.

Glancing briefly at the shipping label, Giovanni Bersei couldn't help but notice the port of origin printed in large bold print: STAZIONE BARI. Bari was an eastern coastal city whose lure to tourists was twofold: its claim to owning the bones of Saint Nicholas and its spectacular seaport where wealthy Italians docked their oversized yachts.

The crate's interior was covered by thick layers of bubble wrap. 'We need to get these two side panels off,' Conte said, claiming one and pointing to the side closer to Bersei.

Bersei stepped forward and lifted the panel easily up and out along grooved tracks, exposing more of what lay inside.

Charlotte moved in closer.

'Don't be shy, just tear it away,' Conte instructed both scientists, pointing at the thick layers of bubble wrap.

As her hands peeled back the last layer of wrapping, Charlotte's fingers ran over a hard flat surface, cold and slick. She glimpsed blue-tinted plastic.

Seconds later a rectangular surface shrouded in the blue material was revealed.

Rubbing his hands together, Donovan looked up at them. 'We'll get it over to the workstation,' he said to Bersei. 'Dr Hennesey, could you please set that rubber matting on top of the table?' He pointed to a thick rubber sheet sitting on a nearby counter.

'Sure.' She noticed that Donovan seemed visibly relieved. She laid the sheet out on the nearest workstation while Conte wheeled the dolly closer.

Following Conte's cue, Bersei crouched down, cupping his hands round the corners. It felt very solid. 'How heavy is this?'

Conte's hard eyes met his. 'Thirty-three kilos. Lift on three.' The mercenary counted down and they manhandled it up.

Halfway into the lift, Bersei's fingers suddenly slipped along the plastic cover, and the load jerked sharply to one side. Charlotte lurched forward to help, but Conte was able to thrust his arm out just in time to stabilize it.

Conte glared at Bersei. 'Not good, Doc,' he chastised in Italian. 'Let's keep it together.' He nodded to the scientist to continue, and they shifted it over onto the matting.

'If there's nothing else you need,' Conte grumbled, '*I* need a drink.'

'That'll be all, Mr Conte,' Donovan replied, trying his best to be cordial. 'Thank you.'

Before leaving, Conte turned to face the priest with his back to the scientists. He pointed to his left eye, then at Father Donovan. The message was clear. *Remember, I'll be watching you.* Then he was gone.

Turning back to the scientists, small beads of perspiration had welled up on Donovan's forehead. 'That was the hard part. Now let's get this plastic off.'

'Just a moment,' Bersei said. 'I think we should clean this up before we unwrap that.' He pointed to the empty crate sitting on the dolly and the splintered mess surrounding it.

'Of course,' Donovan hesitantly agreed. He'd waited this long . . .

Ten minutes later, the lab was once again tidy, the dolly and neatly packed debris rolled out into the corridor; the floor swept, vacuumed, and wiped with a damp mop.

Bersei disappeared into the rear room. Within seconds, he re-emerged holding a newly pressed lab coat. He handed it to Donovan. 'You should wear this.'

Putting it on, the coat hung awkwardly on Donovan's frame.

'And these,' Charlotte passed over a box of latex gloves. 'I hate them too, but we don't want to contaminate the specimen.'

Each scientist took a pair, pulled them over their hands and donned sterile masks and caps.

Charlotte passed Donovan an X-Acto knife from the work-station's tool drawer. 'Would you like to do the honours?'

Drawing a deep breath, the Vatican librarian nodded, took the knife, and began slicing through the plastic shroud. When he finally drew the wrap apart, what he saw made his eyes light up in wonderment.

12.

Father Patrick Donovan devoured what lay before him. Only weeks ago, he'd acquired an astounding manuscript whose ancient parchment pages chronicled the origin of this magnificent relic, complete with detailed sketches and maps to locate its secret resting place. He had tried to imagine what the box would look like in person, but nothing could have prepared him for this. *Astonishing*.

Giovanni Bersei was circling round the box, squinting. 'This is a burial casket – an ossuary.' His voice was muffled by his mask.

Goosebumps ran up Charlotte's arms.

'I hope Santa Claus isn't inside,' Bersei said in a barely audible mumble.

'What?' Charlotte looked at him, puzzled.

'Nothing,' he said.

Bathed in bright halogen light, the ossuary's ornate features seemed to come to life. On the front and rear faces, rosettes and hatch patterns had been painstakingly etched, not by cutting into the surface, but through chipping the soft stone into relief. The lid was arched and bevelled along its edges. The short sides were flat, one blank, the other bearing a simple relief of a dolphin wrapped around a trident.

Hennesey was momentarily transfixed by the image. 'Father Donovan – what does this symbol mean?'

Still trying to calm himself, Donovan studied it briefly then shook his head. 'Not sure.' It wasn't a complete lie. But – vitally – the symbol identically matched the manuscript's meticulous description of the box.

Dr Bersei's head was pressed close. 'It's beautiful.'

'Certainly is,' Donovan agreed. The ossuary's craftsmanship was impressive, far surpassing any other relic he'd examined from the Holy Land. Using the stylus to shape the soft limestone, the carver's technique had been masterly. There were no cracks or imperfections. The decorative work easily rivalled that of master Roman sculptors – a feature that alone made the relic extraordinary.

Bersei ran a gloved finger over the thin gap along the lid's edge. 'There's a seal here.' He pressed it cautiously. 'Most likely wax.'

'Yes. I see that,' Donovan confirmed.

'It's a good indication that what's inside has been well preserved,' Bersei added.

'I'd like to open this now,' Donovan said. 'Then we'll discuss details of the analysis you will perform.'

Hennesey and Bersei looked at each other, knowing that their seemingly diverse disciplines had indeed found common ground. Opening a sealed burial box implied one thing.

A corpse.

Each peering through Orascoptic Telescopes – protective goggles equipped with flip-down miniature telescopes – Charlotte and Bersei worked the lid's edges with their X-Acto knives, loosening the tight seal of wax that, despite its age, maintained a tight bond with the ossuary.

'Can't you just melt the wax?' Donovan enquired.

Bersei shook his head. 'You can't apply heat to the stone. It could crack or discolour. Plus the wax would drip, making a mess inside.'

Minutes passed and the only sound other than the hum of the ventilation system was of the two blades carefully scratching against the ossuary's seal.

The priest watched the scientists from a discreet distance. His thoughts swung violently between the astounding secrets that the manuscript promised were contained within this ossuary and the firefight in Jerusalem that had claimed so many lives. Not until he could verify the contents with his own eyes would he feel any relief.

Bersei took a deep breath as he made the final cuts. 'Almost there.' The Italian was practically lying across the table finishing off the rear seam.

Charlotte completed the front side and removed her goggles. Seconds later, Giovanni Bersei set down his knife and did the same.

'Ready?' Bersei asked both of them.

Donovan nodded and moved to the head of the table.

The two scientists took position on either side of the box. With fingers hooked underneath the edge of the lid, they squeezed and applied steady upward pressure, gently moving it from side to side to loosen the remaining wax. There was a small pop as the ancient seal gave way, followed by a hiss of escaping gas. Even through their masks they all detected an acrid smell.

'Probably effluvium,' Bersei observed. 'By-product of decaying bone.'

The three exchanged glances.

Donovan swallowed hard, anxiously motioning them to continue.

They removed the lid in tandem and placed it on the rubber mat.

13.

Attached to a rail on the side of the workstation, Charlotte slid over what looked like an oversized desk lamp and swung its retractable arm so that the light was directly over the ossuary's exposed cavity.

Beneath his surgical mask, Father Patrick Donovan was grinning from ear to ear. Staring back at him from inside the cavity was a neatly stacked pile of human remains. Each bone had a dark, grainy finish resembling carved maple.

Charlotte was the first to reach out and touch one, running her finger along a femur. 'These are in extraordinary shape.' She silently wished that her own bones might look so good when her time would come. It almost seemed like a cruel joke that she had been called halfway around the world for *this*. After all, the one refuge that diverted her thoughts from her horrible prognosis was her work. *So much for that.*

Intrigued, Bersei turned sharply to Donovan. 'Whose remains are these?'

'We're not sure.' The librarian avoided eye contact. 'And that's precisely the reason you've both been selected, to help us reconstruct the skeleton's identity. As I mentioned earlier, the Vatican lacks the professional resources to analyse such a unique artifact. That is why you have both been hired.' He touched both his gloved hands down gently on the ossuary's rim and stared down at the contents again. 'We have reason to believe that this amazing relic may help us to better understand the historical context of the Bible.'

'In what way exactly?' asked Charlotte. She preferred people to say what they meant.

Donovan's eyes were frozen to the bones. 'We won't know until we can accurately date this specimen, determine the cause of death through forensic analysis, and reconstruct the physical profile.'

Bersei hesitated, sensing the same thing as Charlotte. The priest seemed to be holding back. 'Much of the success of understanding antiquities relies on knowing specifics relating to its origin. Isn't there anything you know about how this ossuary was procured? Where it came from perhaps? An archaeological dig?'

Donovan shook his head and finally glanced up at them and straightened. 'We've been provided with little background. You can imagine an acquisition like this has to be approached very cautiously. The price is substantial.'

Charlotte's expression was muddled. Two prominent scientists lured here to validate bones, both having to sign letters of confidentiality. Obviously the Vatican believed the ossuary and its contents were valuable. Why else would they have gone to so much trouble and expense?

'We'll perform a complete study,' Bersei assured him. 'A full pathology report. Physical reconstruction. The works.' He glanced over at Charlotte.

'And I'll be wanting to do a carbon dating analysis and draw up a complete genetic profile,' she added. 'It's a fantastic specimen. From what I can see here, so far it looks like you've made an excellent acquisition. I'm confident the results will be impressive.'

'Excellent,' said Donovan, clearly pleased. 'Please let me know when you're ready to report your findings. If possible, I'd like to present a preliminary report in the next few days.'

The scientists exchanged glances.

'That should be fine,' Bersei said.

Donovan stripped off his gloves, mask, and lab coat. 'Please direct any activity through me. I can be reached by using the intercom,' he pointed to the small control panel near the entryway, 'or dial extension two-one-one-four on the phone.' Donovan looked at his watch – 6:12. 'Well, it's late. Why don't we call it a day and you can both start fresh tomorrow morning. Say around eight o'clock?'

The two scientists agreed.

'Dr Hennesey, have you had a chance to see the basilica since you've arrived?' the priest enquired.

'No.'

'You can't stay in Vatican City without seeing first-hand its heart and soul,' he insisted. 'Nothing else compares. Many say its like stepping into Heaven itself.'

'He's right,' Bersei agreed.

'Would you like to see it now?'

Her eyes lit up. 'If you have time, I'd love that.'

'Visiting hours are just winding down, so it shouldn't be too crowded. Giovanni, would like to join us?'

'Sorry, but I must get home to my wife,' he humbly declined. 'She's making osso bucco for dinner.' Bersei leaned closer to

Charlotte and whispered loud enough for Donovan to hear, 'You're in good hands. He's the best tour guide in the Vatican. No one knows this place better.'

14.

Outside the Vatican Museum, the sun was low over western Rome. Cypress trees swayed in a gentle breeze. Ambling beside Father Donovan, Charlotte breathed in the garden's fragrant smell that seemed to capture the complex aroma of a bouquet of flowers.

'Tell me, Dr Hennesey,' Donovan said, 'now that you've seen the relic, are you comfortable with this project?'

'I have to admit that it's not at all what I would have expected.' That was an understatement. Human bones didn't seem like the typical acquisition for the Vatican Museum. And a librarian wasn't exactly the person she would expect to handle their procurement. 'I'm pleasantly surprised, though,' she added. 'Should be very exciting.'

'It will be exciting for us all,' Donovan promised. Nearing the rear of the basilica, he gazed up at it, reverently. 'In the first century, this place where Vatican City now stands was the Vatican Circus, later called Nero's Circus. It was a forum where the emperor Nero held chariot races. Ironic, since he's best known for his persecution of early Christians.'

'He blamed them for the fire that burned down Rome in 64 AD. And in 67 AD, he crucified St Peter to entertain the crowds.'

Donovan was impressed. 'You're a Christian then, or just a good historian?'

'There was a time when I was very good at both.'

'I see.' The priest could see that religion was a touchy subject, but ventured to say, 'You know, back in Ireland we had a saying: "I believe in the sun when it's not shining, I believe in love even when I feel it not, I believe in God even when he is silent."' He glanced over at Charlotte and saw that she was smiling. Thankfully, it looked like he had not offended her. 'Sometimes the things we really cherish just need to be remembered.'

Climbing a set of wide marble steps that accessed the rear of the basilica, Donovan led her to one of the largest bronze doors she'd ever seen. He produced a keycard and slid it through the reader on the doorframe. There was a metallic *thunk* as an electromechanical lock turned. With hardly any effort, the priest opened the huge door and motioned her inside.

'We're going in through here?'

'Of course. One of the benefits of being a guest of the papacy.'

With all her media appearances, Charlotte had grown somewhat accustomed to VIP treatment. But nothing compared to this. Crossing through the arched entry, she instantly felt like she was being transported to another world.

Emerging from the entry grotto, Charlotte was blown away by the basilica's cavernous marble nave. On the plane, she remembered reading in her Fodor's that the Notre-Dame cathedral in Paris could easily fit inside this grand basilica. But standing inside it completely distorted her spatial senses.

Her eyes were immediately drawn upward to Michelangelo's

grand coffered cupola. Covered in tiled mosaics, it soared four hundred and fifty feet above the nave with shafts of sunlight spilling in from its west-facing windows to give it an ethereal glow.

Gradually, her gaze panned down to the famous bronze Baldacchino that stood above the papal altar, directly beneath the dome. Designed by Renaissance giant Giovanni Lorenzo Bernini, its four bronze spiral columns rose seventy feet high to support a gilded baroque canopy that stretched another twenty feet upward.

Even the floors were all inlaid with marble and mosaics.

'Wow,' she gasped.

'Yes, quite magnificent,' Donovan concurred, folding his arms and taking it all in. 'I could easily spend a few hours here giving you a tour. There are twenty-seven chapels, forty-eight altars, and three hundred and ninety-eight statues to see. But I find that the basilica is more of a spiritual journey and is best seen alone.' From a wooden kiosk along the wall, he retrieved a map and guidebook then handed them to Charlotte. 'If you see something that interests you, refer to the book for a detailed description. I must be going now. Enjoy.'

After thanking Father Donovan she slowly began working her way along the side aisle along the basilica's northern wall.

Like most pilgrims who came here, she stopped in front of the thirteenth-century bronze statue raised up on a sturdy marble pedestal that depicted a bearded St Peter. Seated on a papal throne, the saint donned a solar halo and gripped a papal key in his left hand, his right hand raised up as if to deliver a blessing. A few visitors were queued up to take a turn in touching the statue's foot. Referring to the guidebook, she read that this ritual was supposed to grant good luck. Typically, she wasn't one to

81

believe in superstition, but she convinced herself that given her current circumstances, every little bit could help.

Less than five minutes later, she stepped forward, staring up into the statue's solemn face, reaching out to place her left hand on its cold metal feet. Then she amazed herself by doing something she hadn't done in over ten years. She prayed, asking God for strength and guidance. Just like Donovan said, maybe she just needed to remember that she had once been a believer.

She had all but abandoned faith eleven years ago, after watching her mother, a devout Catholic, slowly eaten away by stomach cancer. God's compassion, Charlotte quickly surmised, was not guaranteed to the pious, no matter how many novenas were recited, no matter how many Sundays were spent sitting humbly in a pew listening to sermons. Following her mother's death, Charlotte didn't go to church to find answers – she went behind a microscope, convinced that Mom's defect wasn't faith, but simply a genetic imperfection; corrupted coding.

Somehow her father, even after losing his beloved wife so cruelly, had still managed to attend mass every Sunday, still said grace before every meal, thankful for every new day. *How?* Charlotte wondered. There was a time when she had asked him that very question. His response was quick and sincere, '*Charlie,*' – he was the only person, besides Evan Aldrich, who ever called her by that nickname – '*I've made a choice not to blame God for my misfortune. Life is full of tragedy. But it's also full of beauty.*' When he said this, she remembered that he had smiled dotingly and gently touched her face. '*Who am I to question the force behind such wonder? Remember, sweetie, faith is all about believing that life means something, no matter how hard things might sometimes seem.*'

Maybe now she really did want to believe that there was some divine reason for her own misfortune. But regardless of her dad's spiritual resolve, she still didn't have the heart to tell him about her own illness, knowing that it was just the two of them now.

Lacking the structure of religion made her feel spiritually empty – particularly as of late. Did Charlotte Hennesey believe in God? There was no place on earth that could push that question like *this* place. Perhaps she would find that answer here. Maybe coming to Rome *was* fate.

After ducking into countless other grottos and niches to admire yet another beautiful shrine, she neared the front of the basilica where Michelangelo's famous sculpture, the *Pietà*, was given its own marble-clad chapel, shielded behind glass. The image was dramatic and eerily lifelike – the fallen son draped across the mourning Madonna's lap. For a long minute she stood there captivated by the emotions such an image evoked: suffering, loss, love, hope.

Almost forty minutes later, she was circling back beside the Baldacchino again where she came across a haunting sculpture that made her stop dead in her tracks. Tucked into a multitoned marble alcove flanked by massive colonnades, Bernini's *Monument to Pope Alexander VII* loomed above her. Perched high up on a pedestal, the late pope was immortalized in white marble, kneeling in prayer. Beneath him were various statues depicting Truth, Justice, Charity, and Prudence as human figures.

But Charlotte's horrified gaze had instantly blocked those images out and had sharpened on the shrine's central figure – an oversized winged human skeleton forged from bronze, holding out an hourglass in its right hand. A flowing veil of red marble shadowed its ghoulish face that was directed up at the pope, taunting him with his imminent demise.

The Angel of Death.

The basilica seemed to fall into complete silence, the image coming to life like a demonic countenance, swooping out to dump more of its wretched cancer into her body. She swore she could see the sand in the hourglass counting down. For a moment, she didn't breathe and she could feel tears welling up in her eyes. How could this evil depiction be *here*? She almost felt violated, as if it was purposely meant for her.

'Creepy, isn't it,' a voice cut into her thoughts.

Surprised, she gasped. Turning, she saw a figure that seemed equally ominous. Where the hell had *he* come from?

'Bernini was eighty when he designed that one,' Salvatore Conte said, full of himself. 'Guess he was feeling bitter about his golden years.'

Charlotte tried to give him an obligatory smile, but it didn't happen.

'Did you know this place was built by selling indulgences?' Conte glared up at the central dome, disapprovingly. 'Back in the fifteen hundreds, Pope Leo X ran out of money to finish the project, so he basically raised funds by selling Catholics "get-out-of-Hell-free" cards. Rich people got to pre-pay for God's forgiveness. They even had a saying for it: "*as soon as the coin in the coffer rings, the soul from Purgatory springs.*"'

She felt like saying: *How many indulgences would you need to buy to free your soul?* Conte certainly looked like the type who needed a lot of forgiving. It made her wonder why he was even in Vatican City and what at all he had to do with the ossuary. Earlier, Father Donovan had looked more like a hostage in his presence, not a co-worker. 'I take it you don't go to Church every Sunday,' she sardonically replied.

Leaning closer, he dropped his voice an octave and said, 'After all that I've seen, particularly inside these walls,' he said, 'I'm willing to take my chances.'

She tried to understand what he really meant, but there was nothing in his eyes and she certainly wasn't about to ask him to expound. 'Are you visiting or just stalking?'

The remark took him off guard. 'Just seeing the sights,' he replied, looking away.

'Well, I've got to get going. Nice seeing you,' she lied. Turning to go, Charlotte felt his hand touch her shoulder. She went rigid and turned back to him with icy eyes.

Realizing his miscalculation, Conte threw his hands up. 'Sorry. I know American women are sensitive about their personal space.'

'What do you want?' She pronounced each word clearly.

'I was going to see if you wanted company for dinner tonight. I thought, you're here alone . . . I don't see a wedding ring,' he added, eyeing her hands. 'Maybe you'd like some conversation. That's all.'

For a long moment, she just stared at him, unable to process the idea that he was actually hitting on her in St Peter's Basilica. Suddenly she felt bad for any woman that had been charmed by this character. Handsome – yes – but everything else was severely lacking. 'I've got a boyfriend and I've already made plans, but thank you.' Uncertain as to how much she would need to interact with Conte during the coming days, she tried her best to be polite.

'Some other time, then,' he confidently replied.

'Good night.' She turned and made her way for the exit.

'Enjoy your evening, Dr Hennesey. *Buonasera*.'

TUESDAY

15.
TEMPLE MOUNT

The rising sun cast a faint glow of deep blue and purple over the Mount of Olives as Razak made his way across the Temple Mount esplanade toward the Dome of the Rock Mosque's golden cupola, its crescent-shaped finial delicately pointing toward Mecca.

No matter how many times he visited this place, it always affected him deeply. Here, history and emotion seemed to drip like dew.

In the seventh century, Temple Mount had virtually been forgotten and its bare esplanade was devoid of any great monument. All of its previous architecture had been destroyed many times over. But in 687 AD – only a few decades after a Muslim army led by Caliph Omar had conquered Jerusalem in 638 – the ninth Caliph, Abd al-Malik, began construction of the Dome of the Rock Mosque as a testament to the site's rebirth – and Islam's physical claim over the Holy Land.

Throughout the centuries that followed, Islam had periodically lost its hold over the Temple Mount, most notably to Christian Crusaders whose occupation spanned the twelfth and thirteenth centuries. But it was once again under Islamic control and the Waqf had been entrusted to enforce and legitimize that role. It wasn't easy, especially in the wake of mounting political instability that threatened Islamic exclusivity to the place – a privilege that had almost been lost after the Six Day War in 1967.

Razak tried to imagine how it would feel if the political situation had been reversed: Muslims reduced to worshipping a retaining wall with the Jews possessing a shrine on its holiest spot; Jews in occupied territories and the Palestinians in full control.

He scaled a flight of steps to the mosque's raised platform. Outside the entrance, he removed his Sutor Mantellassi loafers, then made his way into the shrine. Hands crossed behind his back, he worked his way around the blood-red carpet of the octagonal ambulatory glancing up at the elaborate inner dome that sat high atop glassy marble columns. Directly beneath the cupola, cordoned by railings, lay a bare stone expanse of Mount Moriah's summit known as 'the Rock'.

The Rock marked the sacred site where in Biblical times Abraham made to sacrifice his son to God, and where Jacob had dreamt of a ladder to heaven. The Jews proclaimed that a grand Jewish temple built by King Solomon and improved by King Herod once stood here. And the Christians claimed Jesus had visited that same temple many times to preach.

But the site was most significant to Razak and his people for another reason.

In 621, the angel Gabriel had appeared to the great prophet Muhammad in Mecca, presenting him with a winged horse bearing a human face, named Buraq. Embarking on his *Isra*, or 'Night Journey', Muhammad was carried by Buraq to the

Temple Mount where he was ascended through the heavens in a glorious light to behold Allah and consult with Moses and the great prophets. There, Muhammad was also given the five daily prayers by Allah – a core event in his ministry known as the *Miraj*.

The *Miraj* rendered the Dome of the Rock the third most important religious site in Islam, preceded only by Mecca – Muhammad's birthplace – and Medina where, through great struggle and personal sacrifice, he established the Islamic movement.

Razak gazed up at the cupola's exquisite tile work, taking in the Arabic inscriptions flowing round its base.

Outside, the *muezzin's* call echoed from loudspeakers, summoning Muslims to prayer. In front of the mosque's *mihrab* – the small, arched golden alcove that indicated the direction of Mecca – Razak eased onto his knees, hands splayed over his thighs and bowed in prayer.

After a few minutes, he stood and circled back round the Rock's enclosure, stopping in front of a stairway entrance to a chamber called the 'Well of Souls', where it was said the spirits of the dead convened in prayer. There he envisioned his mother and father shining in the divine light of Allah, awaiting the final Day of Judgement so as to be delivered to *Jannah* – Allah's eternal garden paradise.

On September 23, 1996, Razak's parents had been killed by two masked gunmen while vacationing on the Jordanian side of the Sea of Galilee. Many had suspected that Israeli intelligence agents – the *Shin Bet* – had wrongly targeted his father for purported ties to militant Palestinian groups, but those rumours were later disproven. Although that turned out not to be the case, the killers were never found. Their tragic deaths were a profound loss that had driven – and still drove – Razak deeper into his faith for answers. Fortunately, his education at home and abroad had helped him to avoid political and religious fanaticism – an easy trapping for someone so intimately affected by Israel's lethal politics.

Turning away, his thoughts shifted to the crypt hidden deep beneath his feet, and the mysterious theft that had once again brought bloodshed to this place. When he'd arrived here yesterday afternoon, he had never anticipated that a situation of such gravity would have allied him with a man like Graham Barton.

At the mosque entrance Razak put on his shoes and made his way outside.

He still had a couple more hours until his meeting with Barton. So he strolled down into the Muslim Quarter and had coffee and breakfast at a small café on Via Dolorosa. There, he met some old acquaintances and caught up on all that had happened since his last visit. Naturally, the conversation gravitated to the theft, but Razak was quick to point out that he couldn't comment on the investigation.

By nine a.m., there wasn't the slightest breeze as he crossed the Temple Mount esplanade beneath a scorching sun and descended into the Marwani Mosque. Climbing through the blast hole into the crypt, Akbar – the oversized Muslim guard instructed to watch over Barton – signalled that everything was fine. Razak nodded and waved him out into the mosque.

Graham Barton was crouched in a corner transcribing an inscription on one of the ossuaries.

'Good morning, Mr Barton,' Razak said in English.

The archaeologist sprung to his feet.

'Looks like you've been busy.' Razak eyed the small stacks of rubbings Barton had laid out at intervals along the floor.

'Very much so,' Barton replied cheerily. 'I got here early and Akbar was kind enough to let me get a head start.'

'What have you found out so far?'

'It's an extraordinary discovery. This crypt belonged to a Jewish man named Yosef.' Barton pointed to a box on one end, just as plain as the others. 'You'll notice that each of these ossuaries is inscribed in Hebrew with the names of his family members.'

Unimpressed, Razak sought meaningful information. 'Yosef *who*?'

Barton shrugged. 'That's the problem with ancient Jews. They weren't terribly specific when it came to names. They rarely used family names, at least for burial purposes. And the Hebrew name "Yosef" was quite common back then. Anyway, you see that each ossuary is plainly marked.'

Razak eyed the inscriptions carved into the sides of the nine boxes.

'Each one says pretty much the same thing: whose remains are contained inside each ossuary. Those are his four daughters,' he indicated the cluster sitting at the beginning of the line-up. 'Three sons,' he motioned to the next three, then to the one beside Yosef's, 'plus his loving wife, Sarah.' Barton drew a deep breath. 'But there's an etching on the back wall of the crypt that provides more detail.' Grabbing a flashlight, he motioned for Razak to follow and advanced into the shadowy recess, stopping by the rear wall. The cylinder of light played along the stone. 'See that.' Barton illuminated a wall-mounted tablet framed with ornate stone trim. 'It lists the inventory of ossuaries contained in this chamber.'

The Muslim stepped closer. 'So the missing ossuary should be listed here.' Counting nine lines of text, Razak's eyes were drawn to a deep gouge scarring the polished rock beneath the last line. Confused, he stared at it for a long moment. 'I'm only seeing nine entries.'

'Correct. And those nine are the names that match the remaining ossuaries. But this entry here,' Barton trained the light on the disfigured rock, 'probably identified the tenth ossuary.' He tapped it with his finger.

Razak studied it critically once more. 'Won't do us much good now.'

'Agreed. Another dead end.'

Razak strolled around the chamber holding out his hands. 'Why here?'

'What do you mean?'

'Of all places, why would the crypt be located here?'

He had a good point, Barton thought. 'Normally we'd expect crypts to be outside the city walls. But it's certainly possible this site was chosen for security reasons. In fact' – he paused to for-mulate the idea – 'in the first century, Antonia Fortress, the Roman garrison, was situated adjacent to the northern wall of Temple Mount. The esplanade above us' – he pointed up – 'would have been a very public area – all sorts of activities going on. Raised portico walkways ran all along the perimeter of the platform and looped around to the garrison. The Roman centu-rions would pace up and down to police the crowds, ready to quell any disturbances.'

Barton refrained from explaining that, in the first century, the primary reason for the Temple Mount's popularity was the grand Jewish temple that once stood in place of the Dome of the Rock Mosque – a claim that the Waqf had systematically denied for centuries in order to secure its hold over the site. Since no archaeological evidence supported the scriptural reference to the temple, their position had remained strong.

'And what do Roman centurions have to do with this crypt?'

'Everything. Remember, in ancient times there were no safes or lockboxes. That's why plundering was the easiest way to get rich. Assets were vulnerable.'

Razak was eyeing Barton intently. 'The only way to protect treasures or valuables was with an army?'

'Correct.'

'Then perhaps the tenth ossuary didn't contain human remains. Could it have protected some kind of treasure?'

'It's plausible.'

'Certainly more believable than human remains,' Razak continued. 'I'm not seeing why anyone would go through such great trouble to steal bones.'

Barton could sense that Razak was pleased with his own reasoning and in the absence of further evidence, he wasn't about to challenge the idea. 'As far as I can see,' he added, 'it's impossible to draw conclusions as to what the stolen ossuary may actually have contained. But inside these remaining nine boxes,' he gestured toward the ossuaries, 'we may find some more clues.' He handed Razak a pair of rubber gloves. 'Which is why you'll need these.'

A horrified look came over the Muslim.

16.

VATICAN CITY

The two scientists convened in the lab at eight a.m., both heading directly to the rear break room where Giovanni Bersei was instructing Charlotte Hennesey on how to use what he considered to be the lab's most vital piece of equipment – the Gaggia automatic coffee machine, which pumped out customized brew at the touch of a button.

'Tell me. How was your visit to the basilica last night?'

Rolling her eyes, she gave him a quick summary that ended with her retelling of an unpleasant encounter with Salvatore Conte. She told him that it had disturbed her so much she'd decided to skip going out all together. Having settled for a tuna sandwich from the Domus's cafeteria, she'd turned in early. Not the most exciting night, she admitted, though she was happy to have caught up on her sleep. 'And how did your wife's osso bucco turn out?'

He made a sour face. 'Not so good. Carmela is many things, but a good cook is not one of them. In fact, she may be the worst cook in all Italy.'

She hit him lightly on the shoulder. 'You're terrible, Giovanni. I hope you didn't tell her that.'

'Are you crazy? I value my life.'

They both laughed.

Bersei checked his watch. 'Ready to begin?'

'Let's do it.'

Refilling their cups, they moved back into the main room and stood at the workstation, both donning lab coats. The ossuary, with its mysterious skeleton, was just as they had left it yesterday.

Bersei handed Charlotte a new mask and latex gloves and she put them on. He did the same.

Staring at the bones, Charlotte half expected a hand to pop out holding an hourglass.

After putting on his own mask and gloves, Bersei retrieved a Canon EOS digital camera, turned it on, snapped some pictures, then set it down.

Positioned on opposing sides of the workstation, the scientists began removing the bones one piece at a time, carefully placing them onto the rubber matting. Slowly the reassembled skeletal frame came together: the longer bones of the legs and arms, the pelvis and loose bundles of ribs, the segments of spinal vertebrae, and finally the delicate, complex bones of the hands and feet.

With infinite care, Charlotte lifted the skull from the ossuary. Supporting the mandible with one hand and the orb of cranium with the other, she placed it at the end of the completed skeleton.

Bersei performed a quick visual inspection. 'Looks like all two hundred and six bones are here.' He grabbed the Canon and snapped a few more shots of the completed skeleton.

Charlotte peered down. 'Okay. Let's figure out how this man died.'

'Strictly speaking, we don't know we're dealing with a male yet, Dr Hennesey,' he politely challenged. 'Could be female.'

Charlotte tilted her head. 'Sure. But I doubt a woman would've been given such a fancy box.'

Raising his eyebrows, he couldn't tell if she was joking.

'Don't panic. I'm not about to get feminist on you,' she said. 'I'm saving that for later.'

'Just be gentle.'

Both scientists agreed that their initial analysis would be a forensic pathology study determining the cause of death if possible, followed by a reconstruction of the skeleton's physical profile. Charlotte activated the workstation's recording system to document the analysis. Later, their oral notes would be transcribed. From the workstation drawer, she pulled out two pairs of Orascoptic goggles. Giving one to Bersei and putting the other on, she flipped the telescoping lenses over her eyes.

They began with the skull, both bending closer to study it in minute detail.

'Looks perfect,' Bersei said peering through his goggles.

Charlotte sized up the dimensions and contours. 'Square chin, pronounced supraorbital ridges and muscle attachment points. It does look like we're dealing with a male.'

'Maybe you're right,' Bersei admitted. He tilted the skull back and rotated it, examining the inner cavity. 'The sutures are still visible, but have all fused. See here,' he pointed to the seam where the contoured bone plates met along the skull, looking like a jagged zipper that had been smoothed over.

Verifying his observation, Charlie knew the concept. The younger the specimen, the more pronounced the joining lines would appear, looking like the tight joining of two saw blades. The older the specimen, the fusion would advance to the point where the lines would become indiscernible. 'That means we're looking at age twenty to thirty, minimum?'

'I'd agree with that.' Bersei turned the skull over a few times, scanning its surfaces. 'I'm not seeing any indications of head trauma, are you?'

'None.'

Both scientists turned their attention to the mandible.

'These teeth are in magnificent shape,' Charlotte said. 'Hope mine hold up this well. This guy still had a full set. Don't even see an indication of periodontal disease.' For a second, she fussed with a rotating dial on the goggles to increase the magnification of the lenses. 'The enamel's intact. No cavities or uneven wearing.'

'Strange.'

'Maybe he didn't like sweets.'

They moved to the cervical region, analysing intently, searching for abnormalities in the neck.

'I'm not seeing any spurs,' Charlotte remarked. 'No ridging or ossification here.'

'And no fusion either,' Bersei added. 'Actually, the discs don't appear to have degenerated at all.' He delicately rotated the last small section of cervical vertebrae. 'Nothing shocking.' He motioned toward the skeleton's rib cage. 'Let's keep moving.'

Almost immediately Charlotte's eyebrows shot up. 'Wait. That's interesting.'

Following her finger to the centre of the chest area, Bersei focused on the flat bones of the sternum and spotted it immediately. 'That's a huge tear.'

'Sure is.' She studied the separations in the dried cartilage attaching the ribs to the chest plate. 'Do you think that might have happened when the rib cage was detached to fit into the ossuary?'

'Perhaps.' His tone was cautious. Bersei shifted his focus to the adjacent shoulder. 'Look here.'

She followed his lead. 'You've got a good eye. The humerus and clavicle were separated from the scapula?'

'Agreed. But it doesn't look like it happened post-mortem. The tears are fibrous. Where the tissue separated suggests the breakage happened before the tissue dried.' He shifted back to the sternum. 'See here. Looks like the same story. Can you detect where the cartilage stretched, pulled widthwise and tore? When the bones were prepared for burial, some kind of blade was used to cut the tissue.'

Hennesey saw it too. A clean cut bisected the lateral stress tears of torn cartilage. 'Ouch, that looks painful. What do you think . . . a dislocation?'

'A very violent dislocation.' Bersei's tone was troubled.

'That had to really hurt.'

'I'm sure it did. But it certainly didn't kill him. You take those ribs.' He indicated the ones closest to her. 'And I'll take these.'

Time seemed suspended as they worked on the ribs, meticulously analysing each surface.

Charlotte was just starting to ease into the idea of working on bones, focusing on the task at hand rather than unpleasant images of the genetic chaos inside her own body at that very moment. 'You seeing what I'm seeing?'

'The deep grooves?' Bersei's head was down. 'Absolutely.'

Some of the ribs were unscathed, but most looked like they'd been raked with thick nails to produce long, scalloped gouges. The ratty fissures appeared in random groupings.

'What could've done this?' Her voice had sunk to a whisper.

'I think I may know. Do you see traces of metal deposit?'

'Yes. Is this something that happened post-mortem? It almost looks like some kind of animal was chewing on them.'

'I'd have to say no,' Bersei told her. 'You'll notice those marks only appear on the anterior fascia. Teeth would've left marks on both sides, not to mention that most scavengers would have run off with the bone before gnawing on it and wouldn't have left us a complete skeleton.'

'So what do you think did this?' Charlotte straightened.

'Let me put it this way.' He peered over the flip-down telescoping lenses. 'If the bones look this bad, the muscle and skin that covered them must have looked far worse . . . Probably shredded.' Holding her gaze, he drew a breath then said, 'Looks to me like this man was flayed.'

'You mean whipped?'

He nodded slowly. 'That's right. Those markings are from a barbed whip.'

'Poor guy.' The thought of such violence hit her in the gut.

'Let's keep going.' Bersei bent down and began working on the upper segments of lumbar vertebrae.

Charlotte leaned over and started rotating the lower vertebrae of the spine while scrutinizing every bone and cushion of disc material. 'Everything looks good here.'

'Agreed.' Bersei glanced at the compact structure of the pelvic bones that provided definitive clues relating to gender. 'And you were right about the gender. Definitely male.' He ran his fingers along the contours of bone where the genitalia would be. 'The sciatic notch is narrow, the preauricular area's got no indentations and flattens.'

'No babies coming out through there. No infants left motherless, at least.'

So far Giovanni Bersei was pleased. Determining gender

from skeletal remains was never easy as the most obvious gender-specific traits occurred in the soft tissues, not the bones. Depending on a variety of factors, from diet and lifestyle, to the physical stress of the subject's occupation, the female human skeleton could easily morph its soft tissue in ways that conditioned the skeletal frame to appear almost identical to its male counterpart. Increased muscle mass would be an obvious equalizer, demanding thicker bones to support them, especially in areas where ligaments would attach. But the pelvis's birthing canal was fairly discernible in most female skeletons.

'So – arms or legs?' he enquired.

'Arms first.'

They shifted along the skeleton, resuming a minute analysis of the long bones, starting with the humerus and working down to the paired set of each arm's lower half – the ulna and radius.

Something caught her eye and she moved even closer to sharpen the lenses' resolution. There was significant damage to the inner surfaces of the bones joining above the wrist. 'What's this? Looks like they went through a grinder.'

'It's on this side too. The damage is contained to just above the wrist,' Bersei confirmed. 'Do you see oxidation, like long streaks?'

'Yeah, could be metallic residue. Maybe hematite.' She saw something else. 'Hang on.' She repositioned the lens. 'Fibres have been lodged in the bone. Your side?'

'Yes. Get a sample of that. Looks like wood.'

Charlotte went into the tool drawer, removed a pair of tweezers and a small plastic vial, and proceeded to pluck away the fibres from the bone.

Meanwhile, Bersei was already moving down near the skeleton's feet. He bent over to get a better look at something there.

'What do you see?' she asked, standing and setting down the vial and tweezers.

He waved her closer. 'Come take a look.'

Training her lenses on the area just below the shin, the paired set of fibula and tibia looked healthy. But nestled in the upper notches of each foot were deep, gritty patches scooped into the bones. Two bones in the left foot had been fractured.

'Look at the damage between the second and third metatarsals,' Bersei noted. 'It's similar to the arms.'

'Same rust-coloured streaking,' Hennesey added. 'Definitely came from some kind of impaled metal.'

'Judging from the fractures in the second metatarsal on the left foot, it was a nail. Do you see where the point hit the bone and split it?'

Hennesey saw a diamond-shaped indentation stamped in the fissure's midpoint and detected more wood splinters. 'Unbelievable. Looks like the nail missed the first time.' Thinking that one human could inflict this kind of damage on another nauseated her. What kind of animal could be capable of such cruelty?

'Most likely because the feet were nailed on top of one another,' Dr Bersei stated flatly. He noticed another oddity in the area of the knees and positioned himself for a better view.

'What do you see?'

'Look at this.'

When Charlotte focused on the knee joint, the damage was immediately apparent. Just when she thought it couldn't get worse. 'Oh, God.'

'Completely blown out,' Bersei gasped. 'Look at those tears in the cartilage and the hairline fractures below the knee.'

'His knees were broken?'

'Yes, of course.'

'What do you mean?'

Bersei straightened and flipped his lenses up. His complexion was ashen. 'It's quite clear what happened here. This man was crucified.'

17.

TEMPLE MOUNT

'Surely you don't expect me to desecrate the remains of the dead.' Utterly insulted, Razak folded his arms across his chest and frowned at Barton. 'Have you no conscience?'

'It's important, Razak.' He held out the gloves again.

Razak pushed the gloves away. 'I will not permit this!' His voice reverberated loudly off the chamber's walls. 'You'll have to get authorization from the Waqf.'

Akbar peered through the blast hole, looking alarmed.

Avoiding the guard's glare, Barton spoke quietly. 'You and I both know that will yield no results. In the interests of time, we'll need to take some initiative to find answers. That's why we're here.'

Still fuming, Razak turned to Akbar. 'Everything's fine.' He motioned for the guard to go away. He rubbed his temples, then turned back to the archaeologist. 'What good can come of this? They are only bones in those boxes.'

'That's not certain.'

Razak spread his hands. 'If that isn't the case, then why didn't the thieves take these boxes too?' He motioned toward the ossuaries.

'We need to be sure,' Barton remained steadfast. 'Every possibility must be explored. As it stands, the only clues we have are in this room. It would be a major oversight to forgo studying these ossuaries.'

For a few seconds, the crypt was deathly silent.

'All right,' Razak finally yielded. 'One box at a time. But this you will do alone.'

'Understood.'

'Allah save us,' Razak muttered. 'Go on, then. Do what you must.' He turned to face away from the scene.

Relieved, Barton knelt in front of the first ossuary, inscribed with the Hebrew characters that translated to 'Rebecca'. 'This may take awhile,' he called out.

'I will wait.'

Reaching out with both hands, Barton firmly clasped the sides of the flat stone lid. He glanced over at Razak. The Muslim still had his back to him. Drawing a deep breath, Barton jostled it loose, pulling it away.

Two hours after he opened the first ossuary, Graham Barton was just replacing the skeletal remains that he had taken out of the seventh ossuary. Much like the specimens he had found in the preceding six burial boxes, this one was remarkably well preserved.

Though forensic anthropology wasn't his speciality, he had studied enough bones in his time to understand the fundamentals. Certainly, the names on each ossuary eliminated much of the speculation concerning gender, but clues present on the skull sutures, joints, and pelvic bones led him to certain conclusions regarding the age of these skeletons. The four younger females –

the daughters, he guessed – deceased very young, ranging in age between late teens and early twenties. The three younger males – by the same logic, the sons – also seemed to fall into the same range. Typical of families during the first century, the children were numerous and born in rapid succession to ensure family survival.

Yet as far as Barton could tell, their remains showed no outright anomalies. No telling signs of trauma.

Assuming these siblings were all born of the father and mother interred in ossuaries eight and nine, it seemed uncanny that all could have died so young. Even in the first century, where normal life expectancy of those surviving their gruelling early years might have been as low as thirty-five, this seemed statistically improbable. In fact, it appeared as if they'd all died at the same time.

Strange.

Barton stood to stretch for moment. 'Still doing okay over there?' He glanced across the chamber where the Muslim was seated in a meditative position, facing the wall. At one point, he had heard him chanting prayers.

'Yes. How much longer will you need?'

'Just two more to go. Say half an hour?'

The Muslim nodded.

The archaeologist rolled his neck then squatted down in front of the eighth ossuary containing Yosef's spouse, Sarah. Having established a good system by now, he deftly pulled away the lid, flipped it, and rested it on the stone floor so it could be used as a pallet for the extracted bones.

The hollow eye sockets of a glossy smooth skull stared back at him from inside the box, looking like a ghoulish plaster mould painted in beige shellac.

Unsure of what he was even looking for, Barton was starting to lose any hope that anything extraordinary was contained in these remaining boxes. Could the thieves really have known this and purposely left these behind like Razak had suggested? Certainly the contents within the tenth ossuary couldn't have been as pedestrian as these. It had him perplexed as to what the thieves knew about the missing relic and how they could've obtained such specific detail in advance.

Palming the skull, Barton rotated it, then shined the flashlight inside, so that it illuminated like a macabre jack o'lantern. The fusion along the sutures suggested that Sarah had probably been in her late thirties. He set it down on the lid. Then one by one, he plucked the larger bones out and stacked them neatly beside the skull. The small bones that had fallen to the bottom of the box came out in fistfuls. All accounted for and all normal. Aiming the flashlight into the empty ossuary, he carefully examined each surface for engravings, making sure that nothing on the bottom evaded him.

Reverently returning Sarah's bones to her ossuary and replacing the lid, Barton squatted in front of the ninth ossuary with little enthusiasm. 'Come on Yosef, talk to me.' Reaching out, he rubbed his fingertips together for good luck and gripped the lid. This time, he was surprised when the top didn't budge. He tried again. Nothing.

'Hmm. That's odd.'

'What is it?' Razak called out.

'This last ossuary's been sealed with something.' Barton ran the flashlight over its seam. There was definitely something there and it looked like grey caulk.

'Then perhaps you should let it be.'

Is this fellow mad? He hadn't come this far to stop now. Ignoring him, Barton removed a Swiss Army knife from his pocket, flipped out a medium-sized blade and scraped some of the gooey stuff away onto his gloved palm. Looking at the shavings under the light, he determined it to be some kind of fatty wax. It took him under five minutes to loosen the seal enough to free the lid. He folded the blade and slipped it back into his pocket.

'Right then,' he muttered, wiping sweat from his brow. Clasping the lid lengthwise, he coaxed it away, flipped it, and set it on the floor. An unpleasant odor rose up from the box's exposed cavity, making him gasp.

Grabbing the flashlight, he shone it downward. The longest bones were up top and he began unpacking them.

When he came to the skull, he flipped it around and lit it up. Judging from the advanced fusion on the skull's sutures and the substantial wear on the remaining teeth along the jaw line, Yosef had been in his late sixties or early seventies at the time of death. When the last of the bones were taken out from the ossuary, Barton drew breath and poked his head into the box, shining the flashlight inside. On the bottom, he was surprised to see a small rectangular metal plate. Retrieving the Swiss Army blade again, he worked it under the plate, prying it away, uncovering a small niche that had been carved into the ossuary's base. And in it was a metal cylinder no longer than fifteen centimetres. Barton smiled. 'That's my boy.' He grabbed it with his fingers and held it up.

'Did you find something?' Razak's voice echoed across the crypt.

'Oh yes. Take a look.'

Without thinking, Razak turned and barely glimpsed the cylinder when his eyes wandered down to the pile of bones. He snapped his head back toward the wall. 'Unfortunate soul. May peace be upon him,' Razak responded.

'Sorry. Should've warned you about that,' Barton said.

Throwing up a hand and shaking his head, Razak said, 'It's all right. What is that you have in your hand?'

'A clue.' Barton bounced to his feet and walked over to the pole light. 'Come and have a look.'

Springing to his feet, Razak went and stood beside Barton.

Eyeing it closely, Razak noticed that the cylinder – most likely bronze – had small caps on both ends. 'Are you going to open it?'

'Of course.' Without hesitation, he pulled one cap free and tipped the open end to the light, looking inside. He spotted something rolled up. 'Aha. I think we have a scroll.'

Razak was nervously stroking his chin, wondering whether there was a better way to go about all this, but resigned himself to the fact that Barton was the expert.

Tipping it over his palm, Barton tapped the cylinder a few times until the scroll fell out. Verifying that there was nothing else inside the metal tube, he placed it in his shirt pocket. 'Vellum. And excellently preserved.' Very gingerly, he unfurled it. It was filled with ancient text, Greek if he wasn't mistaken. The archaeologist glanced up at Razak.

'Bingo.'

18.

VATICAN CITY

Having spent the past two hours completing a comprehensive journal chronicling the forensic examination – digital photos, written descriptions, case notes – the two scientists sipped their espressos by the coffee machine in the lab's cramped, white-walled break room. Both were steeped in thought.

Bersei scrunched up his face. 'I've seen human remains of every shape and kind, some mummified, others just bones. Some even melted.' He paused. 'But that was an absolute first. Although it's not surprising.'

'Why's that?'

'While it's believed that crucifixion was introduced by the Greeks, in fact it was predominantly practised by the Romans – their typical method of criminal execution until the emperor Constantine banned it in the fourth century.'

'You're certain that what we're seeing here is the result of crucifixion, not some other form of torture?'

'Certain. And I'll tell you why.' Bersei drained his coffee. 'Let's start with the basics. First off, you have to understand *why* the Romans crucified criminals. Obviously it was an extreme method of punishment, but it was also intended to send a message to all citizens that Rome was in control. It was a very public death where victims would be stripped naked and hung along major roadways and prime locations. It was considered a dishonourable way to die . . . utterly humiliating. As such, it was typically reserved for criminals of low social status and enemies of the state. It was the Romans' key method of ruling by fear.'

Charlotte's green eyes flashed. 'So we could be dealing with a criminal here?'

'Perhaps.' He shrugged.

She looked at him curiously. 'How do you know all this?'

'I realize it seems odd, but a few years ago I actually published a formal study on crucifixion, funded by the Pontifical Commission. I tested established theories regarding how it kills the victim.'

Charlotte wasn't sure how to respond. 'I've got to ask . . . why?'

'Look, I know it sounds morbid. But crucifixion was practised for centuries and it's hugely relevant to understanding the early Roman government. I prefer to think of it as a niche,' he smiled. 'It was a popular paper.'

'I'm sure it was. A regular barrel of laughs.'

'Would you like me to continue?'

'Please do.'

'Before they were crucified, criminals were scourged, usually with a cane or whip, making them more compliant for delivery to the execution site. In the case of our man, it seems the scourging was performed with a *flagrum* – a vicious, multi-thong whip with metal barbs.'

'That explains why the ribs were so badly scarred.'

'*Si*. And judging from the depth of the fissures, his flesh must have been severely flayed. This man would have been in tremendous pain and bleeding terribly.'

'That's so cruel.' She fought off the urge to visualize the razor-tipped whip streaming through the air and raking across flesh.

'That was just the beginning I'm afraid. Crucifixion itself was far, far worse. There were a number of variations on this type of execution, basically all for the same lethal effect. The criminal was impaled on a cruciform by long spikes driven through the wrists and feet. A rope was bound around the arms to provide additional support when the body was hung upright. The cruciform could take many forms: a simple tree or post, two beams crossed like an X, or a solid structure built like a capital T. I'd guess that in the case of our victim, the cross was a *crux composita*, consisting of an upright post, or stipe, and a crossbar called a *patibulum*. We know that the familiar images of crucifixion depict victims being nailed to the cross through the hands . . .'

Charlotte knew where this was going. 'But the small bones and weak flesh in the hands couldn't support the weight of a body, right? Nailed through the hands, the body would slip off the cross.' She clenched her hands round the cup.

'Exactly. So to support the weight, the iron spikes – huge things measuring eighteen centimetres or so – would be driven into the wrist, just above the ulna and radius along with a large wooden washer to prevent slippage. Right here.' Bersei pointed to a spot just above the crease of his wrist. 'It would've crushed or severed the median nerve, sending shock waves of excruciating pain up the arm. The hands would have been instantly paralysed. Once both wrists were nailed, the *patibulum*, bearing the full weight of the body, would be violently hoisted onto the stipe. One can't imagine how that must have felt. Unbelievable.'

Hideous images of nails pounding into flesh came into her mind's eye. 'That explains the shoulder dislocation.'

'It also explains the gouge patterns and trace residues of hematite we see in the wrists – evidence of extreme pressure against the bones. Grinding. Like the weight of the body was suspended on nails.'

Hennesey dropped her cup into the sink. 'I can't drink any more.'

Bersei put his hand on her arm. 'Are you okay?'

She rubbed her eyes. Maybe bone cancer wasn't so bad after all. 'Keep going. I'm fine.'

'Once the body was pulled upright,' the Italian continued, 'the feet would have been laid over one another, then nailed into the post. It wouldn't have been easy as the victim would have been flailing about.'

'Probably explains the fracture we saw on the foot. There was a struggle.'

'Yes.' Bersei's voice dropped. 'Sometimes, to avoid that struggle, a supporting peg called a *sedile* was inserted between the legs. A nail was pounded through . . .' – he paused to reconsider this part, but felt the need to be thorough in his explanation – 'the penis and into the *sedile* to secure victims to the cross.'

For a moment Charlotte felt light-headed, as if she was going to faint. Every time Dr Bersei added another layer of detail, she felt herself sinking lower, as if her bones were being picked out from inside her one by one. 'That's unbelievably brutal,' she said in a small whisper. This terrifying knowledge appeared totally at odds with Giovanni's otherwise gentle disposition. She took a deep breath.

Folding his hands, Bersei paused to marshal his thoughts. 'The fact is, in crucifixion no one thing kills the victim. Overall trauma eventually does that. Scourging, impalement, exposure to the elements . . . they all contribute. Depending on the victim's health before execution, death could take days.'

It was impossible for Charlotte to imagine humans being subjected to such extreme punishment. Equally puzzling to her was Bersei's intensity regarding the subject. She couldn't help but think that men had an innate curiosity for this sort of thing. 'And we already know that this man was extremely healthy.'

Bersei nodded. 'The damage we saw to the ribs suggests that the intensity of the scourging alone should have killed him. The skin and muscle structure would have been left in tatters, possibly exposing the internal organs. It's incredible that this person could have persevered – he must have suffered horribly. Which brings me to my last point.'

Charlotte's stomach contracted. She knew he was about to lay it on her even thicker.

'If the criminal wasn't moving through the process quickly enough,' Bersei continued, 'death would be speeded up – they'd break the knees with a large metal club.'

That visual came quick and she felt her own knees wobble. 'Just like we're seeing here,' she replied. Fighting to remain objective, Charlotte pondered the consequences of the punishment's final stage. 'Without the support of the legs, the full weight of the body would pull across the rib cage. Is that why the cartilage in the chest was torn?'

'Quite so. With the lungs constricted, the victim would struggle desperately to breathe. Meanwhile what little blood remained would begin to settle lower into the legs and torso.'

'Then basically the criminal would have expired from asphyxiation and heart failure, right?'

'Right. Dehydration and trauma could also speed up the

process.' He paused and pursed his lips. 'The victim would be kept on the cross for days, until death came. It would have been unspeakably painful.'

'Then what?'

Lips pulled tight, Bersei offered his explanation. 'The corpses would be tossed to the ground, then vultures, dogs, and other beasts would take turns feeding on them. Any remnants were burned. The Romans were very systematic about all of this. It reinforced the last stage of the punishment – refusing a criminal proper burial – a huge blow to just about all religions of that period. By burning the bodies, the Romans were actually denying victims any possibility of eventual afterlife, reincarnation, or resurrection.'

'The ultimate punishment.' She cast her eyes to the floor.

'Indeed. The body was completely annihilated.'

'Must've scared the crap out of people to see all this. What a sight that must've been – walking along a roadway and seeing all those bodies impaled on posts. Talk about suggestive advertising.'

'Rome's forte. It certainly left an impression . . . kept the subjugated taxpayers orderly.'

A moment of silence fell over the break room.

'Who do you think this guy was?' she finally asked.

Bersei shrugged and shook his head. 'It's far too early to tell. Could be any one of thousands crucified by the Romans. Prior to this, the only crucified remains ever found was a heel bone with a nail driven through its side. The fact that what we're looking at represents the first intact crucified *body* recovered makes it an extraordinarily valuable relic.'

Charlotte inclined her head. 'That explains why the Vatican's gone to so much trouble to bring us here.'

'Absolutely. Makes perfect sense. A find like this is monumental.'

'But we only opened the ossuary today and if it was sealed, how on earth could they have known the man inside had been crucified? How did they know they'd need your expertise?'

Bersei considered this. 'It's no surprise they called me here. Having worked in the catacombs for years, I've come across many skeletons, many relics associated with burial. As for you . . . well, I don't need to tell you that using DNA to examine human remains is a tremendous tool. But let's hold off on the theories until we study the ossuary further. After all, the physical remains tell only part of the story.'

19.
VATICAN MUSEUM

Down the corridor from the lab, in a cramped space normally used as a storage closet, a network of cables cascaded down to the computer hard drive, feeding live video and audio transmissions from the laboratory and its adjoining break room. Wearing headphones wired to the bank of surveillance equipment, Salvatore Conte was diligently recording all of the scientists' activity, as directed by the Vatican Secretary of State, Cardinal Santelli.

Two separate wireless links also monitored all phone calls in and out of Charlotte Hennesey's dorm room (thanks to a simple patch into the Vatican's main phone server) and Giovanni Bersei's personal residence. He had paid a special visit to Bersei's house last night. While the anthropologist was busy eating his wife's overcooked veal shanks, Conte was outside splicing a transmitter into the phone line junction box on the side of his house – electrical engineering skills, compliments of his previous employers.

Though he found all the science-talk only mildly interesting, most of his attention was focused on the attractive American geneticist. She was hot. Normally, guys like him didn't get girls like her. But it never hurt to try. And no one tried harder than Salvatore Conte. Perseverance was everything.

Studying Hennesey again – face, lips, hair, body – he had decided that one way or another, he would have a taste of her. He would just need to wait a little longer, until the job here was complete.

On a separate computer monitor, he brought up the computer's web browser and linked to the home page for the Cayman Islands bank where he had opened a new account under one of his pseudonyms. Entering his user name and password to access his account summary screen, he paused to make sure that Santelli had made good on his end of the bargain.

Earlier that morning, he'd had a very candid discussion with the cardinal concerning a bonus payment for expedited delivery of the relics as well as additional hazard pay for himself and his colleagues (Doug Wilkinson excluded). He made it clear that he would be 'uncomfortable' leaving Vatican City without seeing that the payment had been made. Surprisingly, the cardinal hadn't protested, readily agreeing that such an efficient operation was well worth the additional expense.

The money was wire transferred through one of the Vatican's outside banking affiliates, bearing no audit trail back within these walls, Conte was sure. The bank hadn't even contacted him regarding the sum and the funds had cleared immediately.

As a teen, Salvatore Conte had been a high achiever at Nunziatella Military School in Naples and upon graduation went off to fulfil the State's mandatory eight-month military conscription. It wasn't long before his unique abilities – both physical and intellectual – caught the attention of his commanding officers whose high commendations earned him a position in the Servizio per le Informazioni e la Sicurezza Democratica, the

Italian Secret Service. There, he had learned the core skills that helped him to become a free agent. Assassinations, hostage situations, infiltrating terrorist cells – Conte took any job thrown at him and he excelled at all of them. He'd been loaned out to assist on collaborative operations throughout Europe and in the United States.

His decision to leave the SISDE almost five years ago had been a good one. Having already established plenty of contacts during his years with them, there was never a shortage of clients seeking vengeance against a foe or scheming to 'procure' new assets. They always paid in cash, and they always paid on time.

However, he had targeted a small group of clients whom he considered the most lucrative prospects. Among them was the Vatican – a tiny country that considered itself virtually impregnable with its high walls, its nifty security system, and its mercenary army. Conte had taken the liberty in paying a visit to its top guy to remind him that no system was impenetrable. Not the pope, of course – that wouldn't have been wise. No, Conte had chosen Cardinal Santelli – the man who he knew had truly been the brains of the operation.

He could still recall the look on the old bastard's face when Santelli came strolling into his office that morning, whistling, only to see Conte sitting at his impeccably organized desk playing solitaire on his computer, which he had hacked into with a portable password unscrambler. He was dressed completely in black – standard attire for a night-time incursion.

Appalled, the cardinal had yelled, 'Who the hell are you?'

'Your local security consultant,' Conte quickly replied in kind, standing and rounding the desk to offer a personalized business card with his alias and an encrypted mobile telephone number. 'I was in the area and wanted to introduce myself personally to go over some obvious deficiencies in your country's security systems.'

The truth was, getting into Vatican City hadn't been easy at all. Stuffed into a backpack beside Santelli's desk was a bevy of gear: grappling cables, rappelling harnesses, glasscutters, night-vision goggles, the works. He'd had to scale the city's northern rampart, shoot a grappling line over to the Vatican Museum rooftop, pull himself across the gap, traverse the top of the building to the Apostolic Palace, scramble the security system (using an electromagnetic pulsing device he had lifted from SISDE), rappel down to Santelli's office window, cut the glass, and unlock the latch. Once inside, he'd eaten a mortadella, prosciutto, and mozzarella panini and drank a Pellegrino Chinotto and waited for sunrise.

It had taken a minute or two for Santelli to calm down, to try and rationalize how anyone could have circumvented the Vatican's tight security layers. All the while, he had been con-templating the intercom on his desk. Then, after explaining the myriad services he could provide to a *'powerful man such as your-self'*, Conte verbally ran through a laundry list of available services that the cardinal pretended to be offended at. But Conte knew better. Having seen the file on this guy when he was work-ing at SISDE – particularly the one related to the infamous Banco Ambrosiano scandal – he knew the cardinal was no stranger to nefarious deeds.

'And what makes you think I won't have you arrested right now?' Santelli had threatened.

'Because I'll detonate the C-4 that's hidden in this building before your guards even get through that door.'

The cardinal's eyes had gone wide. 'You're bluffing.'

Conte held out a small remote transmitter. 'The pope is

upstairs right now, isn't he? Do you really want to take that chance?'

'All right, Mr Conte. You've made your point.'

'Keep my card. Trust me . . . someday you'll be needing my help.' He went over and snatched up his bulky backpack. 'I'd appreciate it if you could escort me out. Lots of stuff in here that might set off your metal detectors,' he said, patting the bag. 'Once I'm safely outside, I'll tell you where to find the C-4. Deal?'

As far as Conte's parents were concerned, they were convinced that real estate investing was the secret to his success, but Maria, his thirty-five-year-old sister wasn't as easily fooled and it always made for an interesting dynamic at family gatherings.

His work didn't allow for permanent relationships. Not that Salvatore Conte was capable of such a thing. For the next few years, there would be no steady girlfriends . . . forget about a wife or kids. That kind of reckless behaviour destroyed the very notion of anonymity and created too many potential complications. For now, there were plenty of other women who were willing to satisfy Conte's more immediate desires. All it took was money. And seeing the pay-off from this latest job, there would be plenty of women in the near future. Entrepreneurship had treated him well.

Smiling, Conte was wide-eyed as he read the account balance: €6,500,000.00. After deducting overhead expenses and the cut owed to his six remaining team members, he was left with a cool net of four million euros. Not bad for a few days' work.

And he didn't even get shot. Another bonus.

20.

CHINON, FRANCE
MARCH 3, 1314

In a dim, cramped cell beneath the Fort du Coudray, Jacques DeMolay sat limply against the dungeon's cold stone wall watching three enormous rats fight over the scrap of bread he had thrown to them.

There was a damp chill in his bones that he couldn't lose. The smell of excrement hung heavy in the air. This place was more than a prison. It was Hell.

Now seventy years old, DeMolay's heavily scarred body – once robust – had turned haggard. His flowing beard, shocked to pure ivory, grew out from sunken cheeks, matted and greasy, crawling with lice.

For two decades, he had held the pre-eminent post within the Order – Grand Master. Now humiliation was his reward. For six years he'd been festering in this godforsaken pit, having fallen victim to the scandalous political ploys of France's young, ambitious King Philip IV and his colluding cohort, the Holy Roman Pope, Clement V.

Not a day had gone by that he didn't think back to his

conversation with Tibald DeGaudin at Kolossi Citadel. Perhaps he should have heeded the coward's advice.

Outside the iron bars he heard sounds emanating from down the passage, a heavy door groaning open on its hinges, metal keys jingling, approaching footsteps. Seconds later, a cloaked figure materialized outside the cell bars. Without looking up, DeMolay had already identified the visitor. The heavy smell of cologne left no doubt that Pope Clement V had finally made an appearance, flanked by two burly prison guards.

A nasal, French voice cut the air. 'You look like hell, Jacques. Even worse than usual.'

DeMolay glared up at the corpulent pontiff who shielded his hooked nose with an embroidered handkerchief. Gold jewel-encrusted rings, including the papal fisherman's ring, covered his soft, manicured fingers. He wore flowing vestments beneath a heavy black hooded cape and his dangling gold pectoral cross winked in the light of a nearby torch. DeMolay spoke, painfully forcing his cracked lips to move. 'You look . . . pretty.'

'Now, now, Grand Master. Let us not make this personal.'

'Too late for that. It has never been anything *but* personal,' DeMolay reminded him.

Clement lowered the handkerchief and smiled. 'What did you want to talk to me about? Are you finally ready to confess?'

DeMolay's icy gaze drilled into the Pope – a man two decades his junior. 'You know I will not disavow my brothers and my own honour by submitting to your scheme.'

Four years earlier, DeMolay had been presented with no less than one hundred and twenty-seven accusations against the Order, outlandish charges that included devil worship, sexual perversion, and myriad blasphemies against Christ and Christianity. And just two years ago, on the 22nd of March,

1312, Clement himself had issued a papal bull entitled '*Vox in excelso*', which formally disbanded the Order.

'You have already taken our money and our land.' DeMolay's tone showed his disgust for this man. 'You've tortured hundreds of my men to extract false confessions, burned alive another fifty-four – all honourable men who dedicated their lives to preserve the Church's Holy throne.'

Clement was impervious to his barbs. 'You know that if you do not end this stubbornness, you will be killed by the Inquisitors . . . and it will not be pleasant. Keep in mind, Jacques, that you and your men are as archaic as what you stand for, honour or no honour. I believe it has been more than twenty years since your legions lost control over the Holy Land and destroyed over two centuries of progress.'

Progress? For an instant, DeMolay considered lunging toward the cage, thrusting his hands through the bars and around the pontiff's neck. But the two guards stood to either side of him, watching vigil over this secret meeting. 'We both know that Rome was unwilling to support our efforts. We needed more men and they weren't sent. We were outnumbered ten to one. It was money then and it's money now.'

The pope waved his hand dismissively. 'Ancient history. I would hate to think I have travelled this far merely to dredge up old misgivings. Why am I here?'

'To make a deal.'

Clement laughed. 'You are in no position to bargain.'

'I want you to reinstate the Order. Not for my sake, but for your own.'

'Come now, Jacques, you cannot be serious.'

DeMolay forged on, determination flickering in his gaze. 'After Acre had fallen, there was no time for us to return to

Jerusalem. We had left many treasures behind. Valuable treasures that could easily fall into Muslim hands.' These days, if there was one thing that Clement responded to, it was anything that could help the Papal State's impending economic collapse.

'Which relics might you be referring to?' The pope pressed his face close to the bars mockingly. 'The head of John the Baptist? Christ's cross? Or perhaps the Ark of the Covenant?'

DeMolay gritted his teeth. The extreme secrecy of the Order had many speculating as to how they had acquired their tremendous wealth and was the reason why it had been so easy for the pope and the king to demonize them and fabricate their vicious falsities. But hearing some of them coming out of Clement's womanly mouth was torturous. 'I want you to listen to me very closely. Because the entire future of your great Church could be in jeopardy.'

The pope looked at him quizzically, moving back slightly from the cage. He sized up the prisoner – a man who, despite recent tribulations, he had never considered a liar. 'I am listening.'

With a knot tightening in his stomach, DeMolay couldn't believe what he was about to do. But having waited for six long years, he had come to the dismal conclusion that the surviving Templars would not endure another year if something drastic did not happen. With remorse, he had resigned himself to divulging the Order's most coveted secret – the very thing the monastic brotherhood had sworn a secret oath to protect. 'There is an ancient book that has remained under the protection of the Order for over two centuries. It is called the *Ephemeris Conlusio*.'

'The *Journal of Secrets*?' The pope's tone was impatient. 'What secrets?'

For the next fifteen minutes, the Templar Grand Master

recounted a remarkable story of a discovery so profound that if it were true, history itself hung in the balance. And the details were far too precise to be anything but real. The pope listened intently because for centuries, the Catholic hierarchy had circulated rumours of just such a threat.

When the Grand Master had finished, he sat perfectly still, waiting for the pontiff to respond.

After almost a minute of brooding, Clement finally spoke, his tone less confident now, almost afraid. 'And you left this book in Jerusalem?'

'We had no choice. The city had already been seized.' The truth was, they had never intended to remove the relics. The Templars had merely secured them. That was God's will.

'That is quite a story,' Clement admitted. 'Why now do you tell it to me?'

'So you can reverse the injustice that has befallen the Order. We need to raise a new army to reclaim what has been lost. If not, I think you realize the consequences.' DeMolay could see by Clement's expression that he did.

'Even if I were to exonerate the Templars,' he thought out loud, 'I would have to convince Philip to do the same.' Doubtful, he shook his head. 'After all that has happened, I do not think that he will concede.'

'You must try,' DeMolay urged. He knew that he had succeeded in finding Clement's one vulnerability. The pope was seriously considering his recommendation. 'Give me your word that you will try.'

Clement had expected today to be the day when he would finally break DeMolay and thus put an end to this whole charade. Suddenly, he realized he needed the old man more than ever. 'As you wish,' he surrendered. 'You have my word.'

'Before you leave here, I want it in writing. I need reassurance.'

'I cannot do such a thing.'

'Without my support, you will never recover the book . . . and what it is meant to find,' DeMolay insisted. 'I am your only hope.'

The pontiff considered the idea for a long moment. 'So be it.' He instructed one of the guards to fetch his scribe. 'And if Philip does not agree to this?'

'Then it is of no matter what fate holds for me or my men . . . for you, King Philip, and all of Christendom will be doomed.'

21.
VATICAN CITY

In the Apostolic Palace, Father Patrick Donovan sat at a heavy oak desk in an expansive library that could only be entered by passing through a biometric retinal scanner, a complex series of key-encrypted entryways and a contingent of Swiss Guards.

The *Archivum Secretum Apostolicum Vaticanum* – the Vatican Secret Archive.

Over the years the Vatican had enhanced the security system here, recognizing that there were no treasures in Vatican City more valuable than its secrets.

Newly installed hulking fireproof metal cabinets lined the walls, reaching toward the main room's lofty frescoed ceiling, housing over 35,000 vellums and manuscripts within airtight glass compartments. From rejected scriptural works blending philosophy, pagan mythology, and the Christ story, to Renaissance heretics like Galileo, the Vatican Archive was a depository for centuries of heretical works banned by past pontiffs, as well as Vatican City's land deeds, depository certificates, and legal documents.

Contrary to popular belief, the Vatican still actively sought new additions to its vast holdings. Heresy was considered very much alive and well in the twenty-first century; the attacks against Christendom ever more sophisticated – the secular chasm growing ever wider. And the fact remained that many pre-biblical scriptures, rife with controversial writings that undermined the integrity of the gospels, still managed to evade the Vatican's grasp.

Throughout Catholic history, a select few have been entrusted with maintaining this daunting archive. Donovan still marvelled at how he had become its most trusted custodian.

It was a long road that had brought him from Belfast to Rome.

Straight out of the seminary, Donovan had joined Dublin's Christchurch Cathedral as a resident priest. But his passion for history and books had soon earned him recognition as a biblical historian. Two years later, he had begun a highly successful Biblical History programme at University College, Dublin. His legendary lectures and papers on early Christian scriptures had eventually caught the attention of Ireland's pre-eminent Cardinal Daniel Michael Shaunessey. Shaunessey was quick to have Donovan accompany him on a visit to Vatican City where he introduced him to the cardinal who oversaw the Vatican Library. Collaborative projects followed, and less than four months later, a compelling offer was extended to Donovan for a position inside Vatican City, managing its archives. Though it was difficult leaving his ageing parents in Ireland – his only remaining family – he had graciously accepted.

That was twelve years ago. And never did he expect that one day he would be intimately involved in the single largest scandal in Church history – and all because of a book.

Poring over the yellowed, parchment pages of the archive's latest acquisition, Donovan was scanning the leather-bound ancient codex entitled the *Ephemeris Conlusio* – the *Journal of Secrets*. In recognition of the blood spilled acquiring the relic now being studied in the Vatican Museum, he needed reassurance that the ossuary had met all the criteria described in the text. Pausing to study a meticulous drawing of the ossuary, Donovan exhaled with relief when his eyes came across a precise match of the unique symbol that had been carved onto the box's side.

It was almost impossible for the librarian to imagine how he had come to this juncture – a shocking series of events that had been set into motion by a single phone call he received one rainy afternoon just two weeks earlier . . .

Oblivious to the unseasonable rain drumming against his office window, Donovan was deeply absorbed in an eighteenth-century study on the nature of heresy when the phone rang. Levering himself out of the chair, he had answered on the fourth ring.

'Is this Father Patrick Donovan, the curator of the Vatican's Secret Archive?'

The voice was laced with an accent Donovan couldn't quite place. 'Who is this?'

'Who I am is of no concern to you.'

'Really.' It wasn't the first time a reporter or frustrated academic had called under the guise of a potential seller to access some of the earth's most coveted books.

'I possess something that you want.'

'I don't have time for opaqueness,' Donovan responded. 'Be specific.' He was about to dismiss the caller as a crank, when three words escaped from the receiver: 'The *Ephemeris Conlusio*.'

'What did you just say?'

'I think you heard me. I have the *Ephemeris Conlusio*.'

'That book is a legend,' Donovan's voice cracked. 'Pure myth.' How could anyone outside the walls of the archive or Jacques DeMolay's prison cell in Chateaux Chinon have discovered its existence? He began pacing nervously as he awaited a response.

'Your legend is now being held in my hand.'

Donovan fought a wave of panic. It was only two years ago that a similar caller had offered up the Judas Papers – ancient Coptic writings that recast the infamous disciple as secretly acting on Jesus's behest to faciliate his crucifixion. But the Vatican had considered the document's provenance to be highly suspect, forgoing the opportunity – a grave miscalculation since shortly thereafter, the writings were published worldwide by *National Geographic*. Donovan was sure the Vatican wouldn't want to repeat that mistake. 'If you really do possess the *Ephemeris Conlusio*, tell me in what language is it written?'

'Greek, of course. Care to be more specific?'

He detected a rhythmic tapping at the other end. 'Who is the author?'

The caller told him and Donovan was amazed.

'Catholicism's prime enemy, am I not correct?' The caller paused. 'Surely you can be more sophisticated than this?'

Outside the window, the sky darkened and the rain intensified.

On the spot, Donovan decided that only if the caller could reveal the book's most profound contents would he consider the claim credible. 'Legend has it the *Ephemeris Conlusio* contains a map. Do you know what it's meant to locate?' His heart was racing.

'Please don't patronize me.'

Donovan's lower lip quivered as the caller elaborated, providing a precise description of the legendary relics.

'Do you want to sell the book?' Donovan's mouth was dry. 'Is that the purpose of your call?'

'It's not that simple.'

Now Donovan feared the worst, painfully aware that this stranger could potentially wound the Church very deeply, perhaps even fatally. Before proceeding, it was essential to determine the caller's motive. 'Are you trying to blackmail the Vatican?'

The man cackled. 'It's not about money,' he hissed. 'Consider the possibility that I might be looking to help you and your employers.'

'Neither your attitude nor your motive seems philanthropic. What is it you are after?'

The man had answered cryptically. 'Once you've seen what I have to offer, you will know what I'm after. And what you have to do . . . and will want to do. *That* will be my payment.'

'The Vatican would need to determine the book's authenticity before any terms could be discussed.'

'Then I shall arrange for delivery,' the caller had replied.

'I'd need to see a sample before that could happen. A page from the book.'

The line was silent.

'Fax me a page now,' Donovan insisted.

'Give me your number.' The caller was hesitant. 'I will stay on this line.'

Donovan twice repeated his office's private fax number.

A long minute passed before the fax machine rang, picking up on the second ring and feeding paper from its tray. The printed message was spat out seconds later. Donovan held it close to the light. When he had finished silently reading the remarkably authentic Greek text, the words left him momentarily breathless.

Shaking, he returned the phone to his ear. 'Where did you find this?'

'That is not important.'

'Why have you come to me in particular?'

'You are probably the only man at the Vatican who can understand the profound implications of this book. You know that history has tried to deny its existence. I have chosen you to be my voice to the Holy See.'

There was another long pause.

'Do you want the book or not?'

There was a pause.

'Of course,' he finally said.

Donovan had made arrangements to meet the anonymous caller's messenger two days later in the Caffè Greco on Via Condotti, near the Spanish Steps. Two armed plainclothes Swiss Guards sat at a nearby table. The messenger appeared at the agreed time and introduced himself by first name only, presenting a business card for any later questions. Donovan had sat with the man only briefly. No indication was given as to the identity of who had dispatched him.

A leather satchel had been discreetly passed over to him.

Though no explanations were provided, Donovan intuited that the man knew nothing of the satchel's contents. There had been no drama requiring the guards' intervention – just a quick, impersonal transaction, and both men had left on their separate ways.

Opening the satchel in the sanctuary of his office, Donovan had found a handwritten note on plain paper and a newspaper clipping. The note had read: '*Use the map to find the relics. Act quickly to find them before the Jews do. Should you require assistance, call me.*' A phone number was listed below the message. Salvatore

Conte had later told him that it had been a one-time use cell phone and that each of his subsequent communications with the insider was routed to a new phone number or anonymous one-time use website – all untraceable. Apparently, using these secure channels, the insider had coordinated with Conte to procure explosives and certain tools needed to extract the ossuary.

The Jews? Confused, the priest read the clipping from the *Jerusalem Post* and realized exactly what had prompted this meeting. Digging deeper inside the satchel, his hands had come upon the smooth leather covers of the *Ephemeris Conlusio*.

22.

JERUSALEM

Outside Temple Mount's northern gate, Barton avoided the chaos of the Western Wall Prayer Plaza, angling along the narrow cobblestone streets that webbed gently down Mount Moriah.

He had actually managed to persuade Razak to let him take the scroll back to his office to see if he could translate its text. Apparently, the Muslim was anxious to find some answers.

Passing through the busy Muslim and Christian Quarters, he entered the Jewish Quarter along Tiferet Yisrael and banked left into the open expanse of Hurva Square, the harsh noonday glare sharper in the absence of any breeze. He glanced over at the sweeping Hurva Arch – the square's focal point and sole remnant of the grand synagogue that had once stood here.

Hurva – literally meaning 'destruction' – was well named, Barton thought. Much like Jerusalem itself, the synagogue had been destroyed and rebuilt many times, the result of endless disputes between Muslims and Jews. On the eve of Israel's birth in 1948, the synagogue had been occupied by Jordanian Arabs and dynamited – its final death blow.

Almost six decades later, the same violent struggle for control continued far beyond its confines – a bitter turf war between Israelis and Palestinians. And somehow he now found himself caught directly in the middle of it all.

Though the main offices of the Israeli Antiquities Authority were located in Tel Aviv, a temporary satellite facility had been set up just three weeks earlier, here, inside the Wohl Archaeological Museum – very near the apartment rented by the Temple Mount suspects.

Parked in front of the building stood a gold BMW saloon with police markings. Barton inwardly groaned as he hurried to the front door to be met by his intern assistant, Rachel Leibowitz – an attractive twenty-something with flowing black hair, olive skin, and hypnotic blue eyes.

'Graham,' she was urgent. 'Two uniformed men are waiting for you downstairs. I told them to stay outside, but they insisted –'

'It's all right, Rachel.' Barton held up a hand. 'They were expected.' He caught himself staring at her lips. If the IAA was trying to do him a favour by assigning him such an attractive assistant, they weren't helping matters. At fifty-four, Graham Barton wasn't exactly the dashing young man he had once been. But in his small circle, he was a legend and that seemed to make good for an ageing facade. And eager students like Rachel would do anything to get closer to him. 'Please don't put through any calls for the time being.' Smiling, he moved past her, trying to avoid the intoxicating smell of her perfume.

There had been no formal invitation for anyone to visit that day, but Barton knew his inspection of the crime scene would have the police and IDF breathing down his neck. Of course, they'd want to know every iota of his findings.

Descending into the Wohl's subterranean gallery, he moved past the restored mosaics and ritual baths of a lavish, excavated Herodian-era villa.

The IAA had recently launched a huge digitizing campaign to catalogue its enormous collection – from vellums to pottery, pagan statuary to ossuaries – creating a database with every relic's historical profile and 3-D images. Internet-based tools needed to be developed to allow the field archaeologists to decrypt ancient inscriptions. Having pioneered similar programmes in the UK, Barton had been the ideal candidate to head up the initiative. It was here where he had begun piloting the digitizing programme to establish a good workflow before continuing through the Israeli museum network, ending with its most famous Israel Museum.

Heading to the rear of the gallery, he made his way into a featureless square room painted in a dull white satin, his temporary office. Waiting for him there were the two men who had visited him only yesterday to ask for his help in the investigation – the Jerusalem District police commissioner Major General Jakob Topol and the IDF's head of domestic intelligence, Major General Ari Teleksen. Each had claimed a metal folding chair on the guest-side of his makeshift desk.

'Gentlemen.' Barton put down his briefcase and sat opposite them.

Teleksen was in his late fifties, thickset, with the face of a pitbull – heavy jowls and puffy eyelids. He sat with his arms folded, making no effort to conceal the two missing fingers of his left hand. As Israel's most celebrated veteran counter-terrorism agent, he retained a coldness befitting someone who'd seen far too much. Olive fatigues and a black beret displayed the IDF's insignia – a golden Star of David bisected by an intertwined sword and olive branch, the epaulettes on each shoulder marking out his rank. 'We'd like to hear the results of your preliminary analysis.' His voice echoed off the bare walls.

Barton stroked his chin as he gathered his thoughts. 'The explosion breached the rear wall of the Marwani Mosque. The blast hole was very precise, very clean. Definitely professional.'

'We know that,' Teleksen impatiently replied, spinning his bad hand. 'But for what purpose?'

'To access a hidden burial crypt.'

'Crypt?' Topol was staring at him. Clearly the junior of the two, his uniform more befitted a commercial jet pilot – a powder-blue collared shirt with rank-marking epaulettes on each shoulder, and navy blue trousers. Centred on his policeman's cap lay the Israeli police insignia – two olive leaves wrapped around a Star of David. Middle-aged with a thick frame, his face was angular with deep-set eyes.

'A crypt,' Barton repeated, as he pulled out one of the rubbings he'd taken. 'See here. There was a tablet on the wall that listed all of their names.'

The eyes of both lawmen leapt to the rubbing.

'What was stolen?' Topol's voice was gruff.

'I'm speculating, but it seems to have been a burial box. An ossuary.'

Teleksen threw up his disfigured left hand. 'Burial box?'

'A small stone vessel about this big.' Barton outlined the ossuary's dimensions in the air. 'It probably contained a disassembled human skeleton.'

'I know what a burial box looks like,' Teleksen replied. 'What I'm interested in here is motives. You mean to tell me that we've lost thirteen IDF men for a box of bones?'

Barton nodded.

Teleksen made a dismissive motion. 'Feh.'

Topol coolly looked back at the image, pointing at the Hebrew names. 'So which one did they take?'

Knowingly, Barton pointed to the defaced image on bottom. 'This one. But as you can see, it's now illegible.'

'I see,' Topol said, clearly trying to mask his puzzlement. The night of the theft, when he had personally first visited the scene with his detectives, he specifically recalled the strange image that had been there – a carved relief depicting a dolphin entwined over a trident. Such an odd symbol wasn't easily forgotten. Yet on Barton's rubbing, the symbol was gone. If the thieves hadn't done this, then who had? 'What do you think the motive could have been?'

'I'm not sure yet.' Barton drew breath. 'The theft seems to have been coordinated by someone who knew exactly what the box contained.'

'Motive, shmotive. What good would a box of bones be to anyone?' Teleksen interjected, making no effort to temper his scorn. He dipped into his jacket's breast pocket and pulled out a pack of Time Lites. Tapping out a cigarette, he skipped the formality of asking Barton if smoking here was okay and lit it up with a silver Zippo.

'Difficult to say,' Barton replied. 'We'd have to speculate on what could have been inside.'

There was a very long silence. The two lawmen exchanged looks.

'Any theories?' Teleksen enunciated each word slowly. Holding the cigarette in his bad hand, he took a deep drag and exhaled, the smoke curling in tendrils from his nostrils.

'Not yet.'

Topol was more level-headed. 'Is it at all possible that this wasn't a burial box? Was there anything else that could've been in the crypt?'

'No,' Barton was emphatic. 'It wasn't customary to leave valuables in crypts. This isn't ancient Egypt, Major General.'

'Did you find any evidence that could lead us to the perpetrators? Anything that might suggest Palestinian involvement?' Teleksen persuaded.

It seemed they would never understand that – unlike many native Israelis – Barton wasn't motivated by either religious or political allegiance. 'As of yet, nothing obvious.'

'Isn't there any way of tracking down this ossuary?' Teleksen was losing patience.

'Perhaps.' Barton regarded both men levelly, though Teleksen's sour demeanour and cigarette smoke were eroding his patience. 'I'll be monitoring the antiquities markets closely. That's the most likely place it'll turn up.' He reached into his briefcase for another sheet of paper and pushed it toward Topol. 'Here's a basic drawing of what the ossuary probably looks like, along with the dimensions and approximate weight. I suggest you circulate this among your men, particularly at checkpoints. And here are pictures of the other ossuaries found in the crypt.'

Topol stowed them away.

'I think you might be missing a very important part of all this,' Barton added quietly.

Both commanders raised their eyes.

'A crypt beneath Temple Mount would reinforce the Zionist notion that a Jewish temple once stood above it. Perhaps you should share that information with the prime minister.' Barton was playing off the idea that every Israeli Jew – orthodox and secular alike – clung to the hope that one day solid archaeological

141

evidence supporting Jewish exclusivity to Temple Mount would be discovered.

Teleksen shifted uneasily, the metal legs of his chair scraping against the floor.

'So don't be too surprised if this investigation leads to a much larger discovery,' Barton added.

'Anything else?' Topol queried.

For a split second, he thought about divulging his discovery of the scroll now back inside its cylinder, safely secured in his pants pocket. 'Not at this point.'

'I hardly need to remind you what's at stake here,' Teleksen said firmly. 'We're teetering on the verge of a very unpleasant confrontation with Hamas and the Palestinian Authority. Plenty of people on their side are ready to use any excuse to accuse us of a terrorist act against Islam.'

Barton looked at them. 'I'll do all I can to find the ossuary.'

Teleksen took a final drag that burned the cigarette down to its filter. 'If you find this box, notify us both immediately. You'll have complete access to any necessary resources.' He tossed the butt onto the floor and stubbed it out with his right foot. 'But please keep in mind that next time we meet, we'll require more than just a lesson in archaeology.'

Both men stood and made their way out into the gallery.

Once he buzzed Rachel upstairs to confirm that they had left the building, Barton quickly closed the door and excitedly pulled out the cylinder. Uncapping it, he tapped the scroll out onto a clear area of his desk. From boxes on a nearby shelf, he retrieved a pair of latex gloves and a plastic Zip-loc bag. Sitting at the desk, he swung the retractable arm of a desk lamp closer, then slipped on the gloves.

After delicately opening the vellum, he slid it face-up into the plastic bag, then gently ironed it flat with his hand. Neatly hand-written in a large font, Barton didn't require a magnifying lens to make out the text. However, he confirmed that he was certainly going to need a translator, because Greek was not his strong point.

And as far as he was concerned, there was only one man in Jerusalem whom he considered an expert.

23.

VATICAN CITY

Charlotte Hennesey was still grappling with the notion that the ossuary's skeletal remains suggested that the thirty-something male subject – otherwise in pristine health – exhibited multiple signs of trauma resulting from crucifixion.

She and Bersei were now preparing to establish further evidence reinforcing the subject's identity, estimating date of death. Carbon dating would need to be performed on the bone, and the ossuary itself would need to be examined closely for any telling clues.

Standing in front of the ossuary, they examined its limestone shell.

'I found some information about an ossuary similar to this discovered in Israel in 2002,' Bersei said. 'On the basis of its inscriptions it was initially thought to have once contained James, the brother of Jesus. Though the ossuary itself was judged authentic, the inscriptions were determined a forgery. Reviewing the forensic analysis on that relic, I've got a pretty good understanding of what to look for here.'

'How did they know it was a forgery? What's the difference between genuine carvings and fakes?'

'Occasionally it's a leap of faith,' Bersei responded. 'But it's mainly the integrity of the patina that legitimizes inscriptions.'

'This stuff?' She pointed to a thin layer of muted grey-green sediment that evenly covered the stone.

'Yes – kind of like the greenish oxidation that occurs on copper. In the case of stone, moisture, sedimentary drip and airborne material builds up naturally over time to form a residue.'

'And the patina's organic composition would indicate the type of environment where the ossuary would have been found?'

'Precisely.' He put on his reading glasses, peered down at a notepad and read from a list of notations. 'Last night, I did some research about ossuaries and it seems that the practice of using them occurred mainly in Jerusalem during the first century BC, and didn't last very long – only a century or two.' He glanced up at her. 'Therefore, I'd expect that this limestone, like the James ossuary, was quarried during that period somewhere in Israel.'

'Right, the patina's mineral content should then be consistent with geological elements in that region,' she said. 'But wait a second, Giovanni. Assuming this ossuary falls into that category, that would mean this is about two thousand years old.'

'Correct. And seeing as crucifixion was commonly practised during that period, it appears that we're on track.'

Hennesey peered closely at the patina. 'So if the stone was tampered with, wouldn't the patina be disrupted?'

'Correct again,' Bersei smiled.

'Is there any way to date the stone?'

He considered this for a second. 'It's possible,' he admitted, 'but not very useful.'

'Why not?'

'We're not really concerned with when the limestone was formed. The stone itself will be millions of years old. We'd be much more interested in when it was quarried. The patina and inscriptions are probably our best gauges determining its age.'

'Aha.' Charlotte pointed to the fused symbol of the dolphin and trident. 'Think we'll be able to determine what that means?'

'I'm fairly certain it's a pagan symbol,' Bersei continued. 'It's funny, I know I've seen this somewhere before. First, let's figure out if this patina's legitimate.'

'While you finish analysing the ossuary, I'll work on preparing a bone sample for carbon dating.' She motioned across the room to the skeleton.

'Sounds good. By the way,' Bersei reached for his notepad and jotted something down. 'Here's the name and number of my contact at an AMS lab here in Rome.' He tore off a sheet. 'Tell him I referred you. Say we're doing work for the Vatican and need immediate results. That should get his attention. And request that he call back with the results straight away. The dating certificate can be sent later.'

Hennesey read it. 'Antonio Ciardini?'

'Pronounced Char-dini. Old friend of mine, plus he owes me a favour.'

'Okay.'

'And don't worry, his English is pretty fluent.' Bersei glanced at his watch: a quarter after one. 'Before you do that, how about taking a lunch break?'

'I'd love to. I'm starving.'

'The tuna sandwich didn't appeal to you?'

'Not my idea of Italian cuisine.'

24.
JERUSALEM

Graham Barton turned off Souk El-Dabbagha in the Christian Quarter and stopped briefly to admire the magnificent facade built by twelfth-century Crusaders that masked the original crumbling edifice of the Church of the Holy Sepulchre.

Christian pilgrims flocked to Jerusalem to retrace Christ's footsteps along the fourteen 'stations' from flagellation to crucifixion – the 'Way of Sorrows', better known as the 'Stations of the Cross'. The journey would begin at a Franciscan Monastery on the Via Dolorosa, just beneath Temple Mount's northern wall – the site where many Christians maintained that Christ had taken up the cross after being scourged and crowned with thorns. Stations ten through fourteen – where Christ was stripped, nailed to the cross, died, and was taken from the cross – were commemorated in this church.

After all that had happened in Jerusalem over the past few days, Barton wasn't surprised that there weren't many tourists here today. He made his way into the main entrance.

Beneath the church's massive rotunda high above two tiers of circular Roman colonnades, Barton walked a circle around a small mausoleum embellished with elaborate gold ornamentation. Inside this small structure was the most sacred site in the church – a marble slab that covered the rock where Christ had been laid out for burial.

'Graham?' a warm voice called out. 'Is that you?'

Barton turned to face a corpulent old priest with a long white beard, dressed in the ceremonial garb of the Greek Orthodox Church: a flowing black soutane and a substantial black pipe hat.

'Father Demetrios.' The archaeologist smiled.

The priest clasped Barton with both his pudgy hands, fingers like sausages, and pulled him slightly closer. 'You look good, my friend. So what brings you back to Jerusalem?' He spoke with a heavy Greek accent.

It had been almost a year and a half since Barton first met the priest to arrange for an exhibit of some of the Sepulchre's Crusader-era crucifixes and relics in the Museum of London. Father Demetrios had graciously loaned the items to the museum for a three-month period, in exchange for a generous donation.

'Actually, I was hoping you'd be able to help me translate an old document.'

'Of course,' the priest cheerily replied. 'Anything for you. Come, walk with me.'

Strolling beside Father Demetrios, he eyed the numerous clerics milling about the space. The Greek clergy was compelled by a long-standing Ottoman decree to share this space with the church's other resident sects – Roman Catholics, Ethiopians, Syrians, Armenians, and Copts – and throughout the Sepulchre, each had erected their own elaborate chapels. It was a haphazard arrangement both physically and spiritually, Barton thought.

From somewhere in the church, he heard a requiem being chanted.

'Rumour has it that the Israelis have called you in to assist in the investigation over at Temple Mount,' the priest whispered. 'Is there any truth to that?'

'I'd rather not say.'

'I don't blame you. But if it is true, please tread lightly, Graham.'

The priest led him into the Greek Orthodox chapel known as 'the Centre of the World', named for a stone basin in its centre that marked the spot ancient mapmakers had designated as the divide between east and west. From his last visit, Barton knew that Father Demetrios felt most comfortable here, on his own turf.

On the side wall stood a Byzantine shrine, covered with gold ornamentation and dominated by a massive gold crucifix boasting a life-sized, solar-haloed Christ, flanked by two Marys looking up in mourning. At the altar's base was a glass enclosure encasing a rocky outcropping where Christ had supposedly been crucified. Golgotha.

The twelfth station of the cross.

In front of the altar, the priest made the sign of the cross, then turned to Barton. 'Show me what you have, Graham.' He reached beneath his vestment and produced a pair of reading glasses.

Barton pulled the plastic-sealed vellum from his breast pocket and handed it over.

The priest fingered the Ziploc bag. 'Good to see you've employed the latest technology. Now let's see what you have here.' Putting on his glasses, he held the document higher against the ambient glow of an ornate hanging candelabrum and

149

studied the text intently. Seconds later a blanched expression came over him and his lower lip sagged. 'Oh my.'

'What is it?'

The priest looked concerned. Scared.

He peered at Barton over his glasses. 'Where did you find this?' he asked quietly.

Barton considered telling him. 'I can't say. I'm sorry.'

'I see.'

By the look in his eye, it was obvious that the priest already knew the answer. 'Can you tell me what it says?'

Father Demetrios scanned the chapel. Three rival priests, dressed in Franciscan cassocks, were loitering close by. 'Let us go downstairs.' He motioned for Barton to follow.

Father Demetrios led him down a wide staircase that wound beneath the nave.

Barton was pondering how the ancient words could have so spooked the old priest. Deeper they went, until stone walls gave way to cool, hewn earth.

Standing in what looked like a cave, the priest finally stopped. 'You know this place?'

'Of course,' Barton said, scanning the low-hanging rocky ceiling that bore telltale marks of mining activity. 'The old quarry.' His eyes wandered briefly to the wall behind the priest where hundreds of Knights Templar equilateral crosses had been carved into the rock – twelfth-century graffiti.

'The tomb,' the priest corrected him, pointing to the long burial niches carved into the far wall. 'Though I know your reservations in wanting to accept this idea.'

Where Helena was also lucky enough to unearth Christ's cross, too, he wanted to say, but curbed his response. The fact that Constantine's elderly mother had personally selected this site –

formerly a Roman temple where pagans once worshipped Venus – left little doubt that its authenticity was questionable. Though he was no stranger to the divergent views of the historical versus the religious, he wasn't about to offend him with blasphemy.

'There's another very sacred tomb just above us,' Father Demetrios reminded him with a serious face.

'And why have you brought me down here? Is it something about this scroll?'

'Everything about it.' His voice was solemn. 'I don't know where you found this, Graham. But if it wasn't from here – and I know it's not – I caution you. Be very, very careful. You know better than most how words can be misconstrued. If you promise me you'll remember what I've said, I will write down your translation.'

'You have my word.'

'Good.' The priest shook his head and let out a deep breath. 'Let me have your pen and paper.'

25.

VATICAN CITY

Each time Father Patrick Donovan walked down the Apostolic Palace's grand corridor he felt intimidated. This was the gateway to the Vatican's royalty – the physical apex of Christendom's hierarchy. Adjoining the far end of the Vatican Museum, it housed the offices of the pope and the secretary of state, while an upper floor contained the pope's lavish Borgia apartment. The entire complex, as big as an airport concourse, felt like an extension of the museum itself with its floor-to-ceiling frescos, marble floors, and baroque embellishments.

Here the Vatican City's military was most evident, expressionless Swiss Guards posted at even intervals and seeing them only added to his nerves.

Tall porticos ran along one side of the corridor, overlooking the Piazza San Pietro – Bernini's massive, elliptical courtyard, which had been completed in 1667. Four sweeping arcs of colonnades embraced the space, pinpointing at its centre Caligula's obelisk that had been plundered from the Nile Delta in 38 CE. The relic sharply reminded Donovan of the pillaging done in Jerusalem only four days ago.

Large rectangular windows on the hall's opposite side were sheathed in iron grating, serving notice that this building had been initially designed as a fortress.

The looming double door at the corridor's terminus was flanked by two Swiss Guards in full costume – billowing gold and Medici blue-striped tunics and pantaloons, red berets, and white gloves. *Conte's buffoons.* Each carried an eight-foot long pole called a 'halberd' – a sixteenth-century weapon that combined speared tip, axe blade, and grappling hook. Donovan noticed that both soldiers also carried holstered Berettas.

He stopped two metres in front of the doorway.

'*Buona sera, Padre. Si chiama?*' The tall guard to his right demanded his name.

'Father Patrick Donovan,' he responded in Italian. 'I have been summoned by His Eminence, Cardinal Santelli.'

The guard disappeared into the room beyond. A few uncomfortable moments passed while Donovan stared vacantly at the floor, the remaining Swiss Guard stood at attention in perfect silence. The first guard re-emerged. 'He is ready to see you.'

The librarian was ushered into an expansive antechamber furnished in marble and wood where Santelli's personal assistant, the young Father James Martin manned a lone desk, his face blank and withdrawn. Donovan smiled warmly and exchanged pleasantries with him, trying to imagine just how mentally taxing it must be for him to be at the beck and call of a man like Santelli.

'You may go right in,' Father Martin said, motioning to a huge oak door.

Opening the door, Donovan moved into the lavish space beyond. Across the sumptuous room, he saw a purple skullcap and the familiar mound of thick silver hair poking over the back of a tall leather chair.

The Vatican secretary of state was facing a window that neatly framed St Peter's Basilica, a phone held to his right ear, frail hands gesticulating. Swivelling round, Donovan was met by the bloodshot eyes, bushy eyebrows, and heavy jowls of Cardinal Antonio Carlo Santelli. The cardinal motioned him toward an armchair in front of the substantial mahogany desk.

Donovan plunked himself down, the upholstery groaning as he shifted in the seat.

As the Vatican's highest-ranking cardinal, Santelli was charged with overseeing the political and diplomatic issues of the Holy See, effectively acting as prime minister of the Roman Curia, accountable only to the pope himself. Though even the pope occasionally acquiesced to Santelli's demands.

The man's political skills were legendary. As a newly appointed cardinal in the early 1980s, he'd steered the Vatican through the murky recesses of the Banco Ambrosiano scandal and the murder of Roberto Calvi, the so-called 'God's Banker', who had been found hanged by the neck under Blackfriars Bridge in London.

While the cardinal wrapped up his conversation, Donovan took in this inner sanctum of the pontifical machine. Santelli's immense desk was bare, save for a short stack of crisp reports arranged at a perfect perpendicular, and an oversized plasma monitor mounted on an arm. The screensaver was on – a golf-green, its flag fluttering against a virtual breeze reading: '*All We Need is Faith*'. A great enthusiast for IT, Santelli had been the main advocate for the installation of the Vatican's sophisticated fibre-optic network.

In the corner, a marble-topped credenza supported a replica of Michelangelo's *Pietà*. Dominating the space to his right was a large tapestry depicting Constantine's battle at

Milvian Bridge. To Donovan's left three Raphaels hung – almost casually – against the wine-coloured wall.

His gaze circled back to Santelli.

'Advise him the final decision will be made by the Holy Father,' the cardinal was saying in thick Italian. Santelli was always direct. 'Call me when it's done.' He replaced the phone. 'Prompt as always, Patrick.'

Donovan smiled.

'After the appalling mess left behind in Jerusalem, I trust you're bringing me good news. Tell me all our efforts have been worthy of such sacrifice.'

Donovan forced himself to look Santelli in the eye. 'There's enough evidence to lead me to believe the ossuary's genuine.'

The cardinal grimaced. 'But you're not certain?'

'More work needs to be done. More tests.' Donovan knew his voice was wavering. 'But so far, the evidence is compelling.'

There was a small silence.

The cardinal cut to the chase. 'But is there a body?'

Donovan nodded. 'Just as the manuscript suggested.'

'Splendid.'

'Will the Holy Father be told?'

'I'll handle that when the time's right.' Elbows on the chair's armrests, Santelli had woven his fingers together, as if in prayer. 'When will these scientists be ready to make a formal presentation?'

'I requested that they prepare something for Friday.'

'Good.' The cardinal saw that Donovan was preoccupied. 'Cheer up, Father Donovan,' he said, spreading his hands. 'You've just helped give this great institution new life.'

26.

Returning from lunch, both scientists felt refreshed. The afternoon had turned out to be mild and the sunshine rejuvenating. Bersei had taken Charlotte to the San Luigi café on Via Mocenigo, only a short walk from the Vatican Museum entrance. The soft music and inviting nineteenth-century décor complemented the lobster ravioli Bersei recommended – a quantum leap over last night's tuna sandwich.

With Charlotte phoning the AMS lab he recommended, Bersei was once again suited up as he began his analysis of the ossuary. Dimming the lights above the workstation, he swept each surface of the ossuary with an ultraviolet light wand. Looking through the Orascoptic's crisp lenses, key areas – particularly the etched grooves forming the intricate designs – were tightly magnified.

The first thing he noticed was that the patina had been scuffed in many areas, particularly along the sides. Glowing under the black light, the abrasive marks were long and wide, in some areas leaving an impression of woven fibre. Straps, he guessed, though no trace fibres had been left behind. Probably new nylon webbing. Confirming that there was zero sedimentary build-up on top of the impressions, he concluded that the marks were fresh.

It wasn't that shocking. He'd often seen relics that had been handled improperly during excavation and shipment, but this type of disregard for the past always offended him. He had read that the James ossuary had been cracked during shipment. By comparison, the damage here was forgivable and probably wouldn't devalue the ossuary either.

After mounting the digital camera on a tabletop tripod, powering it up and deactivating its flash, he snapped some shots. Then he turned off the black light and set the workstation lighting higher.

Next, painstakingly inspecting every edge and surface, Bersei hunted for any evidence that the patina had been manually transplanted with tools. Had the box been inscribed after it was found, the geological residue would exhibit obvious inconsistencies. It took considerable time, but lengthy examination showed no suspicious scrapes or gouges. The patina was bonded tightly and evenly across the ossuary's limestone surfaces, including the relief carved onto the box's side.

As he stood to straighten his cramped shoulders, he flipped up the Orascoptic lenses, taking a moment to once again admire the ossuary's decorative patterns. His twenty-fifth wedding anniversary was quickly approaching and that intricate rosette design might look nice on a piece of jewellery. After so many years together with Carmela it was becoming increasingly difficult to find an original gift.

Leaning over the ossuary again, he used a small blade to scrape samples from selected areas, placing the material on glass slides and clearly marking each one. After collecting fifteen samples, he organized the slides neatly on a tray, moved to another workstation equipped with an electron microscope and loaded the first specimen.

Super-magnified and projected onto an adjacent computer monitor, the dried minerals and deposits that formed the patina looked like greyish-beige cauliflower. He saved a detailed profile of the sample in a database, removed the first slide and continued along the tray. When the last sample image had been captured, the entire group was displayed side by side on the monitor.

He entered a command to cross-check for inconsistencies. After a few seconds of calculations that compared biological content, the program detected no significant differences between the samples. If any part of the patina had been artificially 'manufactured' – the most common method, using chalk or silica diluted in hot water – the program would have spotted inconsistent isotopic ratios or possibly even foreign traces of microscopic marine fossils that could appear in household chalk.

As anticipated, all the samples were high in calcium carbonate, with nominal levels of strontium, iron, and magnesium. According to Bersei's online research, these results were consistent with the patinas on similar relics removed from subterranean Israel.

Bersei pulled the last slide from the microscope.

As far as he could tell, these results substantiated that the ossuary's etchings pre-dated the formation of the patina. It was more than reasonable to conclude that the mysterious pagan symbol on the ossuary's side did indeed date from the same time as the bones. There was a chance that if he could figure out what exactly it meant, it might help identify the crucified man.

27.

Watching Giovanni Bersei at work on the other side of the lab, Charlotte picked up the cordless phone, and dialled the number he had given her. The ring tone – so uniquely European – chimed endlessly. Just when she thought she needed to redial there was a response.

'*Salve.*'

For a moment, she didn't know what to say. She'd expected a switchboard or assistant – perhaps even voice mail – and wondered if she'd accidentally dialled someone's residence.

'*Salve?*' The voice was more insistent.

She eyed the note again where she'd jotted the phonetic spelling. 'Signore Antonio Ciardini?'

'*Si.*'

'This is Dr Charlotte Hennesey speaking. Giovanni Bersei suggested I contact you. I'm sorry – I didn't know I'd be calling your home.'

'You've dialled my mobile. Quite all right.' There was a small pause. 'You are American?'

His English was impressive. 'I am.'

'What can I do for my good friend Giovanni?'

Everyone seemed to like Dr Bersei. 'He and I are working on a unique project here in Rome. In the Vatican, actually—'

'Vatican City?' Ciardini cut in.

'Yes. We've been asked to examine an ancient bone sample. And to be thorough in our analysis, we'd like to date the specimen.'

His voice went up a notch. 'Bone specimens in the Vatican? That's an odd pairing. Though there are those tombs beneath St Peter's Basilica where they bury the popes,' he tried thinking it through.

'Yes, well . . .' She couldn't elaborate. 'I hate to trouble you, but Dr Bersei was wondering if you might be able to speed up the results.'

'For Giovanni, sure. The bone – is it in good condition? Clean?'

'It's extremely well preserved.'

'Good. Then I suggest you send a sample of at least a gram.'

'Got that. And . . . would this be all right? . . . there's a wood splinter that we'd like to date as well.'

'Preferably ten milligrams for wood, though we can go as low as one milligram.'

'Ten is no problem. Is there some kind of form you'll need me to fill out?'

'Just address the package directly to me with your name – that's all. I'll handle the paperwork. Indicate where you'd like the dating certificate sent.'

'That's very kind. I know I've asked too much of you already, but Dr Bersei was wondering if you could call us as soon as the results are available?'

'So that's why he had you call, Dr Hennesey.' Ciardini let

loose with a big belly laugh. 'I'll process the samples as soon as they arrive. Normally it takes weeks to get results. But I'll do my best to get them done within a couple of hours. I'll give you the address.'

Ciardini repeated the street address slowly while Hennesey jotted it down.

'Thank you. I'll send the Vatican courier. The samples will be with you in couple hours. *Ciao*.'

Returning the receiver to its wall-mounted cradle, she went back to the workstation.

Studying the skeleton, she finally settled on a splintered fragment from the left foot's fractured metatarsal. With a pair of tweezers, Charlotte carefully broke away a small piece and sealed it in a plastic vial.

To determine its age, and thus the age of the skeleton, this sample would need to be incinerated. Then, the carbon gases could be collected, scrubbed, and compressed, in order to quantify any remaining carbon 14 – the radioactive isotope in all organisms that, upon death, begins halving in quantity exactly every 5,730 years. Though the process seemed simple to her, she had learned that the complex array of equipment required for this test – known as an Accelerator Mass Spectrometer – demanded substantial investment and maintenance. Most museums and archaeological groups opted to outsource to independent specialist AMS labs like Ciardini's.

From the drawer, she retrieved the wood splinter she had taken during the initial pathological analysis.

Placing the two specimens in a padded envelope, she prepared a second envelope with a Vatican City shipping label. Seeing the label's embossed papal crest, she smiled inwardly feeling like an extra – or maybe a player – in a detective story. It all seemed a million miles from her daily routine back home. When she was analysing samples at BMS, at the very least she knew their age and where they came from.

To thoroughly recreate the skeleton's physical profile, Charlotte would also need to sample the skeleton's deoxyribonucleic acid, or DNA. Contained within the core of all human cells, the ribbon-like nucleotide acids held the coding that determined every human physical attribute. She'd read studies suggesting that in the absence of harsh conditions and contamination, DNA could remain viable in ancient organisms. Scientists had studied it in Egyptian mummies almost 5,000 years old. Judging from the skeleton's remarkable condition, she was confident that its DNA would not have degraded beyond the point of being able to study it.

Like carbon studies, genetic examinations required sophisticated equipment. And without doubt, Charlotte knew the fastest and most reliable facility for such testing was at BioMapping Solutions, under Evan Aldrich's watchful eye. BMS had patented new systems and software to efficiently analyse the human genome using improved laser scanning techniques, and she'd been an integral contributor to the system's technological development.

Glancing at her watch, she picked up the phone and dialled Phoenix. A quarter to five. Even with the eight-hour difference, she knew Evan was an inveterate early bird.

After three rings the phone was wrestled from its cradle. 'Aldrich.'

That was the way he always answered: to the point. Another thing she loved about him. 'Hey there. It's the Rome field office calling in.'

Hearing her voice, he immediately sounded cheerful. 'How are operations at Christianity Central?'

'Good. How are things back home?' She touched one of her earrings, remembering he had given them to her for her last birthday – emerald, her birthstone. He had told her they matched her eyes.

'Same old. So what's shaking at the Vatican? Figuring out how to make the pope live for ever?'

'It's amazing. I've been analysing ancient skeletal remains. Standard forensic stuff so far, but fascinating. I wish you could see this.'

'Back in the trenches then. Hope it's worth our time.'

'Too early to tell. But it is extraordinary work. Anyway how often do you get a call from the Vatican?'

'True.' He paused. 'I'm assuming you didn't call just to chat.'

After her abrupt – make that *icy* – departure last Sunday, she knew he was referring to relationship issues. Evan had slept at her house the previous evening. A night of passion that led to an early morning discussion about 'taking things to the next level'. Still not having told him about her cancer, she'd been quick to dodge the issue, much to his frustration. The limo had arrived in the thick of it all and she hadn't left on the best of terms. Fixing things between them was important, but now was not the time. Luckily, Evan was still pretty good at separating work and pleasure.

'The specimen's bones are in incredibly good shape and I was hoping to impress the locals with some DNA-mapping magic,' she explained. 'I want to reconstruct the physical profile. Think BMS might be interested?' There was a brief pause that she knew was most likely disappointment.

After a long moment, he said, 'Sounds like it would be good PR.'

'Is the new gene scanner ready?'

'We're already in the beta testing stage. That's why I'm in so early – I've been poring over the data.'

'And?'

'It's very promising. Get me your sample and I'll run it through. It'll be a good test.'

'I've got a whole skeleton here. What piece would you like?'

'Play it safe – something small like a tarsal. When can I expect it?'

'I'll see if they'll let me send it for overnight delivery. Hopefully I can get it to you by tomorrow.'

'It will be processed immediately. In fact, I'll handle it personally.'

'Thanks, Evan.'

'Say hi to the pope for me. And Charlotte . . .'

Here it comes, she thought. 'Yeah?'

'Just want to let you know it isn't just my best scientist I miss around here.'

She smiled. 'I miss you, too. Bye.'

Charlotte returned to the workstation, trying like hell to fight off a sudden surge of regret welling up inside her. She should have told him why she couldn't be with him in that way – the way he wanted. Drawing a calming breath, she resigned herself to the fact that when she returned to Phoenix, she would tell him everything. Then they would need to figure out how to move forward. Lord knows she didn't want to scare him away.

Back to work.

Bagging the metatarsal, she stuffed the sample into a DHL box. As she wrote BMS's address on the shipping label, she tried to suppress a sudden bout of homesickness, realizing how far apart she was from Evan.

As she completed the form, Dr Bersei joined her. He put his

hands on his hips. 'Far as I can tell, the patina wasn't tampered with. It's the real thing. You?'

'I had a nice conversation with Signore Ciardini,' she said, managing a smile. 'Very charming man. He'll have the results for us tomorrow.'

'What's that package you're working on?'

'Another sample I hope will provide a genetic profile for our man.' She held it up. 'I'm sending it to Phoenix for analysis.'

'DNA?'

'Mm.'

Bersei glanced at his watch – just past five. 'We got a lot done today. I've got to get home for dinner. My oldest daughter is stopping by tonight.'

'What's Carmela making?'

'Chicken saltimbocca.' He raised his eyes and began stripping off his mask and gloves, then lab coat.

She laughed out loud and it felt good. 'Good luck with that.'

'Watch out or I'll bring you the leftovers,' he threatened. 'Anyway, tomorrow maybe we can take a look inside the box, and I'll see if I can't decipher that symbol. I'll also show you an instrument that will be a nice complement to your DNA analysis. See you in the morning – just hope my daughter doesn't tempt me into a second bottle of wine.'

'You have a good evening, Giovanni. Thanks again for lunch.'

'You're welcome. And try and get some sleep tonight, eh? I don't want you getting sick on me.'

Too late for that, she thought. She smiled and waved. '*Ciao.*'

As the door closed behind him, just for a moment, Charlotte Hennesey envied him.

When she finished preparing the packages, she buzzed the

intercom for Father Donovan. He responded almost immediately, as if he knew she was still in the lab.

'Good evening, Dr Hennesey. What can I do for you?'

She told him about the packages and he assured her that if she left them in the lab, he would have the courier handle both. She also confirmed with him that sending the overnight DHL package was okay, despite the hefty cost for overseas delivery.

Once the business issues were resolved, he asked her, 'Are you going into Rome tonight?'

'It is a beautiful evening. I thought I'd take a walk and get dinner somewhere.'

'If you don't mind splurging a bit, I could give you a recommendation for a superb restaurant.'

'Sure. That would be great. You know what they say – when in Rome . . .'

28.

As Charlotte exited the Vatican Museum through the upstairs service door, the early evening sun was still warm. She'd decided that her khakis and blouse were good enough not to have to trail all the way back to her room to change. Besides, she had to adhere to the Vatican's strict dress code or she wouldn't be allowed back in. That didn't leave many other wardrobe options.

She ambled along the walkway between the towering northern city wall and the Vatican Museum's severe edifice and headed down to the Sant' Anna Gate and was cleared by the Swiss Guards to leave the premises.

Father Donovan had indicated that the restaurant didn't open until seven-thirty. Unlike the States, Italians preferred to eat dinner late, he reminded her. With an hour to kill, Charlotte stayed close by, but enjoyed walking the side streets, venturing over to the Tiber River, taking in the richness that was Rome.

A while later, following Donovan's directions, Charlotte zig-zagged back to the imposing six-storey facade of the Hotel Atlante Star. She saw the sign indicating the hotel's *Les Étoiles* restaurant. Already she felt underdressed. Entering the foyer, she rode an elevator to the top floor.

As soon as the doors opened, she was greeted by the maître d'. He was a young man and elegantly dressed – perhaps in his mid-thirties she guessed – with dark features and thick black hair.

'*Signora Hennesey . . . Buona sera! Come sta?*' He switched to English. 'Father Donovan called ahead. I was expecting you.'

'*Buona sera*,' she said, peering into the restaurant.

'My name is Alfonso,' he bowed slightly. 'Please follow me, Signora. You have a reserved table on the rooftop.'

She was guided through the dining room and up a staircase that led onto a terrace adorned with a sea of colourful flowers. Alfonso stopped in front of a small table by the railing.

Rome's skyline left her momentarily breathless. The huge dome of St Peter's Basilica sat only a short distance away behind the eastern walls of the Vatican Museum. On the opposite side she spotted the curved edifice of Castel Sant' Angelo. Across the Tiber lay the old city marked by the domed Pantheon.

Charlotte was helped into her chair. A white linen napkin was plucked from her plate and draped across her lap.

'If there is anything you need, Signora Hennesey, please don't hesitate.'

'*Grazie.*'

A sommelier silently appeared and presented her with an intimidating leather-bound wine list.

Through all the activity, discovery, and suspense of the day, Charlotte realized that she'd barely had a moment to take stock. Suddenly she felt almost lonely. Or did she? Wasn't everything perfect? She stared out across the river – she couldn't have asked for a more idyllic setting.

But she knew everything wasn't perfect.

The wine waiter was back at her side and she ordered a half bottle of *Brunello di Montalcino*. Alcohol wasn't advised, but this evening she wasn't going to deny herself.

The sound of scooters echoed up from the street below.

When the sommelier returned, he went about his wine presentation, showing the label, then opening the bottle and having Charlotte give it the sniff test. Finally, he poured some into a glass and asked her to taste it. She sloshed it around the glass, more for show, knowing that the medication she'd been taking would give the wine a slight metallic aftertaste no matter how refined its vintage.

When he left, her thoughts settled into their own direction, leading her back to Evan Aldrich. She reminded herself that making any long-term emotional commitment to him would be irresponsible. Yet, the doctors had told her that research was advancing all the time. Answers would soon be found. But how soon was soon?

And what about kids? At thirty-two she was already feeling the pressure that she might never have any of her own. Having researched later, more aggressive treatments that might include bortezomib injections – known to cause birth defects in unborn children – her anxiety had only deepened, knowing that might well be an unattainable dream.

She cast her eyes idly over the neighbouring tables. Happy-looking couples, a laughing family to her right. Maybe they weren't happy at all. Appearances rarely told the whole truth – she knew that better than anyone. Oddly, it made her think about Salvatore Conte and Father Patrick Donovan. What was their story? How had a box of bones brought such a mismatched pair together?

She thought about the bone sample sent to Ciardini – how it

would be incinerated during the carbon dating test to determine its age.

Bone being destroyed.

'Has Signora decided?' It was Alfonso.

'I'm glad you're here. I need your help.'

Despite the fact that the restaurant had a name Charlotte swore was French, its menu featured Italian cuisine. After a few quick questions about her likes and dislikes, Alfonso steered her to a Sorrento scialatielli – 'sumptuous homemade pasta with creamy Alfredo seafood sauce full of lobster and crab. Absolutely delightful.'

From the first bite of her pasta, she knew he was right on target. Addicted to the Food Network channel, Charlotte was a huge fan of Rachel Ray's '30 Minute Meals'. She wished the peppy half-Italian host could be here now to enjoy this with her – it was simply delicious. She'd finally found something that had awakened her pill-muted taste buds.

Eating pasta, drinking wine, surrounded by sweet-smelling flowers, and looking out over the city that had practically moulded Western culture succeeded in bringing Charlotte's mind to another place. After she had finished eating, she just sat and took it all in for another hour. Content. Happy.

When the hefty bill came, she was sure to pay with her corporate American Express card – restitution for last night's tuna sandwich.

Outside the hotel, she ambled back along Via Vitelleschi toward the rugged edifice of Castel Sant' Angelo. Continuing around the castle's perimeter, she saw the Tiber come into view. Crossing busy Lungo Castello, she strode on to the Ponte Sant' Angelo, which spanned the river in five elegant arches.

Rome could boast so much history and culture, she thought.

Even this bridge was a sublime work of art, and in its own way the Vatican had helped make it all possible. Admiring Bernini's marble angels posted along the bridge, her gaze was immediately drawn to one that was cradling a huge crucifix. A day ago, she wouldn't have thought twice about it. Now she would never be able to look at a cross in the same way ever again. Such an utterly normal object, almost prosaic – but now it seemed gruesome. And the fact that they happened to be everywhere if you looked hard enough was not helping matters.

The one thing she failed to notice was that a comfortable distance behind her, Salvatore Conte was watching her from the shadows of the castle wall.

WEDNESDAY

29.
JERUSALEM

Sipping *qahwa*, Razak sat on the veranda of his apartment in the Muslim Quarter overlooking the Temple Mount and its Western Wall Plaza. Throngs of protestors had been gathered since sunrise and now he could see news crews from around the world queuing to get past the police cordons.

Tuned to *Al-Jazeera*, the volume on Razak's TV was set low, providing a quiet buzz in the background. The mood in Jerusalem was tense, and even worse in Gaza's Palestinian settlements where mobs of young men were already engaging in low-level *intifadas*, challenging police with stones. Armoured vehicles were now posted at all Israeli checkpoints, as well as the main gates to Old Jerusalem. The IDF had doubled its border patrols.

People were demanding answers, needing someone to blame. Israel was gearing up its defence, ready for yet another confrontation. Hamas was issuing statements, smearing the Israeli authorities.

Razak tried to focus on formulating a plan for diffusing the tension, at least temporarily. Damage control. Sometimes the problems of this place seemed intractable and the sensitive history surrounding the heart of Jerusalem's thirty-five-acre shrine embodied them.

The mobile phone interrupted his thoughts.

'Sorry to bother you. It's Graham Barton.'

It took him a moment to recall he'd voluntarily given the archaeologist his business card. 'What can I do for you?'

'I've got the transcription back on that scroll we found.'

'What does it say?'

'Something astounding,' Barton promised. 'But not something we should discuss over the telephone. Can you meet me to go over this?'

'Of course.' It was hard for Razak to deny the upbeat archaeologist's infectious enthusiasm. 'When?'

'How about noon at *Abu Shukri* on El-Wad Road? Do you know where that is?'

Razak glanced at his watch. 'Yes, I've been there many times. I will see you at noon.' Maybe, thought Razak, this is the break I've been waiting for.

30.

VATICAN CITY

Charlotte Hennesey turned to see her alarm clock's digital read-out blinking 7:00 in thick lines of annoying red light. The sun was glaring through the thin drapes that covered the windows and she dropped her head back onto the pillow. Though the small bed was quite comfortable, she imagined that its previous occupant had probably been a cardinal.

Hanging on the wall directly above her head was a crucifix. Her eyes locked onto it. Against her will, images of hammers pounding huge nails through skin and muscle again crept into her thoughts. Get used to it, she told herself.

Dragging herself out of bed, she stumbled to her travel bag and wrestled the cap off a bottle of Motrin. The wine had really done a number on her. Out from the small refrigerator, she grabbed the bottle of Melphalan, popped its lid, took out one of the tiny white pills and swilled it down with some water. Next came a fistful of vitamins and supplements to counteract the havoc it would wreak on her immune system.

After brushing her teeth, she showered and dressed. She strapped her money belt containing her cash and passport beneath her blouse (her travel guide had strongly suggested it since Rome was notorious for pickpockets). Pocketing her cell phone, she made her way out of the door.

Entering the lab Charlotte saw Giovanni already well into his work, hunched over a metal cabinet and fiddling with some computer cables.

He looked up and smiled. 'Ah. I see you're looking rested today.'

'Still catching up, but doing better.' She eyed the device. 'What's that?'

He waved her over. 'You're going to like this. It's a laser scanner used for 3-D imaging.'

The rectangular unit was compact, standing about three feet high, with an empty inner chamber and glass door. The controls were mounted on the side.

Charlotte eyed it critically. 'Looks like a mini bar,' she said.

He gave it a cursory glance and laughed. 'Never thought of that. No bags of peanuts inside, though. Why don't you get settled and have some coffee? Then I'll show you how to work this,' he said, connecting a USB cable from the back of the unit into his laptop's data port.

Less than five minutes later, Charlotte had returned suited up and ready to go.

'With this we scan every bone one at a time and reassemble the skeleton in the computer's imaging software,' Bersei explained. 'Then the CAD program analyses them and the associated ligament attachment points, calculates the associated muscle mass each bone supported, and attempts to recreate the image of what our mystery man looked like when he was flesh and blood. I'll do the first one; you can do the rest.'

Bersei reached out for the skull, cradling its toothy mandible with one hand, globular mass in the other, and mounted it in the scanning chamber. 'Just put this in the minibar . . .'

Charlotte laughed out loud.

Smiling, Bersei shifted to his laptop. 'Then click the "*COMINCIARE SCABIONE*" button . . .'

'Is the whole program in Italian?'

Bersei looked up and was amused when he saw her mildly distressed expression. 'Oops. Forgot about that. I'll switch it over to English.' Working the mouse, it took him a few seconds to adjust the program settings. 'Sorry. As I was saying, click on the "START SCAN" button – like so . . .'

The scanner hummed as lasers inside the chamber formed a matrix around the skull, detailing its every feature. Less than a minute later, a perfect digitized replica of the skull popped up on the laptop screen, shaded in white and grey.

'There you go. A 3-D copy. Now the image can be manipulated however we want.' He ran his finger over the laptop's touchpad so the on-screen skull rotated and flipped on command. 'Save the image and the program will ask you to label the bone using this drop-down menu.'

Bersei opened the list of labels and scrolled down until he found CRANIUM – WITH MANDIBLE and clicked on it. 'Then you click "NEXT SCAN". Why don't you try one?' He opened the scanner door and removed the skull. 'Put on gloves and a mask and take a bone.'

Charlotte tossed her coffee cup into the rubbish bin and pulled on a pair of latex gloves and a paper mask.

She picked up a segment of spine from the skeleton, and closed it in the scanner. Clicking the 'SCAN' button, she watched the luminescent lasers as they played over the bones. She had quick, uninvited thoughts of CT scans and radiation therapy, but forced them away. 'Tell me. How did Carmela do with the chicken saltimbocca?'

'Actually, it wasn't that bad,' he said, surprised. 'But my daughter did manage to talk me into that second bottle of wine. Oh, *mamma mia*,' he said, holding his head.

After a minute, the imaging was complete. As Bersei watched over her shoulder, Charlotte used the touchpad to play with the image. She saved it, labelling the scan VERTEBRAE – LUMBAR. She clicked 'NEXT SCAN'.

'*Perfetto*. Let me know when you're finished. Then I'll show you how to piece it all together.'

Bersei made his way across the lab and disappeared into the break room.

She worked on scanning another spinal segment. A minute later, Bersei had returned holding two espressos.

'More Italian jet fuel.'

'You're a lifesaver.'

'Let me know if you have any problems,' he said, going over to the ossuary.

Placing himself at the workstation, he peeked into the ossuary to examine the thick coat of dust about half an inch deep that coated the base of its interior. He would need to empty the material out and analyse its composition using a microscope, then pass it all through the lab's spectrometer to identify element-specific light signatures. Using a laboratory scoop, he began emptying it over a screen-covered rectangular glass dish to sift out the small bone fragments that had fallen to the bottom of the box. He assumed that he would find some desiccated flesh and loose stone dust – perhaps trace amounts of organic material, such as the flowers and spices traditionally used in ancient Jewish burial rituals.

What he didn't expect to find was the small, circular object that was mixed into his next scoop. Removing it with gloved fingers, and lightly dusting its surface with a delicate brush, Bersei saw that the textures on its two oxidized surfaces were deliberate. Stamped metal.

A coin.

Taking a stiffer brush from the tool tray, he beckoned Charlotte over.

'What is it?'

'Take a look.' Centred on the palm of his hand, Bersei held the coin out for her.

Her green eyes narrowed as she peered down at it. 'A coin? Good stuff, Giovanni.'

'Yes. It'll make our job far easier. Obviously coins can be extremely useful for dating accompanying relics.'

He passed her the coin and swivelled back to the computer terminal, keying in the search criteria: 'roman coins LIZ'.

Charlotte studied it intently. It wasn't much bigger than a dime. On its face was a symbol that looked like a backwards question mark, circled by a ring of text. The flip-side revealed three capital letters – LIZ – centred inside a crude floral image resembling a curved, leafy branch.

'Here we go,' Bersei murmured. The first hits had come back instantly. Coming from a generation when thesis papers were still tapped-out on a typewriter, the efficiency of technology and the Internet, particularly for research, simply amazed him. He clicked the most relevant link, which brought up an online coin seller named 'Forum Ancient Coins'.

'What did you find?'

Scrolling down a long list of posted ancient coins for sale, he found an exact image of the coin Charlotte had pinched between her fingers. 'Though ours is certainly in better shape, I'd say that's a match.' He enlarged the picture and indicated the front and back snapshots that were almost perfect replicas of their coin. 'Interesting. Says here it was issued by Pontius Pilate,' Bersei pointed out.

Charlotte was taken aback as she bent over to get a better look. '*The* Pontius Pilate . . . as in the guy in the Bible?'

'That's right,' Bersei confirmed. 'You know, he *was* a real historical figure.' Bersei silently read some on-screen text that accompanied the image. 'Says Pilate issued three coins during his decade-long tenure, which began in 26 AD,' he summarized. 'All were bronze *prutah* minted in Caesarea in the years 29, 30, and 31 AD.'

'So these Roman numerals L-I-Z tell us the specific date?' She thought she remembered L being fifty and I being one. But Z was drawing a blank.

'Technically, those are *Greek* numerals. Back then, Hellenic culture was still very influential on daily life in Judea. And yes, they do indicate the actual date of issue,' Bersei explained. 'However, this coin was made hundreds of years before our modern Gregorian calendar existed. In the first century, Romans calculated years according to the reign of emperors. You see those ancient Greek words encircling the coin?'

She read them – *TIBEPIOY KAICAPOC*.

'Mm-hmm.'

'That says, "of Tiberius Emperor".'

She noted that he hadn't read that off the screen. 'How do you know that?'

'I happen to read ancient Greek fluently. It was a common language in the early Roman Empire.'

'Impressive.'

He grinned. 'Anyway, Tiberius's reign began in the year 14 AD. Now the L is just an abbreviation for the word "year". The I is equal to ten, the Z is seven – add them together and you get seventeen. Therefore, this coin was minted during the seventeenth year of Tiberius's reign.'

Looking a bit confused, Charlotte ticked off the years on her fingers. 'So it's from 31 CE?'

'Actually, the Greeks left out the zero. The year 14 CE is actually "one". I'll save you the recount – the correct date is *30 CE*.'

'And what about this other symbol – this reverse question-mark thing?'

'Yes. It says here the *lituus* symbolizes a staff that was held by an augur as a symbol of authority.'

'An augur?'

'A kind of priest. Likened to an oracle and commissioned by Rome. The augur raised the *lituus* staff to invoke the gods as he was making predictions about war or political action.'

When it came to predictions, nowadays Charlotte was more inclined to envision uptight doctors in white coats trying to interpret lab results. She inspected the coin again. 'Aside from the Bible, what do you know about Pontius Pilate?'

Bersei looked up and grinned. 'A lot actually. He was quite a bad guy.'

'How so?'

He related what he knew. Tiberius Caesar opposed the idea of a Jewish king ruling coastal Judea since Roman troops needed to be fluidly moved down toward Egypt without hindrance. Plus, Judea was a major trade route. Tiberius ousted one of King Herod's sons and replaced him with Pilate, outraging the Jews. Pilate routinely massacred rebellious Jews. According to one well-documented account, when unarmed crowds gathered outside his Jerusalem residence protesting at his theft of temple money to fund an aqueduct, he sent soldiers dressed in plain clothes amongst them. On Pilate's command they drew concealed weapons and butchered hundreds of Jews.

'And that's only one incident,' Bersei continued.

'Nasty.'

'Pilate mostly lived in a lavish palace in the northern town of Caesarea, overlooking the Mediterranean – what you would call in America his beach house. I've been there . . . beautiful place actually. It's where these coins were minted, under his watch.'

Looking back to the monitor, Charlotte noticed the remarkably low bid price for Pilate's relic. 'Twenty-two dollars? How could a coin almost two thousand years old be worth only that much?'

'Supply and demand, I guess,' Bersei explained. 'There are quite a lot of these things floating around out there. Back in the day, this would have been the equivalent of your American penny.'

Her brow furrowed. A *penny*? 'Why do you think *this* was in the ossuary?'

'Easy. Placing coins on the eyes of the dead was part of Jewish burial practice. Kept the eyelids closed to protect the soul until the flesh decayed. After the tissue was gone, they would have fallen into the skull.'

'Hmm.'

Reaching into the ossuary, he fished around for a few seconds then plucked something from the dust and held it up. A second coin. 'Two eyes. Two coins.' Bersei examined both sides. 'A perfect match.'

She considered the new information for a moment. 'So the bones must have been buried in the same year, right?'

'Not necessarily. But most likely, yes.'

Deep in thought, she gazed back at the skeleton then down at the coin. 'Pontius Pilate and a crucified body. You don't think . . .'

Immediately, Bersei held a hand up, knowing what she was about to suggest. 'Let's not go there,' he urged. 'Like I said, the Romans executed thousands by crucifixion. And, I'm a good Catholic boy,' he added with a smile.

Sensing no reservation in his strong eyes, she could tell that Bersei wanted to remain objective.

'Have you finished scanning the skeleton?'

'All done.'

'Great.' Standing, he snatched a printout of the web page from the printer. 'Let me show you how to put it all together.' He gestured to the skeleton laid out on the workstation. 'Then we can see what that guy really looked like.'

31.

TEMPLE MOUNT

At precisely twelve o'clock, Razak strolled over to the square wooden table where Graham Barton was seated in front of the tiny open-air café, drinking black coffee and reading the *Jerusalem Post*. Seeing Razak, Barton folded the paper and stood to greet him.

Razak proferred a humble smile. 'Good morning, Graham.'

Barton offered a hand and Razak accepted. '*Assalaamu 'alaykum,*' Barton said in respectable Arabic.

Razak was impressed. '*Wa 'alaykum assalaam.* We'll need to work on that, but not bad for an infidel,' he said, smiling.

'Thank you. I appreciate that. Please sit.' The archaeologist motioned to the chair on the table's opposite side.

'This was a fine choice.'

'I thought you'd like it.' Barton had purposely selected this popular, small café in the Muslim Quarter since, as of late, he'd been hearing rumblings that Jewish shopkeepers weren't taking kindly to Muslim guests – more fallout from the theft's aftermath.

Pulling in his chair, Razak was immediately approached by a

young male Palestinian waiter, painfully thin, just sprouting a sparse beard.

'Will you eat, Graham?'

'Yes, if you have time.'

'Any preferences?'

'Whatever you recommend.'

Razak turned to the waiter and rattled off a few dishes – the restaurant's famous *hummus* with black beans and roasted pine nuts, pita bread 'hot please,' he specified, *falafel*, two *shwarma* kabobs – and asked for a pot of *shai* mint tea 'with two cups,' purposely in English so as not to make Barton uncomfortable.

Once the waiter had jotted everything on his pad and read it back, he retreated to the rear kitchen.

'Tell me, what have you found out?'

Barton's face lit up. 'Something quite extraordinary.' He reached into his shirt pocket and anxiously pulled out a folded sheet of paper. 'See here,' he opened the paper and laid it out for Razak. 'On top is a photocopy of the original text, below it, the English cipher. Why don't you take a moment to read it for yourself?'

Briefly, Razak admired the beautiful handwriting of the ancient script. Then his eyes skipped down the page to the translation.

Having fulfilled God's will, I, Joseph of Arimathea and my beloved family wait here for the glorious day when our fallen Messiah shall return to reclaim God's testimony from beneath Abraham's altar, to restore the holy Tabernacle.

Razak's expression showed his confusion. 'Who is this Joseph?' The waiter returned with a steaming pot of tea and Razak covered the document with his hand while the young man poured out two cups.

Barton waited for him to leave. 'Joseph is the man whose skeleton is in the ninth ossuary. You see, the Hebrew name "Yosef" translates in English to "Joseph".' He gave Razak a moment to let that sink in and continued, 'Have you ever heard of Joseph of Arimathea?'

Razak shook his head.

'I'm not surprised. He's an obscure first-century biblical figure who appears only briefly in the New Testament.'

Sipping his tea, Razak suddenly looked uneasy. 'And what does the book say about him?'

The Englishman spread his hands on the table. 'Let me first say that most of what we hear about Joseph of Arimathea is purely legend. That's what's most interesting about this find.' Barton was speaking quickly, but in a hushed tone to avoid being overheard. 'Many say he was a wealthy tradesman who supplied metals to both the Jewish aristocracy and Rome's bureaucrats, both of whom needed steady supplies of bronze, tin and copper to produce weaponry and mint coins.'

'An important man.'

'Yes.' Tentative, Barton continued by saying, 'In fact, the Gospels of Mark and Luke state that Joseph was a prominent member of the *Sanhedrin* – the council of seventy-one Jewish sages who acted as the supreme court of ancient Judea. The Gospels also suggest that Joseph was a close confidant of a very famous, charismatic Jew named Joshua.'

The name didn't register with Razak, but Barton was looking at him like it should. 'Am I supposed to know this Joshua?'

'Oh you know him,' Barton confidently replied. 'Some Hebrew translations also refer to him as "*Yeshua*". The original

188

Greek gospels referred to him as "*Iesous*".' He could tell Razak was growing impatient with the name game. 'But surely you know his Arabic name . . . "*Isa*".'

Razak's eyes went wide. 'Jesus?'

'And though Joshua – or Jesus – was the second most popular name here back in the first century, I don't think the Jesus I'm referring to needs any explanation.'

Razak shifted in his chair.

'Following Jesus's death, Joseph was said to have gone to Gaul – modern-day France. Accompanied by the disciples, Lazarus, Mary Magdalene, Philip, he preached Jesus's teachings. Supposedly around 63 CE, he even spent time in Glastonbury, England, where he acquired land and built England's first monastery.'

Sipping more tea, Razak raised his eyebrows. 'Go on.'

'Fast-forward to the Middle Ages and Joseph becomes a cult hero with monarchs fabricating lineal ties to share his fame. And during this time another story surfaces, claiming that Joseph possessed Jesus's crown of thorns and the chalice he drank from at the Last Supper.' Barton paused to let Razak absorb all the details. 'Some believed that Joseph collected the blood of Jesus's crucified body in that cup.' He noticed Razak's lips purse at the words 'crucified body'. 'Better known as "the Holy Grail", the cup was believed to possess healing powers and granted its owner immortality.'

'Those certainly are fantastic stories,' Razak stated. 'Surely you're not suggesting that the thieves thought the missing ossuary contained the Holy Grail?'

Pursing his lips, Barton made a dismissive motion with his hand. 'There *are* some fanatics out there,' he admitted, 'but no. I'd certainly not push that idea.' He continued tentatively. 'I

189

decided to do a bit more research on Joseph of Arimathea using the most convenient and relevant handbook available.' He held up a book.

Razak's eyes bored into its title: *The King James New Testament*. 'More legend,' he said cynically.

Knowing that the New Testament would be a touchy matter, Barton expected this reaction. Any discussion of Jesus had to recognize that Muslims revered him as one in a long series of human prophets that included Abraham, Moses, and Allah's final servant, Muhammad. Under no circumstances would Islam accept any man or prophet as an equal to God himself. It was this pillar of Islamic faith that to Muslims rendered the Christian concept of the Trinity absolute blasphemy, creating the most significant rift between the two faiths. And this book was considered by Muslims as a gross misinterpretation of Jesus's life.

Ignoring the jab, Barton forged on, 'Of the twenty-seven books in the New Testament, four give detailed historical accounts of the prophet Jesus: Matthew, Mark, Luke, and John. Each specifically mentions Joseph of Arimathea.' Barton flipped open the Bible to a section marked by a Post-It note, trying his best to steady his now trembling fingers. What he was about to propose was amazing. He leaned closer across the table. 'All four accounts essentially say the same thing, so I'll just read this first excerpt from Matthew twenty-seven, verse fifty-seven.' Then he slowly read the passage:

As evening approached, there came a rich man from Arimathea, named Joseph, who had himself become a disciple of Jesus. Going to Pilate, he asked for Jesus's body, and Pilate ordered that it be given to him. Joseph took the body, wrapped it in a clean linen cloth, and placed it in his own new tomb that he had cut out of the rock. He rolled a big stone in front of the entrance to the tomb and went away.

Barton raised his eyes from the pages. 'I'll read that one sentence again. *"Joseph took the body, wrapped it in a clean linen cloth, and placed it in his own new tomb that he had cut out of the rock."'*

Razak's mouth gaped open. 'Surely you don't think—'

The waiter suddenly appeared and Razak stopped midsentence, waiting for the young man to set down the plates and leave before continuing.

Razak took a deep breath. 'I see where you're going with this, Graham. It is a very dangerous theory indeed.' He took some bread and scooped hummus onto his plate. It smelled spectacular.

'Please hear me out,' Barton continued softly. 'We have to at least entertain the idea that the thieves may have truly believed that the missing ossuary contained the remains of Jesus. And this scroll we found in the ninth ossuary clearly references the messiah. It's far too precise to ignore.'

As he explained this to Razak, Barton was beginning to feel the full weight of Father Demetrios's subtle warning. The words on this scroll could potentially undermine traditional commemoration of Christ's mysterious benefactor, because the *loculi* deep beneath the Church of the Holy Sepulchre were believed to have belonged to Joseph.

Razak stared at the archaeologist. 'You should eat your bread while it's hot.'

'Look. I'm not saying I believe all this.' Barton tore off some bread and spooned some hummus onto his plate. 'I'm simply suggesting a motive. If we're dealing with a fanatic who believed all this to be true, it would make that missing ossuary the ultimate relic.'

Razak finished chewing, swallowed, and said, 'I'm sure you'll understand that I can't possibly accept the idea that this missing ossuary contained Jesus's body. Remember Mr Barton, unlike the misguided men who wrote that book,' he pointed at the Bible, 'the Qur'an speaks the literal words of Allah using the great prophet Muhammad – peace be upon him – as his messenger. As Muslims we've been told the truth. Jesus was spared the cross. Allah protected him from those who sought to bring him harm. He didn't die a mortal death but was reclaimed by Allah and ascended to Heaven.' He raised his eyes skyward. 'And remember, the men to whom I am accountable will react much worse than me. They won't hear of such ideas.' He dipped his bread in hummus and popped it into his mouth. 'Besides, don't the Christians claim Jesus rose from the dead and ascended into heaven? Isn't that what the Easter holiday is all about?'

'Absolutely,' Barton said.

Chewing, Razak looked at him quizzically.

Barton grinned. 'The Bible says a lot of things,' he admitted. 'But the gospels were drafted decades after Jesus's ministry, following a long period of oral tradition. I don't need to tell you how that can affect the integrity of what we read today. Since Jesus's disciples were themselves Jews, they incorporated a *midrashic* storytelling style, which, quite frankly, focuses more on meaning and understanding – often at the expense of historical accuracy. I might also point out that ancient interpretations of resurrection had much more to do with a spiritual transformation than a physical one.'

Razak shook his head. 'I don't understand how anyone could believe those stories.'

'Well,' Barton carefully countered, 'you need to keep in mind that the target audience for the gospels were pagan converts.

Those people believed in divine gods who died tragically and resurrected gloriously. Life, death, then rebirth was a theme common to many pagan gods including Osiris, Adonis, and Mithras. Early Christian leaders, particularly Paul of Tarsus – a Hellenistic, philosophical Jew – knew Jesus needed to fit these criteria. He was selling this new religion in a very competitive environment. We can't discount the idea that he embellished the story. And of twenty-seven books in the New Testament, he alone is thought to have written fourteen of them. Quite influential, I think you'd agree. It's prudent, therefore, for us to put these accounts into their proper historical and *human* context.'

Razak eyed him approvingly. 'You're a very complex man, Graham. Your wife must enjoy you very much,' he said, half sarcastic. He pointed to the gold wedding band on the archaeologist's right hand.

'If you think I've got a lot to say, you should hear her. Jenny is a barrister.'

'A lawyer?' Razak's eyebrows raised up. 'A professional debater. I'd hate to see the two of you fight.'

'Luckily that's an infrequent occurrence.' The truth was, outside the courtroom she was anything but a contender. Lately, they'd been drifting apart across an ever-widening sea of silence.

'Do you have any children?'

'A son, John, twenty-one. Good-looking lad, with more brains than both his parents put together. Attends university at my alma mater in Cambridge. We also have a lovely daughter, Josephine, twenty-five years old. She lives in the States, in Boston. She's a lawyer, like her mum. And you? Wife and children?'

Razak smiled shyly and shook his head. 'Unfortunately Allah has not granted me a suitable wife as of yet.'

Barton thought he detected something in the Muslim's eyes.

Pain? 'Maybe it's not Allah's will, but because you're stubborn,' Barton said.

Razak pretended to be offended, then burst out laughing. 'Ah yes, perhaps you are right,' he said.

Once they had finished eating, Razak turned his attention back to the transcription. 'And what about the rest of this . . . what does it all mean?' He read the second part of the transcription: *"To reclaim God's testimony from beneath Abraham's altar, to restore the holy Tabernacle."*

Barton was hoping to avoid this part of the discussion. 'Ah.' He paused. 'Abraham's altar is most likely referring to Mount Moriah.'

'Where the prophet Ibraham was told to sacrifice Ismaeel, son of Hagar,' the Muslim stated flatly.

'Okay.' Barton let the interpretation slide. Though the Torah clearly stated that Abraham was to sacrifice *Issac*, the son of his wife Sarah, Muslims traced their lineage back to Ismaeel – the son born to Sarah's hand servant, Hagar. It was yet another example of the two religions trying desperately to claim as its own the Old Testament's most revered patriarch – the man credited with monotheistic faith and complete submission to the one true God. After all, that's what Islam literally meant, Barton thought: *submission to the will of Allah*.

'And this reference to *"God's testimony"*,' Razak added. 'Sounds as if it is a physical thing that is *"beneath Abraham's altar"*. I don't understand.'

A shiver ran down Barton's arm. 'I'm still trying to determine what that means,' he lied. 'I'll need to do a bit more research.'

Looking sceptical, Razak nodded. 'I trust you'll let me know what you discover.'

'Of course.'

'So where do we go from here?'

Barton thought about it. Oddly, his thoughts kept drifting to Father Demetrios – the visit to the Sepulchre's lower crypt that had supposedly belonged to Joseph of Arimathea. It got him thinking again about the chamber beneath Temple Mount, how it lacked some of the features typical in first-century crypts. 'Actually, I think we'll need to go back to the crypt. There's something I may have overlooked. When do you think we can get back in there?'

'Let's hold off on that until tomorrow morning,' he suggested. 'I received a very interesting call late this morning from a good friend in Gaza who heard I was involved in this investigation. He says he has some information that might help us out.'

'What kind of information?'

'I'm not sure, actually,' Razak said. 'He wouldn't say over the phone.'

'Which means it's probably good stuff.'

'That's what I'm hoping. Anyway, I was going to take a drive . . . to go and see him this afternoon. If you're not too busy, maybe you should come along.'

'I'd like that. What time?'

'I just have something to attend to first. Won't take me long.' Razak looked down at his watch. 'Can you meet me in the car park outside the Jaffa Gate around two?'

'I'll be there.'

Razak reached into his trouser pocket and pulled out his wallet.

'Please, Razak,' Barton insisted, motioning it away. 'Let me get this. You run ahead and I'll see you at two.'

'Thank you, Graham. That's very generous.'

*

Opposite the café on El Wad, a forgettable young man was seated on a bench reading a newspaper and sipping coffee, enjoying the mild afternoon. Occasionally he inconspicuously glanced over to the archaeologist and Muslim delegate. The small headphones plugged into his ears, seemingly connected to an iPod, were transmitting the amazing conversation that was taking place to the IDF's Jerusalem outpost.

32.
VATICAN CITY

Bringing up the skeletal scans in full-screen view, Giovanni Bersei scrolled down the grid of miniature images, pausing occasionally to enlarge and analyse a bone in more detail. 'That's great, Charlotte. Looks like you got the ribs right too. Not easy. All we have to do now is ask the computer to assemble the skeleton,' he clicked the menu options.

Charlotte Hennesey stood behind him as a small window popped up:

PLEASE WAIT WHILE YOUR SAMPLE IS PROCESSED.
25% complete . . .
43% complete . . .
71% complete . . .

He turned to her. 'No errors so far. Not bad for a first try.'

98% complete . . .
100% complete.

Twenty seconds later, the screen flashed back a three-dimensional image of the skeleton. The program had scrutinized each bone's smallest detail to recreate the condition of joints and cartilage attachments, providing an accurate picture of the fully reassembled skeletal frame. It had even maintained the minute, awful detail resulting from crucifixion – the gouges on the ribs and damage to the wrists, feet, and knees.

'Extraordinary.' Bersei eyed the on-screen image – an assembled version of what lay on the workstation behind them. For a moment, he was again awestruck by the amazing capabilities of computer technology. 'That's probably just the way our man looked prior to being placed in the ossuary.'

'What about the flesh?'

He held his hands out as if trying to slow a speeding car. 'One step at a time.'

'Sorry. Too much coffee.'

'We like to take things a bit slower over here,' he joked. 'Helps longevity.'

Charlotte cringed.

Bersei worked the mouse again. 'Next we'll ask the computer to assign muscle mass to the skeletal frame. The software will measure every bone to estimate its density and recreate its ligament attachment points.'

She knew the basic concept. 'Larger muscles place more stress on the bones they're attached to, requiring stronger ligaments and connecting points?'

'Quite so. Call it reverse engineering. Granted, the program can't account for every soft tissue abnormality. But it can detect a skeleton's structural anomalies. If that happens, the program will attempt to recreate it, or we'll get an error message. That said, let's get some muscle on this frame.' He refocused on the screen.

The progress window reappeared:

PLEASE WAIT WHILE YOUR SAMPLE IS PROCESSED.
77% complete . . .
100% complete

The screen refreshed.

This time the program had clothed a fibrous weave of lean musculature over the skeletal form. The image was gruesome but anatomically correct – a de-skinned human, the muscles various shades of red, the ligaments a disturbing bluish-white. The man had been extremely well formed and perfectly proportioned.

Charlotte leaned in closer. 'Looks very fit,' she said matter-of-factly.

'No McDonald's back then,' he said as he manipulated the mouse.

'Or osso bucco for that matter.'

They both laughed.

Settling down, Giovanni looked back at the screen. 'Okay, let's add some skin here.' He clicked a command.

Almost instantly the screen refreshed again, the 3-D image looking like a Bernini marble sculpture with its smooth 'flesh'. The enhanced image omitted all hair, including eyebrows. The eyes were smooth, colourless orbs.

Charlotte was transfixed. Now the study had entered a new realm where an otherwise unnamed, faceless specimen seemed to take on an eerie, lifelike quality. They were bringing these ancient bones back from the dead.

'This is where your DNA analysis will help fill in the blanks,' Bersei continued. 'The program accepts genetic information – it recreates everything from eye and skin colour to hair density, hairline, fingernails, body hair, and so on. We can also approximate body fat content within an accurate range. Thus far, I think his most impressive feature is this.' He pointed to the lower right corner of the screen where basic statistics were reported, including one line reading:

HEIGHT (in./cm.): 73.850 / 187.579

'Extremely tall for his day,' Bersei observed. 'Odd. If this man died in the beginning of the first century, he would have really stood out.'

'People were shorter back then, right?'

'It's a commonly held belief that their nutrition wasn't adequate. But I wouldn't give that much credit. Many would argue it was actually better. But even by modern standards this man would turn heads. Your genetic data may help shed light on this.'

'Go in on the face.'

He held the mouse button to drag a white-lined frame around the image and clicked to zoom.

A ghostly form filled the screen, its features well defined, yet soft, with a long sloping nose, full lips, and a strong chin. There was a pronounced jaw line with a firm brow and wide eyes.

Bersei seemed satisfied. 'For now this is the program's best recreation. He was a handsome devil.'

Charlotte was mesmerized by the haunting features. 'I wonder how accurate this is.'

'I've used this same program to reconstruct identities on similar skeletons for homicide investigations,' Bersei said in a confident tone, 'and it's always proved very accurate when eventually matched with a victim's known profile.'

The intercom suddenly came to life. Father Donovan apologized for the interruption, but was patching through a call from a Signore Ciardini.

'Probably our carbon dating results,' Bersei said. 'Why don't you take that call and I'll continue my work on the ossuary.'

'Sounds good,' she said as she made her way over to the phone.

Bersei returned to his workstation.

Once he had finished removing the powdery dust layer from the bottom of the ossuary, something there caught his eye.

A thin outline.

Grabbing a small brush, he bent closer, dusting the grooves until a rectangular form gradually emerged.

Trading the brush for a small blade, he inserted it along the rectangle's edge, carefully levering under what looked like a metal plate. With the plate removed, a hollowed-out compartment was revealed. Inside were the shadowy forms of three long, tapered objects.

He thought his eyes were playing tricks, and adjusted the overhead lighting. Reaching into the ossuary, he worked his fingers along the compartment. Giovanni sensed metal through the latex as he withdrew one of the objects. It was surprisingly heavy, easily eighteen centimetres long and black as coal with a knobby, blunted end that tapered into a shaft of wrought edges.

A nail.

Placing it on a tray, he stared at it, disbelief flooding back.

He pulled two remaining nails from the bottom of the ossuary, and aligned all three on the tray. Three more items that would substantiate the skeleton's identity. There had been many moments in Bersei's career that served as reminders of his passion for discovery. But these revelations transcended all rationality. 'Oh my,' he gasped, sinking back into his chair.

Across the lab Charlotte had just hung up the phone.

'You've got to see what I've just found,' he called over to her. His eyes were locked on the tray.

Charlotte approached the workstation. By Bersei's blanched look she knew that the ossuary had offered up yet another of its secrets.

He pointed mutely to the tray.

She saw three metal objects lying on the tray's shiny steel surface. 'Railroad spikes?' Staring down at the jagged points of the nails made the whole ghastly process of crucifixion even more real.

Bersei broke the silence. 'I think it's safe to say that these would have been the nails used to crucify this man . . . whoever he was.'

'Where did you find them?'

'Take a look.' He pointed with his chin.

She positioned herself above the ossuary, scanning its exposed cavity – a hollowed-out limestone shell.

'The dust was concealing it.'

That's when her eyes caught the faint outline of something else hidden deep inside the ossuary. It looked like a second recess carved even deeper into the compartment. 'Wait,' she called sharply, swinging the retractable lighting arm over the ossuary, light flooding its interior. 'Looks like you missed something. There. It looks like . . .' Under the harsh glare she could discern it better. '. . . a cylinder?'

33.

JERUSALEM

Razak found Farouq in the small upstairs room in the Grammar College building the Waqf had converted into its temporary office. He'd just finished a phone call.

Before he could open his mouth, the Keeper cut across: 'Topol says no recorded shipments over the past couple of days come close to matching the ossuary.' He drummed his fingers on the desk. 'This isn't going well.'

Razak took a seat. Farouq looked as if he hadn't slept in days as he turned to face him at an angle that perfectly superimposed the Keeper over the window-framed backdrop of the Dome of the Rock Mosque.

'Hamas and the Palestinian Authority,' Farouq continued, 'both confirmed that the helicopter used to transport the thieves from the Haram esh-Sharif was definitely Israeli. When I confronted Teleksen about it, he claimed it had been hijacked from the Sde Dov airbase near Tel Aviv. A Sikorsky UH-60 Black Hawk.'

If Razak's memory served him correctly, Israel had purchased several of the assault helicopters from the Americans in the late 1990s.

'Seems that the Israeli Air Force shares the Sde Dov airfield with commercial carriers,' Farouq added.

'No wonder it was so easy for someone to sneak onto the base.'

'Let's not jump to conclusions.' His tone was razor sharp. 'There's always the possibility that the helicopter wasn't actually stolen.'

Not liking the fact that Farouq's objectivity seemed to be waning, Razak shifted gears. 'At least they've finally admitted to it. Quite an embarrassment for them.'

'Assuming it was an accident, of course.'

'Did you ask Teleksen why we weren't informed sooner?'

'Of course I did.'

'And what was his response?'

Farouq folded his arms. 'He was concerned the information would be leaked to the media.'

Razak had to admit that if the tables had been turned, the Palestinians would also have done their best to conceal any information that could initiate hostile retaliation. It all just seemed like a never-ending game. 'You don't actually think the Israelis arranged for the theft, do you?'

'It's too soon to tell. But obviously I'm suspicious.'

'But what about all those Israeli soldiers murdered?' He shook his head. It just didn't gel with what Barton had presented. Why would the Jews be interested in the supposed relics of a false messiah or some ridiculous legend about the Holy Grail? 'What could their motive possibly be?'

'What has the Israeli motive ever been? These people are always looking to destroy peace.'

The same response Razak would expect from Hamas. 'So how will you proceed?'

'I'm not sure. For now, we'll await more information.' Farouq laced his fingers together and pressed them against his lips. 'Tell me, what is going on with the English archaeologist . . . this Barton character?'

Surely this was not the time to fuel the old man's growing frustrations with the other side. As it stood, the archaeologist's wild theories remained just that – untamed. 'He's asked to see the chamber again. He feels he may have missed something.'

Trying to hide his concern, the Keeper seemed unfazed. 'Like what?'

'I'll tell you as soon as I find out.' Razak stood to leave. 'By the way, I'll need to borrow your car. I'm meeting someone who may be able to give us some good information.'

'Fine.' Farouq opened his desk drawer and gave Razak a key to the Mercedes S500. 'I just had it cleaned. Where will you be going?'

'Gaza City,' Razak coolly replied.

'I see.' Farouq's face went limp as he considered asking for the key back. 'You know how things are over there right now.'

'I'll be careful,' Razak assured him. 'I'm taking Barton with me. It will be fine.'

Clearly unconvinced, Farouq nodded. 'Just remember that we're trying to solve a crime here, Razak. An act of terrorism. We're not making a documentary. Make sure Barton stays on track.'

'Yes, yes.'

After Razak left, Farouq sat in silence for some time, staring emptily out of the window at the gold-leafed cupola of the Dome of the Rock – the structure that single-handedly defined Islam's claim to Palestine.

Even the name of the site was one neither side could agree on.

To Jews, it was the Temple Mount. To Muslims – the Haram esh-Sharif.

Everything in Jerusalem had at least two names, even the city itself – *Al Quds*.

How could such a small country have redefined the Middle East and sparked the counter crusade – *jihad*? Centuries of conflict. So many disputes. To Farouq, religion was no longer the cause he championed. It was far more than that now.

He thought back to his days on the front line. He'd been a soldier during the Six-Day War in 1967, when the Arab nations – Egypt, Syria, and Jordan – had formed a united front to cast the Israelis into the sea, once and for all. But Israel's lethal air force – purchased from the United States – had been underestimated, pre-emptively striking the Egyptian airfields before the offensive even began. The conflict had ended with terrible consequences for the Palestinians. Israel had managed to wrest control over the Golan Heights, the West Bank, and the Sinai Peninsula. But even after that disastrous conflict, the Temple Mount had remained under Islamic control. Even the heavily armed Israelis knew that an attack against this site would escalate conflict to entirely new levels.

In 1973 Farouq had once again fought for his people when Egypt and Syria joined forces to reclaim the occupied territories, launching a sneak attack in Sinai and the Golan Heights during the holiest of the Jewish holidays – Yom Kippur, the Day of Atonement. For two weeks the Arab forces pushed deeper and deeper into the region, almost breaking the Israelis. But the tide soon turned, with the United Nations enforcing a ceasefire.

Farouq's hand migrated to his chest and massaged the scar beneath his tunic where an Israeli infantryman's bullet had almost taken his life.

Though a major conflict hadn't occurred in over three decades, Palestinian *intifadas* had been prolonged and frequent. Israel had strengthened its hold over the land, monopolizing the weaponry. It was a poorly kept secret that Israel had nuclear weapons, while Palestinians protesting on the streets had resorted to throwing stones.

But the emergence of extremist militant groups – like Hamas and Islamic Jihad – had transformed the conflict to a psychological offensive designed to starve the Israelis of peace and security. Highly visible suicide bombings had become the new voice of Palestinian freedom. Whether one called them terrorists or martyrs, the message was clear – the Israelis were only visitors in this place.

There would never be peace in Israel and wise men like Farouq who had fought on the front line for independence knew why. To give up Palestine was to surrender to Western ideology. Just as Saladin had pushed the Crusaders out of the Holy Land in the twelfth century, the Palestinians would soon rise again to reclaim the region.

And no controversy resulted in more bloodshed than those resulting from Israeli meddling with the Temple Mount. The archaeological digs initiated by Israelis and Palestinians in 1996 had resulted in scores of deaths. In 2000 Ariel Sharon had tried to reassert Israeli control over the site by marching into the esplanade with hundreds of IDF soldiers. Once again the Palestinians interpreted these actions as a religious attack, and much bloodshed had ensued.

Though he no longer wielded a rifle, Farouq remained a soldier on this new battlefront. The Temple Mount – the region's most valuable asset – was an archaeological treasure, a time capsule of world faith and politics. And no matter how sophisticated

Israeli weaponry became, they would never reclaim the site while he lived and breathed. With all Farouq had fought for in the past, he would rather die before that day passed.

Picking up the phone, he placed a call to the news department at Gaza City's Palestinian TV. Owned and operated by the Palestinian Authority, Palestinian TV underscored the extreme discontent at Israeli occupation. Its message had struck such a chord in right-wing Israeli circles that its director had been killed, shot at close range in the chest and head. The Mossad was suspected.

His call was routed to his inside contact – a young, ambitious Muslim named Alfar. Farouq provided detailed information about the helicopter – ammunition for what would prove to be the network's most contentious media bombshell ever.

Farouq hung up.

Emanating from the network of loudspeakers across the Haram esh-Sharif esplanade, he heard the call of the *muezzin*. It was time for midday prayer.

The Keeper eased himself onto his knees, faced south toward Mecca and began his recitation.

34.

VATICAN CITY

Standing to get a better look at what Charlotte had found, Bersei could see that nestled in a carved niche at the very bottom of the ossuary was something that resembled a metal test tube.

Above the white fabric of their masks, the two scientists exchanged looks.

'I've just about had all I can take right now,' Giovanni motioned to the cylinder. 'You do the honours.'

Charlotte reached down as if into a black hole. Her fingers closed around smooth metal. Slowly, and with infinite care, she withdrew it from the ossuary.

Turning her hand over, she rolled the tarnished tubular casing along her latex covered palm – a stark contrast of old and new. Both ends were sealed by round metal caps. There were no distinguishing marks or inscriptions.

'A container of some kind?' She inspected each end in turn. Her eyes were on him, searching for an explanation, but Bersei could not speak. 'Giovanni, I think you should open this.'

He waved her away.

Charlotte rotated it. The metal looked similar to the coins.

Was it bronze? 'Okay. Here goes.' She held the cylinder over an empty section of the tray. Clenching her teeth, she took hold of the cap sealing one end, applied equal pressure in the opposite direction and twisted. At first it didn't budge. But an instant later, a muffled cracking sound indicated the wax seal had broken.

The cap came free.

Fellow conspirators, the two scientists gazed at one another. Tilting the cylinder closer to the light, she glimpsed something rolled up inside.

'What do you see?' Bersei's voice was hoarse with tension.

'It looks like a scroll.'

He balled his hand into a fist, pressing it against his chin. 'Handle that extremely carefully.' His voice was loud. 'It's probably very brittle.' First the coins, now this, he thought. It was getting to be overwhelming.

Gently tapping the unopened end of the cylinder, Charlotte coaxed the scroll from the tube. Sticking at first, it slid out suddenly, landing on the tray with a small thump. They both froze. 'Shit! I didn't think that would happen so easily.'

Bersei reached out and gingerly rolled it back and forth with his index finger, assessing the damage. 'No harm done.' He exhaled heavily. 'Looks like it's in excellent condition.'

'Is that parchment?'

Bersei studied it. 'Most likely calfskin.'

'Have you ever handled ancient documents?'

'Personally, no,' he admitted.

'We can't just unfurl it, can we?'

'We'd have to research that. It looks remarkably well preserved, but of course it will be frail. There will be strict procedures. We can't risk any damage.' He was trying to imagine what it might reveal. 'Don't you think there's just too much evidence here?' His expression hardened.

'Perhaps. But I've got some really interesting news for you.' Charlotte had his complete attention.

'The radiocarbon dating results?'

She nodded. 'That bone sample I submitted to Ciardini.'

He studied her face intently. 'What did he find?'

'Ready for this? The sample was so good that it's 98.7 per cent certain the bones date from between 5 and 71 AD.'

Uncertainty was growing in Bersei's eyes again. That narrow time range was almost incredible. With his left hand, he massaged a cramp that was setting into the base of his neck. Stress. 'This is compelling news.'

'And the wood splinter – which, by the way, is from a type of walnut tree indigenous to a region in Israel. There's an 89.6 per cent degree of certainty it dates from between 18 and 34 AD.'

Bersei's eyes jumped over to the skeleton as if it had suddenly come to life. 'When do you think you'll have the results of the genetic analysis?'

'We might have it tomorrow.'

He stared down at the rolled calfskin. 'Good. Let's go ahead and document all this,' he suggested.

Charlotte got the digital camera, turned it on and started snapping shots of the ossuary's interior.

Locked in thought, Bersei knew that something about all this felt very wrong. No wonder Father Donovan had wanted to call in leading scientific expertise. The priest had to know more than he was letting on. After Charlotte captured an image of the rolled scroll, Bersei carefully returned it to its metal housing, and sealed the cap.

35.

EREZ CROSSING, ISRAEL

An hour south-west of Jerusalem, the lush farmlands of Israel's transformed desert began to fade back into arid landscape as Razak drove down Highway 4 toward the Gaza border.

'Have you ever been on that side of the fence?' Barton motioned with his eyes through the distant tall posts and steel wiring of the separation fence that ran along the Gaza Strip's fifty-one kilometre border, cutting away the tiny sliver of land from Israel's southern coast.

'Only once,' Razak replied in a dreary tone. He did not elaborate.

A sour taste came into the back of Barton's throat. Seeing as he'd be only one of a handful of Europeans in the tiny place inhabited by almost 1.3 million Palestinians, he would have preferred a more reassuring response from Razak – especially since Westerners were prime targets for abduction by Islamic militants, like the El-Aqsa Martyrs Brigade.

Up ahead, the roadway was snarled for almost three kilometres with idling vehicles – taxis, cars, and vans awaiting clearance through the Erez Crossing. Pulled off to the side of the road, many had already overheated. With no cover in sight, the scorching sun beat down unforgivingly on the stranded motorists.

Even with the windows up, the sounds of crying children and the choking stench of exhaust fumes permeated the Mercedes's air-conditioned interior.

'Who exactly is this contact we're meeting?' Barton asked.

'An old school friend of mine. A man who shares many of my concerns for the future of the Middle East,' Razak explained. 'If you don't mind, I'd like to request that you let me do all the talking.'

'Agreed.'

It took almost two hours before they reached the expansive metal canopy resembling a doorless hangar that shielded the IDF border patrol guards from the sun. Cement barricades and barbed wire lined the road. Tanks and armoured vehicles were positioned on both sides of the gate.

Razak turned to Barton. 'Do you still have that letter the Israeli police gave you?'

'Certainly.'

'Good. I have a feeling we may need it.' Razak tried his best to disregard an Arab taxi driver who was being interrogated by a gang of IDF soldiers on the exiting side of the roadway. A pair of German shepherds sniffed the car for explosives. He remembered hearing that the Israelis were particularly suspicious of lone drivers coming out of the Gaza Strip, many of whom had been suicide bombers.

Finally the IDF soldiers, wearing full combat gear, waved Razak forward, making no effort to point their rifle muzzles down. Surveillance cameras were mounted high up on the steel beams that supported the shelter, glaring down. A scrawny young Israeli soldier stepped forward. 'Open your rear compartment and let me see your papers,' he stated in rough Arabic, taking a moment to admire the Mercedes's smooth lines.

Razak pushed the boot release button and handed over their passports to the guard.

Two soldiers paced along either side of the car, running mirrors under the chassis, eyed the interior, and made their way to the rear to inspect the boot.

The guard crouched slightly to get a look at Barton. He shook his head. 'Not from here, I see.' Grimacing, he shifted his gaze back to Razak and said, 'You must be crazy going in there, especially now. This car. Him.' He made a smug face as he eyed Barton. 'What's your business?'

The trunk slammed shut, making the Englishman jump.

Presenting Barton's letter, Razak explained that the Israeli police had commissioned them to aid in the Temple Mount investigation. The guard seemed satisfied.

'Go, but be careful in there,' he warned. 'Past this gate, you're on your own.'

Razak nodded seriously, then pulled ahead. Letting out a prolonged sigh of relief, he manoeuvred the Mercedes through more cement barricades positioned below a concrete guard tower.

Fifteen minutes later, heading south down the region's main highway, Gaza City's unimpressive skyline came into view. The concentration of buildings tightened as Razak drove mindfully through the crowded downtown streets where the bombed-out facades of some structures still lay in ruins. Lasting reminders of Israel's frequent missile attacks.

For a long while, both men remained quiet, each taking in the bleakness of it all.

'This is awful,' Barton finally said.

'Over a million people packed into a tiny parcel of land.' Razak's tone was grim. 'Horrible sanitary conditions, political instability, a devastated economy . . .'

'The perfect recipe for discontent.'

Parking along the kerb, Razak paid a Palestinian boy with a round face forty Israeli shekels to watch the car. The streets were mobbed. The hot, lifeless air smelled of sewage.

Getting out of the car, Barton tried to avoid eye contact with the curious Palestinians who passed by.

'We'll be meeting him over there,' Razak said, motioning subtly with his eyes to a tiny outdoor café situated on the busy street corner in the shadow of a formidable mosque whose minaret stabbed defiantly into the blue sky. 'Let's go.'

The contact – a Palestinian with a sturdy frame and a bearded, smooth face – was already seated at a table, sipping mint tea from a clear glass. He called over to Razak.

Smiling, Razak greeted the man with a blessing and a handshake, then introduced the man to Barton by his first name – Taheem.

Barton smiled and extended a hand in greeting. He couldn't help but notice that the forty-something contact was well dressed in a neatly pressed linen suit – a sharp contrast to the majority of Palestinians here who donned traditional Islamic dress. Many of the women even wore the *burka* that covered them from head to toe.

Taheem's grin noticeably faded as he looked around before reciprocating the gesture. 'Please, sit.'

'Will it be all right if we speak in English?' Razak asked.

Bouncing his stern gaze off Barton once again, Taheem hesitated. 'Of course.'

'So tell me, my friend. How are things here?'

Shaking his head, Taheem rolled his eyes. 'You'd think the Israeli pullout would have helped matters. Far from it. The parliament is overrun by fundamentalists looking to formally wage war on Israel. Funding from the UN and the West has dried up. And now, with this incident in Jerusalem . . .' His eyes shifted to somewhere off in the distance.

'I know it must be difficult.'

'I'm just happy that I have no family here,' Taheem added. 'And you? How are things? As good as that fancy car you drive?' He motioned with his head down the street about thirty metres away where the young boy was urging some pedestrians away from the Mercedes.

Razak grinned. 'Everything's fine.'

'Glad to hear that.' He called for the waiter to bring two more teas.

'As you might imagine,' Razak said in a hushed tone, 'I'm anxious to know what you've heard about the theft.'

Taheem eyed Barton once again.

'It's okay,' Razak reassured him. 'Graham is not an Israeli. He's looking to help us.'

Taheem paused while the waiter set down the two glasses for Razak and Barton, waiting until he was out of sight to continue. 'You know about the helicopter, I presume?'

'Yes,' Razak said. 'The Israelis are still trying to find it.'

He looked surprised. 'Then you *don't* know.'

Confused, Razak's face scrunched up.

'They've already found it,' Taheem added.

'What?'

216

Sipping his tea, Barton listened in silent astonishment, trying to ignore a series of bullet holes that ran a neat line along across the café's cinderblock facade.

'I heard that a Palestinian fisherman caught some things in his nets three days ago, a few kilometres off the coast. Pieces from a helicopter – seat cushions, flotation vests . . . and the head of a dead pilot wearing an Israeli flight helmet.'

Shocked, Razak was speechless. 'How can it be that no one knows this?' At a minimum, he was sure that *Al-Jazeera* would have taken a shot at the story – facts or no facts.

Taheem scanned the area before answering. 'Rumour has it that the Shin Bet killed the fisherman before he spoke to the media. But not before he had told his brother – a dear friend of mine who will remain nameless, for obvious reasons.'

'But why was the helicopter in pieces?'

'The night of the theft, many heard it flying low over the rooftops and watched it go out over the sea. Minutes later, some even had a chance to see what looked like an explosion out over the horizon.'

Suddenly feeling helpless, Razak knew that Taheem's story confirmed his lingering fear that both the ossuary and the helicopter were long gone. He exchanged an uneasy glance with Barton.

'There's more,' Taheem said. 'As you know, when the Israelis pulled out of Gaza, they had given the Palestinian Authority control over the southern border crossing into Egypt. Since then, many weapons and explosives have flooded into Gaza. Many have found their way over the fence.'

Razak was confused. 'I thought the fences were equipped with sensors and electrical charges that could detonate explosives?' Effective deterrents that had largely thwarted most suicide bombers from getting into Israel, he remembered.

'Let me explain.'

Barton could see that Taheem was beginning to sweat more.

'Not long before the theft in Jerusalem took place, a helicopter was flying along the border fence.' Pointing west, the Palestinian subtly traced the air with his finger, out over the city. 'A routine occurrence,' Taheem admitted. 'However, some say that it hovered for a few minutes, just over the fence . . . into Gaza. A bold move for an Israeli helicopter, one might think, since such an easy target might attract a rocket-propelled grenade.' His voice cracked and he took a sip of tea. Clearing his throat, he continued. 'Anyway, I was told that some cargo was hoisted up from the ground and loaded onto the helicopter.'

A look of alarm widened Razak's eyes. Of course! The only way to circumvent the checkpoints was to avoid them all together.

Taheem leaned in closer. 'I was also told that someone inside Jerusalem coordinated the whole thing.'

'But –'

Before the words escaped Razak's mouth, Taheem's face suddenly exploded outward, spewing blood and fleshy chunks onto the wall, instantly followed by something ricocheting off the wall. Instinctively, Razak catapulted forward onto the ground, pulling Barton out of his chair and down beside him as Taheem's lifeless torso teetered forward and landed hard on the tabletop.

A few nearby pedestrians screamed and scurried away.

'Jesus!' Barton yelled, shaking in fear. 'What on earth was that!'

The silent shot had been so precise, Razak knew instantly. 'Sniper.'

A second round hammered into the thick wooden tabletop, piercing through just above Razak's head. Both he and Barton flinched. A third snapped off the pavement in front of them, almost grazing Barton's arm.

'We've got to get out of here right now.' Razak's head spun down the street toward the car. 'We're going to have to make a run for it.'

Barton's breathing was heavy, sweat dripping from his chin. He nodded. 'Okay.'

Scrambling to remove the car key from his pocket, Razak said, 'We'll split up and meet at the car. Run fast and low through the crowd.' He pointed along the pavement where most of the pedestrians had yet to work out that shots had been fired. 'I'm heading for the opposite side. It's our only chance. Go!'

Both men sprung out from beneath the table, racing off in opposite directions. Razak barely missed being run down by a dilapidated Ford hatchback as he darted across the street.

Barton did his best to avoid running into the pedestrians, feeling remorseful as he strategically kept them in the sniper's line of fire. Fully anticipating being taken down by the gunman, he was surprised when he came nearer to the Mercedes without registering another shot. Out of the corner of his eye, he could see Razak cutting swiftly through the throngs across the street.

The Mercedes's lights blinked as Razak remotely disengaged the door locks.

Barton scrambled to open the car door. Diving inside the Mercedes and pulling the door shut, he glanced over to see the young Palestinian boy holding the driver's door open as if he were a valet. A split second later, Razak weaved deftly through the traffic and spilled into the car. He thrust the key into the ignition as the boy closed the door behind him. Razak waved the clueless kid away just as the sniper managed a clean shot through the boy's temple, toppling him onto the pavement.

Now the pedestrians had worked out what was happening and pandemonium broke out – people running off in all directions.

Throwing the gearstick into drive, Razak slammed his foot on the accelerator.

No more shots came.

Breathless and pumped full of adrenaline, both men exchanged glances.

'What just happened?' Barton said, hands trembling.

Glancing over at him, Razak didn't have an answer. For the next few minutes, he focused on angling his way through the narrow streets, backtracking through the city toward the main highway.

Without warning, the Mercedes's rear lurched to the right amidst the deafening crunch of metal and glass as Razak and Barton were jerked sideways, almost out of their seats.

Somehow, Razak managed to regain control of the Mercedes, only after running up onto a kerb and steering back onto the roadway. His head swivelled to glimpse the late model Fiat saloon with a mangled front end that had spun out in the inter- section and was in the process of manoeuvring to continue its pursuit. Razak could see the driver and a second man riding in the passenger seat. Both were wearing hooded masks. When he saw that the passenger leaned out the window, aiming at them with an AK-47, he yelled over at Barton, 'Get down!'

The archaeologist sank below the seat and huddled below the dashboard just as a string of bullets took out the car's rear window and windscreen, glass fragments showering down on him. Two of the bullets burrowed deep into the stereo console, spewing out a shower of electric sparks.

Moving his head lower, Razak sped through two more inter- sections before swinging a wide turn onto the highway, heading north. More shots loudly strafed the driver's side of the car in rapid succession and Razak felt one dig into the side of his seat, almost clipping him beneath the armpit.

The road opened up with no traffic. Adrenaline buzzing through him, Razak pressed the gas pedal all the way to the floor. The Mercedes's engine revved hard and pulled him back in his seat. Miraculously, the car's rear end had endured the collision, though the steering wheel was pulling hard to the left and was vibrating fiercely. He quickly glanced down at Barton who, understandably, looked completely shaken up. 'You okay?'

'Are they still behind us?'

Razak eyed the rear-view mirror. 'Yes. But I don't think they'll be able to keep up.'

More shots pinged off the rear of the car.

Racing past the cement barricades of abandoned checkpoints, Razak kept an eye on the pursuers. As he anticipated, the Fiat – now spewing grey smoke out from its twisted grill – was quickly losing ground.

Sighing in relief, Razak tried to settle his breathing. His thoughts drifted momentarily to Farouq who would clearly not be pleased with the condition of his cherished Mercedes.

A half-kilometre from the border crossing, Razak watched the rear-view mirror as the pursuers came to an abrupt stop. Up ahead, there was no long queue of cars waiting to cross over to Israel – probably what the gunmen were hoping for, Razak thought – one last opportunity to have a clean shot. 'You can come up now,' he told Barton.

'I can understand why you haven't come back here until now,' Barton said, settling back into his seat and carefully shaking glass fragments out of his hair.

Decelerating, Razak wound the car through the barricades

below the watchtower. Stopping in front of the guard shelter, he waited until the soldiers signalled for him to pull forward. Alarmed by the condition of the Mercedes, they cautiously surrounded the car, rifles drawn, commanding the occupants to remain still.

Then the same young guard that had allowed them entry into Gaza stepped forward. Grimacing, he slung his rifle over his shoulder and put his hands on his hips, raking the Mercedes's marred exterior with his eyes. He crouched down beside Razak's blown-out window and smugly said, 'That was fast. Hope you enjoyed your stay.'

36.

Just after five o'clock, Father Donovan entered the lab.

'Working late again, I see,' he said, flashing a friendly smile.

'We want to make sure that the Vatican gets the best value for its money,' Bersei replied.

'Is there anything that the two of you need? Anything I can help with?'

The scientists exchanged glances. 'No,' Charlotte replied. 'The lab's very well equipped.'

'Excellent.' Donovan's curious eyes wandered over to the skeleton and the opened ossuary.

Bersei spread his hands. 'Would you like a quick overview of what we've found so far?'

The priest visibly perked up. 'Yes, indeed.'

For the next fifteen minutes, the scientists gave Donovan a basic summary of the forensic study and carbon dating results, and showed him the additional relics hidden in the ossuary's secret compartment. Bersei maintained a clinical, objective demeanour and Charlotte followed his lead.

Judging from the priest's reaction to the preliminary findings –

ranging from genuine surprise and intrigue, to tempered concern over the nature of the skeleton's telling signs of crucifixion – Charlotte sensed that maybe he had no advance knowledge of the ossuary's contents. She noted that the bronze cylinder seemed to capture his attention more than anything else, a lingering concern bleeding into his puzzled gaze. Trying to gauge Bersei's take on the matter, she felt that he too was catching the same vibe from Donovan.

'I'll tell you, Father Donovan,' Bersei added, 'this is one of the most remarkable archaeological discoveries I've ever laid eyes upon. I'm not sure what sum the Vatican has paid to acquire all this, but I'd say you have a priceless relic here.'

Watching the priest closely, Charlotte saw that Donovan's expression showed that he was pleased, but even more so, relieved.

'I'm sure my superiors will be delighted to hear that,' the priest said, his eyes wandering once more over to the skeleton. 'I don't want to rush things, but do you think you might be able to formally present your findings on Friday?'

Bersei looked over to Charlotte to see if she concurred with the idea. She nodded agreeably. Turning his attention back to Donovan, he said, 'It will take some preparation, but we can do it.'

'Very good,' Donovan said.

'If there's nothing else, Father,' Bersei said, 'I'll have to be on my way. Don't want to keep my wife waiting.'

'Please, don't let me keep you,' the priest said. 'I very much appreciate both of you taking the time to update me.'

Bersei disappeared into the break room to hang up his lab coat.

'He's quite the family man,' Charlotte whispered to Donovan. 'His wife is very lucky.'

'Oh yes,' Donovan agreed. 'Dr Bersei is very kind . . . a gentle soul. He's been quite helpful to us over the years.' The priest paused for a moment and added, 'Tell me, Dr Hennesey, have you ever visited Rome before?'

'No. And honestly, I haven't really had time to venture across the river yet.'

'Can I suggest a tour for you?'

'I'd love that.' She genuinely appreciated the priest's hospitality. Living the cloistered life of a cleric, he was quick to offer activities that were geared to a lone traveller.

'If you don't have plans this evening, I'd highly recommend the Night Walking Tour,' he energetically offered. 'It begins at Piazza Navona, just across the Ponte Sant' Angelo Bridge, at six-thirty. Takes about three hours. The tour guides are fantastic and you'll get a great overview of all the major sights in the old city.' He peered down at his watch. 'If you leave directly from here, you can make it on time.'

'Sounds perfect.'

'Normally you have to book these tours two days in advance,' he explained, 'especially this time of year. But if you're interested, let me make a call to reserve you a ticket.'

'That's very kind of you,' she replied.

Bersei was just emerging from the break room. 'Dr Hennesey, Father Donovan, I wish you both a good evening,' he said eyeing them in turn and bowing slightly. Then he turned to Charlotte and said, 'I'll see you tomorrow morning, same time. Make sure not to stay out too late.'

37.
ROME

Crossing the Ponte Sant' Angelo Bridge, Charlotte strolled down Via Zanardelli to its terminus and made a couple quick turns before entering the expansive Piazza Navona, laid out like an elongated oval racetrack. Striding toward the immense Italian baroque fountain that was its centrepiece – *Fontanna dei Quattro Fiumi* – she spotted the six-thirty tour group already assembling around a lanky Italian man with a laminated badge, presumably the tour guide. Reaching them, Charlotte waited patiently on the fringe, admiring the fountain's huge obelisk and four Bernini marble sculptures representing the great rivers – the Ganges, the Danube, the Nile, and the Rio de la Plata – as muscular male giants.

Moments later, the tall guide came over to her, looking down at a list of confirmed attendees. Glancing up, he smiled brightly, doing a double take when he saw Charlotte's amazing eyes. 'You must be Dr Charlotte Hennesey,' he said cheerily in near-perfect English, placing a check next to a handwritten note at the bottom of his roster.

'That's right,' she replied. With a perfect smile and soft eyes, his face was young and pleasant, topped with a thick quaff of long, yet well-groomed black hair.

'My name is Marco,' he told her. 'Father Donovan called ahead for you. It's a pleasure to have you join us this evening.'

'Thank you for taking me on such short notice.'

A strong voice, with a heavy trace of Italian, suddenly came at Marco from over her left shoulder.

'Perhaps you have room for one more?'

Both Charlotte and the tour guide turned at the same time. Her smile disintegrated when she saw Salvatore Conte standing behind her, grinning.

Marco looked insulted by the interruption. 'Your name?'

'Doesn't matter,' Conte retorted. 'How much for the ticket?'

Sizing him up, the guide pointed to his list and said abruptly, 'Sorry. We're already booked. If you'd like to leave me your name, I can see if we can get you onto Saturday's tour.'

Agitated, Conte spread his hands and dramatically peered around the piazza, then back at the guide's name badge. 'Come on . . . Marco, it's not exactly like you can't accommodate one more body. Plenty of room here, right, Charlotte?' Raising an eyebrow, he stared at her expectantly.

Amazed at his crassness, Charlotte looked away and said nothing.

Conte made a move for his wallet. 'How much?'

Shaking his head, Marco crossed his hands behind his back, still holding the clipboard. He could see that the man was making the Vatican guest uncomfortable. She wouldn't even make eye contact with the guy. 'I don't make the rules, Signore,' he calmly told Conte in Italian. 'Please be kind enough to contact our main office to voice your concerns. This is not the place.'

Pressing his tongue against the inside of his cheek and making a smug face, Conte jabbed a finger at the guide's chest and said in Italian, 'You should have a bit more respect for your fellow countrymen, tour guide. It's no wonder you make a living walking the streets and telling stories to tourists. Well, I've got a story for you.' He pressed his face close. 'Watch out, because at night, the streets in Rome can sometimes be dangerous. You never know who you might encounter in a dark alley.' He savoured the man's discomfort. 'It's a ticket, not a fucking bar of gold.'

Charlotte didn't understand what Conte was saying, but the guide's face revealed a growing concern.

Conte's eyes drifted over to her. 'Just thought you'd like some company,' he said, playing the martyr. 'Have a good night, Dr Hennesey.'

With that, the mercenary paced back two steps, spun and strode across the piazza.

'Sorry about that,' she said to the guide.

It took Marco a few nervous swallows to regain his voice. 'Friend of yours?'

'Far from it,' she replied quickly. 'And thanks for not giving in. That would've ruined my night.'

'Well then,' Marco finger-combed his mane of hair as he composed himself, 'I guess we'll be on our way.'

As Marco formally introduced himself to the group and briefly ran down the tour's itinerary, Charlotte scanned the piazza for Conte, sighing in relief when she didn't spot him. Who exactly was this character? How could such a creepy guy be connected with the Vatican?

It took almost an hour for Charlotte to forget about the crazy encounter at Piazza Navona. But slowly, she had lost herself in

Rome's extraordinary history, retold effortlessly by Marco. He had led the group on an amazing journey through the city's famous circular temple, the Pantheon, completed in 125 AD by Emperor Hadrian. There, Charlotte had marvelled at its expansive inner dome that seemed to defy the rules of physics, as the sun melted through the wide oculus that hovered at its centre.

Then it was off to the junction of three roads – *tre vie* – to admire Nicola Salvi's enormous baroque Trevi Fountain with its seahorse-riding tritons guiding Neptune's shell chariot. Nearby, they passed the Piazza di Spagna just below 138 steps that climbed up the steep slope to the twin bell towers that flanked the Trinità dei Monti church.

A few blocks further came the white Brescian marble Il Viattoriano, an eye-catching (most Romans wouldn't be as polite) monument that most compared to a colossal wedding cake plunked down in the centre of Old Rome, inaugurated in 1925 to honour Victor Emmanuel II – the first king of a unified Italy.

By the time the tour had made its way up Capitoline Hill – the only prominent remainder of ancient Rome's famed Seven Hills – and through the crumbled arches and columns of the Imperial Forums, the sun was starting to fade over the horizon and a new moon became visible in the clear night sky. Charlotte Hennesey had finally completely lost herself in the shadows of an ancient Empire.

Once the tour group had traversed Old Rome to the Colosseum, the entire city had taken on a new persona, basking in glowing lights. Walking the outside of the forty-eight metre high, circular amphitheatre with its three tiers of travertine porticos, Charlotte swore she could hear the clash of gladiators and roar of lions.

Then, imagination turned instantly to cold reality when she caught a fleeting glimpse of a modern-day gladiator disappearing into the shadows. Though she wanted to believe her eyes were tricking her, there was no doubt. Salvatore Conte.

THURSDAY

38.
TEMPLE MOUNT

Just after nine a.m., Barton negotiated his way past Akbar, and through the blast hole. Razak was already in the crypt standing with arms folded, wearing neatly pressed chinos and a white collared shirt. If Barton didn't know any better, he could have sworn that the Muslim was trying to make some kind of peace with this place. 'It's getting bad out there.'

'Yes.'

Barton dusted off his trousers. 'Tell me, how did Farouq react when he saw his car?'

Razak cringed. 'Not well.' That was an understatement. Last night, Farouq had berated him when he saw that his prized Mercedes was beyond repair. *'I shouldn't have let you go! Completely irresponsible! You should have known better, Razak. And for what? What did you gain by going there?'* It was like being a mischievous teenager again. 'Luckily, he has insurance, which, believe me, isn't so easy to get if you're a Palestinian.'

'Did you tell him what we discovered?'

Razak shook his head and held a finger to his lips, pointing toward Akbar. He drew Barton by the arm toward the rear of the chamber. 'I don't think he's ready for that just yet,' he whispered. Last night, Razak had barely slept, trying to figure out who'd sent the sniper. He could only guess that the Shin Bet was looking to tie up some loose ends. Now, there was a good chance that he and Barton might share Taheem's fate if they didn't move quickly to find answers. 'Remember what we discussed – you mustn't tell anyone what we heard or what happened yesterday. We don't know what the consequences could be.'

Barton nodded.

Razak let go of his arm. 'So what brings us back here?'

The archaeologist collected his thoughts. 'As I mentioned yesterday, I've given the concept of a crypt considerable thought. There are certain facts that simply don't add up.' Barton moved to the centre of the room, his eyes roving the walls. 'I have been thinking about Joseph of Arimathea – his status, power, and money. I'm troubled that this crypt lacks many of the features I'd have expected to see in the tomb of a wealthy family.'

'Such as?'

'Refinement, for one. There's nothing here to suggest position or wealth. It's just an ordinary stone chamber – no ornate carvings, no pilasters, frescos, or mosaics. Nothing.'

Razak inclined his head, trying to remain patient. To a Muslim it wasn't striking. 'Perhaps this Joseph was a man of humility?'

'Maybe. But remember how I explained to you that the body was allowed to decompose for twelve months before being placed in the ossuary?'

Razak nodded. 'Hard to forget. But I hope there's a point to all this.'

'Believe me. In ancient Jewish crypts, you'd expect to see at least one small niche called a *loculus* – a small tunnel about two metres deep.' He envisioned the tomb Father Demetrios had indicated in the bedrock beneath the Church of the Holy Sepulchre. 'Where the body would have been laid out.'

Razak eyed the walls. 'I don't see one.'

'Precisely,' Barton agreed, striking a finger into the air. 'Which made me wonder about this crypt's design. With ten ossuaries, many trips in and out of here would have been required. At the very least there would have been one visit to place the body here after each family member's death, another to practise the sacred rituals of the *tahara*, and then a final trip to transfer the expiated bones to the ossuary. That's a minimum of three visits per body.'

'Okay.'

'And when I studied these remains the other day,' Barton motioned to the ossuaries, 'I had a feeling that this family all died at once.'

Razak's brow furrowed. 'How could you tell?'

'Granted, I'm not an expert when it comes to forensic anthropology. But these remaining skeletons seem like they came out of a family photo.' He eyed the nine ossuaries. 'The age gaps show a very normal progression with no apparent overlap – an old father, a slightly younger mother, and none of the children making it past their late twenties. One would expect a large family to decease in a more random pattern where at least some of the children reach their later years.'

'That is odd.'

'Furthermore,' Barton's eyes canvassed the space, 'do you see any sign of an entrance?'

Razak scanned the bedrock surrounding him on all but one side. 'Looks like the only way in and out was that opening covered by the stone wall.' He pointed to the blast hole.

Barton nodded. 'Exactly. And look at this.' Moving toward

the blast hole, he motioned for Razak to follow. 'See?' Barton spread his hands, indicating the depth of the wall. 'This wall's about half a metre thick. But look here. See how these stones' — he tapped the side facing them — 'are the same style as those stones?' He tapped the other side of the wall facing into the mosque. Then he pointed out into the cavernous, arched room and Razak's eyes followed. 'And it's the same stone that was used to construct this entire room. Coincidence? Perhaps not.'

Razak was getting it. 'Wait a second.' He moved in closer, bending at the waist. His head circled all the way around the inner circumference of the blast hole. Sure enough, the walls had a purposeful design to them. 'You're saying both sides of the wall were erected at the same time?'

'Absolutely. Sealed away from *that* room,' he said, pointing out into the Marwani Mosque again, 'during its initial construction. Look at the opening that led into this chamber before the wall was erected.' Barton paced back and spread his hands to emphasize the width where carved bedrock transformed to stone.

Razak moved back to see what the Englishman was implying. Turning toward the blast hole again, he studied the space that the stone wall had filled. Certainly it was wide, but no larger than twice the width of an average doorway. 'What do you think this means?'

'It strongly suggests that our thieves weren't the first intruders here. It seems clear to me that this room wasn't designed to be a crypt.'

The Muslim stared at him blankly.

'This room is a *vault* specifically built for concealment and security,' Barton explained. 'Somehow it was built in conjunction with Solomon's Stables. And I think I know who was responsible.' In his mind's eye, he saw the graffiti that hovered in the bedrock over Father Demetrios's stout form – the image that helped him postulate this new theory.

Razak thought it through, mulling over the history that he knew about this place. One thing that clearly stuck out in his thoughts was the notion that the area now converted into the Marwani Mosque was supposedly used as a horse stable centuries earlier. And supposedly, it was built by . . . Suddenly his face slackened. 'The Knights Templar?'

Barton smiled and shook his head knowingly. 'Correct! It's a long shot, but most archaeologists credit them with constructing Solomon's Stables. How familiar are you with Templar history?'

Clearly not thrilled that the archaeologist was venturing into history again, Razak told him what he knew from his surprisingly extensive reading around the subject. After all, he thought, to understand the modern struggle between East and West, one must open a history book.

The Poor Knights of Christ and the Temple of Solomon had been founded in 1118 CE, after the first Christian Crusade. The Knights Templar were an order of militant, monastic mercenaries commissioned by the papacy to protect the reclaimed kingdom of Jerusalem from neighbouring Muslim tribes, ensuring safe passage for European pilgrims. They were notorious, feared for their lethal tactics and their fanatical oath to never retreat from the battlefield and fight to the death in the name of Jesus Christ. The Templars had remained in control of the Temple Mount until slaughtered by a Muslim force led by Saladin at the Battle of Hattin in the twelfth century. They'd even used the Dome of the Rock Mosque as their headquarters, giving it the Latin name *Templum Domini*, or 'Temple of the Lord'.

Barton was impressed by Razak's knowledge and said so. Not

many Jews, or even Christians for that matter, could readily display such command of the finer points of history. 'These ossuaries were transferred here from another site where the proper rituals would have initially taken place. If we go with the theory that this is a vault,' Barton continued, 'it would suggest the Templar Knights might have constructed it to protect the ossuaries.'

'Or treasure.' Razak responded swiftly, spreading his hands. 'Let's not forget that possibility.' He wasn't thrilled about the archaeologist's determination to link the theft to a revered prophet's remains. 'After all, weren't they very rich? Looting Muslim mosques and homes, bribing public officials . . .'

'True, the Templars amassed a fortune, mostly plundered from conquered enemies. The papacy even allowed them to levy taxes and collect tithes. Eventually, they became bankers. The Templars were the medieval equivalent of . . . say . . . American Express. You see, prior to embarking on their journey to the Holy Land, European pilgrims would deposit money with a local Templar lodge where they'd be given an encrypted depository note. Upon their arrival here in Jerusalem, they'd exchange the note for local currency.'

'Then how can you be so sure this vault didn't contain their loot?'

'We'll never know for sure,' Barton admitted. 'But it seems highly unlikely they'd seal away assets so permanently knowing they'd need it for such frequent transactions.'

'Not good for liquidity,' Razak agreed, 'But it would ensure safety for assets not needed in the short term.'

'Touché,' Barton admitted. 'However, those etchings on the rear wall don't make reference to anything else. Just the names of those whose remains are in these boxes.' He ambled over to the ossuaries again, scrutinizing them, searching for an explanation. 'If these were transferred here to be locked away, then where were they originally found?' he muttered quietly, thinking aloud.

'I'm still confused.' Razak spread his hands. 'How could a secret vault have been excavated beneath such a public place?'

'I've given that a lot of thought and this is where it all gets interesting.' Barton looked at him closely. 'In the first century, the House of the Sanhedrin – where the Jewish authorities congregated and held trials – was located directly above Solomon's Stables. And back then the platform beneath it was rumoured to be honeycombed with secret passageways.' *Many leading to the temple's inner sanctum*, he thought. 'As a member of the Council, Joseph would have had access to those areas and stairs leading directly to the vaulted chambers beneath the platform, allowing him to construct the vault in complete secrecy.'

'This Joseph of Arimathea. I'm assuming he was from somewhere called Arimathea – correct?'

Barton nodded. 'That's what the scriptures imply.'

'Then perhaps the original crypt was in Joseph's own land, where his family lived?'

'Perhaps,' Barton replied unenthusiastically. But it made him think: *could the real tomb really have been beneath the Church of the Holy Sepulchre?* It didn't seem possible since the basilica had been there long before the Crusaders arrived. 'The problem is that no one knows what place Arimathea really referred to. Some think it was a Judean hill town. But that's all conjecture.'

'Assuming you're on the right track, how do you suppose the thieves found this place?' Visualizing Taheem's horrid, blown-out face, Razak felt an urgent sense of linking this to something the authorities would find useful – something that could help to bring closure to their investigation.

Barton let out a long breath and ran his fingers through his hair. There was so much to consider. 'The only thing I can think of is that the thief got hold of a document of some kind. This burial spot must have been accurately described in an ancient text. The entry was far too precise – it had to have been measured.'

'But who could possess something like that?'

'I'm not sure. Sometimes these ancient scrolls or books have been lying around in plain sight, untranslated, in museum rooms – for decades. Maybe some fanatical Christian museum employee,' he said half-heartedly. But then he wondered if it wasn't that far-fetched after all.

Razak looked sceptical.

'And you've seen nothing in the antiquities markets yet for the ossuary?'

Barton shook his head. 'I checked again this morning for any new items. Nothing.'

Without warning, the floor of the chamber shook beneath their feet, instantly followed by a distant, reverberating drone. Alarmed, both Barton and Razak instinctively reached out for something to steady themselves.

Then as quick as it came, it had disappeared. Though it might easily have been confused with a low-level earthquake, both men immediately grasped that it was something else all together.

39.

VATICAN CITY

Shortly after nine a.m., Father Donovan buzzed the lab intercom, announcing a call for Charlotte from the United States.

'Well, go get it,' Bersei urged.

She made her way to the phone, sliding the mask off her face. She pressed the speakerphone button. 'Charlotte Hennesey speaking.'

'It's me, Evan.'

Hearing his voice come through the small speaker, her stomach fluttered. 'Hi, Evan. What time is it there?'

'Very early, or very late, depending on how you want to look at it. Anyway, I just finished running a scan on your sample.'

Something in his voice didn't sound right. Hennesey heard Aldrich rustling some papers.

'Wait,' she said. 'I'm on speakerphone. Let me pick up.' She snapped off her lab gloves and grabbed the receiver. 'Okay,' she said.

Aldrich jumped right in. 'I began with a simple spectral karyotype to get a preliminary idea of the DNA's quality. You know what we'd

241

be looking for . . . basic plot of chromosome pairs. That's when I noticed something very odd.'

'What is it? Is something wrong?'

'Yes, Charlotte. The result was forty-eight XY.'

In a spectral karyotype, dense DNA strands called chromosomes are marked with fluorescent die and colour-sorted into pairs to detect genetic aberrations. Since every human inherits twenty-two chromosomes from each parent, an X sex chromosome from the mother, and an additional sex chromosome from the father, a typical result would be forty-six XX for females and forty-six XY for males.

Forty-*eight* XY? Hennesey twisted an earring between thumb and forefinger, trying to let that one sink in. The good news was that the gender was definitely male. That agreed with all the forensic evidence. But Aldrich was suggesting that an extra pair of non-sex chromosomes, or 'autosomes', had appeared in the molecular structure of the sample. Such aberrations were typically linked to serious diseases like Down's syndrome where an extra chromosome twenty-one was present. 'So it's aneuploidy?' Charlotte whispered.

'Right. We have a mutation here.'

'What kind?' She kept her voice low so as not to draw Bersei's attention. Glancing over at him, she could see that he was paying her no attention, analysing the skeletal scans.

'Not sure yet. Got to adjust the gene scanner to handle the additional strands. I wasn't expecting something like this the first go-round, but it shouldn't take me much longer. I was able to pull basic coding for the genetic profile. I've posted it to your e-mail account.'

'Great. That'll give me a good head start.'

'How much longer do you think you'll be in Rome?'

'I don't know. I think most of the major work is done. I'll have to make a presentation, of course. Maybe a few more days. I might want to take a couple more just to explore Rome. It's wonderful here.'

'Has the Vatican briefed you fully about the work?'

'Yes, but we're being told everything here is in strictest confidence. I had to sign a letter of confidentiality. So I can't really say anything about it.'

'That's okay, Charlie – I don't need to know. I figure if there's anyone we can trust it's the Vatican. I just don't want BMS involved in anything shady.'

What had he discovered that made him so nervous? she wondered. 'One more thing. Did you happen to run the genetic profile against our database to determine ethnicity?'

There was a brief silence. 'Actually, I did.'

'Oh.' She was surprised he didn't mention that. 'And what did you find?'

'That's the other weird thing about all this. I found nothing.'

'What are you talking about?' What he was saying sounded almost ridiculous. Though ninety-five per cent of all humans shared the same genetic coding, less than five per cent of the genome accounted for differences relating to gender and ethnicity. It wasn't difficult to spot the variations.

'No matches.'

'But that's impossible. Did you include Middle Eastern profiles?'

'Yeah.'

The ossuary was part of Jewish burial customs. Perhaps she needed to be more specific. 'How about Jewish profiles?'

'Already checked it. Nothing there.'

How could that be? It wasn't at all consistent with their other findings. 'Could it have something to do with the anomaly you found?'

'I'd say so. I'll let you know what I find. Anything else?'

She hesitated, huddling closer to the wall. 'I miss you,' she finally whispered. 'And I'm really sorry that I didn't leave on a better note. I just . . . I'd like to talk to you when I get back. There's some stuff you really need to know.'

At first, he didn't respond. 'I'd like that.'

'I'll see you soon. Don't forget me.'

'Impossible,' he said.

'Bye.'

Bersei appeared beside her as she returned the phone to the cradle. 'Everything all right?'

'Seems so,' she said, flashing a smile. 'I got the DNA profile from the lab.'

'And?'

'We have the missing information we need.'

Bersei watched over her shoulder as Charlotte brought up the web browser and accessed her e-mail account. Within seconds, she'd retrieved Aldrich's data file, and opened it for Bersei to inspect – a dense spreadsheet of data.

'Okay. Here it is.' She switched places with him.

He scrolled through the data. Three columns identified a universal code for each gene sequence, a layperson's interpretation of the coding, such as 'hair colour', and a numeric value specifying those attributes. In the case of hair colour, a numeric value in the third column corresponded with a specific hue on a universal colour chart.

'How does it look?'

'Incredibly specific. Looks like I can plug the data right into the program.'

She smiled to herself. *Thank you, Evan.*

Bersei opened the imaging software and located the file containing the skeletal scans and tissue reconstruction – the ghostly marble statue awaiting its final touches: the genetic 'paint'. 'For now, I'm going to go with the basics. The computer will fill in hair colour, but not hair style, of course,' he explained as he formatted the data file for import.

Aldrich's discovery of a mutation had prompted Charlotte to start thinking through a long list of possible diseases. Since most attacked the body's soft tissues and didn't affect the bones themselves – unlike the one raging inside her own bones that was determined to leave its mark – she couldn't even begin to imagine what he could have detected. Her extraordinary desire to see the completed picture was now replaced by a sudden foreboding.

Bersei imported the genetic data and clicked to update the profile.

For a few agonizing seconds, it seemed like nothing was happening.

Then the enhanced reconstruction flashed back onto the monitor.

It wasn't what either scientist expected.

40.
JERUSALEM

When Ari Teleksen's cell phone rang, he already knew the purpose of the call. In the IDF's downtown Jerusalem headquarters, he stood at the wide plate-glass window of his eighth-floor office with its panoramic view of the city. Just a few blocks away, his grey eyes were glued to the sickening plume of thick, black smoke that billowed up from street-level like the devil's breath.

'I'll be there in five minutes,' he said grimly.

Just last night, he had heard the first wave of news stories reporting that the Temple Mount thieves had stolen an Israeli helicopter. With a growing sense of foreboding, Teleksen knew that the Palestinian response had just begun.

Without setting foot in the area, he retained an uncanny ability to foresee the aftermath of a bombing and the reverberations he had felt rattle his chest only minutes ago told him that there would be many casualties.

He hastily made his way down to the parking garage and jumped into the driver's seat of his gold BMW. After turning on the ignition, he grabbed the magnetic blue police light from the floor and stuck it on the car's roof. Peeling out of the parking garage, he jammed his foot down on the accelerator and rocketed down Hillel Street.

As his BMW approached the Great Synagogue, the chaotic scenes on King George Street looked all too familiar – the panicking crowds being held back by IDF soldiers and police, the site's perimeter already cordoned off by wooden barricades. A fleet of ambulances had arrived, with emergency crews racing to tend to survivors.

Teleksen threaded the BMW through the mob, a young IDF soldier waving him forward, and parked a comfortable distance away. When he opened the car door, the air smelt of burnt flesh.

Even at fifty metres he could see tattered chunks of bloody tissue and bone stuck to the walls of buildings adjacent to the scene, looking like wet confetti. The blast had stripped tree limbs and cast shrapnel, pockmarking the vicinity. Almost every window had been shattered.

At first glance structural damage seemed minimal. Compared with many other scenes he'd witnessed, this one was fairly low-level. But deep down, he knew many more would follow if the rising discontent stemming from the Temple Mount theft was not soon remedied.

One of the investigators recognized him and introduced himself. The man was in his fifties, with a mop of silver hair.

'Detective Aaron Schomberg.' He couldn't help looking at Teleksen's three-fingered left hand.

'What have you found out, detective?' Teleksen lit up a Time Lite.

'Witnesses say a young Arab woman, dressed in plain clothes, ran into a crowd as they were leaving the synagogue and blew herself up.'

With Schomberg at his side, Teleksen walked toward the epi-centre. He eyed the medical workers bagging human limbs and remnants too small for stretchers – the bomber's ripped-apart remains, most likely.

'How many dead?' Cigarette smoke spun out of his nostrils.

'So far eleven with another fifty or so injured.'

He took another heavy drag. 'No one saw her coming?'

'The bombs were strapped beneath her clothes. It happened too quickly.'

Ruing the time when terrorists had been easier to detect, Teleksen turned to Schomberg. 'What did she say?'

The detective was confused. 'Commander?'

'Sacrificial death is never without preamble.' Pinching the cigarette between the remaining fingers of his left hand, he pointed the lit end at the detective to emphasize the point. 'Martyrs don't give their lives in silence. Did anyone hear what she said before she detonated herself?'

Schomberg flipped through his notepad. 'Something along the lines of "Allah will punish all those who threaten him."'

'In Arabic or English?'

'English.'

They had reached the spot where witnesses told Schomberg the suicide bomber had positioned herself only a few metres from the synagogue's entrance. At first, it seemed like an odd place for the bomber to detonate since the explosives were typ-ically designed to be most effective in closed spaces, like buses or cafés. Studying the close proximity to the building's ravaged cement facade that looked more like a bank than a place of wor-ship, Teleksen quickly realized that it actually wasn't a bad choice. He could see that the victims strewn across the steps had been corralled in, and the looming cement wall behind them had actually amplified the blast wave. So if the bullet-like shrapnel hadn't killed them, the blast's crushing shock wave would have done the job by pulverizing their internal organs and bones.

Teleksen's cell phone rang, and he saw from the display it was Topol. He flicked the cigarette butt onto the sidewalk. 'Yes?'

'How bad?' The policeman's voice was urgent.

'I've seen worse. But all the more reason why we need to resolve this issue quickly. When can you get here?'

'I'm only a few blocks away.'

'Be quick.' Hanging up, Teleksen wondered how much more of this would happen before they came up with real answers for Friday's theft.

The clutch of media vans momentarily distracted him. The Palestinian TV channel was particularly troublesome. Hatred and discontent required little stimulation. The pressure was really on.

Thirteen Israeli soldiers and two helicopter pilots killed. Now innocent Jewish civilians had died.

And for what? he wondered. The English archaeologist, supposedly the best in his field, insisted it was a relic. Teleksen knew ancient relics fetched huge prices – particularly those from the Holy Land. There was no telling what some people would do to realize them. But hijack helicopters? Kill soldiers? How could an ossuary possibly be worth that much? He had seen dozens of them in Israel's museum galleries and they weren't nearly as well hidden or protected. What could make this one so special? It made no sense.

His best intelligence people kept insisting that only an insider could've been capable of such an elaborate heist. Teleksen knew what they meant. To secrete weapons into Jerusalem was like walking on water. One would need to be able to circumvent checkpoints, metal detectors, and myriad other logistical hurdles. Few could accomplish that.

Of course, the helicopter had proven to be a tremendous tactical weapon. Was its theft intended to mock Israel's security system? Luckily, his agents had managed to prevent the Palestinians and the media from discovering the true fate of the Black Hawk. But knowing that beyond these borders many were unwilling to cooperate with Israeli intelligence, Teleksen was deeply troubled by the fact that the thieves had so quickly reached international waters. Because if the relic had been taken out to sea . . .

Something rubbery beneath his left foot interrupted his thoughts and he looked down. Lifting his shoe, he realized he had been standing on a human ear. Scowling, he stepped sideways.

Was there any way out of this? Barton was supposed to be coming up with answers, but only seemed interested in peddling wacky theories about ancient history. The archaeologist was proving to be a real problem.

Then an idea suddenly came to Teleksen, and he was sure Topol would approve of it. Far from being a liability, Barton might actually be the solution.

41.

VATICAN CITY

Both scientists stared in amazement at the screen.

The scanned skeletal frame had been calibrated to reconstruct muscle mass with a layer of colourless skin applied. Now this new data had transformed the statue-like image into a complete 3-D human apparition.

Astonished at the final result, Bersei's hand was covering his mouth. 'What would you say is his ethnic origin?'

Charlotte shrugged. It looked like maybe Aldrich had been correct after all. 'I'm not sure he has one.' Her words sounded totally implausible.

Blending dark and light, the assigned skin pigmentation added an eerily life-like quality, defining muscles and highlighting features.

Giovanni zoomed in on the face.

Though unmistakably masculine, the image exuded a subtle androgyny. With their hypnotic aquamarine irises, the eyes were wide, tapering slightly upwards in the corners beneath slender eyebrows. The long nose broadened slightly above full, mocha-coloured lips. Blackish-brown wisps formed a thick hairline that pinched in hard corners at the temples. The facial hair was similarly coloured and thick, mostly evident along the angular jaw line.

'Quite a handsome specimen,' Bersei said in a very clinical tone.

'I'd say he's perfect,' Charlotte replied. 'I don't mean in a male model or movie star sort of way . . . but he's unlike anyone I've ever seen.' Looking for anything anomalous, nothing about the image suggested a genetic defect, unless perfection was considered a flaw. Now she wondered what Aldrich's analysis had actually detected. Could the prototype scanner have malfunctioned? Had the imaging software misinterpreted the data?

Tilting his head sideways, Bersei said, 'If you took all the typical ethnic characteristics of humanity and put them in a blender, this would probably be the end result.' Face tight, he held his hand out at the computer, still overwhelmed by what he was seeing. 'It's absolutely fascinating that any one human being could display such complexity.'

'Now what?'

Bersei looked haunted, as if the image was almost torturing him. 'I'm really not sure.' Tearing his eyes from the monitor, he glanced up at her with tired eyes. 'We've performed a full forensic examination' – he began counting off with his fingers – 'carbon dating, a complete genetic profile. The only major item left is the symbol on the ossuary.'

'Well, if you want to look into that,' Charlotte suggested, 'I can begin preparing our preliminary presentation for Father Donovan. I'll compile all the data, the photos, and start writing a report. Then maybe tomorrow we can tell him what we've found so far. See what he recommends.'

'That sounds like a plan. Who knows, maybe that symbol has something to tell us about this guy.'

Bersei returned to his workstation and turned on the digital camera. Humming softly to himself, he proceeded to snap several close-ups of the ossuary's single relief, uploading the images onto the computer terminal.

Marvelling at the quality of the engraver's work, he ran his finger over the raised symbol carved onto the ossuary's side:

From the onset, this image had perplexed him. The ossuary was clearly used almost exclusively by Jews in ancient Judea. Yet he remembered both the dolphin and the trident as being primarily pagan symbols, adopted by many early Roman cults. It was clearly in contradiction to the relic's supposed origin.

Back at the computer, he brought up the web browser. He

began with simple search criteria: *trident*. Almost instantly, a flood of hits came back at him. He began clicking through the most relevant ones.

The trident itself had many meanings. Hindus called it the *trishul*, or 'the sacred three', symbolizing creation, preservation, and destruction. In the Middle East, it was associated with lightning. Its alter ego, the pitchfork, later found its way into Christian art to symbolize the devil – an early attempt at discrediting pagan imagery.

Singularly, the dolphin was equally mysterious. In ancient times, the intelligent mammals were revered for their devotion to saving the lives of shipwrecked sailors. Romans also used dolphins to signify the journey souls would take far to the ends of the sea to their final resting place on the Blessed Isles. The dolphin was also strongly associated with the gods Eros, Aphrodite, and Apollo.

But certainly, the symbol engraved into the ossuary fused the two for a more purposeful meaning. But what could it be?

Bersei tried to find more references that could explain the dolphin twined around the trident.

The dolphin and trident seemed to first appear together in Greek mythology, both symbolizing the power of Neptune, the sea god. His trident was a gift from the one-eyed titans, the Cyclops. When the god was angered, he'd pound the ocean floor with it to stir the oceans, causing storms. Able to morph into other creatures, Neptune frequently chose to appear to humans in the form of a dolphin. The Romans later renamed the Greek sea god Poseidon.

Bersei was certain there had to be more that he was missing.

Another hit came back, linking to ancient coins minted by Pompey, a Roman general in the mid-first century BC. On the front of the silver coin was an effigy of the general's laurelled head flanked on both sides by a dolphin and a trident – not blended together, but certainly depicted side by side. And Bersei recalled that early in Pompey's career, he had invaded Jerusalem.

He leaned forward.

Following his siege of Jerusalem in 64 BC, he had ordered the crucifixion of thousands of Jewish zealots – all in a single day. It was said that so many crucifixes were needed, that the general had stripped away every tree from the city's surrounding mountains.

Crucifixion. Jerusalem.

Could this be the connection? Could the ossuary be linked to the notorious Roman general?

Considering this for a long moment, Bersei still wasn't satisfied. He still vaguely recalled seeing this exact depiction somewhere else. And somehow, he strongly believed it was linked to Rome.

The hunt continued.

Using various search phrases, like 'dolphin around trident', he finally found a clear hit. Clicking the link, he was astounded when the exact image on the ossuary filled the screen.

A smile broke across the anthropologist's face. 'Now we're getting somewhere,' he muttered.

Scrolling down, he read the text that accompanied the image.

The words hit him like a stone. He read it again, dumbfounded, his entire world caught in the screen's contours. 'Charlotte,' he called out. 'You have to see this.' He slumped back into his chair, covering his mouth with his hand in disbelief.

Two seconds later, she was at his side. His face drained, the Italian pointed at the computer screen.

'What is it?'

'The meaning behind the relief on the ossuary.' Bersei's voice was quiet as he pointed again to the monitor.

Seeing his bewildered expression, she scrunched her face and said, 'Looks like it did have something to say after all.'

'I'd say so,' he muttered, rubbing his eyes.

Leaning closer, Charlotte read the text aloud: 'Adopted by early Christians, the dolphin intertwined around the trident is a portrayal of . . .' she paused.

The low drone of the ventilation system became suddenly pronounced.

'. . . Christ's crucifixion.' Her voice trembled as she uttered the words, which seemed to hang in the air like vapour.

It took Charlotte a moment until the full impact hit her. 'Oh my God.' A vice tightened in her stomach and she had to look away.

'I should have known.' Bersei's strained voice sounded tormented, weak. 'The dolphin shuttles spirits to the afterlife. The trident, the sacred three, representing the Trinity.'

'No way. This isn't right.' She looked down at him.

'I *know* the ossuary's patina is genuine,' Bersei protested. 'Every single part. Consistent throughout, including the residue covering this relief. Plus I've established that the mineral content could only have come from one place – Israel. And the evidence we saw on the bones reinforces that message. Scourging. Crucifixion. We even have the nails and bits of wood,' he emphasized, throwing his hands up in surrender. 'Just how much more obvious could all this be?'

Her mind went momentarily blank, as if a cord powering her rational thought had been unplugged. 'If this is really the body of . . . Jesus Christ' – it almost hurt for her to say it – 'think about it – how profound this is.' Charlotte saw the crucifix hanging over her bed. 'But it *can't* be. Everyone knows the crucifixion story. The Bible describes it in minute detail and it doesn't agree with this. There are too many inconsistencies.' She strode briskly to the workstation.

'What are you doing?' Bersei was out of his chair.

'Here. See for yourself.' She jabbed a shaking finger at the brow of the skeleton's skull. 'Do you see any evidence of thorns?'

He looked up at her then straight back at the skull. Giovanni knew what she was implying. Scrutinizing it intently, he failed to detect even minute scratches. 'But surely it's hardly likely that thorns would inflict damage on the bone itself?'

Moving around the side of the workstation, Charlotte was now down by the legs. 'What about this? Broken knees?' She pointed at them. 'I don't remember these being mentioned in the Bible. Wasn't it a spear in Jesus's side that finished him off?' Here she was trying to renew her lost faith at a time when she most needed to believe in something bigger than herself, and Bersei – of all people – was tearing it down again. Worst of all, he was using science to do it.

The anthropologist spread his hands. 'Look, I understand where you're going with this. I'm just as confused as you are.'

She studied him intently. 'Giovanni, you don't *really* think these are the remains of Jesus Christ, *do you?*'

He ran his fingers through his hair and sighed. 'There's always the possibility that this symbol was only meant to honour Christ,' he offered. 'This man,' he pointed to the skeleton, 'could merely have been some early Christian, a martyr perhaps. This could all be a tribute to Christ.' He shrugged. 'It's not exactly a name on that box. But you saw the genetic profile. It's not like any man we've ever seen. I'd have to say that I'm pretty certain about this one.'

'But it's only a symbol,' she protested. 'How can you be sure?'

Bersei was taken aback by the American's passionate denial. He wished he could feel as strongly. 'Come with me.' He motioned for her to follow.

'Where are we going?' she called after him, pacing behind him into the corridor.

Without stopping, he turned back to her. 'I'll explain in a minute. You'll see.'

42.

PHOENIX

Evan Aldrich threaded his way past the workstations heaped with scientific gadgetry, making for the glass-panelled enclosure to the rear of BMS's main laboratory.

Once inside, he closed the door, reached into his lab coat and removed a sealed glass vial, which he set down next to a high-powered microscope. The prototype scanner sat on an adjacent desk, looking like a streamlined photocopier. He pulled on a pair of latex gloves.

There was a brief knock and the door opened.

'Morning, Evan. What's happening?'

Glancing over, he found Lydia Campbell, his managing technician for genetic research, poking her head around the doorframe. Aldrich's hand reflexively moved to cover the vial. 'Got some samples I need to look at.'

'The ones you were working on yesterday?' She looked down at the vial beneath his hand. 'Thought you'd finished with them.'

'Yeah, I'm just having another look at something.'

'Well, you know where I am if you need anything. Coffee?'

He shook his head with a smile and the door closed behind her.

An hour later, he slipped the vial – now filled with a clear serum – back into his pocket. Feeling an overwhelming urgency to tell Charlotte what he'd found, he reached for the phone . . . but pulled back. This was something that needed to be done in person. What he needed to tell her was far too sensitive – far too *astounding* – for an open phone line or an unencrypted e-mail. He remembered her saying that she might extend her stay a few extra days. But this couldn't wait until then.

Leaving the lab, Aldrich headed directly for his office and plunked himself down in front of his computer. Bringing up the web browser, he logged onto his Continental Airlines frequent-flier account page and booked a first-class ticket on the next flight to Rome.

43.

JERUSALEM

Farouq had just hung up his phone, in utter disbelief, his hands shaking. It was no coincidence that the call came mere hours after the early morning bombing at the Great Synagogue.

The caller had been a voice from the distant past – a dark past that still haunted him on many sleepless nights. The last time he'd heard that unmistakable baritone was just past six p.m. on November 11, 1995. That was the day the Shin Bet – Israel's most secret and lethal intelligence branch – abducted him on a side street in Gaza, pulling him into the back of a van. They had bound his limbs and slipped a black hood over his head.

As the van sped off, the interrogation began, carried out by the man who now held the second highest position in the IDF power structure. Back then the ambitious Israeli had been assigned the impossible task of hunting down the Engineer – a Palestinian rebel named Yahya Ayyash who, assisted by militant groups, recruited suicide bombers to launch numerous attacks on Israeli civilians in the mid-nineties. The Israelis were closing in, thanks to information forcefully extracted from key informants. One of their prime suspects was Farouq, who had alleged ties to the Engineer's primary supporter – Hamas.

By the time he'd been tossed from the van in a desolate location not far from the Israeli border, Farouq had suffered three broken ribs, four fractured fingers, cigarette burns to the chest, and seven missing teeth.

But he smiled, blood oozing through his broken mouth, knowing that he had not uttered one word about the whereabouts of the Engineer. No Israeli would ever break him.

He also took great pleasure in knowing that the blood on his face was not only his own. Even hooded and bound he had managed to bite Teleksen's hand, clamping his teeth into the despicable Israeli flesh, harder, harder, cranking his head sideways until nerves severed and bones cracked. The Israeli had whimpered like a dog.

Shortly after the Engineer was assassinated in his Gaza safe house by a rigged explosive cell phone, Ari Teleksen was promoted to *Aluf* – Major General. Farouq had seen him a few times since then – news reports mostly – always identifiable by the hand the Keeper had disfigured that night long ago in Gaza.

Now Teleksen had the audacity to call with what initially seemed to be a request for a favour. But after a lengthy explanation, it had become clear that the request would benefit Farouq's cause equally well.

'Akbar,' Farouq called out to the corridor, struggling to compose himself.

A moment later, the hulking bodyguard appeared in the doorway.

Farouq's eyes briefly sized him up. 'You're a strong boy. I need you to do something for me.'

44.

VATICAN CITY

The two scientists rode the elevator up one level and the doors opened into the main gallery that stood above the lab – the Vatican Museum's Pio Christian Gallery.

As they exited the elevator, Bersei quietly explained, 'You see, Charlotte, for three centuries after Jesus's death, early Christians did not portray his image. However, these early Christians did use other familiar images to depict Jesus.'

'How do you know that?'

'We have archaeological evidence. And much of it is here,' he said, motioning with his eyes to the art collection that spread out before them. 'Let me show you something.'

As Charlotte strolled beside him, she eyed the Christian-themed marble reliefs that were mounted on the walls like massive stone canvases.

Bersei waved a hand at them. 'Are you familiar with this collection?'

She shook her head.

'They're relics from the early fourth century,' Bersei explained, 'a time when Emperor Diocletian began his campaign of persecution – burning churches and killing Christians who wouldn't denounce their faith. It's also a time when early Christians secretly convened in the catacombs outside Rome to pray amongst the dead martyrs and saints laid to rest there – some in ornate stone coffins.' He pointed to one mounted on a sturdy platform.

'A sarcophagus,' observed Charlotte, admiring the craftsmanship.

'Yes. A sort of cousin to the Jewish ossuary we're studying. Many early Christians were converted Jews who undoubtedly developed what were to become Christian burial rituals.'

They had stopped in front of a three-foot-high marble statue. 'Here we are.' Bersei turned to her. 'Do you know what this image portrays?'

Looking at it, she saw a young man with long curled hair, dressed in a tunic. A lamb was slung over his shoulders and he was holding its legs with both hands. Hanging at his side was a pouch containing a lyre.

'Looks like a shepherd.'

'Not bad. It's actually called "The Good Shepherd". It was found in the catacombs. This image is how early Christians depicted Jesus.'

Charlotte gave the statue another once-over. 'You're kidding me.' The shepherd was boyish, with smooth features, its design Greco-Roman – not biblical.

'No. Ironic isn't it? But keep in mind that this representation blended mythology with the Jesus story. This wasn't intended to resemble him. It was an attempt to embody the ideal he represented – the protector, the shepherd. Orpheus, the pagan Greek god of art and song, was also blended into this image of Christ. Just as Orpheus's heavenly music could calm and soothe even the most wild of beasts' – he pointed to the lyre hanging at the shepherd's side – 'Jesus's words could tame the souls of sinners.'

'Just like the dolphin and the trident represent salvation and divinity.' Now she knew why he had brought her up here.

'Exactly.'

'Why though? Why didn't they worship icons or the crucifix?' They were everywhere, she thought. Especially in this place. It was hard to imagine Catholicism without its gruesome cross.

'First off, it would've sent a clear message to the Romans that they were indeed Christians. It wouldn't have been wise in an era of systematic persecution. And second, the early Christians didn't embrace the notion of iconography. In fact, Peter and Paul forbade such things. That's why images of the crucifix didn't exist back then. That didn't happen until Constantine came along.'

'That guy again.'

'Sure. He's the forefather of the modern faith. Constantine changed all the rules. Crucifixions and even the catacombs themselves were abandoned when he came to power in the fourth century. That's also when Christ was transformed into a true cult hero – a divine being. Crucifixes sprouted up, grand cathedrals built, and the Bible formally compiled. Literally, the faith went from underground to national stage.'

'It's amazing – Constantine wasn't really covered in my history classes – and I went to a Catholic high school! I really don't know anything about him.'

Bersei took a deep breath, relaxing his shoulders. 'In 312 AD, the Roman Empire was split between two factions of emperors – Constantine in the west, and his ally Licinius in the east, versus Maximinus and Maxentius. Constantine had decided that the sun god, Sol Invictus, had preordained him to be the sole ruler of the entire empire. So with an army made up of an obscure group known as Christians, he battled his way all the way through northern Italy to within ten miles of Rome to the only bridge that crossed over the Tiber river . . . Milvian Bridge. When rumours spread that Maxentius's army outnumbered Constantine's by ten to one, the Christians quickly became demoralized. The dawn before his final push into Rome, Constantine was paying tribute to Sol Invictus, when in the sky above, he saw a miraculous sign shaped like a cross – the over-lapping X and P, the Greek chi and rho, which were the first two letters of 'Christ'. He immediately roused his troops and pro-claimed that their saviour, Jesus Christ, had told him that 'with this sign you shall conquer'. Constantine ordered the black-smiths to emblazon the symbol on all the shields and the men had regained their courage. Later that day, the armies clashed in a bloody battle and miraculously Constantine emerged victori-ous.'

'And his army attributed the victory to Christ's intervention?'

Bersei nodded. 'Yes. And owing a debt to his soldiers, perhaps even inspired by the intoxicating power and persuasion of their passionate faith, Constantine later embraced their religion at the national level. Of course, one must also note that the "one god" worshipped by Christians blended well with Constantine's self-concept as the sole Roman emperor. However, to honour Sol Invictus and to appease the pagan masses throughout the empire who had yet to assimilate into the new religion, Constantine craftily blended many pagan concepts into early Christianity.'

'Such as?'

'Let's start with the simple things.' Bersei laced his fingers together, eyes scanning the gallery. 'The solar halo for instance. Just like our coins from Pontius Pilate, Constantine had minted coins in 315, while his alliance with Licinius was falling apart and about ten years before Constantine took over the entirety of the empire. But Constantine's coins depicted Sol Invictus on them – a *solar-haloed* Sol Invictus in a flowing robe that looks remarkably similar to later Jesus iconography.'

'Interesting.'

'Constantine also cleverly coincided the celebration of Christ's birth with the December twenty-fifth pagan winter solstice celebration of Sol Invictus's birthday. Of course, I think you won't be surprised when you hear that the Christian day of worship, once celebrated on Saturday, the Jewish Sabbath, was also moved to a more special day of the week.'

'*Sun*day.'

He nodded. 'Known in Constantine's time as *dies Solis*.' Giovanni's expression darkened. 'And then something even more profound emerges during Constantine's reign. The emphasis on Jesus's physical rather than spiritual resurrection.'

'What do you mean?'

'The early Greek Gospels used wording that suggested Christ's body wasn't necessarily reanimated, but transformed.'

'But in the Bible, Jesus walked out of the tomb and appeared to the disciples after his death, didn't he?' All those years of Catechism and Catholic school had drilled this stuff into her head.

'Sure. Jesus disappeared from the tomb,' he readily agreed. Then a knowing grin swept across Giovanni Bersei's face. 'Though none of the Gospels say *how*. In the Gospel accounts that follow the empty tomb, Jesus also had the ability to walk through walls and materialize from out of nowhere. And if you recall from the Bible, many whom he appeared to hadn't even recognized him. Those aren't attributes associated with a reanimated physical body.'

'Then why does the Church emphasize his physical death and physical resurrection?'

He smiled. 'My guess goes something like this. Egypt, particularly Alexandria, was a very influential cultural centre in the Roman Empire. There, cults worshipped Osiris, the god of the underworld who was horribly murdered by a rival god named Seth – cut to pieces in fact. Osiris's wife, the female goddess of life named Isis, collected his body parts and returned them to the temple and performed rituals so that three days later, the god resurrected.'

'Sounds a lot like Easter,' she concurred. 'Are you suggesting the Gospels were altered?'

An older couple were dawdling close by, intrigued by the two people in white lab coats. Bersei drew closer to Charlotte. 'Largely untouched, but perhaps reinterpreted in key areas,' he clarified. 'I suppose some of this could all be coincidence,' he said with a shrug. 'Anyway, the point to be made here is that in the fourth century, Christianity was being practised inconsistently throughout the Empire. Hundreds of scriptures were circulating out there, some legitimate, many wildly embellished.'

'Which meant scrapping all the inconsistent scriptures,' she deduced.

'Right. You can't blame the guy,' Bersei said in his defence. 'Constantine was trying to unite the empire. The Church's infighting only undermined that vision.'

'Makes sense,' Charlotte admitted. It seemed like Giovanni actually admired Constantine, she thought.

'Anyway, that's where it all began. The Church became more intertwined with the empire, one symbiotically serving the other.

Crucifixions had disappeared from the roadways, but one enormous crucifix was erected above the altar and Rome's fearmongering evolved from ruling by the sword, to ruling by fear of damnation for sinners. All thanks largely in part to one brilliant Roman emperor who reshaped the face of Western civilization.'

She sighed and shook her head. 'I thought you said you're a good Catholic boy?'

'I am,' he assured her.

'Even though you know all this stuff?'

'*Because* I know all this stuff. You have to understand that if what we're looking at downstairs is the physical body of Christ, it doesn't contradict the original Gospels. But it certainly creates a big problem for a Church that's taken some liberties in its scriptural interpretations.'

'I'd say,' she readily agreed. 'What do you think Christians would think if our findings were made public?'

'They'd think what they want to think. Just like you and me. The evidence is remarkable, but inconsistent. So the faithful would remain faithful, like they have through other controversies. Don't get me wrong, it would certainly be an enormous dilemma for Christianity. And a public relations nightmare once the press got hold of it.'

'Any possibility this could be a fake?'

Bersei exhaled. 'It would have to be one hell of a hoax, but you never know.'

45.

JERUSALEM

By the time Graham Barton returned to his second-floor rented flat in a luxury high-rise conveniently located on Jabotinsky Street in modern Jerusalem, it was already eight-thirty in the evening. After all that had happened today, he was looking forward to a full glass of cabernet sauvignon, a call to his wife to let her know that he was okay, and a long night's rest.

The bombing at the Great Synagogue had derailed the entire day's plans. After confirming what had happened, Razak had immediately left to consult with the Waqf on how to handle the incident. Mostly everyone else in Jerusalem had spent the day glued to a television, awaiting updates on the blast. So Barton spent the remainder of the afternoon at the Wohl, catching up on the work he had been neglecting. It took everything in his ethical arsenal to decline a six p.m. invite from Rachel to join her and a friend for drinks. The truth was that he would have loved the diversion.

All day, images of Templar crosses flitted through his thoughts like taunting furies, trying to convey a message and reconstruct a miraculous story that beckoned to be unlocked. Having touched the bones of Christ's benefactor, he was agonizing over the possibilities of what the missing ossuary might have contained and who could have possibly known how to find it.

Now, seeing the violence that was unravelling this city, he felt obligated to come up with real answers that might help the situation. But after the harrowing experience he and Razak had endured in Gaza, he was wondering if the Israelis knew more than they were letting on. He was also concerned that the gunmen might still be anxious to find him and Razak. Who were they working for? he wondered.

The truth was that so far, he had come up with nothing meaningful for the investigation – at least as far as the authorities would be concerned. As promised, he had been making enquiries to his international contacts in the antiquities markets. But nothing suspicious had yet turned up.

Surely Topol and Teleksen would soon be reaching out to him to turn up the pressure.

As he inserted his key into the front door lock, he barely registered three figures coming up the stairwell. He leaned back to get a better view. That's when Topol and two burly, uniformed officers rounded the corner and came closer in rigid strides.

Topol gave him a cursory nod. 'Good evening Mr Barton.'

A sense of foreboding swept over the Englishman. Sooner than anticipated, an evening visit from policemen and to his residence. Nothing good could come of that, he thought. He eyed their holstered handguns. Coming from the UK, the sight of so many weapons openly paraded around was unnerving. 'Good evening to you, commander.'

'I'm glad you're here.' Topol's dark eyes were hard, unblinking. 'It will make our visit more meaningful.'

Heart drumming in his chest, Barton replied, 'Why would that be?'

'Please, let's talk inside.' The major general motioned to the door.

Hesitantly, Barton made his way into the apartment and switched on the lights, the policemen crowding in behind him.

The apartment that had been secured by the IAA as part of his generous retainer had a roomy reception area where he invited the guests to sit. Only Topol accepted while his two cronies stood at either side of the door like bookends.

Topol got right to the point. 'I've been asked to search your residence and I'd like your cooperation.'

Stupefied, Barton was unsure how to respond. 'What? Why would you want to do that?'

'I'd rather not get into that just yet. I have secured proper authorization.' He flashed an official looking document and handed it to Barton. 'You can read this while we proceed.' It was in Hebrew, of course. Topol nodded to the two bookends and they disappeared into the next room.

'Can I please have everything from your pockets?'

'What is this? Am I am being arrested?' Barton hadn't expected that the call to his wife would be a request for her legal representation. He didn't have a clue as to his civil rights in this country. Should he protest?

'For now, we're just talking,' Topol explained. 'If you'd feel more comfortable at the station, we can go there now.'

Barton nodded compliantly.

'I received a very disturbing phone call from the Waqf.'

'Oh?'

'Your pockets, please,' Topol insisted, pointing to the table.

One way or another, the major would have his way, Barton realized. Trying not to look alarmed, he began emptying the contents of his pockets onto the table: a wallet, UK passport, keys to the Wohl, bus tickets.

'It seems some things have gone missing,' Topol went on.

The sounds coming from the rear of the apartment were less than subtle – drawers being opened, furniture being moved around. Signs that nothing was safe from Topol's rigorous inspection.

With enormous reservations, Barton dipped into his breast pocket and withdrew the bronze cylinder, certain it would ignite the policeman's curiosity. Lastly came the plastic sealed vellum and its accompanying folded transcription. Setting it down on the table, he tried to gauge Topol's expression.

Eyebrows raised, the major's head cocked slightly to one side – like a curious dog – as he eyed the vellum's strange text, but for now, he let it go. 'Since the inception of this investigation, I've had suspicions that an insider could have helped organize this theft. The head of the Waqf expressed similar concerns. And after hearing what he had to say earlier today, I must admit I'm inclined to agree with his assertions.' Topol recalled his late-night discussion with Teleksen the previous evening. A quick solution was essential to prevent more bloodshed.

Barton's shoulders sank. 'I'm not sure I understand what you're implying.'

'The theft required extremely sophisticated movements of weapons and explosives,' the policeman sneered. 'Not to mention skilled manpower. Only someone with high-level clearance could have handled such transactions. Someone with access to shipping. Someone extremely well-versed in Temple Mount's history. And someone who knew precisely what treasures lay buried in that vault. The Waqf suggests that person is you.'

Barton felt suffocated. 'You must be joking. I know this bomb-ing has escalated the need for concise action, but this is –'

Topol's hand cut the air. 'An Israeli helicopter and two pilots are still missing . . .'

Barton saw the major's eyes shift down when he said this. Could he have known about the meeting in Gaza? Did he know about the fisherman and the recovered debris from the Black Hawk?

'Sources indicate these pilots may have been involved in the theft . . . helped make it all happen,' Topol elaborated. 'Perhaps someone on the inside approached them? Gave these people some incentive.'

Barton remained steadfast. 'You know there's no way I'm involved in this.'

The major was stone-faced. 'I've been told you've made quite a name for yourself procuring rare antiquities for European clients.'

'Museums,' the archaeologist clarified.

'Quite a lucrative service you provide. Isn't that right?'

Barton wasn't about to get into this discussion, not without a lawyer present.

'Given the nature of your work with the IAA, you've also been given high-level clearance in the Old City. You've been moving equipment in and out at will . . . many times without inspec-tion.'

'How could I have got explosives into the city?' Graham Barton's tone was stronger now. 'There are detectors all over the place.'

'Apparently quite easily. Our chemists analysed the residue of the plastic explosive. Seems it was missing the chemical marker that would allow it to be detected – dimethyl dinitrobutane. You see, Mr Barton . . . those explosives were military grade. Perhaps provided to you by our missing pilots.'

One of the officers stormed into the room to momentarily break the tension. He was hauling something in a large plastic sheath.

Barton was confused as he warily eyed the package. What the hell was in the bag? It looked like something very substantial.

Still sitting, Topol removed the plastic and read aloud the model name on the black motor housing – Flex BHI 822 VR. 'A European manufacturer, I see.' Topol ran his finger over the long hollow drum attached to its chuck. Its circular tip was razor sharp. 'A coring drill. This part of your toolbox?'

Shortly following the theft, when Topol's forensic crime team initially had analysed the blast area, they'd found the drill abandoned on the floor. No prints. That morning, Topol had ensured all documentation concerning it had been struck from records.

The archaeologist's complexion turned grey. 'I've never seen that thing before in my life,' he said weakly. Voices were starting to sound hazy, as if everything was happening in slow motion. Could this really be happening?

'And what do you have here?' Topol leaned over and snatched the vellum off the table, eyeing it curiously. 'Seems to be an ancient document.' He unfolded the sheet of paper containing the photocopy and accompanying transcription. 'I'm no biblical scholar Mr Barton, but this looks to me like something that implies a burial chamber hidden beneath Mount Moriah. And if I'm not mistaken, wasn't Joseph of Arimathea somehow connected to Jesus Christ? Isn't he the subject of legends about the Holy Grail – a priceless relic for those who believe?'

There was a sarcastic tone to Topol's voice that only reaffirmed his suspicion that somehow, he already knew about the scroll. Perspiration started to bead on his forehead. The walls were closing in.

'You were given access to the crime scene and in return you tampered with key evidence – scratching inscriptions from the wall, removing the remaining ossuaries.'

'What?' Barton was aghast. 'Are you completely out of your mind?'

'You heard me. The Waqf insists that the remaining nine ossuaries have mysteriously vanished. It seems that the thief is still among us.'

That the ossuaries had suddenly vanished was truly disturbing, but something about the major's first accusation struck even harder. 'Scratching inscriptions from the wall? What does that mean?'

Topol was prepared for this. From his jacket, he produced a picture and handed it to Barton. 'See for yourself. That picture was taken by my forensic team a day before you arrived.'

Stunned, Barton saw that the clearly framed image was the stone tablet affixed to the crypt wall. Nine names were listed . . . and one perfectly clear relief depicting a dolphin intertwined around a trident. He had seen this symbol before, and knew its origin well. Its implications shook him to the core. But he couldn't deal with that now; he needed to save himself first. 'Being framed is not what I had in mind when I signed up for this project.'

Topol dodged that comment. The second officer returned and he motioned them toward Barton.

46.

PARIS, FRANCE
MARCH 18, 1314

Hands bound behind his back, Jacques DeMolay was escorted by guards up the steps of the wooden scaffold in front of Notre-Dame Cathedral. Glancing up at what had once seemed a transcendentally grand work of architecture, DeMolay saw only the stone skeleton of a mammoth demon – the flying buttresses were giant ribs, the twin spires horns, the fiery rose window an enormous evil eye. He heard the sound of the River Seine as it looped around Ile de la Cité, carving the tiny island away from the rest of Paris as if it were a cancer.

Gazing down to the cathedral's front steps, he scanned the assembled papal prelature seated there and tried to find Clement's ugly face. Having failed miserably in his appeal to King Philip to reinstate the Order, the damned traitor did not have the nerve or decency to make an appearance. Three cardinals sat centre stage to officiate and act the role of executioners.

A large crowd had gathered to watch the impromptu trial, eager to lay eyes on a fallen hero about to meet a tragic end. DeMolay felt like an actor, alone on an ominous stage, until moments later, three other Templar dignitaries were pushed up the wooden stairs and herded beside him.

With pride, Jacques DeMolay glanced over to them: Geoffroy DeCharnay, Hugues DePairaud, and Geoffroy DeGonneville – all honourable men who had served the Order nobly. Unfortunately, they too had been in France almost seven years earlier when King Philip had ordered his armies to secretly round up the Templars.

Minutes later, the farce began with fiery testimonies from sharp-tongued priests inciting the crowd with their farrago of accusations and false charges levied against the Knights Templar. Particular emphasis was paid to lurid accounts of homosexuality and devil worship, since those fabrications played well with the crowd's emotions. Then, as DeMolay listened in utter amazement, the priest read a document to the crowd that itemized DeMolay's signed confessions to the charges – a document he had never seen before.

The lies seared DeMolay's ears like burning embers, but he remained defiant, occasionally glancing up at the stone gargoyles leering down from Notre-Dame's facade.

Silence fell abruptly over the scene when one cardinal stood, pointed at the Grand Master, and yelled: 'And you Jacques DeMolay, the very evil who leads this ungodly Order, what say you to the charges presented herewith? Do you once and for all profess your guilt by affirming that these confessions are your true testament so that you may reclaim your dignity in the presence of God?'

DeMolay eyed the cardinal curiously, amazed that he had once so loyally served men like this. So many Templars had died in the name of Christ in the Holy Land. He felt like shouting out the lies that these sanctimonious bastards had propagated through the centuries to undermine that sacrifice. But no one would ever believe the amazing things he had learned and the equally amazing relics still hidden beneath the site of Solomon's Temple in Jerusalem that attested to those truths. Without proof, he would merely tarnish his reputation further and play into the hands of his executioners. DeMolay took solace in knowing that some day the truth would be discovered . . . and woe to all who tried to deny it, he thought. He knew that these men were determined to destroy him. Whether it happened today, or after more years slowly rotting to death in some vile prison cell, he was doomed – the target for the king's malicious scheme.

The Grand Master looked deep into the eyes of his three friends and saw a common resolve beneath a thin veil of fear. The brotherhood would endure until the very end.

Clearing his throat DeMolay stared back at the cardinal. 'It is only right that when my life is to be taken by those I have so loyally served, that I should make known the deceptions here presented and that I tell only the truth from my own lips. Before God and all who witness this injustice' – his eyes panned over the crowd – 'I admit I am guilty of a gross iniquity. But not one fabricated by my accusers.' He swung his gaze back at the cardinal. 'I am guilty only of the shame and dishonour I have endured through torture and threat of death to induce these disgusting charges laid against the Templar Order. I declare before you now that the noble men who have served this Church to protect Christianity have been unjustly demonized. Therefore, I disdain to disgrace my brothers by grafting yet another lie.'

Astounded at the prisoner's brazen rebuttal, the cardinal stood mute for a long moment before declaring, 'By denouncing this sworn confession, you leave me no choice but to invoke the decree of King Philip that you shall perish by fire.'

DeMolay smiled thinly. Finally, the end would come.

Then the cardinal addressed the remaining three Templars, sentencing all to life imprisonment. DeMolay was shocked when Hugues DePairaud and Geoffroy DeGonneville confessed to the charges.

Then the cardinal asked the same of Geoffroy DeCharnay.

Suddenly possessed, DeCharnay bared his teeth and yelled: 'I too renounce all charges brought against me! For God as my witness, these lies serve only a contemptuous pope and an equally villainous king. The only just man who stands here today is Jacques DeMolay. I have followed him into battle and I will follow him to God.'

The cardinal was fuming. 'You shall have your wish!'

Jacques DeMolay and Geoffroy DeCharnay were then taken to a boat for the short journey to the neighbouring Ile des Javiaux, the site where dozens of Templars had already been burned alive.

The sun melted into the distance and darkness crept over Paris.

As the two prisoners were escorted to the two stakes, both already blackened by charred flesh, DeMolay turned to his Templar brother. The years of torture and imprisonment had rendered DeCharnay to a shadow of the robust warrior he had known in the Holy Land, but the man's expression was surprisingly resolute. 'Remember what we leave behind in Jerusalem,' DeMolay told him. 'Your service and sacrifice will be justly rewarded by Him. And His day of justice is soon to come, Geoffroy. You have done the most noble deed a man can do. You have served God. Leave this broken body behind and don't look back. Tonight, your soul will be free.'

'Bless you, Jacques,' DeCharnay said. 'It has been my honour to serve with you.'

As the French soldiers forced DeMolay against the post, he turned to them. 'I am no threat to you now,' he insisted. 'Unbind my hands so that I may pray in my final moments.'

Reluctantly, the guards cut the ropes from the old man's wrists, but used heavy chains to bind his body to the stake. The wood heaped around DeMolay was still green. By express order of King Philip, his death was to be prolonged by slow fire.

Looking over his shoulder, DeMolay gave his last thanks to DeCharnay, shackled to the post behind him. As the pyre was ignited, Notre-Dame's bells began to toll.

The heat crawled up the old man's feet and legs. Then the tongues of flame began to slowly broil his lower body. When the fire intensified, his flesh roasted into red blisters, blackening his feet. As the inferno grew, DeMolay screamed out in agony, the flames licking their way higher up his legs. He could barely register DeCharnay's screams. Weaving his hands together, he threw them to heaven and yelled: 'May evil find those who have wrongly condemned us! May God avenge us and cast these men into Hell!'

As his body was consumed Jacques DeMolay felt his spirit lifting.

The Templar Grand Master was swallowed by the inferno, his mortal remains a brilliant torch against the night sky.

FRIDAY

47.

ROME

Opening the front door of his quaint townhouse overlooking Villa Borghese's manicured park, a robed and barefoot Giovanni Bersei retrieved the morning's delivery of *Il Messaggero* from the front step. The sun was barely glowing a deep blue over the neighbouring rooftops, and the lamp posts lining the empty street were still casting a warm glow. This was his favourite time of the day.

Turning to go back inside, he paused to glance over at the iron railing that still hung loosely from its mount on his home's stucco facade. Carmela had been after him for three weeks to fix it. Today would be the day the job would get done, he vowed. Closing the door, he went directly to the kitchen.

The coffee pot, dutifully set on a timer, was already full. He poured himself a cup and sat for a long moment to enjoy the silence. Cupping the heavy porcelain mug in his hands, he sipped the black coffee slowly, savouring the deep, rich flavour. What was it about a great cup of coffee? He swore there was no better elixir.

Last night, he hadn't slept well at all, his mind endlessly

churning over the ossuary, the skeleton and the shocking symbol that accompanied the relics. The mere possibility that he had touched the physical remains of Jesus Christ had left him feeling ashamed and vulnerable, searching for an explanation. Bersei was a practising Catholic – a believer in the most powerful story ever told. He went to church each Sunday and prayed often. And later this morning, he was going to be asked by the Vatican to explain his findings. How could anyone explain what he had witnessed over the past days?

Scratching the grey stubble on his chin, he put on his reading glasses and began scanning the newspaper's front page. A headline on the bottom of the front page read: MUSLIMS AND JEWS ENRAGED OVER RUMOURED THEFT AT TEMPLE MOUNT. He ignored it, flipping directly to the funnies. Then, almost as an afterthought, he turned back to the front page.

Though articles sensationalizing the tenuous political problems in the Holy Land were regular media fodder, these past few days he noticed that it had dominated the headlines even more than usual. Perhaps all the lab-talk concerning ancient Judea, Pontius Pilate, and crucifixion made him consider this one more closely. The piece's accompanying photo showed Israeli soldiers and police trying to hold back violent protestors just outside the famous Wailing Wall – the Temple Mount's western wall.

He read the report.

Following Friday's violence at Jerusalem's Temple Mount, Islamic officials are pressuring the Israeli government to release details concerning the mysterious explosion that inflicted serious damage to the site. Resident Jews are demanding answers as to why thirteen Israeli Defense Force soldiers were killed during a firefight that erupted shortly after the explosion. Thus far, authorities have only confirmed that an Israeli military helicopter had been used to transport the alleged attackers from the site . . .

'That's not good,' he muttered.

. . . Many have criticized Israeli officials for ignoring rumours that the incident involved religious artifacts stolen from the site.

'Religious artifacts?'

'What, love?' Carmela emerged from the doorway, donning a powder blue robe over her silk pyjamas. She bent to kiss him on the head before making her way to the cupboard for a mug, her fuzzy pink slippers scuffing along the tile floor.

'Probably nothing. Just reading about all this turmoil in Israel.'

'They'll never get along,' she said, pouring coffee into her favourite mug, shaped like an animated elephant head with a curved snout as its handle. 'They all just want to kill one another.'

'Seems so,' he agreed. Seeing her without make-up and her hair tousled, he smiled to himself. So many years together.

He directed his attention back to the newspaper. The article went on to say that efforts toward a more formal and lasting peace accord between Israelis and Palestinians had once again been tabled.

'Will you be home early tonight?'

'Should be,' he said, preoccupied.

Carmela pushed down on the newspaper to get his attention. 'I was hoping maybe you could take me out to that new bistro Claudio and Anna-Maria were talking about the other night.'

'Of course, sweetheart. That would be wonderful. Would you make a reservation for eight o'clock?'

'Maybe you can find some time to fix that railing before we leave.'

Grinning, Bersei said, 'I'll see what I can do.'

'I'm going up to take a shower.' Sipping her coffee, she shuffled away.

Bersei turned to where the article continued. Immediately, he felt like he had been punched in the gut. Staring up at him was a photofit rendition of a man that looked all too familiar.

Reading the caption beneath, he mouthed the words aloud: '"The suspect is said to be a Caucasian male, approximately 180 centimetres tall and 88 kilos. Authorities state he is travelling under the assumed identity of Daniel Marrone, and are looking for any information concerning his whereabouts."'

Suddenly, everything was moving in slow motion. He collapsed back into his chair.

The only possible explanation could be that the Vatican was somehow involved in what was happening in Israel. But that was *impossible*. Or was it?

Bersei tried to reconcile the timing of the events over the past few days. According to the news report, this theft in Jerusalem had occurred last Friday. A week ago. Both he and Charlotte had arrived in Vatican City shortly afterwards. She'd flown into Rome on Sunday afternoon. He arrived on Monday morning, shortly before Father Donovan and Salvatore Conte returned with the mysterious crate.

Of course. Recalling the woven impressions left on the ossuary's patina, he no longer suspected a careless extraction. He suspected a *rushed* extraction. A theft?

He remembered Father Donovan's expression when he

288

opened the crate – anxiety . . . and something else playing in his eyes. The crate's Eurostar shipping label was still imprinted into his brain. Bari, the final resting place of Saint Nicholas. The vibrant tourist spot on Italy's east coast faced the Adriatic with direct sea routes to the Mediterranean . . . and Israel. Bari was 500 kilometres from Rome – probably less than five hours by rail, he guessed. But it had to be at least 2000 kilometres from Israel.

You'd need an awfully fast boat for that, he thought. But cruising at twenty knots – just over thirty-seven kilometres an hour – it was manageable in perhaps two days. Conservatively allowing for two and a half days at sea and another half-day traversing Italy, the shipment fitted comfortably into the time frame.

He went back to the news article. Thirteen Israeli soldiers killed. The thieves had been sophisticated and no meaningful clues had been found.

Was the Vatican *really* capable of pulling off an operation like that? But an Israeli helicopter employed in the theft? It didn't make sense. Certainly Father Donovan – *a cleric for Christ's sake!* – wasn't capable of such a thing.

But Salvatore Conte . . . He eyed the photofit again and felt nothing but fear.

Bersei considered a second theory. Maybe the Vatican had bought the ossuary from whoever stole it and had been unwittingly caught up in the incident? Even so, that could prove very problematic for the Vatican. They could be drawn into this mess as an accomplice. One thing was certain: somehow the relics sitting in the Vatican basement had a very questionable procurement.

He wrestled with how to deal with all this. Should he consult with Charlotte? Or should he go to the authorities.

You can't make wild claims without adequate proof, he told himself.

Setting the paper down, Giovanni went over to the phone and asked the operator to connect him to the local substation for the *Carabinieri* – Italy's military police force that walked the streets of Rome with submachine guns as if the city was under a constant state of martial law. A young male voice picked up the call and Giovanni requested to speak with the resident detective. After a few brief questions, the young man informed Giovanni that he'd need to speak with Detective Armando Perardi who wasn't expected in the office until nine-thirty.

'Can I have his voice mail, please?' Giovanni requested in Italian.

The line clicked and went silent for a few seconds before Detective Perardi's glum greeting came on. Giovanni waited for the tone, then left a brief message, requesting a meeting later in the morning to discuss a possible Roman link to the theft in Jerusalem. He left his mobile phone number. For now, he didn't make any reference to the Vatican. That would only confuse the issue since the Vatican was its own country. Ending the call, Bersei hurried upstairs to put on his clothes. He would need to act quickly.

Parking his Vespa in the personnel car park outside the Vatican Museum, Giovanni quickly made his way through the Pio Christian gallery's rear service entrance.

As the elevator doors opened into the basement corridor, he experienced a wave of panic, hoping that no one else had decided to come in early this morning. He checked his watch – 7:32.

What he needed to do had to be done alone. Charlotte

290

Hennesey couldn't be dragged into this. After all, what if he was wrong?

As he moved out of the elevator, the corridor seemed to come alive, as if he were Jonah being swallowed by the whale. He lightly treaded his way to the lab and used his keycard to unlock the door. Looking over his shoulder to see that the corridor was still clear, he ducked inside and went directly to the workstation.

The spikes and coins sat on the tray. Beside them lay the last of the ossuary's mysteries – the scroll cylinder. There was something about it that stirred him. If his foreboding about all of this were correct, there'd be no future opportunity to read it. And something prompted him that it contained critical clues about the relic's provenance.

Careful study of the ossuary and its contents had left him in little doubt the ossuary originated from Israel. The stone and patina were both specific to the region. He eyed the skeleton laid out on the workstation – the bones, too, supported the relic's provenance. Crucifixions had been commonplace in Judea during the first century. And studying the ossuary one last time, he ran his fingers over the early Christian symbol for Christ – the very thing that had broken down his final wall of doubt.

All were damning facts, pointing to the Vatican. Bersei punished himself for not making the connection sooner. But it had all seemed too fantastic.

From the tray, he picked up the cylinder and removed the unsealed cap. Then he teased out the scroll. As he gently unfurled the calfskin his heart was pounding. Glancing quickly around the room, he swore he felt invisible eyes boring into him.

Lingering questions bothered him. How could such a profound discovery have remained secret for so long? If the bones were truly those of Jesus – or even one of his contemporaries – why hadn't it ever been documented? And no matter who this man had been, how was it that the Vatican had discovered the secret only now, two thousand years later?

Back to the matter at hand.

Delicately smoothing out the calfskin scroll, Bersei experienced a flurry of conflicting emotions. He was convinced that this ancient document might provide a final clue – perhaps even confirm or deny the dead man's true identity.

Just like the bones and other relics, Bersei could immediately see that the calfskin scroll had been magnificently preserved. There were countless possibilities of what this document might contain. The last will and testament of the deceased? A final prayer sealed away by those who buried the body? Perhaps even a decree explaining why this man had been crucified.

His fingers were shaking uncontrollably as he held it up.

Neat text was written out in some kind of ink. Studying it more intently, he saw that it was Koine Greek, the dialect sometimes referred to as 'New Testament Greek' and the unofficial *lingua franca* of the Roman Empire up until the fourth century.

The first implication was that the author had been well educated – a Roman, perhaps.

Below the text was a very detailed drawing that looked remarkably familiar.

As he read the ancient message – clear and brief – his extreme tension began to subside and for a moment, he sat there in silence.

Refocusing his attention on the accompanying drawing, the anthropologist again felt as though he'd seen this imagery before. His brow tightened as he studied it intently. Think. *Think*.

That's when it hit him. Bersei's face blanched. *Of course!*

He had definitely seen this image before, and the place it was meant to depict was only a few kilometres away on the outskirts of Rome, deep beneath the city. Instantly he knew that he would need to go there as soon as his business here was complete.

Scrambling over to the photocopier that sat in the corner of the room, he flattened the scroll onto the glass, closed the lid and made a copy. Returning the scroll to the cylinder, he placed it beside the other relics. Then he folded the copy and stuck it in his pocket.

As he focused on gathering evidence to substantiate his claim against the Vatican, paranoia about his own safety quickly returned. But he needed information that could be used by the *Carabinieri* to investigate the case.

Nerves ablaze, Bersei linked his laptop to the main computer terminal and began copying files onto its hard drive – the skeleton's complete profile, pictures of the ossuary and its accompanying relics, carbon dating results – everything.

He eyed his watch again – 7:46. Time was running out.

When the last file had finished copying, he folded the laptop and packed it into its carrying bag. Removing anything else would seem overly suspicious.

'Hey, Giovanni,' a familiar voice called over to him.

He spun around. Charlotte. He hadn't even heard her come in.

Walking past him, she noticed that he looked awful. 'Everything okay?'

He didn't know what say. 'You're here early.'

'I didn't sleep well. Are you going somewhere?' Looks awfully nervous, she thought.

'I have an appointment I need to go to.'

'Oh.' She looked at her watch. 'You'll be back for the meeting, right?'

He stood and slung the bag over his shoulder. 'I'm not sure, actually. Something important has come up.'

'More important than our presentation?'

He avoided her eyes.

'Something's wrong, Giovanni. Tell me what it is.'

His eyes combed the walls, as if he were hearing voices. 'Not here,' he said. 'Walk out with me and I'll explain.'

Bersei opened the main door and poked his head out into the corridor. Everything was clear. He motioned for her to follow.

Quietly, he slipped outside and Charlotte followed, easing the door closed behind her.

In the makeshift surveillance room, Salvatore Conte sat perfectly still until the footsteps in the corridor had faded away. Then he snatched the phone from its console.

Santelli answered on the second ring and Conte could tell by his groggy voice that he'd woken the old man.

'We have a real problem down here.'

The cardinal knew what was coming. He cleared his throat. 'Have they found out?'

'Just Bersei. And right now he's on his way out the door with copies of everything on his way to the *Carabinieri*.'

'Very unfortunate.' A slight pause and a sigh. 'You know what you must do.'

48.

Bersei didn't say a word until they were safely outside the museum's confines. He headed straight for his parked Vespa as Charlotte paced quickly to keep up with him.

'I think the Vatican is involved in something bad,' he said to her in a hushed tone. 'Something to do with the ossuary.'

'What are you talking about?'

'Too much to explain right now and I don't even know if I'm right about all this.' Stowing the laptop bag in the scooter's rear compartment, he put on his helmet.

'Right about *what*?' He was starting to scare her.

'It's best that I not tell you. You need to trust me on this. You'll be safe here, don't worry.'

'Giovanni, please.'

Mounting the Vespa, he put a key in the ignition and turned the engine on.

She grabbed his arm tightly. 'You're not going anywhere,' she said over the noise of the puttering engine, 'until you tell me what you're talking about.'

Sighing heavily, Bersei looked at her, his gaze filled with

concern. 'I think that ossuary was stolen. It may be linked to a theft in Jerusalem that left many people dead. There's someone I need to speak with about what we've found.'

For a moment, she said nothing. 'Are you sure about this? That seems a bit extreme, don't you think?'

'No, I'm not sure. That's why I'm trying to leave you out of this. I know we've signed confidentiality agreements. If I'm wrong, this could turn out badly for me. I don't want you being dragged down too.'

'Is there anything I can do to help?'

Bersei flinched when he thought he saw a face looking out from behind the shadowy glass of the museum door. 'Just pretend we didn't have this conversation. Hopefully I'm wrong about everything.' He looked down at her hand. 'Please, let me go.'

She loosened her grip. 'Be careful.'

'I will.'

Charlotte watched as Bersei rode off around the corner of the building.

As the elevator doors slid apart, Charlotte hesitated before stepping out into the basement corridor. Folding her arms across her chest, she proceeded forward, fighting off a sudden chill.

Surely the Vatican couldn't be involved in a theft, she tried to convince herself. Then again, why would they consort with a goon like Salvatore Conte? It was quite evident that *he* was capable of violence and just about any other act of bad behaviour. But what if Giovanni was right? Then what?

Halfway down the corridor, she noticed that one of the solid metal doors was slightly ajar. It hadn't been earlier – she was sure of that. Until now, every door down here had been closed – presumably locked. Was someone else down here with them?

Curious, she stepped up to the door and knocked. 'Hello? Anyone in there?'

No answer.

She tried again. Nothing.

With her left hand, she reached out and pushed, swinging the door open smoothly on well-oiled hinges.

What she saw inside was puzzling.

Stepping into the tiny room lined with empty shelves, she stood in front of a very peculiar workstation – a bank of monitors, a computer, a set of headphones. Her eyes followed a bundle of wires that led out from the computer, crept up the wall, and disappeared into a darkened opening in the ceiling where a panel had been removed.

The system was in sleep mode. The screensaver depicted a slide show of naked women in a variety of pornographic poses. Charming.

Sitting in a chair positioned in front of the equipment, she tried to imagine what purpose this all served. Obviously, it had all been done in haste, because this room looked like a closet – not an office.

Finally, she couldn't help but reach down to press a key on the keyboard.

The monitors flickered and hummed as the screensaver disappeared and the computer woke up.

Seconds later, the software activated what appeared to be the last program that had been in use. It took Charlotte a moment to piece together the familiar collage of camera images that spread out before her. On one of the on-screen viewing panels, there was a chambermaid cleaning a small room. Charlotte's stomach sank when she saw her own luggage – a red, rectangular carry-on and matching garment bag – beside the bed. The maid moved into the bathroom, which projected real-time on a second panel. A familiar set of toiletries lined the vanity, complete with a hefty bottle of vitamins.

'Conte,' she seethed horrified at what she was seeing. 'That fucking pervert.'

She studied a number of other hidden cameras transmitting from the lab and the break room – live feeds, judging by the time and date counters on the bottom of each panel. He'd been watching and listening the whole time.

In that moment she knew that Giovanni had been right.

49.

In the Secret Archive, Father Donovan placed the *Ephemeris Conlusio* codex next to the plastic-sealed document bearing reference number *Archivum Arcis, Arm. D 217* – 'The Chinon Parchment' – and closed the door. There was a small hiss as a vacuum pump pulled all the air out from the compartment.

Secrets. Donovan was no stranger to them. Perhaps that was why he felt so connected to books and solitude. Maybe this archive somehow mirrored his soul, he thought.

Many who were drawn to the Catholic priesthood would attribute their decision to some kind of vocational calling – a special closeness to God, possibly. Donovan had turned to the Church for a more sobering cause – survival.

As a young boy, he'd grown up in Belfast during the tumultuous sixties and seventies when violence in Northern Ireland peaked between the Nationalist Catholics seeking independence from British rule, and Unionist Protestants who were loyal to the crown. In 1969 he watched his house, and dozens of others around it, burned to the ground by rioting loyalists. He could also vividly recall the IRA's retaliatory bombings, which were a regular occurrence – 1,300 in 1972 alone – and claimed hundreds of civilian lives.

At fifteen, he and his friends had been lured into a street gang that ran errands for the IRA and acted as the 'eyes and ears' of the movement. On one memorable occasion, he'd been asked to drop a package outside a Protestant storefront. Unbeknownst to him at that time, the bag actually contained a bomb. Luckily, no one had been killed in the subsequent blast that levelled the building. Somehow, he'd even managed to avoid being arrested.

But it was a fateful evening on his seventeenth birthday when Donovan's life was changed for ever. He was drinking at a local pub with his two best friends, Sean and Michael. They had got into a shouting match with a group of drunken Protestants. Donovan's crew left an hour later, but the Protestants – five in all – followed them outside and continued haranguing. It hadn't taken long for fists to start flying.

Though no stranger to street fighting, Donovan's wiry frame and swift hands had been no match for the two men that teamed up on him. While one of the Protestants had pinned him to the ground, the second landed body blows, seemingly intent on beating him to death.

It was hard to forget the suppressed rage that had flooded into him as he envisioned the glowing embers of his home. Donovan had reacted on instinct, fighting his way back onto his feet, flipping open a jackknife and plunging it deep into the stomach of the attacker who had held him down. The man had fallen to the pavement, horrified as he tried to hold back the gush of blood flooding out of his abdomen. Seeing the rage in Donovan's fiery eyes, the second man had backed away.

Dazed, Donovan turned to see Sean, blood-soaked and baring his teeth, had also taken a man down with his own knife. The remaining Protestants had stood frozen in disbelief as the Catholics fled.

He remembered the awful dread he had felt the next day when the newspapers and TV reported that a local Protestant man had been stabbed to death. Though there had been some doubt as to which of the two fallen Protestants suffered the fatal blow, Donovan quickly came to terms with the fact that he needed to leave Belfast behind before he became its next victim.

The seminary had provided him with a safe haven from the streets, providing hope of God's forgiveness for the horrible things he had done. Though not a day had gone by that he couldn't see the bloodstains on his hands.

Despite his past, he'd always been a good student and the solitude of priesthood had reignited his passion for reading. He found peace in history and scripture. Guidance. Seeing his remarkable dedication to learning, the Diocese of Dublin had sponsored his extensive university training. Perhaps, Donovan thought, it was his obsession with books that had helped to save him.

Now, it was a book that seemed to threaten everything he held sacred. The very institution that had protected him was under attack.

For a long moment he stared behind the glass panel at the *Ephemeris Conlusio* – the lost scripture that had set in motion the momentous events leading to the theft in Jerusalem. It was hard to grasp that it was only two weeks earlier that he had presented this incredible discovery to the Vatican secretary of state. He saw the meeting with Santelli as clear as day, as if a movie played in his memory.

*

'It's not often I receive such urgent requests for an appointment from the Vatican Library.' Cardinal Santelli's hands lay folded on his desk.

Seated opposite, Father Donovan clutched his leather satchel. 'Apologies for the short notice, Eminence. But I hope you'll agree that the reason I've come here warrants your immediate attention . . . and will justify why I have chosen not to involve Cardinal Giancome.'

Vincenzo Giancome, the *Cardinale Archivista e Bibliotecario*, was Donovan's superior and acted as the supreme overseer of the Vatican Secret Archive. He was also the man who'd tabled Donovan's fervent request to acquire the Judas Papers. So after much deliberation, Donovan had made the unorthodox decision of not including Giancome in on this matter – a bold move that could potentially backfire and cost him his career. But he was certain that what he was about to divulge would directly involve matters of national security – not reserve documents. Furthermore, the mystery caller had specifically chosen Donovan for this task and there was no time for delays or bureaucratic infighting.

'What is it?' Santelli looked bored.

Donovan was unsure exactly where to begin. 'You recall a few years back when the Chinon Parchment was discovered in the Secret Archive?'

'Clement's secret dismissal of charges brought against the Knights Templar?'

'Correct. I came to you with further documents detailing the clandestine meeting between Clement V and Jacques DeMolay, the Templar Grand Master.' Donovan swallowed hard. 'The pope's account specifically mentioned a manuscript called the *Ephemeris Conlusio*, supposedly containing information about the Templars' hidden relics.'

'An attempt to restore the Templar Order,' Santelli interjected. 'And a rather crude attempt at that.'

'But I think you'll agree that DeMolay's negotiations had to be quite compelling for Clement to have exonerated the Templars after ordering their disbandment.'

'A fabrication. No book was ever produced by Jacques DeMolay.'

'Agreed.' Donovan dug into his satchel and retrieved the book. 'Because it wasn't in his possession.'

Santelli shifted his chair. 'What is that you have there?'

'This is the *Ephemeris Conlusio*.'

Santelli was bewildered. This was one legend he had always hoped to be pure fantasy. None of the Vatican's darkest secrets began to compare. He clung to the hope that the librarian was wrong, but Donovan's confident gaze confirmed his worst fears. 'You're not suggesting . . .'

'Yes,' he confidently replied. 'Let me explain.'

Donovan recounted the history of Jacques DeMolay's imprisonment, his secret discussion with Clement, his trial in Paris in front of Notre-Dame Cathedral and final execution on the Ile des Javiaux. 'Apparently his dying curse worked,' Donovan explained. 'Pope Clement V died one month later from what many accounts say was severe dysentery – a hideous death. Seven months later, King Philip IV died mysteriously during a hunt. Witnesses attributed the accident to a lingering disease that caused him to bleed rapidly to death. Many speculated that the Knights Templar had exacted their revenge.'

Santelli looked spooked. 'Poisoned?'

'Perhaps.' Donovan shrugged. 'Meanwhile the Holy Land had been fully reclaimed by the Muslims. The European countries and the Church lacked proper funding to stage further crusades to retake it. Pope Clement's documents and the Chinon Parchment gathered dust in the Secret Archive as the papal conclave focused on its two-year struggle to restore the insolvent papacy. The *Ephemeris Conlusio* – this book – faded into history,' Donovan explained. 'Until I received a phone call this week.' Donovan summarized his phone conversation with the mystery caller, then went on to describe the transaction with the caller's messenger in Caffè Greco. Santelli listened intently, hand covering his mouth. When Donovan finished, he waited for the cardinal's response.

'Have you read it?'

Donovan nodded. As the archive's senior curator he was a polyglot – proficient in ancient Aramaic, and completely fluent in Greek and Latin.

'What does it say?'

'Many disturbing things. Apparently this book isn't a Templar document *per se*. It's a journal written by Joseph of Arimathea.'

'I don't understand, Patrick.'

'The entries in these pages chronicle many events specific to Christ's ministry. Eyewitness accounts of miracles, like his healing the lame and lepers. His teachings, his travels with the disciples – it's all referenced here. In fact, after reviewing the language, I'm convinced this book is "Q".'

Biblical historians had long theorized that a common source influenced the *synoptic* – or 'one eye' – Gospels of Matthew, Mark, and Luke since all three spoke of the historical Jesus in a common sequence and writing style. The *synoptic* Gospels, believed to be written between 60 CE and 70 CE, each bore the name of an actual disciple who inspired the work, though all three authors were actually unknown.

Santelli was temporarily encouraged by this, but acutely aware that Father Donovan remained troubled.

'There's much more here, however,' Donovan warned. 'The book describes events leading to Jesus's apprehension and crucifixion. Again, most of Joseph's account is in agreement with the synoptic Gospels . . . with some minor discrepancies. According to Joseph of Arimathea, he himself secretly negotiated with Pontius Pilate to remove Christ from the cross, in exchange for a hefty sum.'

'A bribe?'

'Yes. Probably a supplement to Rome's meagre pension.' Donovan took a deep breath and gathered himself. 'In the New Testament, Jesus's body was supposedly laid out for burial in Joseph's family crypt.'

'Before you continue, I must ask. This Templar relic . . . the book. Is it authentic?'

'I had the parchment, leather, and ink dated. The origin is unquestionably first century. But this book isn't the relic Jacques DeMolay implied. It's merely a means of finding the real treasure he alluded to.'

Santelli stared at him.

'Joseph of Arimathea describes Jesus's burial rituals in vivid detail. How the body was cleaned, wrapped in spices and linen, and then bound. Coins were placed over the eyes.' Donovan's voice sank an octave. 'It claims that the body was laid out in Joseph's tomb . . . for twelve months.'

'*A year?*' Santelli was aghast. 'Patrick, this isn't yet more Gnostic scripture?' In the past Donovan had routinely briefed him on the many pre-biblical writings that presented Jesus quite differently – an attempt by early leaders to entice pagans to adopt the Christian faith. Many of those stories were wildly exaggerated, rife with philosophical interpretations of Jesus's teachings.

'According to Joseph – the man entrusted with burying Jesus – there never was a physical resurrection. You see . . .' There was no subtle way for him to say what needed to be said. He locked eyes with the cardinal. 'Christ died a mortal death.'

It wasn't the first time Santelli had heard this argument. 'But we've been through all this before – assertions about early Christians seeing resurrection as being spiritual not physical.' He gestured at the book dismissively. 'This *Ephemeris Conlusio* is a clear contradiction to scripture. I'm glad you found it. We'll need to ensure it doesn't fall into the wrong hands. We don't need some enemy of the Church rushing off to the media.'

'I'm afraid there's more.'

Santelli watched silently as Donovan reached into his satchel and removed a furled, yellow scroll. He laid it out on the desk.

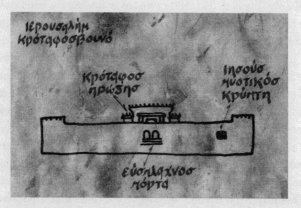

The Cardinal leaned in. 'What is this?'

'A technical illustration – a kind of map, actually.'

He made a face. 'Certainly doesn't look technical to me. A child could have drawn this.'

The one-dimensional style used to draft the image was simplistic, Donovan would agree. But three-dimensional illustrations weren't employed until the Renaissance period, and he wasn't about to belabour the point with Santelli.

'Despite its lack of detail, there are a few critical things you can see here,' Donovan explained. He indicated the elongated rectangular base. 'This is Temple Mount in Jerusalem.' Then he pointed to the image drawn on top of it. 'This is the Jewish Temple that was built by Herod the Great, later destroyed by the Romans in 70 AD. As you know, the Dome of the Rock Mosque is there now.'

Santelli looked up sharply. 'Temple Mount?'

'Yes,' Donovan confirmed. 'This is Joseph of Arimathea's representation of how it appeared in 30 AD during the time of Christ.'

Donovan explained that Joseph's writings described in great detail what the temple looked like – its rectangular courtyards and sacred Tabernacle; its storage houses for oil and wood; the water basins used to consecrate sacrificial offerings and the wooden pyres to burn sacred animals during Passover. He said that Joseph had even noted the temple's sacred threshold beyond which gentiles were forbidden to cross – a railed, outer perimeter called the '*Chell*'. Then there was the account of the Roman garrison that adjoined Temple Mount – the place where Jesus was taken before Pontius Pilate.

'But it's this spot here' – Donovan pointed to the small darkened square that Joseph had drawn inside the gut of the platform – 'that's most important. It's meant to show the location of Jesus's crypt. In the text, Joseph includes specific measurements as to its proximity from the Temple Mount's outer walls.'

Santelli's hand was over his mouth again. For a few seconds he remained perfectly still.

Beyond the window the looming black clouds finally made good on their threat.

'After obtaining the *Ephemeris Conlusio*,' Donovan continued, 'I researched the site in great detail. I'm absolutely certain that the secret crypt is still there. I believe that Crusaders – the Knights Templar, in fact – might have discovered the crypt and secured it.'

'How can you be so sure?'

Donovan reached across the desk and carefully turned the ancient pages, stopping on a group of sketches. 'This is why.'

The cardinal had trouble comprehending what appeared to be a catalogued collection – the drawing style equally crude.

'Those items,' Donovan went on, 'are the relics that Joseph of Arimathea buried in the crypt. The bones, coins, and nails. Plus the ossuary, of course. These are the things Jacques DeMolay was referring to.'

Santelli was thunderstruck. Slowly his eyes settled on an image of a dolphin wrapped around a trident 'That symbol there. What does it mean?'

'It's the reason I'm sure these items are still secure.' He explained its significance.

Santelli crossed himself and set it down.

'If these relics had ever been discovered, without a doubt, it would certainly have been referenced somewhere. In fact, we probably wouldn't even be sitting here having this conversation if they had been.' Donovan retrieved yet another document from his satchel. 'Then there's this recent article from the

Jerusalem Post which our mysterious benefactor included with the book.'

Santelli snatched it away and repeated the *Post*'s headline out loud. '"Jewish and Muslim Archaeologists Cleared to Excavate Beneath Temple Mount."'

Donovan gave Santelli time to absorb the rest of the article, then spoke up. 'Since Israeli peace accords don't permit digging on the site, the Templar Knights are Temple Mount's last known excavators. But in 1996 the Muslim trust that oversees the site was permitted to clear rubble from a vast chamber beneath the platform – a space that was once used by the Templars as a stable, and completely blocked off since their twelfth-century occupation. The messenger who delivered this book was an Arab. Therefore, I'm fairly certain that the *Ephemeris Conlusio* must have been discovered by the Muslims during their excavations.'

'But why have they waited until now to present it?'

'At first, I too was suspicious,' Donovan confessed. 'Though now I've got a good idea as to why.' From the satchel he retrieved a modern drawing – his own. The final exhibit of the presentation. 'When the areas were cleared, the Muslims converted that space into what is now called the Marwani Mosque. Here's an aerial view of the Temple Mount as it stands today. Using Joseph's measurements, I've calculated the precise location of the crypt.'

On the schematic, Donovan had converted the ancient Roman measuring units, *gradii* – one *gradus* equal to almost three-quarters of a metre – to their modern metric equivalent. 'I've marked in red the area that is now the Marwani Mosque, situated about eleven metres below the esplanade's surface.' The shape of the subterranean mosque looked like a stacked bar chart.

Santelli grasped what Donovan was implying. 'My God, it's right next to the secret chamber.'

'Directly abutting the mosque's rear wall. Muslim and Jewish archaeologists already suspect that chambers exist beneath Temple Mount and they'll be performing surface scans to detect them.'

Santelli's face was drained. 'Then they will find this place.'

'It would be impossible to miss,' Donovan grimly confirmed. 'If the relics described in the *Ephemeris Conlusio* are real, there's a good chance that the physical remains of Christ may be unearthed in a few weeks. That is why I have come here today. To ask you . . . what can we do?'

'I think that's all too clear, Patrick,' Santelli's voice was brisk. 'We must retrieve those relics from beneath Temple Mount. Over one billion Christians depend on the Gospels of Jesus Christ. To disrupt their faith is to disrupt social order. We have a very real responsibility here. This isn't just a matter of theology.'

'But there's no diplomatic way to obtain them,' Donovan reminded the cardinal. 'The political situation in Israel is far too complicated.'

'Who said anything about diplomacy?' Santelli reached over to the intercom mounted on his desk. 'Father Martin? In my phone list, you'll find the number for a "Salvatore Conte". Please summon him to my office immediately.'

50.

Veering off congested Via Nomentana through the Villa Torlonia park entrance, Giovanni Bersei slowed along a narrow bike path, the Vespa's engine purring softly.

Here, beneath the sprawling English gardens where a flurry of joggers and cyclists went about their exercise regimens, a labyrinth of Jewish crypts formed just over nine kilometres of what had recently proved to be Rome's oldest catacombs – the burial grounds that ancient Rome insisted be well outside the city walls. And somewhere in this subterranean realm, he was certain, lay part of an ancient secret tied to Jesus Christ.

Glancing up at the weathered neoclassical edifice that made this place famous – the palatial villa where Benito Mussolini had once resided – he angled toward a set of low buildings adjacent to the building's rear courtyard. Here were the stables where excavations in 1918 had accidentally uncovered the first burial chambers.

Outside the Villa Torlonia catacomb gateway, Bersei killed the Vespa's engine, dismounted, and rocked the scooter onto its kickstand. Opening the rear cargo box, he removed his laptop bag and a sturdy flashlight, then stowed his helmet inside.

Though he'd been caught up in rush hour traffic for the past forty minutes, it was still only ten minutes to nine. Most likely, the place would still be locked up.

Bersei tried the door. It opened.

Inside the crude foyer an elderly docent sat behind a desk, reading a Clive Cussler novel. There was a large boat on the cover caught in a massive whirlpool's swirling vortex. The old man's deep-set, hazy eyes shifted up, squinting over thick bifocals. A smile broke across his face – an exterior as aged and historically complex as Mussolini's villa.

'*Ah, Signore Bersei*,' he placed his book down and spread his hands. '*Come sta?*'

'*Bene grazi, Mario. E lei?*'

'Better and better every day,' the old man boasted in thick Italian. 'It's been a while.'

'It has. Glad you're an early bird. I thought I'd be standing outside for a while.'

'They have me here at eight nowadays, just in case anyone feels motivated to get some work done. They've been trying to speed up the restoration.'

The Soprintendenza Archeologica di Roma still denied tourists access to the Jewish catacombs due to the intensive conservation efforts that were still under way – a project now spanning more than a decade. Noxious gases still present in the deep recesses of the subterranean labyrinth of crypts had only prolonged the delay.

Bersei pointed to the book. 'I see you're keeping busy.'

The docent shrugged. 'Catching up on my reading. Still haven't got word that we'll be opening any time soon. I need to find action somewhere else.'

Bersei laughed.

'What brings you back here?' The old man stood, stuffing frail hands into his pockets. Mario's frame was mostly bone, dramatically stooped by age.

It had been a while since Bersei's last visit. Two years, in fact. This was only one of over sixty Roman burial sites he had surveyed for the Pontifical Commission over the years. 'The latest carbon dating results have me second-guessing some of my original assumptions. Just want to have a second look at some of the *hypogea*.'

The story was a good one. Only a few months ago, a team of archaeologists had carbon dated charcoal and wood fragments embedded in some of the crypt's stucco. The remarkable results dated the site as far back as 50 BC – over a century earlier than the city's youngest Christian catacombs. The implications of such a discovery were profound, strongly supporting prior theories about Jewish influence on Christian burial rituals. But what was most fascinating was that mingled with the Judaic motifs were symbols closely tied to the early Christian movement. And these vague recollections had brought Bersei back here.

'I see you've got your flashlight.'

The anthropologist held it up proudly. 'Always prepared. Do you need my card?' Bersei pulled out his wallet, flipping it open to a laminated identification card granting him full access to most of the city's historic sites. Few academics had earned this status.

Mario waved it away. 'I'll log you in,' he said, pointing to a clipboard at his side.

'No one else down there?'

'You've got it all to yourself.'

Somehow, that wasn't sitting right with him. He smiled uneasily.

The docent passed him a piece of paper. 'Here's an updated map for you.'

Bersei eyed the revised plan of tunnels and galleries. Now it was even more evident that the passageways had evolved haphazardly over centuries of expansion. The complicated representation looked more like a pattern of cracks in a crazed piece of pottery. A web. 'I won't be long. Would you mind if I left this with you for a little while?' He held up the laptop bag.

'No problem. I'll keep it behind the desk.'

Handing the bag over, he made his way across the foyer and flicked on the flashlight, angling it low to illuminate the stone steps that plunged into pure blackness.

At the base of the steps, Bersei fought off a shiver and paused to adjust his breathing to the frigid, damp air – the brutal conditions that challenged restoration. It was remarkable that so many frescos and etchings had been preserved down here, in an unforgiving environment that had completely ravaged the corpses that once occupied its thousands of niches. Barely any bones had been uncovered during excavations in these tombs, most having been stolen centuries earlier by unscrupulous charlatans who had turned a profit by passing them off as the relics of martyrs and saints. Ironic, he thought, seeing as the place was constructed like a maze specifically to avoid looting. So much for protecting the bodies for eventual resurrection. Come Judgement Day, there would be plenty of disappointed souls.

He pointed the light down the narrow passageway – barely a metre wide and less than three metres high – where it dissolved into total darkness only a few metres ahead. Almost two thousand years ago, the *Fassores*, a guild of diggers, had hand-carved this labyrinth of tombs out of the soft volcanic rock or *tufa* that formed Rome's foundation. Burial slots called *loculi* layered the walls on both sides. In ancient times, bodies had been shrouded and laid out on these shelves to decompose for *excarnation* – the ritual rotting of flesh that expiated earthly sin. All were now empty.

These subterranean galleries had been layered into the earth, with three levels of similar tunnels running beneath this one. Luckily, the chamber he was most interested in viewing was in the catacomb's upper gallery.

The *necropolis*, he thought. 'City of the dead.' He shielded his nose from the mouldy smell and hoped that nobody was home. Swallowing hard, Giovanni Bersei pushed forward.

'*Desidera qualcosa?*' Mario set down his book for the second time and studied the rugged-looking man, standing in front of his desk. The man looked preoccupied. Mario tried English. 'Can I help you?'

Aggravated by the formality, Conte didn't reply. Following Bersei here, he'd been wondering why the hell the scientist had turned into this park. Now as he read the signage hanging behind the docent's desk, he was starting to make better sense of it. Jewish catacombs? His eyes panned over to the other doorway, opening to a darkened stairwell. Most likely, it served as the exit too. He liked that. 'No lights?' Conte queried in Italian.

'You need a flashlight down there,' the old man replied.

Again, Conte was pleased.

'But the exhibit isn't open to the public,' the docent continued, smiling wryly. 'And unless you have proper identification, I'll have to ask you to leave.'

Power wielded by the powerless. Conte disregarded the request, ogling a clipboard on the desk. A visitor's sign-in sheet. And only one name was listed there; the only name that mattered. Besides his quarry, it was clear that the place was empty. This was going to be even easier than he thought. He slid his left hand into his coat pocket and calmly withdrew a small syringe.

As the menacing figure circled the desk in three quick strides, Mario Beneditti was just starting to realize the danger he was in. Cornered, the old man froze.

'Pathetic,' Conte muttered. He threw out his right hand, clasping the docent by the back of his neck, while his left hand swiftly arced through the air, thrusting the needle deep into neck muscle, depressing the plunger to inject a concentrate of Tubarine – a drug used during heart surgery to paralyse the cardiac tissue. Never knowing when he might need it, Conte always kept a lethal dose in his possession.

As the old man crumpled to the floor, Conte stepped smartly away.

The toxins instantly invaded Mario Beneditti's bloodstream and he clawed at his constricting chest with leaden fingers. His face contorted in agony as his heart seized up like a blown engine. His body gave a last, shuddering convulsion and lay still.

Salvatore Conte always marvelled at this method's lean efficiency. Whoever found the old man would assume he'd had a heart attack. Any basic autopsy would come to the same conclusion.

Clean. *Very clean*.

After securing the deadbolt on the inside of the entry door, and pocketing the empty syringe, Conte rummaged through the desk drawers until he found the docent's flashlight. He noticed Bersei's laptop bag had been set aside and made a mental note to take it with him on his way out. Then he reached down to the corpse and yanked away a set of keys.

From beneath his coat, he drew his Glock 9mm. He'd try his best to avoid shooting Bersei. That wouldn't be clean and he wasn't looking for complications.

Flashlight on, Conte stepped down into the darkness and pulled the door shut behind him, engaging its meaty lock.

51.

For fifteen minutes, Giovanni Bersei worked his way deeper into the Villa Torlonia catacomb, stopping intermittently to refer to the map. The chill in his bones was impossible to shake and the absolute silence down here crushed his ears. At every turn, history's long legacy of death swirled around him. Not exactly ideal working conditions, he mused.

Without the diagram, this zigzag of tunnels would have been impossible to navigate. So many of the passages – most of which terminated in dead ends – looked the same, and being underground he had little sense of direction. By no means claustrophobic, Bersei had been in many subterranean lairs more daunting than this. But he had never been alone . . . in a gigantic tomb.

Judging from the map's scale he figured he'd walked just under half a kilometre from the entrance. His destination was very close now.

Ahead, the left wall gave way to a sweeping archway – an entrance to a chamber called a *cubiculum*. In the opening, Bersei paused and referenced the map again to confirm that he had found the right cell. Pocketing the map, he let out a long breath and moved into the space beyond.

Running the light over the walls, he scanned the spacious square chamber, hewn out of the porous *tufa*. There were no *loculi* here, just workspaces where bodies would once have been laid out to be prepared for interment. Sitting in a corner were a couple of ancient *amphoras*, which had probably once contained scented oils and spices.

The floor was ornately tiled, the walls plastered and covered in more Judaic design, primarily menorahs and even strong depictions of the Second Temple and the Ark of the Covenant.

In the centre of the floor, Bersei craned back his head and aimed the flashlight upwards. If he remembered correctly, what he'd most wanted to see would be here. The moment his eyes adjusted to the amazing fresco that covered the lofty vault, he felt the breath pulled out of his chest.

His flashlight momentarily switched off, Salvatore Conte listened intently for the distant sounds echoing through the stone maze. Strangely comfortable in darkness, the fact that for the second time in a week he found himself in a tomb had no effect on his resolve.

Totally unaware of his pursuer, the anthropologist was making no effort to conceal the scraping sounds of his footsteps against the rough tunnel floor. And stopping occasionally to view a map only compounded his predicament.

Conte was close now. Very close.

He poked his head around the corner of the wall. About forty metres down the narrow passage, a faint glow spilled out from an arched opening.

Reaching behind his back, he tucked the Glock into his belt. Keeping the light off, he quietly removed his coat and shoes, placing them beside the wall with the flashlight. The Minotaur was moving again.

Giovanni Bersei's gaze was transfixed on the images floating above him.

In the centre was a menorah contained within concentric circles like a sunburst, centred upon a large cross – a cruciform – wrapped by grapevine tendrils.

On the ends of the cross were circular forms containing other symbols – a *shofar*, the ceremonial horn used to usher in the

Jewish New Year; *etrogs*, the lemon-shaped fruit used by Jews during *sukkot*, the feast of the sacred Tabernacle – all imagery that paid homage to the lost temple.

Between the equal arms of the cross were four half circles that he swore had been purposely arranged to match the points of a compass. Each contained the symbol carved onto the ossuary's side – a dolphin wrapped around a trident. The early Christian symbol for Jesus Christ, the Saviour – the dolphin who shuttled spirits to the afterlife superimposed over the physical incarnation of the Trinity.

Trembling, Bersei tucked the flashlight in his armpit and reached into his breast pocket for the photocopy of the scroll.

'My God,' Bersei muttered. The same exact image – a virtual reproduction of the ceiling fresco – was drawn beneath the Greek text written almost two millennia earlier by Joseph of Arimathea. It was this image that had drawn him here. As far as Bersei had been aware, this fresco was one-of-a-kind.

Impossible.

This commingling of Jewish and Christian motifs was overwhelming enough, but the fact that Joseph was somehow linked to this place was mind-boggling. Bersei lowered the light along the wall to a fresco of the Ark of the Covenant. Surely all these images were related. There was a clear message Joseph had left here. But what did he and Jesus have in common with the Tabernacle and the Ark of the Covenant? The possibilities were tantalizing.

Turning his attention to an opening in the *cubiculum*'s rear wall, he made his way into another chamber. If the place followed standard crypt design, this funerary preparation room would adjoin a burial room, or *cella*. Therefore, it was reasonable to assume that the corpses of the family who owned the *cubiculum* would have also occupied the *cella*.

321

He could barely control his excitement. Had he found the crypt of Joseph of Arimathea?

He moved forward into the rear chamber. As anticipated, the walls of this space were cleanly carved into *loculi*.

Amazing.

The beam of light shifted as Bersei counted the niches. *Ten.*

Nine of the shelves were fairly plain, spare some ornamental stone mouldings. But on the rear wall, one *loculus* stood out. Most anthropologists would have quickly surmised this to be the burial spot of the family patriarch. But having seen the Jesus ossuary up close, Bersei immediately noticed the intricate rosettes and hatch patterns that framed this particular niche. Undoubtedly, it was the handiwork of the same stone craftsman who had decorated the ossuary.

Awestruck, Bersei paced forward, mouth agape. His imagination running wild, he pointed the light into the carved grotto, just large enough to store a prostrate body. Empty, of course. Now the light caught a symbol carved into the top edge of the frame. A dolphin wrapped around a trident.

Extraordinary.

Could Joseph of Arimathea have really transported Christ's body back to Rome after the crucifixion? And if so, why? Bersei tried to wrap his head around the gigantic idea. Protection perhaps? But wasn't there an empty tomb near Golgotha in Jerusalem? Maybe this could explain why the Gospels said it had been found empty.

It actually seemed to make some sense. If Joseph's family lived in Rome's Jewish ghetto, it would have certainly been much safer to secrete Christ's body here, far away from the watchful eye of the Jewish Council and Pontius Pilate. Especially if customary burial rituals were to take place: rituals that involved shelving the corpse for up to a year.

'Dr Bersei,' a sharp voice abruptly invaded the dead silence.

Startled, Bersei jumped and pivoted, swinging the light behind him. Half-expecting to see a ghastly apparition looking to punish him for his invasion of the tomb, he was even more terrified when the cylinder of light played on Salvatore Conte's hard features. Having appeared without the slightest sound and dressed completely in black, it was as if Conte had materialized from the wall of the crypt.

'Do you mind?' Squinting, Conte motioned at the flashlight.

Heart thundering hard against his ribs, Bersei lowered the beam to the floor. He noticed Conte wasn't wearing shoes. At first glance, it also appeared that he wasn't armed. 'How did you get down here?' He feared he already knew the answer.

Conte ignored the question. 'What are you looking for, doctor?'

Bersei didn't answer.

Conte strode up to the anthropologist and snatched the photocopy from his hand.

'It's merely research. Nothing more.' Cursing the fact that he was a horrible liar, Bersei retreated a step, his back pressing against the crypt wall.

'You must think I'm an idiot. I know you've taken files from the lab. Do you intend to give them to Detective Perardi too?'

Bersei went mute. How could Conte have known about Perardi? That call was made from his home. A sinking feeling came over him. Could the Vatican have been so ruthless as to tap his telephone?

'Stealing's one thing. Stealing from the Vatican . . . Now that's just un-Christian. You surprise me, Dr Bersei. But you are a smart man . . . I'll give you that.' Conte turned and stepped away to the centre of the chamber purposely displaying the Glock stuffed in his belt for dramatic effect. 'Come here and give me some light.' He moved out into the centre of the cubiculum.

Reluctantly, Giovanni Bersei shuffled into the antechamber and shone the light high up into its vault. The beam oscillated in his shaking hand.

Conte absorbed the fresco's complex imagery for a few seconds, then compared it to the image on the paper. 'So this is what you've found,' he said, impressed. 'Good work. Who would have thought that box had origins here? I guess Joseph of Arimathea was pretty worldly after all.'

Bersei frowned.

'I take it you think he brought Jesus's body here first,' Conte continued, 'before boxing the bones and shipping them back to that sandbox in the Holy Land. I don't even think the librarian or the pope's cronies could have thought this far ahead.'

Bersei was stupefied by Conte's candour, and his casual disregard for what this all really meant. More so, he was horrified that Conte had just confirmed his suspicions of the Vatican's knowledge of the theft. Now he was certain they were directly involved and, somehow, Salvatore Conte had made it all possible. The master thief. The silent stalker. The Israeli death count scrolled through his mind's eye. Thirteen dead. What was one more life for a man like this? Especially after what amounted to an admission of foul play. Immediately, his thoughts jumped to his wife, and three daughters. His mouth went dry.

Calmly, Conte folded the paper and slipped it into his pants pocket. Then he was coolly reaching behind his back for the Glock.

Correctly anticipating what was coming, Bersei reacted on survival impulse, slamming the flashlight against the stone wall behind him. There was a harsh clatter of metal and breaking glass as the element shattered, plunging the cubiculum into utter darkness.

An instant later, Conte squeezed off a shot, the muzzle flash strobing the darkness, just long enough to see that the scientist had already scrambled away on his knees. Conte paused briefly to gauge the sounds of his movement before firing again – another flash, followed by a perilously close ricochet that almost clipped Conte's ear. Though his intention was merely to scare the scientist, not actually shoot him, he'd have to take better care aiming.

'Fuck,' Conte screamed out loud. 'I hate this fucking game.' The game, of course, was the futile attempt of any quarry to survive the likes of a seasoned hunter like Salvatore Conte. He listened again, hoping Bersei would double back to the catacomb entrance. But to his surprise, a sloppy fall and fast-moving steps confirmed that the anthropologist had gone the opposite way – deeper into the maze.

Before Conte began his pursuit, he felt his way back a few metres to retrieve his flashlight and shoes. Slipping them on, he flicked on the flashlight and sprinted along the narrow tunnel, the amber glow of his light swinging with each pump of his arms.

Giovanni Bersei had a good head start, but the uncertainty of the catacomb's layout, filled with long tunnels that ran hundreds of metres to dead ends, had him panic-stricken. He needed to keep his wits about him, above all to remember the map . . . or else. He shook the thought away.

Running through the uneven stone corridors, each footfall echoed loudly behind him, an aural trail for Conte.

There was something otherworldly about moving so quickly through pure black; disorienting. With nothing for his eyes to focus on, Bersei held one arm out like he was running a touchdown in an American football game, all the while praying he wouldn't crash face-first into a wall. To make matters worse, as he progressed deeper, the air was harder to take in, putrid with the acrid smells of wet earth and chemicals he couldn't quite identify – most likely the noxious gases that were the catacomb's greatest natural hazard.

His right shoulder bounced off the wall and he spun slightly, almost tripping over himself. Slowing momentarily to regain his balance, he began to move again, only to career into a wall face-first. Panting wildly, he thrust his arms to the right, groping, searching for an opening, praying that this wasn't a dead end. Nothing except the hollow niches of *loculi*. For a split second, he considered hiding in one, but knew his uncontrolled breathing would give him away. He spun a one-eighty and paced over to the other wall. More stone.

Jesus, don't do this to me.

Feeling his way along the wall and moving right, his hands found a void. The passageway hadn't terminated; it simply angled hard to the left.

Just as Bersei rounded the corner, he swore he glimpsed a distant light that looked like a star in the night sky. He heard the steady drum of Conte running, louder by the second.

Bersei sprinted through the darkness, running purely on faith that he wouldn't crash again. Seconds later, his feet tangled on something low to the floor. His legs buckled and he slammed hard onto the stone paving. He'd landed on what felt like paint cans, his head colliding loudly against some kind of metal case.

A blinding light shot into his eyes as intense pain racked his skull. He swore furiously, thinking the flash was a by-product of the head blow. But opening his eyes, he stared directly into an illuminated work light. Blinking, he saw that he had run directly into a section of the tunnel where restoration was still underway. Tools, brushes, and cans were strewn throughout the passage. A thick cord had lassoed his ankles and downed the pole light onto its switch. He yanked the mess away, snapping back to his feet, barely glimpsing the magnificent frescos that were in the process of repair.

The footsteps behind him were faster now, closing in.

The toolbox that he'd collided with lay open, a ball-peen hammer sitting in its top tray. He grabbed it and ran.

Conte rounded the corner where a mysterious light spilled out into the tunnel. He was beginning to feel a bit light-headed, not from the run, but from the acrid air now filling his lungs. Slowing to navigate the mess of tools blocking the passage, he planted a firm kick on the work light and it fizzled out.

Up ahead, the passage forked in three different directions. Racing to the intersection, he paused, striving to control his breathing, and listened.

Conte levelled the flashlight straight ahead. It appeared to be a dead end. Then he spun right and shone the light down the passageway, which curved gently out of sight. The left tunnel was also curved.

He listened again. Nothing. Finally he had to make a choice.

52.

JERUSALEM

Inside Station Zion's cramped detaining cell, Graham Barton stared hopelessly at the solid metal door. Somehow he'd been framed as the mastermind behind the Temple Mount theft. Deep down he knew that the powers were aligned against him for a reason – perhaps an expedient political one.

Early that morning, Israeli police had finally permitted him to call his wife. Given the seven-hour time difference she'd been agitated when woken from a deep sleep. But after he explained his predicament, she quickly softened.

In Jenny's voice, Barton sensed something that he thought was long dead – concern. She readily believed him when he insisted that he was innocent. 'Come on, Graham, I know you'd never do something like this.' Reassuring him that she would immediately formulate a plan of action, she'd ended the call by saying, 'I love you, darling. I'm here for you.' The words had almost brought tears to his eyes, and in a moment when everything seemed dark and uncertain, he had regained something more precious than his freedom.

The door opened and he looked up at a familiar figure.

Razak.

Clearly upset, the Muslim crossed to the remaining chair as the door closed behind him and was locked from the outside.

'Quite a predicament you're in, Graham,' his tone was disappointed. Razak had always been a good judge of character. Yet the police had presented such strong evidence against the archaeologist that he couldn't help but feel he'd been played for a fool.

'It's a set-up,' Barton insisted. 'I had nothing to do with this crime. You of all people should know that.'

'I like you. You seem to be a good man, but really, I don't know what to think. They said that solid evidence was discovered in your apartment. Things only the thieves could have possessed.'

'Someone planted that drill,' Barton protested. 'And you know as well as me that the scroll was in that ossuary.' He saw the incredulous look on the Muslim's face. 'For goodness sake, Razak. You have to tell them that the scroll was in that ossuary.'

Razak spread his hands. 'I had my back turned,' he reminded him. He couldn't discount the possibility that Barton may have purposely gone through the charade of opening the remaining ossuaries to legitimize the scroll in his possession. But why? For notoriety? To discredit the Muslim claim to Temple Mount by sidetracking the investigation with a territorial dispute? Maybe to divert the blame to a fanatical Christian?

'Right. I see.' Disappointment clouded the archaeologist's face. 'You're part of this, too.'

'What about the other ossuaries?'

Barton was exasperated. 'How could a man my size move nine ossuaries weighing thirty-three kilos each right from under the eyes of the Waqf and police? They're not the kind of things one can slip into one's pocket,' he said sarcastically. 'Haven't you seen this city the past few days? There's surveillance equipment everywhere. All they need to do is play back some video recordings and they'll see that I was never there without you present.'

Razak was silent, eyes cast down.

'And even if I'd been able to take them, where would I have hidden them? In my flat? They've already searched there. Next you're going to assume that I defaced the tablet on the wall of the crypt because I saw it before you did.'

The Muslim's eyes shot up. 'What do you mean by that?'

'The tenth entry on the tablet. Remember it was scratched away?'

Now Razak knew what he was referring to. 'Yes.'

'Well tonight, Major Topol conveniently showed me a photograph taken *before* I was brought in. It showed the symbol that was originally there.'

Razak didn't like that. 'And what was it?'

Barton wasn't in the mood for another history dissertation. 'A pagan symbol. A dolphin wrapped around a trident.'

Razak tried to comprehend what this meant.

'An early Christian symbol for Jesus, representing crucifixion and resurrection.'

Razak didn't know what to say. If this were true, it would certainly strengthen Barton's assertions about the crypt's owner and the perceived contents of the stolen ossuary. He shook his head. 'I don't know what to believe.'

'You must help me, Razak. You're the only one who knows the truth.'

'Truth's a rare commodity in this part of the world.' Razak glanced away. 'Even if it existed, I don't know if I'd recognize it.' He began to feel a keen responsibility for the Englishman. Barton's

330

intuition about the theft had been virtually flawless and he'd perceived things no one else had grasped. Yet here he was awaiting charges. Razak had seen these tactics used many times in the past by the Israeli authorities. But was Barton really just a convenient patsy for the Israelis? This possibility presented an entirely different challenge.

'Is there any hope for me?'

Razak spread his hands. 'There's always hope.' But deep down he knew that there would be no easy way out of this.

'You're not going to pursue this investigation, are you?'

'You have to understand our position.' Razak was beginning to wonder if he understood it himself.

'What position exactly?'

'Peace. Stability. You know what happened yesterday,' he said, referring to the bombing. 'If something doesn't change, that will be just the beginning. Already news of your arrest has started to ease tensions. Discussions are resuming. People have someone to blame – and a man who's not a Jew or a Muslim.'

'Very convenient.' The archaeologist knew nothing more could be done.

'The real problem we're facing is political.' Razak leaned forward. 'I know it's terrible. But if there's no blame, there'll be no solution. Blame a man and one man falls. Blame a country and the problem isn't singular.'

'This is how you're going to let this end?'

'It will never end.' Razak rose to his feet and knocked on the cell door. Before leaving, he paused and turned back to Barton. 'I need to digest all this, Graham. I will do my best to help. But I cannot attest to things that I'm unsure of. I know you can respect that.' With a sinking feeling, he made his way outside.

*

When Razak had entered Station Zion just minutes earlier, the pavements had been empty. But as he emerged out into the harsh sunlight, his eyes adjusted to a completely different scene.

Over a dozen news reporters had materialized. And judging from their frenzied reactions when they saw him, Razak knew *he* was the reason they were here. Shoulder-mounted cameras swung at him as the reporters came at him like a swarm, thrusting their microphones like épées.

'Mr al-Tahini!' one reporter managed to break forward to grab his attention.

Razak froze, knowing that confrontation was inevitable and somehow, necessary. After all, he was the Waqf's designated spokesman.

'Yes.'

'Is it true that the police have arrested the man responsible for the Temple Mount theft?'

As if by some unsigned accord, the entire assemblage of media personnel quieted down in unison, anxiously awaiting his reply.

Razak cleared his throat. 'That is still unclear. As far as we know, the police are still sorting through the facts.'

Another reporter yelled out, 'But weren't you working with this man? The English archaeologist, Graham Barton?'

'It is true that I was assigned to the investigation, as was Mr Barton whose impressive credentials were considered vital to our understanding of the thieves' motives.'

The first reporter squared up again. 'And how do you feel now that he's been singled out as the man behind all this?'

Careful, Razak told himself. *Don't make things worse for Graham. And don't make things worse for your Muslim and Palestinian constituents either.* 'Though I am anxious to come to a resolution, I feel that many more questions need to be answered before anyone should levy accusations against this man.' He glared at the reporter. 'Now if you'll excuse me,' he said, pushing forward through the mob.

53.

ROME

Huddled inside a *loculus* high on the passage wall, Giovanni Bersei was sucking in shallow breaths, desperate to steady himself, hoping that Conte would choose the wrong tunnel and wander aimlessly into the catacomb. If he was really lucky, the assassin might succumb to the fumes and pass out. Bersei only hoped it didn't happen to himself first. He tightened his grip around the ball-peen hammer's handle. *As if this is any match for a gun.*

Minutes passed. Silence returned.

A little more time and he would consider climbing back out into the tunnel. But the idea was short lived, because a faint glow of light suddenly played along the craggy wall opposite the niche. Conte was coming.

Having searched two tunnels unsuccessfully, Conte had backtracked to the area where Bersei had stumbled over the tools. Surely his quarry hadn't returned this way. Bersei couldn't have navigated the mess in the dark without causing a commotion.

Pacing down the third passage, Conte felt the slightest breeze. The air here was less putrid. Maybe there was a ventilation shaft nearby.

He was beginning to entertain the very remote possibility that Bersei might have outsmarted him. However, that could only be temporary since the only door out of this place was locked.

Moving slowly through the tunnel, he detected a dim light far ahead. Daylight?

Panic overcame him. Perhaps it was a ventilation shaft, but it certainly looked wide enough to provide an escape route. Conte broke into a sprint.

About ten metres ahead, a dark form suddenly arced out from high on the wall too fast for even the mercenary to react. It cracked him hard in the right temple and landed him flat on his back, his head slamming hard against the ground with a hollow thud.

The flashlight skittered across the tunnel floor. The Glock, however, remained fast in his grasp. For him, that was pure instinct.

Dazed, Conte barely discerned a figure crawling out from the wall like a reanimated corpse. Hitting the floor, Bersei scrambled for the light.

Suddenly, through blurry double vision, Conte saw something cartwheeling through the air. It struck him hard in the chest. A hammer? Raising the Glock, he blindly squeezed off a shot, just in case Bersei felt like attempting another blow.

The light disappeared down the passageway as Conte tried to pull himself together.

Running to the light source at the end of the passage, Bersei was grateful Conte's shots had missed him. Agonizing over the possibility that this might be a dead end, he focused on the luminous cone of sunlight at the tunnel's terminus that offered some hope of escape. The breeze was blowing stronger now. Maybe, just maybe, he'd get out of this appalling place alive.

But only a couple of metres from the shaft, Bersei slid to a stop, just before the gaping opening in the floor where the sunlight flowed down a wide, ragged shaft. He stared down its throat, four, perhaps five storeys to a rocky bottom.

The lower galleries. Three more levels lay below, he reminded himself. The restorers must have opened the ventilation shaft to help release lingering subterranean gases.

Christ help me.

His eyes drifted up to the light source. The shaft was too wide to climb. Worse, a heavy iron grate sealed the opening high above. Despair closed in on him like a vice.

Suddenly from behind, he heard a slight noise.

Bersei turned just in time to see Conte's body poised in horizontal form, launched in mid air like a projectile. The assassin's feet caught Bersei square in the chest, throwing him back violently across the mouth of the shaft, slamming his body against the wall beyond.

The flashlight tumbled downward end over end until it smashed on the rocks far below.

For a split second, Bersei was suspended on the wall, his feet caught on the small ridge that formed a rim around the opening. But the force of the impact teetered him forward uncontrollably. He reflexively kicked out from the wall, hurling himself across to the other side of the aperture, adrenaline pumping hard. Fingers clawed earth and squeezed. But there was nothing to hold onto.

The jagged rocks pin-wheeled around him as he plummeted

down to collide head first into the *tufa* at the base of the shaft.

Conte stared down into the abyss. Spread across the shaft's rocky bottom, Giovanni Bersei was bent into an unnatural shape, blood oozing from his collapsed skull, broken bones protruding through skin.

The hunter smiled. A clean kill that would appear to be an unfortunate accident. It would probably be days, perhaps weeks, before the body was found. Even the awful smell of rotting flesh could be dismissed down here. After all, that's what this place was designed for.

Backtracking through the tunnels, Conte gathered his shoes, gun, and coat. He even managed to find the Glock's discharged casings. It was a rule to never leave behind solid ballistics evidence. That's why he'd used XM8s for the Jerusalem job. By now, those slugs would have the investigators spinning in circles, trying to figure out how a prototype weapon that should have been stockpiled somewhere in a United States military bunker had wound up in the possession of nameless mercenaries.

Unlocking the door, he made his way into the foyer. Returning the keys to the rigid docent, he grabbed the laptop bag, unbolted the entrance and went outside, closing the door behind him. Taking a moment to let his eyes adjust to the glaring sunlight, Conte proceeded to wheel Bersei's Vespa over to the white Fiat rental van. Opening its rear doors, he manhandled the cycle into the rear compartment, closed the doors, and jumped behind the wheel. For a moment, he eyed himself in the rear-view mirror. A purple lump the size of a walnut had welled up on his right temple. Luckily, Bersei's swing hadn't been perfectly timed or he might have been knocked unconscious.

All things considered, it had been a good job.

54.

VATICAN CITY

At ten to ten, Father Patrick Donovan entered the lab looking like he hadn't slept in days. A leather satchel hung at his side. 'Good morning, Dr Hennesey.'

Seated beside the ossuary, Charlotte forced her eyes up from the relic.

Donovan looked around the lab for the anthropologist. 'Is Dr Bersei here?'

'I was going to call you earlier,' she said. 'He hasn't come in yet.' Bending the truth was not something she was good at. But now, for Giovanni's sake, she found herself trying harder than ever to be convincing.

'That's strange.' Immediately, he suspected that Conte was up to no good, because as Donovan had just come down the corridor, he had noticed that the makeshift surveillance room was unlocked and vacant. Apparently, Conte had left in a hurry. 'I hope everything is okay.'

'I know what you mean. Doesn't seem like him to be late.'

'Especially for something so important,' Donovan added. 'Well, I was really hoping he could be here for the presentation. Think you can handle this without him?'

'Sure,' she replied, her insides roiling. How could she possibly go through with this alone? What if Bersei was right? And what if she *wasn't* safe in Vatican City? The only solace she had was her gut feeling that this priest would watch over her. Rarely was she wrong about someone's character.

Donovan checked his watch. 'We really should get going. I don't want to be late.'

Forcing a smile, Charlotte slung her laptop bag over her shoulder, took the sizeable presentation portfolio in her hands, and followed Donovan out into the corridor. 'So where are we going exactly?'

He glanced over at her. 'To the office of the secretary of state, Cardinal Antonio Carlo Santelli.'

55.

Traversing the Apostolic Palace's grand corridor, Donovan stole a glimpse at Charlotte as she strode beside him, seeing in her eyes the same awe he'd experienced the first time he saw this place. 'Spectacular, isn't it?'

'Yes.' She was trying to calm her nerves as she eyed the heavily armed Swiss Guards stationed along the corridor. 'Amazingly grand.'

He motioned to the lofty ceiling. 'The pope lives one floor up.'

At the guarded entry to Cardinal Santelli's office, Donovan and Charlotte were quickly cleared and escorted by a Swiss Guard into the antechamber where Father Martin stood from his desk to greet them.

He wasn't thrilled about the cardinal's decision to meet here. What was Santelli's motive? To illustrate what was at stake should she actually suspect something?

'Good to see you again, James.' Donovan shook the young priest's hand, trying not to focus on the dark circles under his eyes. He introduced Charlotte, then asked if Martin could buzz the lab to see if Dr Bersei had arrived.

Martin obliged and circled behind the desk to make the call. The ring tones chimed for fifteen seconds with no response. He shook his head. 'Sorry. No one's picking up.'

Donovan turned to Charlotte. 'I guess you're on your own,' he said apologetically.

The intercom on Martin's desk suddenly came to life. 'James,' a rough voice tore through the tiny speaker. 'I asked you for that report ten minutes ago. What the hell are you waiting for?'

The priest rolled his eyes and smiled tightly. 'Excuse me for just a moment.' He leaned over and pressed the intercom's button. 'I have it right here, Eminence. I apologize for the delay. Also, Father Donovan and Dr Hennesey have arrived.'

'Well, what are you waiting for? Send them in!'

Angrily snatching a folder off the desk, Father Martin led them into Santelli's office.

Inside, the cardinal was seated behind his desk, wrapping up a call. He acknowledged the visitors with a nod and motioned to the folder in Martin's hand. After the priest handed it over, Santelli waved him away as if he were a mosquito.

'He's all yours,' Martin whispered to Donovan as he retreated to the antechamber.

Seeing Santelli's intimidating figure behind the desk, Charlotte suddenly realized that she'd been so preoccupied with Bersei's claims and Conte's creepy spy room that she'd failed to discuss etiquette with Donovan. Ending the call, the cardinal stood, tall and rigid, his face pleasant yet firm. Coming round his hulking desk, she could have sworn he exhibited the tell-tale signs of someone who'd recently stopped drinking, though there was no denying he had powerful presence.

'Good morning, Father Donovan.' The cardinal extended his right hand as if to grasp an invisible cane.

'Eminence.' Donovan stepped forward and bowed slightly to kiss Santelli's sacred ring, hiding his disdain for the superior gesture. 'Eminence Antonio Carlo Santelli, may I introduce you to Dr Charlotte Hennesey, a renowned geneticist from Phoenix, Arizona.'

'Ah, yes,' Santelli was grinning widely. 'I've heard much about you, Dr Hennesey.'

A look of panic came over Charlotte as he closed in for a greeting. Perhaps sensing it, he offered her a standard handshake. Relieved, she shook Santelli's enormous paw. She sensed the musky smell of cologne. 'An honour to meet you, Eminence.'

'Thank you, my dear. You're very kind.' Momentarily distracted by her beauty, he held her hand for a long moment before letting go. 'Come, let us sit.' Cupping his hand on her shoulder, he motioned across the office to a circular mahogany conference table.

Santelli kept in step with Charlotte, his hand still connected to her shoulder, Father Donovan in tow.

Donovan was amazed how Santelli could turn on the charm when required . . . a wolf in sheep's clothing.

'I'm anxious to discuss this tremendous project you've been working on,' Santelli stated exuberantly. 'Father Donovan's told me many exciting things about your findings.'

When they had all settled into their leather armchairs, Donovan provided a quick background to bring Santelli up to speed on the relics that had been presented to the scientists. Then he apologized on behalf of Dr Bersei who could not attend the meeting due to a personal crisis.

The cardinal looked alarmed. 'Nothing serious, I hope?'

The librarian was hoping the same thing. 'I'm sure he's fine.'

'That means you have the floor, Dr Hennesey.'

Charlotte handed Santelli a neatly bound report and gave Donovan a second copy. Flipping open her laptop, she waited for it to power up. 'Our first order of business was a pathological analysis of the skeleton . . .' she began, allowing her professional persona to take over.

Step-by-step she walked the two men through a PowerPoint slideshow of crisp, enlarged colour photos of the skeletal aberrations: the gouges, fractured knees, damaged wrists and feet. 'On the basis of what you see here, both Dr Bersei and myself concluded that this male specimen interred in the ossuary – who was otherwise in perfect health – died in his early thirties as a result of . . . execution.'

Santelli managed to look surprised. 'Execution?'

She glanced to Donovan who seemed equally puzzled, but nodded for her to continue. Directing her eyes back to the cardinal she got quickly to the point. 'He was crucified.'

The words hung in the air for a long moment.

Santelli leaned forward to put both elbows on the table and held the geneticist's gaze. 'I see.'

'And the forensic evidence unequivocally supports this,' she continued. 'Furthermore, we also found these objects in a concealed compartment inside the ossuary.' Determined to steady her hands, Charlotte removed the three separate plastic bags from her carrying bag. Laying the first one down, she tried not to let the spikes hit too hard against the burnished tabletop. Next came the sealed bag with the two coins. The third contained the metal cylinder.

Santelli and Donovan examined each object closely.

The nails drew the most attention, but required little explanation. The two men must have been thinking exactly what she did the first time she saw them: what it would have been like to be impaled by them.

Charlotte expanded on the significance of the coins. Surprisingly, neither Santelli nor Donovan had yet to raise a question. Did they already know about these things? Had that bastard Conte been updating them with the findings from his spying? Trying to shake away her suspicions, she informed them that the cylinder contained a scroll that had yet to be studied. This particular relic had once again managed to hold Father Donovan's attention for some time.

'We submitted a bone sample and some wood splinters for radiocarbon dating.' She passed across two copies of the dating certificates Ciardini had sent over. 'As you can see, both samples date to the early first century. The wood turns out to be a rare walnut indigenous to ancient Judea. Organic material from flowers used during the burial ritual and flax were also found inside the ossuary. Again, both are specific to Judea.' She flipped open more images and data.

'Why flax, Dr Hennesey?' Donovan asked.

'Most likely from the linen strips and shroud used to wrap the body during the burial ritual.' She paused. 'Dr Bersei performed a microscopic analysis of the ossuary's patina.'

She moved on to images revealing the varying degrees of magnification applied to the stone's surface.

'And the biological composition was uniform throughout the sample set. Plus the mineral content of the patina is consistent with similar relics found in caves throughout that region. More importantly, no signs of manual manipulation were detected.'

'I'm sorry, but what does that last point mean?' the Cardinal enquired.

'Simply that it's not a fake – the patina hasn't been artificially

344

created by modern chemical methods. And it implies that the ossuary and its markings are authentic.' *But you probably already know that*, she thought. She brought up the 3-D skeletal imaging and swivelled the laptop toward them. 'Scanning the skeleton, we calibrated the specimen's muscle mass.' Working the mouse, she brought up the digitized, blood-red musculature, allowed them both a few seconds to absorb the image, then clicked a command to assign the monochrome 'skin'. 'By incorporating the basic genetic profile found in the specimen's DNA we reconstructed this man's appearance at the time of death. And here he is.'

She tapped the mouse button and the screen refreshed – pigmented skin, eyes alive with colour, the hair dark and full.

Both men were astounded.

'That's absolutely . . . extraordinary,' Santelli muttered.

So far, neither the cardinal nor the priest was letting on about whether they had any advance knowledge of the skeleton's identity or the ossuary's origin. As they studied the image, she eyed both of them in turn. Could these two clerics possibly be involved in a theft that had left people dead? 'Lastly, Dr Bersei was able to decipher the meaning behind this symbol carved onto the side of the box.' She was confident this next exhibit would elicit a reaction. She held up a close-up photo clearly showing the dolphin wrapped around a trident, and explained the significance of each symbol taken separately. 'The fusing of these two pagan symbols was how first-century Christians represented . . . Jesus Christ.'

Santelli and Donovan exchanged uneasy glances.

Mission accomplished, Charlotte thought.

Silence fell over the room.

56.

Cardinal Santelli was the first to break the atmosphere. 'Are you telling us, Dr Hennesey, that you believe these are the mortal remains of Jesus Christ?'

Though she instinctively liked it when people got to the point, this was more than she'd bargained for. Swallowing hard, Charlotte felt a bolt of energy shoot through her system – fight or flight. She actually had to temper the urge to look toward the open door.

Now she was glad that before leaving the Domus that morning, she had put in an hour's reading of a book that was always readily available. In the drawer of the nightstand, in fact. If the report was going to even remotely suggest that these bones might have been those of Jesus Christ, double-checking related parts of the New Testament was prudent.

'At face value,' she began, 'the evidence is compelling. But there are discrepancies in the pathology report and contradictions to accounts in the Bible. For example, we found no evidence that a spear was thrust into the rib cage as the Bible states. And this man's knees were broken.' She went on to detail how the Romans speeded up death with a metal club.

Father Donovan's attention wandered momentarily as he thought about this anticipated inconsistency. He knew Charlotte was referring to the Gospel of John, verse nineteen, which stated that a Roman soldier pierced Jesus's side with a spear to help expedite his agonizing death:

So the soldiers came and broke the legs of the first man and of the other one who had been crucified with Him. When they came to Jesus, they did not break His legs since they saw that He was already dead.

Donovan always mused that two lines included in that passage – thirty-six and thirty-seven – actually concisely explained the incongruent account:

. . . For these things happened so that the Scripture would be fulfilled: Not one of His bones will be broken. Also, another Scripture says: They will look at the One they pierced.

Interestingly, none of the synoptic Gospels – Matthew, Mark, or Luke – made mention of this event. Donovan could only surmise that the Gospel of John included this embellished account to convince Jews that Jesus had been the true Messiah foretold by Old Testament prophets – '*so that Scripture would be fulfilled*'. He was certain that the skeleton laid out in the Vatican Museum was actually telling the truth: Pontius Pilate and the Romans had treated Jesus just like every other faceless criminal that threatened the empire's social order. They had ruthlessly annihilated him and when he wasn't dying quickly enough, they had smashed his knees to speed up the process.

Charlotte forged on. 'I'm sure you're far more aware than I

am about what the Bible says about Jesus's occupation before his ministry.'

Donovan played along with this. 'He'd been a carpenter since boyhood.' In fact, the Bible never made explicit reference to Christ's occupation. Jesus was *thought* to have been a carpenter merely because the Gospel of Matthew referred to him as 'the carpenter's son'. It was assumed he would have been employed in the family business – even though Matthew's Greek word '*tektonov*' – loosely translated as 'carpenter' – really could have applied to anyone who had worked with their hands, from builders to day labourers to farmers.

Charlotte nodded. 'All those years of hard manual work would have resulted in visible changes to the finger joints and wrists, where the bone and surrounding tissue thicken to accommodate increased demand. The joints would have shown signs of premature wearing in at least one of the hands.' She flipped to close-ups of the hands. 'Yet this man's show no obvious changes.'

'That's fascinating,' Donovan managed, almost sounding sincere.

'But most importantly,' she pointed to the monitor, 'his genetic make-up isn't what you'd expect of someone born in ancient Judea. I carefully reviewed the DNA's gene sequencing and it doesn't match any documented Middle Eastern profiles for Jews or Arabs. The Bible states that Jesus Christ was born from a long bloodline of Jews. As you both know, Matthew's Gospel begins by retracing Jesus's lineage – forty-two generations – and all of them Jews. Way back to Abraham. That bloodline would have been flawlessly Jewish. Yet this man's DNA has no identifiable genealogy.'

Now both Santelli and Donovan looked perplexed.

Santelli tilted his head to one side. 'So, Dr Hennesey, are you telling us that you *don't* believe that these are actually Jesus's remains?'

Their eyes met in a silent stand-off.

For an instant, she thought back to her conversation with Bersei – how he'd said that people might have been killed for these relics. Unlike Donovan, the cardinal's shifty gaze was starting to convince her that Giovanni's suspicions might just have been right. 'From what I've seen here, claiming these to be the actual remains of Jesus Christ would be a long shot. The scientific methods available today pose too many questions. There remains a very real possibility that this is some kind of first-century forgery.'

'That's a relief,' said Donovan.

Taken aback, Charlotte looked at him sharply. 'Why's that?'

Opening his satchel he produced the *Ephemeris Conlusio*. 'Let me explain.'

57.

Carefully resting the ancient, weathered manuscript on the glossy mahogany tabletop, Father Donovan turned to her. 'You know, of course, that the Vatican has been extremely concerned about the ossuary's provenance?'

Cardinal Santelli sat back in the chair, hands folded across his chest.

Charlotte eyed the book curiously.

'And there was a very good reason why,' he explained. 'No one outside a small circle within the upper reaches of the Church has heard what I'm about to tell you.'

Judging from the cardinal's body language, she highly doubted that. 'Okay.'

'First, I need to give you some background,' Donovan began. 'Many Jews, particularly those living in ancient Judea, maintained that Jesus – the self-proclaimed son of God – hadn't fulfilled the messianic criteria outlined in the Old Testament. And they were right.'

That's an odd admission, she thought.

'The Messiah foretold by the prophets was supposed to be a

warrior directly descended from King David, empowered by God to militarily reunite the tribes of Israel, thus freeing the Promised Land from tyranny and oppression.' Donovan was speaking quickly, his face animated, hands gesticulating. 'The Messiah was supposed to rebuild the Holy Temple. The Messiah was supposed to conquer Rome. The Jews had been vanquished for centuries and subjugated by all the major empires – Persians, Greeks, and Romans. For the first thousand years of its existence, Jerusalem had known only bloodshed.' Images of dead Israeli soldiers reminded him how little had changed. 'Yet in reading the scriptures, you find Jesus advocating peace. Here was a man telling the Jews to pay their taxes and accept their lot in life. In return he promised them eternity with God. He believed using evil to conquer evil only prolonged a perpetual cycle.'

Charlotte realized that Donovan needed to tell this story and that she needed to encourage it. 'Live by the sword, die by the sword?'

'Exactly. Jesus knew Rome couldn't be defeated. He was trying to prevent a massive Jewish rebellion that would have ended in a massacre by the Romans. But many chose not to listen.' Donovan's voice was solemn. 'Less than thirty years after Christ's death, the Jews finally revolted. The Roman response was swift and it was brutal. They besieged Jerusalem and after they'd taken the city, they slaughtered every man, woman, and child. Thousands were crucified, burned, or simply hacked to pieces. Jerusalem and the second temple were razed to the ground. Just as Jesus had predicted.' He paused. 'Dr Hennesey, are you aware that most theologians estimate that Jesus's ministry spanned only one year?'

She knew that Christ had been in his early thirties when he died. 'I never realized that.'

Donovan leaned in closer. 'I hope you'd agree that regardless of one's faith, or even the degree of one's faith, Jesus was a remarkable human being – a philosopher and teacher – someone who emerged from relative obscurity to bring a lasting message of hope, kindness, and faith that still resonates two thousand years later. No other figure in history has had such an impact.' His eyes on her, Donovan's hands migrated to the *Ephemeris Conlusio* and rested flatly on its cover, as if protecting it.

'That book has something to do with all this?' Charlotte noticed that Donovan had yet to look at Santelli, making it clear that this part of the discussion had been choreographed by the two men.

Donovan answered her with a question. 'You're familiar with Christ's resurrection story, the empty tomb?'

'Of course.' Having attended catechism classes throughout elementary school and having gone to an all-girls Catholic high school, she knew plenty about scripture – more than she wanted to. She gave Donovan the straightforward answer that he'd expect – the one that smoothed-out the inconsistencies within all the Gospels: 'Jesus was crucified and buried. Three days later he rose from the dead and reappeared to his disciples' – *in what form is anybody's guess* – 'before ascending to Heaven.' That summed it up nicely, she thought.

'Absolutely.' Donovan was pleased. 'Which brings us to this most remarkable story.' He gently patted the book's cover. 'This is a journal written by Joseph of Arimathea – a biblical figure intimately linked to Jesus's death and resurrection.'

Charlotte was amazed by the Vatican's secret treasure trove. Had this book been stolen too? '*The* Joseph of Arimathea?'

'Yes. The man who buried Christ.' Father Donovan opened the volume revealing pages in ancient Greek, and looked up.

'For centuries the Vatican has feared rebuttal of Christ's role as the Messiah. And this book provides many reasons why.' Stealing a quick glance at Santelli, Donovan braced himself not to falter or let his voice waver. So far, it seemed that the cardinal was satisfied with his performance. 'Though portrayed as Christ's advocate in the New Testament, in fact Joseph of Arimathea was secretly working to undermine Jesus's ministry. You see, Jesus posed a substantial risk to the Jewish elite. Though he smartly avoided confronting the issues of Roman occupation, he had harshly criticized Jewish authority, particularly those priests who had turned God's house into a travesty. In exchange for donations, the Jewish priests were allowing pagans to make sacrifices on the temple's holy altars. They had turned the temple's sacred courtyards into a marketplace. The temple embodied Jewish faith. Therefore, to faithful Jews like Jesus, its steady decline marked the slow death of religious tradition.'

Charlotte recalled Matthew's portrayal of Jesus entering the Jewish temple, ransacking merchants' and money changers' tables. Understandably, Jesus hadn't been keen on the holy place being used as a market.

'Jesus had certainly found fault with the Jewish ruling class,' Donovan went on, 'and he wasn't afraid to let them know it. It was no surprise that it was the Jewish priests who'd sent their own guards to apprehend him. After Jesus was executed, Joseph of Arimathea was chosen by the Sanhedrin to approach Pontius Pilate to negotiate the release of the body. Convinced by Joseph that it would prevent Jesus's fanatical followers from removing the body from the cross, Pilate granted his request.'

Charlotte knew body language. Though Donovan was telling his story confidently, his eyes were shifting. She recalled Giovanni remarking that removing a criminal from a cross would have been unprecedented. No crucified body had ever been recovered. But given the threat Jesus posed to the Jewish aristocracy – who seemingly had everything to lose should the system be challenged – Donovan's explanation seemed plausible. 'But why would Jesus's followers even want to steal his body?'

'In order to declare a resurrection and portray Jesus as divine.'

'So Joseph of Arimathea procured the body to protect it?'

'That's right.' Donovan forced himself to look at her.

Now she was put in a divisive position. There was an obvious question that needed to be presented at this juncture. Her eyes shifted to the laptop screen where the reconstructed image of the crucified man seemed to be watching vigil over the proceedings. 'And the resurrection?' She swallowed hard. 'Did it really happen?'

Donovan grinned. 'Of course,' he replied. 'The body was secretly placed in Joseph's tomb – a location unbeknownst to Jesus's followers. But three days later it had disappeared.'

'Was it stolen?'

Donovan felt Santelli's judicious gaze digging into him. 'That's where the Bible is correct, Dr Hennesey. Four separate New Testament accounts tell us that three days later Jesus rose up from the tomb. Then he reappeared to his followers and ascended to heaven.'

Charlotte didn't know what to think. She certainly wasn't one to believe everything in the Bible, and her early-morning brush-up reading had reminded her why. One passage in particular that described Jesus's physical death on the cross had driven that point home. It began with Matthew 27:50:

Jesus shouted again with a loud voice and gave up His spirit. Suddenly, the curtain of the sanctuary was split in two from top to bottom; the earth quaked and the rocks were split. The tombs also were opened and many bodies of the saints who had gone to their rest were raised. And they came out of the tombs after His resurrection, entered the holy city, and appeared to many.

Reflecting on it, she saw something disturbingly contradictory to the Easter story. It was this passage that first mentioned 'His resurrection' – with no three-day gap or burial having taken place. It made her wonder: if it was Jesus's spirit that had already risen during the moment of death on the cross, then what part of him could possibly have emerged from the tomb three days later? A lifeless, spiritless shell? If bones were actually left behind, should that have surprised anyone? And what about all those other reanimated saintly corpses? Why had no other historical account made reference to so many resurrected *bodies*? She thought she knew the answer. *Because it wasn't a physical resurrection*. The words laid out in the Gospels were being misconstrued. Looking over at the Vatican's second-in-command, she saw a seasoned bureaucrat who would hear nothing of interpretation. Though she needed to continue cautiously, she still had to address the obvious: 'But what about this ossuary, the crucified corpse . . . and this symbol of Christ? Does this book say what it all really means?'

Composed now, Donovan leafed through the *Ephemeris Conlusio* almost to the end, carefully setting it back in front of her.

Studying the pages, Charlotte took in detailed drawings of the ossuary and its contents.

'After Joseph's secret deal with Pilate,' Donovan explained levelly, 'the disciples caused quite a stir in Jerusalem when they discovered that Jesus's body had gone. The body's disappearance allowed them to claim a resurrection had occurred.

Naturally, Pilate came down hard on Joseph of Arimathea, insisting that he fix the problem.' Donovan pointed to the ossuary. 'And that's when Joseph concocted this idea.'

Charlotte tried to compute what it actually meant. 'If these bones aren't Jesus's . . .'

Smiling, Donovan spun his hands, encouraging her to think it through.

'. . . That means Joseph of Arimathea must have *replaced* the body?'

'Absolutely.'

She thought she heard Santelli sigh in relief.

'According to Joseph's account, he acquired *another* crucified corpse – one of two bodies that still remained on a cross on top of Golgotha . . . a criminal who had been killed the same day as Jesus. The body was subjected to standard Jewish burial rituals and allowed to decay for a year.'

'Thus wiping out the second man's identity.' If Donovan was making this all up, he was doing a hell of a good job.

'Yes. A brilliant fabrication intended to prove Christ never left the tomb. A desperate attempt to discredit early Christianity in order to preserve the Jewish aristocracy.'

She let that sink in. Father Donovan's argument was pretty good, plus he possessed what he stated to be a real document to back up his story. And it did agree with the inconsistencies she'd cited earlier, particularly the odd genetic profile and the clubbed knees. The skeleton could have belonged to some convicted criminal from a backwater Roman province. But the fact still remained that the writings in this ancient book were, quite literally, all Greek to her. The priest's interpretation was all that she had to go by. Maybe that was how he had planned it. But why? She looked at him sharply. 'It's obvious Joseph's plan failed.

So why is it that no one previously discovered all this?' As soon as she'd asked the question, she felt herself tighten up. Was she pushing too hard?

Donovan shrugged. 'I believe Joseph of Arimathea died or was killed during those first twelve months, before the body was finally prepared. Perhaps the Sanhedrin or the Romans murdered him. We'll never really know. Let's just be thankful that his scheme was never carried out. Because unlike today, where skilled scientists like yourself can detect foul play, in ancient times, a physical body could have been extremely problematic.'

'And the ossuary was found only recently?' She braced herself for the answer.

'The *Ephemeris Conlusio* was obtained by the Vatican in the early fourteenth century. But it wasn't taken seriously until a lone archaeologist unearthed a tomb just north of Jerusalem a few weeks ago. Luckily he was smart enough to know that if he approached us discreetly we'd pay him very handsomely for it.'

Momentarily perplexed, Charlotte let the explanation roll over in her mind a couple times. If Donovan was telling the truth, that would mean that this anonymous *archaeologist* might have killed people to get the ossuary and the Vatican may have been none-the-wiser about its procurement. Possibly Bersei had jumped to the wrong conclusion. But he was a smart man – a *very* smart man. She'd personally witnessed that he wasn't the type who'd make hasty assumptions about anything. What had he discovered that made him so sure of his claims? 'A first-century relic of a crucified man bearing the symbol of Christ,' she murmured. 'A priceless artifact . . . for all the wrong reasons.'

'Exactly. This was a seemingly authentic discovery that, without proper explanation, may have caused needless hardship for the Christian faith. We needed to be sure it all matched the accounts in Joseph's journal before finalizing any transaction. And thanks to your hard work, I'm certain we've closed this case.'

Charlotte's eyes wandered back to the opened manuscript where Joseph's drawings inventoried the ossuary and all its contents. Then she noticed something. The scroll cylinder wasn't included there. Her brow furrowed.

'Is something wrong?' Donovan asked.

Taking the plastic-sheathed cylinder in her hand, she said, 'Why isn't this shown there?' She motioned to the drawings.

Donovan suddenly looked nervous. 'Not sure,' he said, shaking his head. He tentatively glanced over at Santelli. He had tried to avoid this, not knowing what the scroll inside might actually say.

'Why don't you open it?' Santelli boldly suggested.

Taken aback, Charlotte said, 'I've never really handled ancient documents before. We were waiting to . . .'

'Nothing to worry about, Dr Hennesey,' Santelli cut in. 'Father Donovan is an expert in handling ancient documents. Besides, I doubt we'll be wanting to put any of this on display in the Vatican Museum.'

'Okay.' She handed the bagged cylinder to the white-faced librarian.

'Go ahead, Patrick,' Santelli urged. 'Open it.'

Amazed that the cardinal could be so brazen, Donovan proceeded to open the bag. Withdrawing the cylinder, he removed the loose end cap and tipped the scroll out onto the table. He exchanged eager glances with Santelli and Hennesey. 'Here we go.' With the utmost care, he unfurled the scroll on top of the plastic and held it flat with both hands. Seeing what was there, he felt instantly relieved and pushed it further along the table so the others could see it too.

All eyes took in what had been inked onto the ancient vellum. It was an unusual drawing that blended all sorts of images. The focal point was a Jewish menorah superimposed over a cross entwined with leafy tendrils. The symbol that was on the ossuary's side was repeated here four times, at the end of each arm of the cross.

'What does this all mean?' Santelli asked Donovan.

'I'm not sure,' he admitted. He tried to conceal the fact that he noticed the edge of the scroll that faced toward him looked freshly scored. Had someone purposely cut away part of the scroll? He rested his thumbs flat over the edge to conceal the marks.

'Whatever it means, it's beautiful,' Charlotte interjected.

'Yes it is,' Donovan agreed, smiling.

'Well then, Dr Hennesey,' Santelli spoke up. 'You've done a brilliant job. We cannot thank you enough and the Holy Father extends his thanks as well. Just please be diligent in adhering to our request to not discuss this with anyone – including members of your own family as well as the press.'

'You have my word,' she promised.

'Excellent. If you don't mind, I'll have Father Martin escort you out. I just have a few items to discuss with Father Donovan. And though your work here is finished, please do feel free to stay with us as long as you'd like.'

58.

Leaving the Apostolic Palace, Charlotte headed directly to the lab to see if Bersei had returned.

Walking along the basement corridor, her eyes were drawn to the door of the surveillance room. It was still ajar. Against her better judgement, she wrapped her knuckles on it.

'Mr Conte. Can I have a word with you, please?'

No answer.

She pushed it open and poked her head inside. It was empty – nothing but bare shelving lining the walls. Even the ceiling panel had been moved back in place. 'What the . . .'

Pulling the door closed, Charlotte proceeded cautiously down the eerily quiet hall. She slid her keycard through the reader next to the lab door, fully expecting that it would not work. But the lock disengaged with an electromechanical tumble and she made her way inside.

For the first time since she'd been here, the lights and air-conditioning in the lab had been turned off. Groping along the wall for the control panel, she flicked a few switches up.

When the lights came on, she couldn't believe what she was

seeing. The entire lab was empty – the ossuary, the bones, the relics . . . all gone. Even the computer CPUs were missing from their bays.

Fearing the worst, she didn't move into the room – just turned the lights off again and doubled-back to the door. That's when she heard footsteps out in the corridor, growing louder as they approached.

Now what? There was no window on the door, so she couldn't see who was coming. Father Donovan? Bersei? She listened closer. She'd strode up and down the corridor with both of them, but couldn't recall this rhythm – this smooth stepping she now heard.

What if it was Conte?

Now that she'd seen the empty closet and lab, the laptop she was carrying – the only remaining proof of the Vatican's secret project – felt like raw meat in the lion's den. Her whole body stiffened, praying that she'd hear a different door open, or that the steps would retreat back down the corridor.

The footsteps stopped and she could see a shadow moving into the light penetrating in from beneath the door.

Lunging back into the darkened lab, she silently felt her way along the first workstation and crouched low to the floor just as the door lock turned.

The hair on the back of her neck prickled as the door creaked open, light from the corridor spilling into the room. She was certain that whoever it was couldn't see her below the table. The intruder paused. Listening?

Charlotte held her breath and steadied the laptop bag with both hands, remaining perfectly still. A very long moment went by. Then there was the flicking sound of switches and the over-head lighting instantly stripped away the darkness.

No movement.

Her legs were starting to cramp up.

Pulling the door closed, the intruder moved slowly into the room, snaked between the workstations and back toward the break room.

Though she couldn't see what was happening, the second she sensed that the intruder had gone into the break room, she sprang up and lunged for the door. Just as her hand turned the handle, she glimpsed Conte as he returned into the lab . . . and his face twisted into a snarl.

59.

Charlotte sprinted down the corridor, the rubber soles of her shoes squeaking urgently as they pushed off the polished vinyl tiles. Without looking back, she could hear Conte in pursuit.

Up ahead, the elevator was closed. Knowing she couldn't risk any delay, she headed directly for the fire exit, shoving the door back hard on its hinges. She practically flew up the stairwell, taking the steps three at a time, clutching the laptop tightly to her side. Halfway up the second flight of stairs, the sound of Conte slamming against the basement door blasted up at her. Climbing higher, she glimpsed his silhouette spiralling upward.

At the top of the landing, Charlotte knew she'd have two choices: the service door leading outside, or the staff entrance accessing the museum gallery. Once she got there, she immediately pushed open the service door so that it swung wide. But instead of going outside, she wheeled toward the staff entrance door and entered the museum as quietly as possible, easing the door closed behind her.

*

Rounding the last set of switchback steps, Conte heard the lock on the service door snap into place as it closed. Charging up the last few treads, he flung the door open and ran outside.

The geneticist was nowhere in sight – not running down the garden walkways, not scampering around the corner of the building. And there was no worthy hiding place anywhere close by. He spun round, making his way back into the building.

Moving quickly through the Pio Christian gallery, Charlotte was determined to get out of Vatican City. That meant heading straight for the Sant' Anna Gate. With her money belt containing her cash, credit cards, and passport secured tightly around her waist, everything in her dorm room could be sacrificed.

Feeling light-headed – not from the run, but from the Melphalan swirling through her system – she took a few deep breaths to get her head together. A quick pang of nausea came and went.

Knowing Conte would only be temporarily thrown off, she struggled with how to proceed. Should she lose herself in the museum's massive galleries? There was plenty of floor space here, no doubt. But with surveillance cameras mounted all throughout the exhibits, she didn't want to chance him calling museum security. Plus in the long hallways that ran the length of the building's mammoth footprint, she'd be easy to spot – the curly chestnut-haired lone tourist with a bright pink blouse and computer bag who wasn't stopping for exhibits.

Luckily, the Pio Christian gallery was in close proximity to the building's main entrance. After scanning the area beyond the glass doors, she slipped outside.

Threading through the crowds loitering in the courtyard, she rounded the corner of the building, hurrying along the walkway that ran along the museum's eastern wall. Conte was still nowhere in sight. But that didn't ease her concern, because she knew first-hand that he wasn't the type to give up.

Through a short tunnel that passed beneath the city's old ramparts, she emerged into the small village that clustered in the shadow of the Apostolic Palace's rear edifice. For a moment, she wondered if Father Donovan was still in there consorting with his puppet master, Santelli. How could such a nice man be involved in all this?

Turning onto Borgo Pio, her eyes reached for the open gate and the Swiss Guards who diligently manned it. She wondered if Conte had called ahead to alert them. Would they try to detain her? She pushed forward knowing she had to take that chance.

Then, only twenty metres from the gate, she saw him. Though she hadn't noticed it before, she could swear that there was some kind of wound on the side of his head.

Hands on his hips and breathing heavily, Conte had positioned himself between her and the gate, daring her to take another step.

But she did just that. Determined that there was no going back, her only hope was to stay the course and push forward. This was a public place. The guards were close. Surely they wouldn't tolerate an altercation here, even if they were on his side.

Then she broke into a sprint, eyes focused on the gate.

Conte reacted instantly, shooting out onto the roadway, just missing a delivery van that was heading into the city. A horn blared, but he ignored it – sights set on his quarry.

She managed another ten metres before Conte drew perilously close. There was no way she'd get around him.

Conte lunged in front of Charlotte, stopping her dead in her tracks. 'You're not going anywhere with that,' he growled, eyeing the laptop bag. For some reason, the geneticist didn't look scared. He noticed that she kept glancing at the huge purple lump on his temple, then over his shoulder toward the gate.

Then she did something he hadn't expected. She screamed.

For a moment, Conte was paralysed.

'Help!' Charlotte screamed again, louder this time.

The guards at the gate heard her. Two of them, dressed in blue coveralls and black berets, were running toward her, drawing their holstered Berettas and pushing through the crowd of startled tourists.

Conte considered grabbing the bag. But where would he go? He punished himself for not having a weapon. 'Remember your confidentiality agreement, Dr Hennesey,' he stated calmly. 'Or I'll have to come and find you.'

When she saw his attention momentarily shift to the approaching guards, she took the opportunity to do something she'd been thinking about since the moment she met this creep. Bending slightly at the knees, she swept a powerful left foot at his crotch, landing a perfect shot.

Conte buckled. Wretching, he had to put his hands to the ground to not fall flat on his face. 'You fucking cunt!' The veins in his red face bulged as he stared malevolently at the American.

The two guards arrived and planted themselves on opposite sides, guns levelled at his head. 'Stay still!' one of them commanded, first in English, then Italian.

Gasping, Conte immediately recognized him as the *cacasenno*, or smart-ass, who manned the gate the day he arrived at Vatican City with Donovan. The guard had made the connection too and flashed a satisfied grin.

'What's going on here?' the second one asked Charlotte in English.

'This man was threatening me, trying to take my bag.' Her voice was urgent.

The first guard was asking Conte for identification.

'I'm not . . .' – he spit out more vomit and bile – 'carrying it on me.' He was sure Santelli wouldn't approve of name-dropping in this situation. Later, he would insist on a phone call to the secretary. He also decided against telling the guards that the laptop contained critical information since that would only lead to bigger problems if they insisted on details. For now, he'd have to play the game.

The second guard had also asked Charlotte for identification, which she readily provided. The ornate papal crest on her guest badge showed she was a guest of the secretariat. 'You're free to go, Dr Hennesey.'

He turned to Conte. 'And you'll need to come with us, *signore*.'

Conte had no option but to comply.

The guards helped him to his feet and remained at his side, Berettas drawn.

Breathing a sigh of relief, Charlotte made her way to the gate. Once safely outside Vatican City, she angled her way to Via Della Conciliazione, waved down a taxi, and told the driver to take her directly to Fiumicino Airport. *Rapidamente!* The car lurched forward as the driver stepped hard on the accelerator, but this was one time she wasn't going to complain about Rome's insane drivers. She couldn't get out of this place fast enough.

Only now did she realize that her entire body was trembling.

Peering out of the rear window, she watched the dome of St Peter's Basilica as it shrank away, fingers still clamped around the laptop bag.

The taxi driver hit the autostrada and Charlotte watched the needle on the speedometer climb to 160 kilometres per hour. She sank back and put on her seat belt. With Rome safely behind her, Charlotte pulled out her cell phone and called Evan Aldrich. So what if it was still the middle of the night in Phoenix? He picked up almost instantly.

'Evan?'

'Hey, Charlie. I was just thinking about you.'

Hearing his voice instantly soothed her. 'Hi.' Her voice wavered.

'Everything okay?'

'No. Not at all.' Lowering her voice and turning away from the driver, she gave him a brief rundown of what had transpired. 'I'm heading to the airport now.'

'I was going to surprise you, but . . . I was actually on my way there to see you. In fact, my flight just arrived at Fiumicino a few minutes ago.'

'What? You're kidding!' Her shoulders relaxed.

'I'm at the baggage carousel right now. I'll tell you where to meet me.'

60.
ABRUZZO, ITALY

An hour north-east of Rome, Salvatore Conte's rented black Alfa Romeo saloon climbed the SS5 autostrada along the Apennine mountain range into Monte Scuncole. The afternoon sky was a dull grey that choked the sun to a fizzled shade of white. A light drizzle sprayed the windscreen.

Trying to settle his thoughts, Patrick Donovan stared out of the misty passenger window at the patchwork of vineyards in the valley below.

Following Charlotte Hennesey's unanticipated and hasty departure earlier that morning, and Conte's embarrassing bail-out from the Swiss Guard detention centre, a profoundly anxious Cardinal Santelli had given him specific instructions about what was to happen next: *'You'll need to see to it that this chapter of the Church's history disappears without a trace – by whatever means necessary, Patrick. I'll have Conte assist you in destroying the ossuary and everything it contains . . . the manuscript too. Without the physical evidence, the only thing that should remain is a legend. Understood?'*

The relics and book could easily have been destroyed in the Vatican laboratory, so he intuited that this drive was about far more than a simple disposal of the ossuary. Glancing at the mercenary, he knew that Dr Bersei's mysterious disappearance coincided all too well with Conte's unexplained head wound.

Conte slowed the saloon and turned right down a narrow unpaved road. Thick grass and low bushes scraped the car's undercarriage. They drove on in silence until the track broadened by a small grove of beech trees. Conte braked, and killed the engine, leaving the keys in the ignition. He pushed the boot release button.

Emerging from the car, both men circled to the back. Shovels and picks had been stowed diagonally behind the ossuary. Conte grabbed them and pushed a spade into Donovan's hands. 'We'll need to dig deep.'

'Now that this thing's over' – Conte wiped away sweat from his forehead with the back of his muddy hand – 'I've got a couple of questions for you.' He thrust his shovel into the soil and leaned on it. The smell of fresh earth filled the damp air. The light rain had resumed.

Donovan peered up at him through foggy glasses. 'Haven't you seen enough to answer your questions?'

The mercenary shook his head. 'Whose bones do you really believe are in that ossuary?' Salvatore Conte wasn't questioning his own faith. That was something he'd abandoned long ago. But the theft of the ossuary and its scientific analysis, along with Bersei's discoveries at the Torlonia catacombs had really piqued his curiosity.

'You've seen the same evidence as me.' Donovan stretched his arms. 'What do you think?'

Conte smiled. 'It's not my job to think.'

'Honestly, I don't know.'

'So why go to all this trouble?'

Donovan considered this. 'The evidence is substantial. For all we know, these are the bones of Jesus Christ. Our duty is to protect the Church. Surely you can see that action had to be taken.'

'Well, if that's Jesus in there' – the mercenary pointed to the car's trunk – 'I'd say you're protecting an enormous lie.'

Donovan hadn't expected a man like Salvatore Conte to understand the broader implications of all this. Two millennia of human history would be fundamentally affected by the ossuary and its contents. Humankind needed truths to bring people together, not controversies. He'd learned that first-hand on the streets of Belfast. Patrick Donovan was supremely well versed in Catholic history, but what he was defending had little to do with old books. There was a moral imperative that needed to be preserved so that what spiritual belief remained in this chaotic, materialistic world could remain strong. 'I'm surprised. You don't strike me as someone who'd really give a shit about that.'

Surprised by the priest's language, Conte shot him a look. Suddenly the task before him seemed easier. 'I don't actually. Besides, if there was a God,' he said sarcastically, 'men like you and me wouldn't exist.' He continued digging.

Donovan was disgusted by the idea that he and Conte shared any commonalities, but knew that perhaps the mercenary was right. *I am part of this.* After all, Conte wasn't operating autonomously – he was merely a foot soldier. And it wasn't Conte who'd beseeched Santelli to take action to retrieve the ossuary – he had done that. Granted, he had never anticipated the extreme measures Santelli would employ, but he hadn't intervened to stop him.

'What really happened to Dr Bersei?' Donovan's tone was forceful. Somehow he knew his own fate was linked to Conte's answer.

'Don't worry yourself about him.' Conte's hard face was twisted. 'He got what he deserved and I spared you the dirty work. That's all you need to know.'

'Why was he in the catacombs?' Donovan felt a swell of anger.

Conte considered dodging the question, but knew that at this juncture, Donovan was no threat. 'The scroll he found in the ossuary had a picture on it – and he figured out that it matched a fresco in the Torlonia catacombs. Apparently this Joseph of Arimathea character had a crypt in Rome. Seems Bersei thought that's where Jesus was originally dried out. Who'd have thought?'

Donovan's eyes went wide. Could it be? Had he found the actual tomb?

'Let me give you a piece of advice,' Conte added. 'Don't get too attached to the girl, either.' He liked it that each revelation weakened the priest's resolve. 'She's only on temporary reprieve.'

'What's that supposed to mean?'

'Santelli told me all that nonsense you fed her about the man-uscript. Nice story. But you're failing to grasp that you've already given her too much information. Did the cardinal tell you she skipped off with her laptop . . . loaded up with all the data?'

'No, he didn't.' No wonder Santelli was a bundle of nerves about all this – the whole thing was on the verge of unravelling. Conte had been sloppy – the reports coming out of Jerusalem now included a computerized photofit image that bore an uncanny resemblance to him. Giovanni Bersei was dead. Now Hennesey had managed to leave with all the proof she needed to implicate the Vatican.

'It's not good. I've got to fix that too and her blood will be on your hands.'

Hatred showed in the priest's eyes.

'Don't look at me like that, Donovan. You're the one who insisted on bringing in outsiders.'

'We had no choice.'

'Exactly.'

'What are you going to do to her?'

Grinning deviously, Conte waited before responding. 'Wouldn't you just love to know. You sound like an infatuated lover, for Christ's sake. Santelli feels that two deaths linked so closely to the Vatican would arouse too much suspicion. But if a freak accident should happen to befall the lovely geneticist back home in the States, the authorities would be none the wiser. Of course, I'll be sure to show her a good time before she goes.' Then we'll see who gets the last laugh, he thought. Conte sighed, as if bored. 'Keep digging.'

Donovan's jaw tensed as he thrust his shovel into the dirt, the latent anger pushed deep down in his soul fighting its way to the surface.

It took them almost three hours to carve out the five-foot-deep rectangular pit.

This pit could easily accommodate the ossuary *and* a body, Donovan thought.

At last Conte threw his shovel to the ground. 'Looks good.' Both men were lathered in dirt and sweat. 'Let's get the ossuary.'

They walked back to the saloon.

Donovan turned to him. 'Why are we burying this? Can't we just destroy it on the ground?'

Without responding, Conte leaned into the trunk and lifted the ossuary's lid. Resting on top of the bones was the *Ephemeris*

Conlusio and two thick grey blocks that resembled moulded clay.

Donovan pointed to the C-4. 'Is that—'

'Oh, I think a man with your background should know. Or didn't the IRA use this stuff to blow up Protestant storefronts in Belfast? Boom!' Conte opened his eyes in mock astonishment and splayed his fingers.

How on earth could he have known that? That had been years ago – another lifetime.

'So best to blow it apart underground, wouldn't you agree?'

Donovan wondered if Conte would hit him on the head with a shovel, then push him into the hole and detonate the explosives. Or was he concealing a gun? Perhaps the mercenary would elect to kill him with his bare hands.

Conte stood to face him. 'You take that end.' He moved to one side, wrapping his hands round the ossuary's base, while Donovan stepped forward to grasp the other end.

They heaved the ossuary out of the trunk, lugging it over to the edge of the pit.

'Drop on three.' Conte counted down.

Father Donovan felt a sudden dread as he watched the ossuary hit the earth with a dull thud. The lid slammed back onto the base, producing a crack along its etchings. He thought about Santelli sitting in his office, working diligently to preserve the huge institution created by the man these innocent bones might have belonged to. He thought about his meeting with Santelli weeks earlier when the initial battle plan had been mapped out. Once again, the Vatican seemed to have emerged victorious.

Conte turned around for his spade. Wrapping his hands around its handle he studied the sharp edges. One solid blow to Donovan's skull should do it. He'd toss the body in with the

374

box. Covered with dirt, the C-4 would do the rest. From the corner of his eye, he noticed that the priest was crouching down as if to tie his shoe.

Rising to his feet, a very different man now faced him. The priest was aiming a silver handgun directly at his chest. Eyeing him disdainfully, as if the gun-wielding curator was almost comical, Conte scrutinized the weapon – a standard issue Beretta, most likely lifted from the Swiss Guard barracks. The safety was off.

Donovan was determined to survive, not just for himself, but more so to preserve the innocent life of Charlotte Hennesey and anyone else he'd unwittingly involved in this fiasco. 'Drop the shovel,' he demanded.

Shaking his head chastisingly, Conte squatted to rest the shovel on the spongy grass, then quickly went for the Glock strapped round his right ankle, beneath his trouser leg.

The first shot was unexpectedly loud, striking Conte in the right hand with appalling force. The slug ripped cleanly through flesh and bone, grazing the mercenary's ankle as it exited. Conte flinched, but didn't scream. Blood bubbled out from the hole and his damaged hand curled into a tight claw. He peered up at Donovan. 'Motherfucker. You're going to pay for that.'

'Stand up,' Donovan demanded, daring to move a bit closer, levelling the gun at Conte's head. Killing the son of a bitch wasn't going to be nearly as hard as he had thought. *Give me strength, Lord. Help me make this right.*

At first, it looked as if the mercenary would comply. But what happened next was far too fast for him. Conte sprang forward, burying a shoulder in Donovan's chest, forcing him back and then down.

Remarkably, the priest managed to maintain his grip on the Beretta. Conte reached for it with his left hand, but miscalculated, cupping the muzzle. A second shot cracked through the air and Conte screamed out in frustration. Now his good hand had been mangled too.

Badly wounded, Conte still managed to force Donovan's gun-hand down to the ground. Cocking his elbow back, he landed a shot just below the priest's wrist, forcing the Beretta away. Next he brought the elbow down hard on Donovan's face, crunching bone and cartilage. The priest's nose instantly spewed blood and he cried out in agony.

Thrashing viciously, Donovan tried to escape from under the assassin, but to no avail. Conte let go of the priest's arm to prepare another elbow-shot. That's when Donovan had a fraction of a second to strike the only vulnerable thing he could see through his blood-splattered bifocals. He jabbed hard with his fist at the purple lump on the side of Conte's head.

It worked. Momentarily dazed, Conte teetered off to one side, allowing Donovan to stagger to his feet. Seeing there was no chance of getting the Beretta, he ran away.

After a few seconds, the blaring pain subsided, but Conte was still seeing stars through a haze of red covering his right eye. Blood poured down his face where Donovan's ring had opened the hammer wound. Shaking his head, he spotted the priest retreating along the track towards the autostrada.

The fumbled Beretta was under Conte's shoulder. He tried grabbing it, but neither crippled hand would obey. If picking the damn thing up was going to be a problem, firing it would be impossible. '*Affanculo! Sticchiu!*' Abandoning the weapon, Conte sprang to his feet in pursuit.

Halfway to the autostrada, Donovan was running frantically,

glancing back over his shoulder. Not only was Conte back on his feet, he was in full sprint, quickly closing the gap. It would only be a matter of time until he caught up. Unarmed, Donovan knew he was no match for the trained killer, wounded or not. *Please, Lord, help me get through this.* Donovan heard Conte's hoarse panting. He was only a couple of paces behind him, ready to pounce. Calling on all his reserve energy, Donovan pushed his body to the limit.

Five metres.

Two metres.

As Donovan's front foot hit the autostrada's tarmac he barely registered a fast-approaching car just on the periphery of his field of vision. A blaring horn. Headlights perilously close. Squealing rubber. He barely saw the yellow-painted line that divided the roadway. By some miracle, the car veered behind him . . . just as Conte's feet touched the roadway.

Collapsing onto the roadway, he watched Conte's legs bend and snap in the wrong direction against the car's front end, his body hurled up onto the hood, striking the windshield, tumbling over the roof and onto the roadway.

Trying to compensate for the sudden manoeuvre, the Mercedes's anti-lock brakes and traction control system simultaneously went into action. But the saloon couldn't defy the physical combination of excessive speed, a sudden turn, and rain-slicked pavement. It careened into a large fir tree, the bodywork crumpling around the trunk in a horrible cacophony of twisting metal and breaking glass. The driver – a young female with long blonde hair who apparently hadn't been wearing a seat belt – was ejected through the windscreen and hung limp across the hood of the car, neck broken, blood everywhere. The sound of the Mercedes's rear tyre spinning and the hiss of a broken radiator played along to the car's radio, still loudly throwing off a techno dance number.

There was nothing Donovan could do for her.

Conte was down, but remarkably, still moving.

Donovan staggered over to the mangled assassin, convinced that a threat still existed. There was no way he was going to gamble that Salvatore Conte was going to have even the slightest chance of making it out of here alive. Looking both ways down the quiet roadway, Donovan clawed for the handgun strapped to Conte's right ankle, tearing it free. The chamber was loaded, safety off. As he jabbed it against Conte's lumpy right temple, he swore he could hear the church bells chiming over Belfast. 'God forgive me.'

Father Patrick Donovan squeezed the trigger.

61.

Donovan dragged Conte's broken body into a thicket of bushes by the side of the road and concealed it beneath a shallow covering of leaves and branches. Stripping the mercenary of his wallet, he came across a syringe and a vial of clear liquid, and pocketed them too.

Next, he ran back along the track to the pit, easing himself down into it. Donovan manhandled the two broken halves of the lid out onto the ground, then carefully pulled the two bricks of C-4 from the ossuary, leaving them in the hole.

Planting both feet firmly beside the ossuary, he crouched low and grabbed beneath it, lengthwise. With little room to manoeuvre, it took him a while to steadily ease it up along the dirt wall, its weight not so much a problem as its awkward dimensions. He managed to coax it up and out, until it rested on the rim of the pit. Sweating profusely and struggling to catch his breath, he climbed out.

Moving the Alfa closer, Donovan made a final effort to hoist the ossuary into the boot and stowed the shovels behind the box. Slamming the lid, he ducked into the driver's seat, a dirty, bloody mess. Fatigue swept over him. His muscles were aching and his smashed nose throbbed painfully. But, all things considered, he felt pretty good, the waning adrenaline still giving him an almost euphoric high. Overall, he was pleased with his performance. It had been a long time since he'd handled a weapon or fought in self-defence. But as his father used to say, *'The Irish forgive their great men only when they are safely buried.'*

God had protected him . . . and he knew why. This injustice needed to be undone.

He wiped the blood and prints from the Beretta and Conte's Glock, both still smelling of burnt gunpowder, and stashed them inside the glove compartment. He'd toss the Glock in the first river he came across, but for now, he'd hold onto the Beretta. Switching on the ignition, he circled the saloon back along the track.

When he reached the autostrada, Donovan paused, surprised that anyone had yet to arrive on the scene. There hadn't even been another car.

Eyeing the brush-covered corpse on side of the roadway, Donovan knew that once discovered, it would be difficult, if not impossible to identify the mangled mercenary. Fingerprints, dental records, or any other forensic identification technique, no matter how sophisticated, would no doubt come up blank. Equally certain was the fact that Conte couldn't be tied in any way to the Vatican. He was a drifter, plain and simple – a man from obscurity, returning to obscurity.

He wondered which way to go.

With little deliberation, Patrick Donovan turned right, heading southwest. As the scene in his rear-view mirror disappeared, he prayed silently for the soul of the woman driver.

62.
JERUSALEM

Seated at his kitchen table, sipping a late afternoon tea, Razak was interrupted by his cell phone. Checking the screen, the caller I.D. flashed 'UNAVAILABLE'. Confused, he picked it up. '*As-Salaam?*'

'I saw you on television.'

The man spoke in English and his voice was vaguely familiar. 'Who is this?'

'A friend.'

Razak set down his glass. Maybe a reporter, he thought. Or perhaps even someone with information. But he swore he'd heard the lilting accent somewhere before.

'I know who stole the ossuary,' the voice stated flatly.

Razak straightened in his chair. 'I don't know what you're talking about.' The caller would need to be more specific before he would confirm what had been taken.

'Yes you do. I met with you only a few weeks ago in Rome. You delivered a package to me at Café Greco. You gave me your card and said to call you if there were any problems.'

In his mind's eye, Razak recalled the bald man with glasses,

381

sitting at the table with wiry fingers wrapped tightly around a pint of lager. He had been wearing black with a white collar – a Christian cleric. Razak remembered that the leather satchel he had given the priest contained a confidential dossier, but he was trying to understand how it had anything to do with the ossuary. 'I do,' he replied tentatively. 'I'm listening.'

'The book contained very detailed information about an ossuary buried deep beneath Temple Mount in a hidden chamber.'

'What book?'

'There were nine other ossuaries there, too. Am I not correct?'

'Okay.' Razak's voice was encouraging. Not quite an admission.

'And I have the tenth ossuary.'

Wishing he could record this conversation, Razak paused, stupefied. 'You killed thirteen men. You desecrated a very holy site.' He stood from the table and began pacing the apartment.

'No,' the caller cut in, insistent. 'Not me.'

Razak sensed the man's sincerity.

'. . . But I know who did,' the voice added.

'And how do I know you're telling the truth?'

'Because I'm going to give the ossuary back to you . . . So you can put an end to this, as you see fit.'

At first, Razak didn't know what to say. 'And why would you do that?'

'I see what is happening there, in Jerusalem,' the man continued. 'Too many innocent people suffering. I know you agree. You're a just man. I could tell that the moment I met you.'

It was almost too much for Razak to comprehend. 'I don't suppose you'll be making the delivery yourself?'

'Unfortunately, there's more work I'll need to do. I'm sure you'll understand that I cannot take that risk.'

'I see.'

A pause.

Razak couldn't help but to ask: 'What was inside the ossuary that made it so valuable?'

There was a long pause.

'Something very profound.'

Razak shuddered when he thought about Barton's wild theory about fanatical Christians. Could the remains of Jesus really have been inside the missing ossuary? Did this mysterious book tell of the relic's ancient origins?

'Will the contents be returned with the box?'

'Unfortunately, I cannot allow that.'

Razak dared another question. 'Was it really *his* remains inside that box?' He tried to prepare himself for the response.

The caller hesitated, clearly knowing whom Razak was referring to. 'There's no way to know for sure. For your own safety, please don't ask any more about this. Just let me know where you'd like it delivered.'

Razak thought about it. He pictured Barton sitting in an Israeli prison cell, awaiting trial. Then he considered how Farouq – the singular force behind the delivery of the book that had set everything in motion – had likely played him like a fool, jeopardizing both peace and lives. Razak decided to give the caller a name and a shipping address. 'When should I expect it to arrive?'

'It will be sent out today, I assure you. I'll spare no expense to have it to you as soon as possible.'

'And the book?' Razak enquired.

'I'll be sure to include that as well.'

'Can you send that to a different address?'

'Absolutely.'

Razak gave him the second mailing address.

'And for the record,' the caller added, 'that English archaeologist being held by Israeli police had nothing to do with all this.'

'I suspected that,' Razak replied. 'And the real thieves? What will happen to them?'

Another pause. 'I think you'll agree that justice has its own way of finding the guilty.'

The line went dead.

SATURDAY

63.
TEMPLE MOUNT

After dawn prayer, Razak headed straight for the El-Aqsa Mosque. He hadn't slept at all last night, his mind mulling over the shocking phone call he'd received from the priest he had met in Rome three weeks ago. The Israeli police were right. Only an insider could have abetted the thieves. Now it was clear that Graham Barton wasn't the insider.

In the rear of the building, he made his way down a service corridor ending at a newly installed metal fire door. Above it, a sign in Arabic read: 'Open only in case of emergency.'

He reached down and turned the handle.

Beyond the door, a freshly painted spiral staircase wound down twelve metres, directly to the subterranean Marwani Mosque. A secret passageway? Could this be the modern equivalent of the one Joseph of Arimathea used two thousand years ago?

Turning his attention back to the corridor, he let the door swing shut.

Off each side of this hallway lay the mosque's storage rooms.

His heartbeat quickened as he went over to the first door and opened it. Inside there were cardboard boxes stacked against one wall and a shelving unit containing cleaning supplies. Another shelf was stacked with fresh copies of the Qur'an, ready to provide spiritual enlightenment to new Muslim recruits. He shut the door and moved on to the next room.

Behind the second door were stacked chairs, a discarded desk, and spare oriental carpets rolled up in plastic, propped against a side wall. Against the rear wall lay the charred remnants of the *mihrab* that had been set ablaze by a young Australian Jew, Michael Rohan, on August 21, 1969. Razak remembered being told that the fanatic had informed Israeli authorities that his act had been inspired by God to expedite the coming of the Messiah and the rebuilding of the Third Jewish Temple.

Closing the door, Razak considered that maybe his theory was wrong. He wanted it to be wrong.

Next he continued down the hall to the door that marked the threshold to the last storage room. Trying the handle, he was surprised to find that it had been locked. He tried it again. Nothing.

Puzzled, he made his way back through the mosque's spacious prayer hall, out into the bright morning sun, and across the esplanade toward the Qur'anic teaching school. If he were to find the Keeper there, he'd insist that the room be opened for inspection.

But upstairs, Farouq's office was empty.

Razak stood motionless for a moment, struggling with what he should do. Then reluctantly, he circled behind the desk and searched its four drawers.

Inside, he discovered a strange array of items that included a compact handgun and a litre of Wild Turkey bourbon that, since the Qur'an strictly forbade drinking alcohol, Razak fervently hoped Farouq had confiscated from someone. There was an ornate bronze casket stashed in the left bottom drawer, but it was locked. Finally, he found what he was looking for: a key ring. Snatching it up, he made his way downstairs and out of the building.

Traversing the esplanade, Razak was unaware of the Keeper trailing discreetly behind him.

Negotiating his way through the El-Aqsa's prayer hall, Razak produced the key ring, stopping at the rear corridor's locked door. One by one, he tried the keys. Coming across a small, tarnished skeleton key, he wondered if it opened the casket that he'd found in Farouq's desk. He continued through the set. Finally, with only two keys left and a waning sense of hope, a silver key slid easily into the lock. Praying silently and holding his breath, Razak turned it.

Clicking, the lock gave way.

Razak depressed the door handle. Beyond the threshold, the windowless room was dark. Moving inside, Razak fumbled for the light switch, leaving the door open. The room appeared empty.

The overhead strip lights crackled and slowly came to life, strobing the room with quick flashes that played with his eyes.

Then the room was aglow.

Instantly, Razak's face slackened in bewilderment.

Along the rear wall, the nine ossuaries, each etched in Hebrew text with the names of Joseph and his family members, had been neatly arranged on the vinyl-tiled floor.

'Allah save us,' Razak muttered in Arabic.

From the corner of his eye he detected a figure in the doorway and spun round.

Farouq.

'You've done well, Razak.' Farouq crossed his arms, stuffing his hands into the loose sleeves of his black tunic. 'You mustn't be troubled by this. They will shortly disappear.'

The Keeper's talent for making things vanish was starting to sicken him. 'What have you done?'

'A noble deed to help our people,' the Keeper stated flatly. 'Don't concern yourself with the small sacrifices that need to be made.'

'Small sacrifices?' Razak stared at the ossuaries. 'You framed an innocent man.'

'Barton? Innocent? None of *them* are innocent, Razak. Not when their motive is to threaten Allah.'

'Did the other council members know about this?'

The Keeper made a dismissive motion. 'Does that matter?'

'You sent me to Rome to deliver a package to the Vatican – a book that led them to perpetrate this unthinkable crime. I feel some explanation is warranted. Many men died for this and an innocent man is now being detained by the police. And what exactly have you achieved?'

'Razak.' Farouq shook his head in disappointment. 'You haven't grasped the seriousness of our situation here. We've achieved solidarity and unity. Our people rely on us to protect both them and their faith. And a faith like ours must remain strong throughout. Here in Jerusalem what we protect isn't just a patch of land or a sacred shrine. Islam is everything. To undermine its teachings is to take away a Muslim's soul. Don't you understand?'

'But this isn't a war.'

'It's been a war since the very beginning. Ever since the Christians and Jews decided to reclaim this forgotten land made sacred by the great prophet Muhammad, Allah grant him peace.

Need I remind you that I've shed my own blood to protect our people and this place? A great number of people have given their lives so that men like you' – he jabbed a finger – 'can still have homes here.'

Razak elected to remain silent. Undeniably a real debt was owed to men like Farouq, men who had vehemently opposed Israeli occupation. But he was tired of the rhetoric, tired of the perpetual hatred that plagued this place. He wanted answers. And Razak knew for certain that those answers would begin with knowing exactly how a book delivered to Rome had divulged the precise location of an ancient crypt concealed beneath Temple Mount for centuries.

'What was it that I delivered to Rome for you?'

Farouq contemplated the question. 'If I tell you, will you feel at peace with what has happened?'

'Perhaps.'

Farouq turned toward the door. 'Come with me.'

64.

Inside Farouq's office, Razak sat anxiously awaiting the Keeper's explanation for enabling Christians to violate the Temple Mount – a deed so vile and deceitful that no motive seemed good enough.

The old man held out his hand. 'My keys, please.'

Razak pulled the key ring from his pocket and dropped it in the old man's palm.

Reaching beneath his desk, Farouq withdrew the small, rectangular casket and cradled it on his lap.

'When we began excavating the Marwani Mosque in 1996,' he began, 'tons of rubble were transferred to dumps in the Kidron Valley, every piece thoroughly sifted through and examined. The last thing we needed was some relic misconstrued as belonging to the Jewish temple.'

'You mean Solomon's Temple?'

He nodded. 'Concise archaeological evidence substantiating that claim has yet to surface and, as such, strengthens our position here.' Farouq's gruff voice rose slightly. 'But as you are aware, the Jews managed to persuade the Israeli government and some Muslim archaeologists to study the whole platform's structural integrity, citing a bulge in the outer wall that appeared during our work – a sign that the foundations could be shifting.' Farouq moved in his seat. 'Myself and several other council members tried to stop them. But the Israeli Antiquities Authority convinced many people – including some of our own – that this work was essential. Their studies were to have begun just days from now.'

It had been hard to avoid the heavily publicized controversy. Razak knew where this was going. 'So you knew that the hidden crypt would be discovered?'

Farouq nodded.

'But how did you know it even existed?'

He patted the casket. 'This extraordinary find was unearthed a few years ago. And very early on in the excavations.'

Razak's eyes combed its stamped bronze exterior. The décor appeared Islamic, but on closer examination the symbols – mainly ornate cruciforms – were undoubtedly Christian. A unique image adorned the cover and he knew immediately from its blasphemous depiction of living creatures that it too wasn't Islamic. 'What does that seal mean?'

'Two medieval knights in full armour, bearing shields, sharing a single lance and one galloping horse symbolizes those who swore to rid this land of Muslim influence. The Christian knights of Solomon's Temple. The Knights Templar.'

Razak looked up sharply. 'So Graham Barton was right?'

'Yes. This was the Templar seal when those infidels first occupied Temple Mount in 1099. You can imagine my surprise when I found it. I was even more surprised when I learned its origins.'

'Where exactly did you find it?'

'Buried beneath the floor of the Marwani Mosque. An earth-moving machine broke a stone slab. A freak discovery.'

'And what was inside?'

Farouq tapped the lid. 'Among other things it contained an ancient manuscript called the *Ephemeris Conlusio*. But you delivered that to Rome three weeks ago.'

Razak recalled that the bald priest he'd met at Café Greco had with him a leather portfolio that bore the symbol of two crossed keys and a papal mitre – the royal crest of the Catholic Church. Vatican City. *Fanatical Christians*.

'We needed the Catholics' help.'

Razak folded his arms. 'I'm assuming that this book indicated the vault's precise location?'

'Among other things, there was a drawing accompanied by precise measurements.'

'And the rest of the manuscript?'

Farouq described Joseph of Arimathea's account. The eyewitness telling of Jesus's capture, crucifixion, and subsequent burial. The revelation of the ossuary and its relics substantiating Jesus's crucifixion and mortal death. Farouq gave Razak time to let it all sink in.

Razak reflected on just how intuitive Barton had been. 'If this was true, it would violate the Qur'an's teachings.'

'Absolutely. You know our position when it comes to Jesus. Allah raised him up to Heaven before his enemies could do him any harm – no arrest, no trial, no crucifixion . . . and certainly no burial. Now do you understand the necessity of eliminating this threat?'

Razak grasped that it wasn't just the Temple Mount that Farouq had been protecting. The implications ran far deeper. 'Couldn't you have gone into the crypt to destroy these things without involving the Catholics? Without killing innocent men?'

'The risks would have been much too high,' he said dismissively. 'We both know the IAA employs many of our own people. People – I might add – who regularly attend prayer service in the Marwani Mosque. All devious tactics on their part, I'm sure. We are not allowed to excavate without explicit Israeli authorization. Had we done so, the death toll from protests would have been far higher than what we've already seen.'

'So you let the Catholics do your dirty work. And it gave you total deniability.' Each new revelation chipped away at Razak's spirit, everything he'd known to be true turned upside down. Once again, religion and politics had become inseparable.

'It was the only way to achieve our objectives,' Farouq continued smoothly. 'And since the threat was even more damaging to them, I knew the Catholics would act quickly to extract this relic. It enabled them to preserve their institution. In return we'd strengthen our own position here by eliminating a threat that contradicts the Prophet's teachings.'

'There must have been a better way . . .' Razak's voice trailed off.

'You're thinking of that archaeologist, aren't you?' Farouq sounded disappointed. 'Razak, we all know that in Israel, regardless of religious affinity, there are only two sides. And Barton is not on ours. Just remember which side *you* are on,' Farouq warned. Brushing his palms together, he continued: 'And before you pass judgement, let me show you one more thing.' He opened his desk drawer and produced a ream of paper. Peeling off the top page, he laid it out for Razak. 'Take a good look at this.'

Razak studied the crude sketch of rectangles that was

accompanied by some text that appeared to be Greek. He shook his head, failing to grasp what it all meant. 'What's this?'

'Joseph's map of Temple Mount – the same map the thieves had used to determine the ossuary's exact location. Notice that structure on top?'

Nodding, Razak felt choked.

Farouq's voice was suddenly frail. 'That's the Jewish temple Joseph so vividly describes in these pages.' He patted the pile of paper.

'Then it did exist after all.' Razak felt the breath sucked out of him.

Farouq smiled. 'Perhaps. One could even argue, just as the Jews have, that the rubble in Kidron Valley contains its building blocks. Maybe now you'll understand my desire to avoid further digging. Following the theft, all discussions of excavations beneath the Temple Mount have been indefinitely suspended.'

'And all archaeological evidence removed.'

'Once we've permanently disposed of the remaining nine ossuaries, nothing will remain.'

Razak was at a loss. If it was true that the Western Wall had definitely once supported a temple, it legitimized Jewish claims to the platform. The Jews' endless mourning hadn't been in vain. But now they'd never know. And unwittingly, he had helped make it all possible.

Farouq reached down again and produced a thick document. 'I had the entire text of the *Ephemeris Conlusio* secretly translated. Read this in your own time,' he set it before Razak, 'then let me know what you'd have done. Make absolutely sure that you burn these pages when you've finished.'

Razak wasn't sure if he could take any more of this.

'There is something you didn't deliver to Rome. Something

you need to know.' Farouq unhinged the casket's lid. 'I found one other document in this Templar box. Another journal, though not one written by Joseph of Arimathea.'

It was beginning to dawn on Razak that the old man's motives were complex, not driven purely by hatred. It only confirmed that circumstances had a cruel way of playing with a man's fate.

'Then whose journal is it?'

From the box, the Keeper pulled out a frail-looking scroll. 'The Templar Knight who discovered the ossuaries in the first place.'

65.

ROME

In their suite at the Fiumicino Hilton, Evan and Charlotte sipped coffee as they relaxed in armchairs facing the sun-filled window, overlooking the airport's busy runways. Not exactly classical Italian romance for a surprise rendevous, but Charlotte had insisted that she wouldn't feel safe going back into Rome.

She pulled her bathrobe snug and eyed Evan affectionately, a light breeze ruffling her hair. Finally, she had achieved a good night's sleep. All it had taken were a couple of glasses of wine and a sleeping pill. The unexpected and utterly gratifying bout of lovemaking hadn't hurt, either. Having told Evan all about the incredible events that had taken place over the past few days, she'd shown him the astounding presentation stored on her laptop. He convinced her that everything would be okay – regardless of any confidentiality agreement she'd signed. Nonetheless, he had booked the room under his own name, just to be safe.

Given BMS's involvement in the analysis, they'd have to be very careful, Evan reminded her. He suggested waiting to see what would come of Dr Bersei's claims against the Vatican, feeling that it was much too early to assume anything fatal had happened to him.

Adoringly, she gazed over at him. 'I really missed you, Evan. And I'm sorry about how I've been acting lately.'

'It's not exactly like I've been on my best behaviour either.' He smiled. 'Hey, I know yesterday wasn't the best time for this, but I've been dying to show you something, Charlie. You have no idea.'

He looked awfully excited, she thought.

Getting up, he slalomed around the room service cart and went directly to his bag. Unzipping its side pouch, she watched him take out a small box, a key ring, and what looked like a vial. He retrieved her laptop from the nightstand and sat back beside her, placing the items on the round table that sat in front of the window.

She shot him a look. 'What's going on?'

'I was going to call you,' he said. 'But I knew that we'd need to talk about this face to face. First off, this is for you. Honestly, it's the real reason I came here.' Smiling, he held out the small box in the palm of his hand.

Seeing it, her heart skipped a beat. It looked like a jewellery box – the perfect size for . . . *Had he come here to propose?* She took it from him and straightened in her chair.

'Go ahead. Open it.'

She glanced at him. Not exactly the most romantic approach.

'It's that bone sample you sent me.'

'Oh,' she said, feeling simultaneously relieved and disappointed. Pulling the lid away, she stared down at the aged metatarsal that could've easily been confused with a fossil. Sitting on a piece of white gauze, there was a perfect hole drilled into its centre where Evan had extracted its DNA. She gently touched it with her index finger.

'You remember that anomaly we discussed?'

'Of course.' She wondered what he could have found that would bring him halfway around the world. 'What about it?'

'First off, did anyone else perform an analysis on these bones?'

She shook her head. 'Just carbon dating at the AMS outfit in Rome, and that sample's been incinerated.'

'How about the rest of the skeleton?'

She pictured the ancient bones reassembled on top of the black rubber matting. Yesterday morning they had disappeared, along with the ossuary and its relics. 'The Vatican still has it.' Or did they?

'Good.' He was clearly relieved. ''Cause when you see what I have to show you . . .' Aldrich uncapped the tiny flash drive that dangled off his key ring and inserted it into the laptop's data port. Flipping up the screen, he brought up a media player window and activated a file. A video clip began loading for playback. 'I thought the scanner was malfunctioning when I saw this,' he explained. 'Almost gave me a heart attack. Turns out the scanner's working just fine. It's the sample that can't be right.' The clip finished loading.

She leaned closer.

'Here we go. The first thing you'll see is the karyotype. I'll pause it when it comes up.' As playback began Aldrich froze the image.

Charlotte's eyes trained on the wormlike chromosomes, arranged side by side in order of length. Fluorescent dyes assigned different colours to each pairing, labelled 1 to 23, X and Y.

'Even here the mutation is evident.'

'Which pair is the anomaly?'

'Look closer,' Aldrich instructed. 'You tell me.'

She scrutinized the image. As soon as her eyes alighted on the twenty-third chromosome set, she spotted something odd. Under a microscope one expected each chromosome to exhibit visible bands along its length. Pair twenty-three didn't have any banding. 'What's with twenty-three?'

'Exactly. Let's keep moving and hopefully it'll start to make some sense.'

Aldrich brought up another screen showing a super-magnified cell nucleus, as it would appear in microscopic view. The chromosomes and nucleotide material were present in their natural, unordered state. The cell's nuclear wall was barely visible along the screen's periphery.

'I marked the twenty-third chromosome pair.' Aldrich pointed it out. 'See?'

Bright yellow circles were drawn around the two anomalous chromosomes.

'Got it.'

'Watch closely, Charlie. Here comes the extraction.'

'What?'

'I'll explain in a sec.' She noticed that Aldrich's left leg was bouncing up and down.

On the screen a hollow glass needle penetrated the nuclear membrane, its sharp angles in stark contrast to the natural cellular construct. Next some chromosome pairs – though not the twenty-third pair – were extracted.

'I was removing the chromosomes for the karyotype.' On top of the media window, the extracted chromosomes appeared along a black bar, in size order and he pointed to them. 'Here are the extracted pairs. So far, so good?'

'Yeah.'

On the screen, the needle retracted from the nucleus and the membrane shrank back over the puncture.

'Now watch this.'

That's when she saw something remarkable unfold. The unbanded twin chromosomes – still inside the cell's nucleus – instantly began to divide, churning out new chromosome pairs to replace the extracted material. The spontaneous regeneration stopped once the nucleus had reached its odd equilibrium – forty-eight chromosomes.

'What did I just see?' She tore her eyes from the screen. '*Evan?*'

He looked up at her intently. 'A huge biological discovery. That's what you just saw. I'll play it again.'

Playback was reset to the point where the needle was extracted. The black bar with the missing chromosomes was on top of the screen again. And then there it was, just as Evan had said – the most remarkable biological process she had ever witnessed – spontaneous genetic regeneration.

Charlotte covered her mouth. 'But that's completely impossible.'

'I know.'

Nothing on earth could explain what she'd just witnessed. 'It's absolutely scientifically impossible for any human chromosome to replicate exact copies of other sets. There's DNA from the mother, the father . . . a complex genetic code.'

'Violates everything we know as scientists,' he stated flatly. 'I had a very difficult time coming to terms with this myself.'

Silence.

'Want to hear more?' He flitted his eyebrows and was beaming again.

'You mean this gets better?'

'Much.' Aldrich collected himself. 'I performed a thorough analysis using the new gene scanner and mapped out the DNA's coding, comparing it with published genome maps. You know what I'd be looking for?'

'Anomalies in the three billion base pairs,' she replied.

The typical genome molecular diagram resembled a spiral ladder or double helix with horizontal 'rungs' formed from pairs of adenine and thymine or guanine and cytosine – otherwise known as the building blocks of life. Three billion of these rungs were spread out over the tightly wound chromosome strands, forming 'genes' – unique DNA segments specific to bodily organs and functions. With the laser scanner, gene sequences could be analysed to detect corrupted coding resulting in mutation.

Aldrich leapt up and paced around. 'Well, I found that the sample you'd sent me registered less than *ten per cent* of the total expected genetic material found in the standard human genome.'

Charlotte eased back into her armchair, shaking her head in disbelief. 'I don't understand.'

'Me neither,' Aldrich replied. 'So I did a lot more testing. Using our new system to compare the genome to all known anomalies, I came up with . . . ready for this? *No matches.* Nothing! Not a single one!'

For a moment her rational mind shut down. No explanation came. 'What does that mean?'

'This sample has no junk DNA!' Aldrich was shouting.

Before the Human Genome Project's completion in 2003, scientists believed human superiority over other organisms – especially in intelligence – would translate to a substantially larger, more complex genetic code. But the human genome had fallen far short of expectation, having only one-twelfth of the genetic content of an ordinary onion. Geneticists attributed the differential to junk DNA – garbage heaps of defunct genes along the DNA strands rendered obsolete by evolution.

It sounded like a scientific fairly tale. But recalling the flawless 3-D physical profile the DNA sample suggested – the absence of a known ethnicity, the androgyny, the unique colouring and features – it made sense. 'Evan, are you seriously telling me that this sample has DNA with a perfect genetic structure?'

He nodded. 'I know it seems too good to be true.'

A flawless genome implied the absence of an evolutionary process. An organism in its purest, most unadulterated form.

Perfection, she thought. But how could a *human* possibly exhibit that kind of profile? It certainly didn't fit with what Darwin or modern science presented as the explanation for human development from primates.

Evan Aldrich waved a shaking hand at the screen. 'This DNA could potentially be used as a template to spot anomalies in comparative samples. And it could be replicated using bacterial plasma.'

Charlotte stared at him. 'Aren't you getting a bit ahead of yourself?'

'It would take stem cell research to an entirely new level. I mean, this is *perfect* DNA in a viral form! Unimaginable.' He spoke slowly. 'A miracle, in fact. It got me thinking about the real consequences of making this public, how the world would respond. At first I thought how many lives could be saved, the effect on disease. Then I envisioned biotech companies scrambling to customize cures for the rich. And designer babies. And rationed healthcare. Biological elitism. It will only benefit the rich – the poor won't get a piece of this. And even if they did – using such a broad brush to wipe out disease would be devastating.

Widespread longevity would lead to unprecedented population growth that would place enormous strain on all the world's resources.'

She felt overwhelmed. 'I see what you mean, but –'

'Let me finish,' he urged. 'There's a point to all this.' He reached over with his right hand and pinched the vial between his fingers, holding it up in front of her. 'This.'

66.

VATICAN CITY

Cardinal Antonio Carlo Santelli stared dejectedly out of his office window at the expanse of Piazza San Pietro and the giant obelisk at its centre that glowed pure white in the morning sunlight. He panned over to the basilica and the statues of saints lining the rooftop. If Catholics knew his noble intentions – to protect the faithful as a true servant of God – would his image too be immortalized and adored there one day? Would he become a modern-day martyr? A saint?

It hadn't been just the high drama of the past few weeks. As far back as the Banco Ambrosiano scandal, the revelations he had witnessed during his tenure in the Vatican had gradually made him question his devotion to the Church. He wondered if his life had truly been in the service of a greater good, or whether he was fast becoming everything he'd once loathed as a young and idealistic priest.

Late yesterday morning, after personally seeing to Conte's release from the Swiss Guard detention cell, he'd given the reckless mercenary the go-ahead to eliminate the last potential complications that could implicate the Vatican in the Jerusalem debacle: the ossuary and its contents, of course; Father Patrick Donovan, next; then Dr Charlotte Hennesey; and finally, her American lover, Evan Aldrich.

Yet more blood on his hands.

Last night, he had expected an update from Conte to confirm that both the relics had been eliminated. No call had come. Now he was starting to worry that the mercenary had double-crossed him, convinced that the next call from him would involve more money – blackmail.

Worse, only minutes ago, he'd heard a news report concerning the death of a docent at the Torlonia catacombs – not exactly the type of thing that made headlines. But the seemingly mundane incident had prompted a routine police inquiry from the only name listed on a visitors' sign-in sheet found in the docent's office. That had led investigators to the visitor's distraught wife who had just contacted the police to report that her husband hadn't come home last night. A search of the catacombs ensued. It hadn't taken the authorities long to find Giovanni Bersei's broken body at the base of a shaft.

Perhaps under better circumstances the incident could have been classified as an accident – a strange intersection of misfortune for two men who happened to be in the same place. However, police had spoken to a witness – a young woman jogger – who had reported seeing a stranger exiting the site and loading the anthropologist's scooter into a van. The photofit she had provided happened to bear an uncanny resemblance to another sketch coming out of Jerusalem.

The media was eating it up.

Any minute now, Santelli expected a call from the investigators.

Another scandal.

In each hand, Santelli held the two halves of the scroll the scientists had found in Christ's ossuary. In his left hand was the sketched ceiling fresco in Joseph's crypt deep within the Torlonia catacombs. In his right hand was the ancient Greek text that preceded the drawing, which he had asked Conte to separate from the picture, fearing the text might contain some overt message. Prior to sending Father Donovan to accompany Conte on his fatal journey, he had asked the priest to translate the Greek message – the last remnant of Christianity's centuries-old threat.

The transcription was penned on a crisp sheet of Vatican letterhead. Leaning over his desk, Santelli pieced together the scroll's halves beside it.

He had considered destroying the scroll, burning it. But now he prayed that something in it might settle him. Drawing a deep breath, he studied the original vellum one more time, then shifted his gaze over to read Father Donovan's transcription:

May faith guide us in our solemn vow to protect the sanctity of God. Here lay his son, awaiting his final resurrection so that God's testimony may be restored and the souls of all men may be judged. Let these bones not dissuade the faithful, for stories are but words written by misguided men. The spirit is the eternal truth.

May God have mercy on us all.

His loyal servant,

Joseph of Arimathea

The intercom came to life, pulling the cardinal from his thoughts.

'Eminence, I'm sorry to bother you, but . . .'

'What *is* it Father Martin?' The young priest sounded flustered.

'Father Donovan is here to see you. I told him you weren't available, but he's refusing to leave.'

Alarmed, the cardinal collapsed into his chair, hands gripping the armrests. *Donovan?* Impossible. Santelli opened the top drawer of his desk, confirming that the Beretta was still there. 'Send him in.'

Seconds later, the office door opened.

As Patrick Donovan made his way into the room, Santelli saw that he had deep bruises under each eye. The priest's nose was crooked and swollen, looking like it had just been pieced back together. He was wearing what appeared to be an old pair of glasses with thick plastic frames rather than his usual wire-rimmed bifocals. Santelli eyed the bulky leather bag that the priest gripped in his left hand.

Donovan sat in the leather chair opposite the cardinal and placed the bag on his lap.

Santelli offered neither ring nor handshake.

Donovan wasted no time. 'I came to show you something.' He patted the bag.

Had Santelli not been sitting in one of the most secure rooms in Vatican City, protected by metal and explosives detectors, he might have thought that inside the bag was some kind of weapon or bomb. But nothing like that could have made it this far. He'd personally seen to that after Conte's unexpected and shocking introduction all those years ago.

'But first, I must ask you why you tried to have me killed?'

'That's a very serious accusation, Patrick.' Santelli eyed the top desk drawer.

'It certainly is.'

'Are you wearing a wire? A recording device? Is that what this is about?'

Donovan shook his head. 'You know that it would have been detected before I made it through the door.'

The priest was right. This inner sanctum was designed to be foolproof. Conversations behind these doors were far too important to risk indiscretions. 'Do you seek retribution? Is that why you came here? Have you come here to kill me, Father Donovan?'

'Let's leave that job to God, shall we?' Donovan was stone-faced.

An uncomfortable moment passed before Santelli motioned to the satchel that looked like it was meant to hold an oversized bowling ball. He half expected it to contain Salvatore Conte's head. But he knew Donovan was incapable of violence. Though it did make him wonder why the assassin hadn't completed his assigned task and why the priest looked like he'd just sparred ten rounds. Was he in on Conte's plot? Had Conte sent him here to extort the money? 'So what have you brought me?'

'Something you must see with your own eyes.' Donovan stood and placed the satchel on Santelli's impossibly neat desk. As the bag settled, something inside it clattered, sounding like wooden dowels. He noticed that the plasma monitor now displayed a new screensaver. The words *Your faith is what you believe, not what you know . . . Mark Twain* scrolled across. Donovan remained standing, glaring at Santelli.

There was a brief stand-off as both men locked stares.

Finally, Santelli levered himself out of his chair, huffing. 'Fine, Patrick. If looking in your bag will make you go away . . . so be it.' Irritated, the cardinal bent over the satchel, hesitated, then slowly opened its zip. There was more clattering as he pulled the sides apart to view the contents.

The cardinal's face went a ghastly white as he stared at the human skull and bones, the ultimate relic. When he looked up again, his eyes had lost their fiery glow. 'You sanctimonious bastard. You'll certainly go to Hell for this.'

'I wanted you to make your peace with him before I perform a proper burial,' said Donovan. He'd felt terrible carrying the sacred bones around in what amounted to little more than a duffel bag. But yesterday afternoon, he had stopped at DHL to arrange for the ossuary to be airfreighted immediately to Jerusalem. The manuscript had been sent separately to Razak, the Muslim courier he'd met in Rome. The spikes and coins were stowed in the rental car's glove compartment alongside the Beretta.

'You son of a bitch,' Santelli's voice was strangely calm.

What happened next was a blur.

Yanking his hands out from his pockets, Donovan clasped the old man's wrist with his right hand, simultaneously revealing the small plastic syringe with his left. Thrusting it deep into the cardinal's upper arm, he pressed down on the plunger.

With a look of utter disbelief, the cardinal tore away, collapsed into his chair, and grabbed the site of the injection. Before he could yell for Father Martin, the Tubarine had clamped down on his heart, bringing it to a grinding halt. Buckling over in agony, Santelli's hands clawed for the pain, trying to tear it from his chest.

Patrick Donovan watched the body give a last convulsive shake. 'God's will,' he said quietly. He wasn't sure what the syringe had contained, but was fairly certain it had been Conte's method for killing the docent found at the Torlonia catacomb's front desk. Within these walls, there weren't many options for a lethal weapon. So Donovan had taken a lucky chance on the needle.

Murder violated everything he held sacred, breaking his vow to God that he had cast aside his horrible past. But unless Santelli was taken down, Charlotte Hennessy would surely die, and he too. The Israelis would never know the truth and an innocent archaeologist would shoulder the blame for a crime he hadn't committed.

Carefully gathering up the satchel, Donovan exited into the antechamber, advising Father Martin that the cardinal wished not to be disturbed and to hold all calls.

Father Martin nodded and eyed Donovan curiously as he hurriedly made his way past the Swiss Guards and out into the main corridor. Once Donovan was out of sight, he quickly made his way into Santelli's office. There he saw the purple skullcap poking above the chair facing the window. Calling out the cardinal's name twice, he slowly rounded the desk.

67.

JERUSALEM

Razak waited for Farouq to put on his reading glasses, all the while staring at the ancient scroll intently.

Clearing his throat, the Keeper began to read out loud.

12 December Anno Dominae 1133

It was Saint Helena who first discovered the true origins of Jesus Christ. She came to the Holy Land in search of historical evidence proving Christ was not a figment of legend or lore. During her pilgrimage, she found what she believed was Christ's empty tomb, and discovered the wooden cross upon which Jesus suffered and died, buried deep beneath the Holy Sepulchre. Today, we carry the true cross in battle to defend our faith and God. Many similar relics have we been rumoured to possess. But what I have discovered on this day is the most wondrous yet.

But first I must explain how this came to be.

In Jerusalem, there has existed for centuries Christians who follow not the words of our Holy Bible. They are a peaceful group who have survived many centuries in isolation, calling themselves the 'Order of Qumran'. I have met them and learned much about their faith. At first, their beliefs shocked me, for their ancient scrolls say many things to contradict God's word. The Order believed that Christ died a mortal death and that only his spirit rose from the tomb to appear to his disciples. They even claimed Christ's body still lay in a hidden place awaiting resurrection to usher in the Day of Judgement and that his bones would once again be reclaimed by God's spirit.

I questioned the origins of their writings. They insisted the teachings and scripture existed long before the 'The book of the Romans'.

Hearing these words, I was inclined to lash out. But, intrigued, I was compelled to learn more. Over time, these people, kind and generous, had become our friends. Through careful study, I began to understand that their beliefs, though untraditional, were rooted in true faith and reverence. Their God was our God. Their Christ was our Christ. Interpretation was all that seemed to divide us.

On the 11th day of October, 1133, Jerusalem was attacked by a band of Muslim warriors. Though we were able to drive them back, it wasn't before our Christian brothers of Qumran had fallen, for they tried to defend their holy city. Their leader, an old man named Zachariah, was wounded severely, and dying when I found him. In his possession was an old book. Knowing that none of his brothers had survived the attack, he gave it to me. He whispered that the book contained many things, including an ancient secret long protected by his people – the location of the chamber where Christ's body had been interred. Then God claimed the old man's spirit.

I employed trusted local scribes to translate the book's

writings, most of which were in Greek. It was then that I discovered that the text was a journal written by a scholarly man named Joseph of Arimathea. In the book, I also found a map drawn by Joseph, marking the location of Christ's body. It was then that I realized the tomb was buried beneath our very feet, under the site of Solomon's Temple.

I ordered my men to find Joseph's tomb. After weeks of digging and breaching three ancient walls, we reached solid earth. Here my hopes would have easily been lost, for nothing would imply man had touched this spot. But Joseph of Arimathea's precise measurements suggested further digging was required. Continuing, we first cleared soft debris, realizing what we had thought to be the face of the mountain was actually a massive circular stone. It took four men to roll it back. Behind it was a hidden chamber, precisely where Joseph had indicated.

Inside I found nine stone boxes inscribed with the names of Joseph and his family. To my amazement, a tenth box bore the sacred symbol of Jesus Christ, and in it were human bones and relics that could only have come from the cross.

To uphold my sworn oath to protect God and his son Jesus Christ, I have secured these wondrous relics beneath Solomon's Temple. For if the old man taught truth, these bones may one day be brought back to life so that the souls of all men might be saved.

I have named Joseph of Arimathea's book *Ephemeris Conlusio*. In it are the secrets to our salvation.

May God forgive me for my deeds.

His faithful servant,
Hugues de Payen

Farouq carefully rolled up the yellowed parchment and returned it to the casket. He removed his glasses and sat back, waiting for Razak's response.

Finally Razak spoke up. 'Tell me if I've got this right. In the twelfth century, the Knights Templar befriended a group of radical Jews – or perhaps Christians – who gave them the *Ephemeris Conlusio*, which led them to Jesus's body, buried in a secret room beneath this very platform. Almost nine hundred years ago the Templars secured the crypt and secreted that casket together with the *Ephemeris Conlusio* beneath the floor. You yourself found the casket during excavations here in 1997.'

'That is all correct.'

Razak tried to absorb it. He was tempted to ask Farouq why the Templars would have hidden such extraordinary relics. But he knew the Keeper would only be able to speculate. It was obvious that the Knights Templar had been protecting an ancient secret. Knowing something of the tenuous relationship between the pope and the mercenaries during that time, it was quite possible that this knowledge had been retained as insurance – perhaps even blackmail – against the Church. It certainly helped explain the Templars' rapid rise to power. But the piety in Hugues de Payen's letter had suggested something else. Perhaps the Templars had retained noble intentions? After all, they too had once been protectors of this place. 'How were you able to convince the Vatican to take action?'

'Easily. I spoke to Father Patrick Donovan, the Vatican Library's head curator. He is the one man I knew of who would have been absolutely aware of the *Ephemeris Conlusio*'s existence and, much more importantly, its implications. I mentioned it by name and he recognized it immediately. A few days later you delivered it to him in Rome. I correctly assumed that he would escalate things fast.'

'What if he hadn't recognized its name?'

Farouq scoffed. 'That wouldn't have really mattered. I would still have persuaded him. The message couldn't have been ignored.'

'You took a very big risk doing all of this.'

Based on that reaction, Farouq thought it best not to inform Razak that he'd further aided the thieves by smuggling explosives into Jerusalem – supplied by his Hezbollah contacts in Lebanon equally eager to topple the state of Israel. A second procurement had also been made at the thieves' behest – a heavy-duty coring drill that Farouq had been told to purchase abroad in cash. Hezbollah had helped with that too.

'Probability, Razak, my friend. It's all about odds on a favourable outcome. In this case the numbers were in our favour, and I acted as I saw fit. I've said before that averting discovery of Jesus's body preserves the teachings of both Islam and Christianity. Very regrettably lives have been sacrificed in the process . . . although they were only Jews. But if we'd done nothing, there would have been a much higher death toll – both physical and spiritual – of both Muslims and Christians. Only the Jews would have gained at our expense. I think you'll agree that this outcome's the best we could have expected.'

Razak had to concede that there was undeniable, yet twisted, logic to Farouq's thinking. It had been extremely devious damage control. 'And how do you feel having learned of these contradictions to our teachings?'

Farouq stared at the ceiling. 'None of this should mean that we question our faith, Razak. It may mean we need to dig deeper for meaning. Even if those stolen bones truly were Jesus's remains, I will not waver in my faith. Not over some old bones.'

Razak recalled Barton saying something about pre-biblical

texts viewing resurrection as a spiritual transformation – not a physical one. Though the word 'resurrection' had survived for centuries, perhaps its meaning had somehow evolved into a more literal definition.

'And Solomon's Temple?'

The Keeper pursed his lips. 'Ancient history. Just like the city of Jebus that King David conquered and renamed Jerusalem one thousand years before Jesus's time. The Jews shed a lot of innocent blood to lay claim to this so-called 'Promised Land'. Yet when the tables were turned, they felt violated. No one truly owns this place except Allah. For now, the Jews have regained control of Israel. But our very presence here, on this site, reminds them that the tide will once again reverse. Ultimately, it is up to Allah to decide who will be victorious.' Farouq circled round the desk and placed a hand on Razak's shoulder. 'Let us go to the mosque and pray.'

68.

ROME

Aldrich moved closer to Charlotte. 'Charlie, what if I told you we could wipe away any disease with one injection – a serum so powerful that it can recode damaged DNA?'

Her mouth opened, but no words came. She stared from the vial, to Evan, and back again. Could it be?

'When I was at your house last week, I saw the medication in your refrigerator – the Melphalan . . . with your name on it.'

A lump settled into her chest and her eyes welled up with tears. 'I've been meaning to tell you, but –'

She collapsed in his arms.

'It's okay,' he said softly.

Her tears came stronger now. Then she sat bolt upright. 'My pills! I left my pills back at the Vatican. I'm supposed to take them every day!'

'Don't worry about that,' he assured her. 'You don't need them. Not any more.'

She was momentarily puzzled.

'Myeloma is one tough cancer,' he explained. 'I know this must be tearing you up. And I know it's probably why you've

419

been distant lately. I pushed too hard last week. You've got so many other things on your mind right now. It was selfish of me.'

Sobbing, she nodded. 'I . . . I haven't told anyone.'

'I think that from now on, we need to make sure that you start opening up a little more before you emotionally implode,' he said with a smile. 'I can take the tough stuff, Charlie. You need to be able to trust me.'

Nodding, she reached over for the tissue box on the night-stand. 'I've got to tell my dad, too.' She dabbed the tears away. 'But I'm just afraid. He's already had to deal with losing Mom . . .'

'You're not going to have to tell him.'

Evan's comments were starting to bother her. 'What are you talking about?'

He cradled the precious vial. 'If I'm right about this, there will be nothing to talk about. There'll be no reason to keep popping Melphalan. I'd like you to be the first in my clinical trial.'

She wiped her eyes. 'Come on, Evan, it can't be that easy.'

'That's what I thought, too. But I think you'll agree that when it comes to genetics, I know what I'm talking about. I'm absolutely certain about this.'

She studied the vial again, this time more seriously. 'But why me? There are so many other people more deserving . . . more *sick*.'

'I'm sure there are. And if we're right, maybe we can think about how to help them. But in order to do that, I need to make sure you'll be around to help make that happen.'

'So . . . if I agree to this, you mean I just shoot this stuff into my body?'

'Yes.'

'That DNA was from a male. Will it turn me into a man?'

420

They both laughed and it lifted some of the heaviness from the room.

'I've already stripped out the gender-specific stuff,' he assured her. 'What you have here is a customized serum that will primarily target your bones, blood cells, and so on. With a perfect genome, we can mix this stuff all sorts of ways.'

'It's incredible,' she muttered.

He looked at the vial, then back at her.

Time seemed suspended as she contemplated the dismal alternative of staying the course with chemotherapy. No doubt, even if she were to control this incurable thing raging in her bones, those treatments would eliminate any hope of having children. Best-case scenario, she might live another ten or fifteen years. She'd never even make it to fifty.

'Well?'

She smiled, knowing that she could trust him. She recalled the angel of death in St Peter's, flipping the hourglass. 'Okay.'

'Great.' He was grinning ear to ear. 'But just answer me one question. Who on earth *was* this guy?'

Father Donovan had fed her the story that the skeleton was a hoax concocted by Joseph of Arimathea, intended to debunk Jesus as the promised Messiah. Now that theory seemed utterly ridiculous. Only a divine being could exhibit such a remarkable genetic profile.

She walked over to the window and silently looked out over Rome. Then she turned to Aldrich, her eyes sad, and she smiled.

69.

VATICAN CITY

St Peter's Basilica had closed promptly at seven p.m. and the vast, dimmed interior was empty, except for one figure toting a black bag, striding hastily along the northern transept.

Father Donovan moved to the front of the towering Baldacchino where a marble balustrade circled around a sunken grotto directly below the papal altar. Pausing to bless himself, he checked to make sure no one was watching, then opened the side gate and slipped through. He pulled the gate closed and crept down a semicircular staircase.

One level beneath the basilica's main floor, an elaborate inlaid marble shrine glowed in the warm light of ninety-nine ornate oil lamps, burning perpetually in tribute to the most holy ground in all of Vatican City – the *Sepulcrum Sancti Petri Apostoli*.

St Peter's tomb.

Peter was the man who, according to Joseph of Arimathea, he had designated to handle two critical, final tasks to serve the Messiah: transferring the ten ossuaries from Rome to a new crypt beneath Temple Mount in Jerusalem, and delivering his precious manuscript – the foundation for the Christian gospels –

to the Jewish zealots who had helped execute Jesus's ambitious plan to restore the temple.

Donovan recalled Joseph's final passage in the *Ephemeris Conlusio*:

On this night, the emperor Nero has made a banquet in his palace. I am to be his guest, and so too, my wife and children have been asked to sit with him. With much sadness, I have agreed, though I know his intent, for his heart is filled with evil. Those who celebrate the teachings of Jesus have refused to pay tribute to him. For this, many he has burned alive.

For my loyal service to Rome, Nero has made known to me that my death and the deaths of my beloved family will be humane. The food we eat tonight will be poisoned.

Rome is vast and there is no place he will not find us. The only protection we have comes from God. Our fate is his will.

It has been agreed that our bodies will be given to my brother, Simon Peter, to be buried in my crypt beside Jesus. Once all have been freed from flesh, Peter will journey back to Jerusalem. Beneath the great temple will Jesus be interred, for this I promised to him before his execution. There too will we share in his glory on the Day of Atonement. Then will the temple be cleansed. Then shall God return to its holy Tabernacle.

These writings I have asked Peter to deliver to our brothers, the Essenes. They will protect this testament to God and his son. They will tell all men that the Day of Judgement will soon be at hand.

Once Peter had fulfilled his duties to the brotherhood, he had returned to Rome to continue preaching Jesus's teachings. Shortly thereafter, he was imprisoned by Nero and sentenced to death by being crucified upside down.

Keep moving, Donovan silently urged himself.

Directly beneath the Baldacchino's base, between red marble columns, was a small glass-enclosed niche containing a golden mosaic depicting a haloed Christ. In front of the mosaic was a tiny golden casket – an ossuary.

Inside this ossuary were the bones of St Peter himself, extracted from a tomb deeper beneath the Baldacchino that was accidentally discovered during excavations in 1950. The skeleton had been found in a communal grave, but caught the eye of archaeologists overseeing the digs because it belonged to an older man whose feet were missing – as would be expected of someone who had been cut down from an inverted crucifix. Carbon dating had been subsequently performed. The male specimen had lived during the first century.

From his pocket, Donovan produced the gold key he had removed from a safe in the Vatican's Secret Archive. He set down the bag, then smoothly inserted the key into a lock on the niche's frame. The hinges let out a low moan as he eased the door open.

He stared down at the ossuary that had been fashioned from pure gold, resembling a miniature Ark of the Covenant – no doubt, a purposeful design. Directly above him, the four spiral columns of the Baldacchino had also been purposely fashioned to reflect the designs of Solomon's Temple.

Knowing that he had little time, Donovan reached out with both hands and firmly grabbed the box's cover. Drawing a deep breath, he jostled it, pulling it up and away.

As expected, St Peter's ossuary was empty.

Following the studies performed on the saint's bones, the skeleton had been returned to the humble Constantine-era crypt where it was originally found. Few knew that this box was only meant to commemorate the first pope.

'God have mercy on me,' he reverently whispered, eyeing the mosaic of Christ.

Reciting the Lord's Prayer, he began transferring the bones from the leather bag into the ossuary, finishing with the perfect skull and jawbone. Then he replaced the lid.

As he closed the glass door and turned the lock, he heard noises emanating from above, within the basilica. A door opening. Urgent footsteps. Excited voices.

Just above the niche was a heavy metal grating that served as a vent for the hollow area beneath the altar. Instinctively, Donovan passed the key through the grate and released it down into the void. He heard the small ting of metal striking rock. Then he remembered the empty syringe in his pocket and got rid of that too.

Grabbing the bag, he ascended the ramp, staying low as he emerged.

'*Padre Donovan*,' a deep voice called out in Italian. 'Are you in here?'

Peering through the balustrade, he could see three figures – two in blue coveralls and black berets, a third in vestments. Swiss Guards and a priest.

Trapped!

For a moment, he considered retreating down the ramp, back into the extensive subterranean papal burial crypt adjoining St Peter's shrine. Maybe he could hide there for a while amongst the hundreds of sarcophagi, wait it out, then try to escape Vatican City.

He wondered how they had found him so quickly. Then he remembered he'd used his keycard to enter the basilica. Each key-swipe logged his location into the Swiss Guard's security system – a safety precaution that apparently served a second, more sinister purpose. The grim reality of the situation flooded over him: he couldn't hide because they already knew he was here.

Trying his best to remain calm, he climbed the rest of the way up the steps and opened the gate. 'Yes, I'm over here,' he called out.

The two guards quickly made their way over to him, with the cleric trailing cautiously behind.

'Just finishing my prayers,' Donovan offered, confidently. They seemed to buy it.

'Father Donovan,' the shorter guard's voice was curt. 'We need you to come with us.'

The curator eyed the guard's gleaming Beretta with newfound admiration and thought about yesterday, when he and Santelli had dropped by the barracks to retrieve Conte. The Swiss Guard's gunsmith had half a dozen weapons set out for maintenance. Amidst all the excitement, no one had even noticed Donovan slip the gun and a few clips of ammunition into his pocket.

Managing a smile, Donovan said, 'Is there a problem?'

'Yes,' the cleric responded, stepping into view.

Putting on his glasses, Donovan saw it was Father Martin. Had Santelli's assistant found the body? Was he bringing the guards to arrest him?

'There's a major problem,' Martin stated severely. 'Shortly after you left Cardinal Santelli's office this evening, His Eminence was found dead.'

Donovan gasped, trying his best to look surprised. His pulse was drumming hard and his palms were moist. 'That's awful.' He prepared himself for what was sure to come next – the cleric's accusation.

'It seems that he suffered a heart attack,' Father Martin explained.

Studying Martin's face, Donovan swore he detected a lie. He let out a long breath, perceived as shock, but actually of relief.

'Very unfortunate,' Father Martin said in a quiet tone, casting his eyes to the floor for a moment, as if in vigil. Earlier that evening, he had listened in on Donovan's discussion with Santelli, using the cardinal's phone as an intercom. And what he heard had been deeply shocking. He was almost certain that Father Patrick Donovan had exacted revenge on the scheming old man, though he could only wonder how. Didn't the metal detectors register all weapons? But no matter, he thought. Had he been in Donovan's position, he would have done the same. Regardless, that bastard Santelli was dead. *Not only is the Church better off without him*, Father Martin thought, *but so am I.* 'We will need your help in collecting his legal papers from the archive.' He sighed. 'The cardinal's family will also need to be notified immediately.'

Donovan raised his head, eyes gleaming. 'Certainly . . . We can go there now if you'd like.'

Martin offered a reassuring smile. 'Bless you, Father.'

SUNDAY

70.

JERUSALEM

Graham Barton had never been so glad to see the dusty streets of Jerusalem. He drew a deep, invigorating breath, savouring the familiar smell of cypress and eucalyptus. It was a lovely morning. He grinned when he saw Razak standing at the bottom of the steps of the police station and his smile grew even wider when he saw that Jenny was standing beside him.

She ran up and threw her arms around him. He could feel her tears as she kissed him.

'I've been so worried about you.'

'All I've been doing is thinking about you. Thank you for coming.'

She smiled. 'I'll always be there for you, you know that.'

'I've heard that in Jerusalem, being framed happens often.' Razak embraced Barton. 'But justice has a way of finding the guilty.'

'It certainly does. Speaking of which,' Barton said, confused, 'how did you manage this? What convinced the Israelis it wasn't me?'

'You'll find out soon enough,' Razak replied. 'I brought a gift for you.' He held out a thick envelope that looked like it contained a large book.

'What's this?'

'A copy of one of the exhibits presented as evidence in your defence,' Razak answered cryptically.

Barton accepted the package.

'There's a lot of history inside that envelope,' Razak promised. 'You should read it. It says many interesting things.'

71.

Farouq sat on his veranda, overlooking the red-tiled roofs and weathered facades of the Old City's Muslim Quarter. It was an unusually mild day, with a flawless sky and a gentle breeze fragrant with the scent of palm.

He felt good. Better than he had felt in a long time, in fact. Israel was once again teetering on the verge of violent confrontation, the struggle for Palestinian liberation was alive and well, and the faith of all – the vital fire required to keep the conflict burning – was strong. Smiling, he sipped his mint tea. In the distance, he could hear the crowds near Temple Mount, though today, the tone seemed to carry a different air, sounding almost . . . celebratory?

Inside the apartment, the phone chimed.

Farouq levered himself out of his chair and went inside to get it. '*As-salaam.*'

'Sir,' Akbar's voice was shaky. 'Have you heard the news?'

'No, I have not. What are you so worried about?'

'Please. Turn on your television . . . CNN. Then call me to let me know what to do.'

There was a click and the line went dead.

Alarmed, Farouq grabbed the remote and turned to CNN. Two commentators were on split-screen – an anchorman sitting behind a news desk, and an attractive blonde woman standing against the backdrop of the Temple Mount. On the bottom of the screen, a text box read: 'Live from Jerusalem'.

Crossing his arms, Farouq remained standing as he listened in.

'I'm sure this is causing quite a stir in Jerusalem,' the male reporter stated in a serious tone. 'Taylor, how are local officials reacting to this news?'

There was a slight delay as the satellite feed bounced the question from New York to Jerusalem.

'Well, Ed, as it stands,' the female reporter replied mechanically, 'we're still awaiting a formal statement from the Israeli government. So far, we've only been hearing reports through local news stations.'

'And has this anonymous informant been identified?'

A longer delay.

'As of now, no,' she replied, cupping her earpiece. 'And that seems to be causing just as much excitement as the relics themselves.'

Farouq's face sagged. *Relics? Informant?*

The anchorman turned to the camera.

'If you're just tuning in, we're live with a breaking story coming out of Jerusalem, where late this morning, Israeli officials recovered a key item linked to last Friday's violent exchange that took place at the Temple Mount, leaving thirteen Israeli soldiers dead . . . and until now, many unanswered questions. Taylor, this

434

book that's been given anonymously to the Israeli police . . . is it certain it's authentic?'

It can't be, Farouq tried to convince himself. Knees suddenly weak, he slumped into an armchair.

'We've been told that the archaeologists working with the IAA – the Israeli Antiquities Authority – have analysed this ancient manu-script and that based on carbon dating studies, yes, they are convinced the document is real. They have invited outside scientists to see the evidence, leading many to believe that the claim is valid.'

'Have you been told what the book says?'

The transmission sputtered for a split second.

'We haven't been told yet,' she replied, shaking her head, 'But the IAA will be holding a press conference tomorrow afternoon to release complete details. Sources close to the investigation suggest that the book contains compelling historical accounts of the Jewish temple that was situated on the Temple Mount in the first century. Equally astounding, the book is said to contain shocking facts about the life and death of Jesus Christ.'

'Shocking indeed.' The reporter's face intensified and his shoulders became even more rigid.

'As you can imagine' – her brow creased tightly – 'this is all nothing short of astounding. Jews here are celebrating in the streets . . . Muslims are not at all pleased. And certainly, the Christians we've spoken to are anxious to learn more. The Temple Mount has long been the centre of an ongoing religious rivalry between the three faiths . . .'

Feeling as if the world were crashing down around him, Farouq al-Jamir stared at the screen. He tried to postulate how the original manuscript could have found its way back to Jerusalem . . . and so suddenly. Certainly, the Vatican wouldn't have offered it up, knowing full well the nasty consequences. Surely, Razak had given the Vatican envoy the original text in Rome, not a copy. Or had he? Could there possibly have been a second book? The odds seemed highly unlikely.

Suddenly, the doorbell rang.

No visitors were expected that morning. Scowling, the old man made his way back inside just as the bell rang again. 'I'm coming!' he yelled impatiently.

Opening the front door, he was surprised to find a yellow DHL delivery van parked out front, the Palestinian driver standing on the stoop in uniform, the white cords of an iPod dangling from his ears. He was holding a chunky rectangular device. Farouq frowned when he saw that the young man was wearing shorts.

'You should dress in proper clothing,' Farouq grumbled. 'Do you have no shame?'

The deliveryman shrugged. 'You have a package.'

The Keeper's face showed his puzzlement. He wasn't expecting anything. 'And what might it be?'

'How would I know?' the young man replied. 'If you'll just sign here, I'll unload it.' He held out the electronic package-tracking module, pointed to an illuminated touch screen signature box, and handed him a plastic stylus. Farouq signed.

'It's large. Heavy, too. Where would you like me to put it?'

Feeling more anxious, Farouq began stroking his beard – an old habit from his days as a soldier. 'In the garage.' He pointed to it. 'I'll open the door.'

Inside, Farouq pushed the garage door button, and groaned as he squeezed past his wrecked Mercedes. The only nearby body shop that was any good was owned by a Jew who, given the current state of affairs, had refused the job. Now the mess would have to sit here until Farouq could find someone who could do the work. Standing with his arms crossed, he pouted as the door slowly rolled back on creaking hardware.

The driver was waiting on the other side with the delivery.

The moment his eyes landed on the crate, the creases in his wooden face smoothed out. He stepped outside and looked both ways down the narrow street.

The driver lowered the crate onto the cement floor of the garage, rolled the handtruck back to the van, stowed it, and drove away.

Farouq eyed the shipping label. The package had come from Rome and the return address was a P.O. Box. The sender's name was a Daniel Marrone.

The Keeper suddenly felt light-headed.

It took Farouq ten minutes to gather the courage to open the crate. And once he started, it hadn't been easy. With the cover off, the box had been filled with bubble wrap. Stripping it all away, his fingers detected the cold touch of stone. A sinking feeling came over him – a profound sense of loss and failure. First the book. Now this? Pulling away the last layer of bubble wrap, he stared vacantly at the beautiful etchings on the ossuary's fractured lid. He immediately recognized the design since he'd seen it in the *Ephemeris Conlusio*.

Without warning, figures suddenly materialized in the garage opening.

'Stay right there,' a voice commanded in Arabic.

Farouq stood bolt upright to see four men, each with a gun targeting his chest. They wore plain clothes and bulletproof vests, but he immediately knew who had sent them. Shin Bet agents. Ghosts from his past. 'What is this?' he demanded.

Ari Teleksen appeared round the corner, his saggy jowls raised on both sides by a sardonic smile. A cigarette dangled between his stern lips. He exhaled a plume of smoke, knowing it would offend the Muslim. 'Farouq al-Jamir,' Teleksen's haunting baritone filled the garage. 'Thought I'd bring you the owner's manual for your delivery. You seem to have left it in your office.' Gripped between the three fingers of his disfigured hand, he held up a plastic-covered ream. 'If you'd like to see the original, maybe I can talk to my friends at the Israeli Antiquities Authority.'

Farouq immediately recognized the photocopy of the *Ephemeris Conlusio*.

'Just like old times, eh?' Teleksen was grinning now. 'Ready to go for a ride?'

For the first time in a long while, Farouq felt afraid. Very afraid.

ACKNOWLEDGEMENTS

With deep gratitude, I'd like to thank those who inspired me and provided me with a bottomless well of emotional support and technical expertise:

To my beautiful wife Caroline for her patience and encouragement, and to my loving daughters, Vivian and Camille, for their daily reminders that family is the most precious gift of all.

To all my friends and family – you know who you are! – who have endured my incessant ramblings and provided the stimulating debates that balanced my thoughts and kept my feet on the ground.

To my literary agents and friends across the pond, Charlie Viney and Ivan Mulcahy, who believed in me and helped me realize my full potential – Jonathan Conway too!

To an amazing editor named Doug Grad whose incredible grasp on his craft is only surpassed by his wit . . . and Alison Stoltzfus who adds even more talent to a winning team.

Finally, to the remarkable body of research that sits on bookshelves, plays in VCRs and DVDs, and floats around cyberspace for all to experience. Explore!